PENGUIN BOOKS

The Truth Will Out

The Truth Will Out

ANNA McPARTLIN

PENGUIN BOOKS

PENGUIN BOOKS

Published by the Penguin Group
Penguin Books Ltd, 80 Strand, London WC2R ORL, England
Penguin Group (USA) Inc., 375 Hudson Street, New York, New York 10014, USA
Penguin Group (Canada), 90 Eglinton Avenue East, Suite 700, Toronto, Ontario, Canada M4P 2Y3
(a division of Pearson Penguin Canada Inc.)
Penguin Ireland, 25 St Stephen's Green, Dublin 2, Ireland (a division of Penguin Books Ltd)
Penguin Group (Australia), 250 Camberwell Road, Camberwell, Victoria 3124, Australia
(a division of Pearson Australia Group Pty Ltd)
Penguin Books India Pvt Ltd, 11 Community Centre, Panchsheel Park, New Delhi – 110 017, India
Penguin Group (NZ), 67 Apollo Drive, Rosedale, Auckland 0632, New Zealand
(a division of Pearson New Zealand Ltd)
Penguin Books (South Africa) (Pty) Ltd, 24 Sturdee Avenue, Rosebank, Johannesburg 2196, South Africa

Penguin Books Ltd, Registered Offices: 80 Strand, London WC2R ORL, England

www.penguin.com

First published in Ireland by Poolbeg 2008
This edition published in Penguin Books 2011
1

Copyright © Anna McPartlin, 2008, 2011
All rights reserved

The moral right of the author has been asserted

Set in 12.5/14.75 pt Garamond MT Std
Typeset by Palimpsest Book Production Limited, Falkirk, Stirlingshire
Printed in Great Britain by Clays Ltd, St Ives plc

ISBN: 978-0-241-95213-9

www.greenpenguin.co.uk

Penguin Books is committed to a sustainable
future for our business, our readers and our
planet. This book is made from paper certified
by the Forest Stewardship Council.

In memory of Ciara Collins

Dedicated to Caroline, Ger and Ashling Collins

1. The wedding: take two

The date was 1 May 2006. It was Harri's thirtieth birthday and the day she was set to marry.

She'd woken up only once the night before, humming 'Get Me To The Church On Time'. *I'm getting married in a few hours. Holy crap, I think I'm going to cry. La-la-lala-la. I wish I wasn't losing my mind.* She wasn't awake for long, just time enough for a mini freak-out, to indulge in a tear or two, blow her nose and hit her head on the Edwardian mahogany headboard with its checked stringing. *Bastard* – the bed, not the fiancé: she loved her fiancé. Harri was just nervous. When she got nervous she got confused – or maybe it was the other way around. Either way, nervousness and confusion usually ended up in minor injury. *Don't be all* My Left Foot *about it, Harri. It'll go beautifully. Everything will be fine. You will not mess this day up. Go back to sleep.* She obeyed herself and, despite a slightly sore head, managed to return to the Land of Nod within minutes, no real harm done.

'Big day.' Her dad greeted her with a wink on the landing.

'Big day, Dad,' she agreed sheepishly, rubbing a particularly stubborn piece of crap from the darkest and deepest corner of her right eye.

'Don't pull your eye out, love,' he warned.

'I'll try not to,' she said, kissing his hairy cheek as he passed with his paper heading towards his en-suite bathroom, where he would spend what he often described as a well-earned hour on the loo.

When she emerged from a pounding shower, her mother was waiting in her bedroom with a full Irish breakfast, including toast, tea, coffee, croissants and cheese.

'Morning, my darling,' she said, with a smiling sigh, placing the breakfast tray on the table by the window. It looked down onto a pretty stone patio and across to an ancient oak tree.

'Morning, Mum.' She held a cloth against the eye she'd all but pulled out despite her earlier promise.

When she took it away from her face, her mother gasped. 'Holy hell, darling, how'd you manage that?'

'Sleep crap.'

'Ah,' her mother beamed, 'so you slept.' She nodded approvingly. 'Good girl. Don't worry, darling. Mona will sort it out. Mona could conceal a baboon's arse stuck out of a white Fiat Uno.'

'Oh, Mum!'

Her mum was laughing. Gloria didn't often curse or engage in conversation she deemed lewd, but when she did she made sure the verbal misdemeanour was for comic effect. Harri, giggling, went to sit on the chair beside the table at the window. The sun shone a bright yellow against a light blue cloudless sky. 'It's a nice day,' she commented, hugging herself in the towelling dressing-gown her mother had given her six years before, when she'd moved twenty minutes down the road to the UCD campus –

'Always buy quality, darling,' Gloria had said, 'anything else is simply false economy.'

Gloria was all about quality. She had expensive taste and found it difficult to tolerate anything but the finer things in life. She had grown up as the only child of a wealthy landowner, and her parents had once owned a quarter of South Dublin. Harri's granddad had died in his late forties, leaving the house to her nana and mum. Nana suffered from epilepsy and because of this Gloria would never leave her. She had met Harri's dad when the house was broken into in the early seventies and he had come to investigate the crime. They had fallen in love quickly and were married within a year.

Harri's dad, Duncan, originated from North Dublin and initially he was uncomfortable with his new wealthy lifestyle. Gloria said he was like a duck in a desert, but his work kept him rooted in the familiar gritty reality that his new-found home life shielded him from so he retained a balance. Also, he was fond of Nana. She was a lady, but she was also as tough as old boots and a whizz at chess – together they played games that lasted up to a month.

Duncan had joined the guards straight out of school. He was the third generation of his family to do so and moved up the ranks quickly, making detective in his early twenties. He had worked on some of the most tragic cases Ireland had seen. Harri often wondered how he managed not to bring all that terror home. Her mum said he wiped his feet on the mat and there he'd leave his day.

Harri only ever witnessed her dad cry once. She was

nine, maybe ten, and he was sitting at his desk in his attic office. She was holding a tray with his lunch and didn't knock before she went in. He was looking at a photograph with his hand held up to his face and tears flowing. He shoved it into the file that lay open on his desk, closed it quickly and spun towards the window, wiping his eyes. In Harri's house they didn't talk about anything that made anyone feel uncomfortable. Duncan's job meant that he had to keep quiet about many things, while Gloria was far too ladylike and – unlike Nana – too fragile for confrontation. Nana didn't believe in discussing anything that verged on boring. Feelings, she had once decreed, were dull. Harri and her twin brother George had grown up in a house that was all about being lovely. Crying had no place in their home so Harri pretended she hadn't seen her father weeping on that day – but years later, if she closed her eyes, she could still see those fat tears splashing on white paper.

'It's a fabulous morning.' Gloria kissed the top of her daughter's head.

'I'm never going to be able to eat all this.' Harri surveyed the ridiculous amount of food before her.

'I know.' Gloria moved to the end of the bed and bent over to pull out a blue box from under it. 'For you,' she said. 'Happy birthday, darling!'

'Thanks, Mum.' Harri grinned. She was thirty but still got giddy around presents. She opened the box to reveal a beautiful art-deco pendant. Gloria loved art deco and Harri did too – Duncan liked to say they were two peas in a pod. She held it up against the window. It was beautiful, gleaming in the light with stones that glistened. 'I love it!' she said.

George came in then and dropped on to the bed. 'So, Mum, where's my present?'

'Under your bed.'

'Aah!' he said.

'What's wrong?'

'That's two floors down.'

'Don't be so lazy, darling. It's a staircase, not blooming Everest.'

'What is it?'

'I'm not telling you,' Gloria said, smiling.

'And how come I didn't get breakfast in bed?' he queried, while examining a strand of his hair.

'Because you're not getting married. Happy birthday, Nuisance. Now, please be an adult.' She often called George 'Nuisance' and was smiling as she said it – she liked it when he acted like a child. It made her feel needed. 'My twins. Both so grown-up, but deep down and where it counts, you'll always be my babies.'

George jumped up and kissed his sister. 'Happy birthday, Harri!'

'Happy birthday, George!' Harri idolized her brother. He was everything she wasn't. George could stand centre stage and hold any room while Harri could only ever be found in its corner. He was adventurous, having travelled around the world, spending summers in the snow and winters in the sun. He surfed, skied and dived. He loved to paraglide and was considering helicopter lessons. Harri was not much of an explorer. Hot sun brought her out in a heat rash and the one time she'd skied she'd broken her wrist. He was athletic; she was bookish. He was loud; she was quiet. He was a playboy; she was a worker. He was gay; she was straight. They didn't even really look alike, except for their thick wavy dark hair. He was tall; she was average. He was broad; she was petite. He had a square face while hers was oval. They were so different in so many ways, yet they didn't need words to communicate. They understood each other. They knew one another. George would have jumped any bridge for his sister. The Ryan twins had always been extremely close.

'Time to let go, little sister,' George said, pulling away from her.

'I'm older.' She smiled.

'You're smaller!' He grinned.

And, really, with the sunny morning, the shiny new jewellery, the big breakfast, Gloria's tasteful décor, her warmth and kindness, that moment depicted a picture-perfect family. The only thing spoiling it in Harri's mind was the impending nuptials.

Stay calm, Harri. Don't mess this up.

But, unbeknown to her, a far greater menace underlay that ideal family on that ideal day.

The dress was slightly too tight and Mona's perfectly coiffed up-style was bringing on a headache but even Harri was forced to admit that she had done a fantastic job, despite a broken finger.

'What happened?'

'Desmond happened.'

6

'I need more.'

'I had a child who turned into a teenager who turned into an arsehole who thinks nothing of leaving a skateboard at the top of a staircase.'

'You're lucky you didn't break your neck.'

'He's lucky I didn't break *his* neck! Seriously, Harri, think before you copulate.'

Harri enjoyed Mona. She was named well for she loved to moan but did so with likeable verve. George called her Moaning, which she seemed not to mind.

'Wow, Moaning, you make breeding sound so romantic!' he chimed in from the doorway.

'Tell me you're going to let me do something with that hair of yours.' Mona was accustomed to ignoring his witticisms.

'What's wrong with it?'

'Nothing – if you're emulating a fop.'

'Well, I was going for Hugh Grant *circa Four Weddings*.' He stood behind her, examining himself in the mirror.

'Well, then, dear, you've achieved the look beautifully.'

'Moaning, you're such a bitch but I love it.'

He sighed and sat in the corner of the sitting room, where Harri was standing in her slightly too-tight wedding dress, with pretty but headache-inducing hair.

Duncan coughed outside, knocked and crept into the room with a camera. 'Oh, now. What?' Duncan often said 'what' out of context as though someone unseen had whispered a query into his ear. He mostly did it when he was happy. 'Fantastic. Fantastic!' He was also given to repeating himself in a tone that suggested childish delight.

'Jaysus, you're smashing. Isn't she smashing?' George and Mona smiled and nodded. The dress made up for in wow-factor what it lacked in comfort, its sheer splendour bringing a tear to Duncan's usually dry eyes. At that point George joked that his father's tears had more to do with cost than visual appeal, and the awkward moment was averted.

Melissa rang. Mona handed Harri the phone with a warning. 'Two minutes.'

'Hi, Melissa.'

'Still with us?'

'I am.'

'Excellent.'

'Where are you?' Harri asked, confused by the sound of passing traffic.

'I'm in the church car park, changing a nappy.'

'You're at the church already?' Harri squeaked, panic in her voice.

'Stop. Breathe. I'm just checking the flowers. You still have an hour.'

'Okay.' She exhaled as much as the dress would allow.

'Jacob, get in the car. Jacob, get in the car. Jacob . . .'

'Melissa?'

'Sorry. Get in the bloody car!'

Shuffling ensued and Harri heard Jacob say something about wanting a sandwich from the car boot. 'You keep sandwiches in the boot?'

'Sandwiches, yogurts, nappies, towels, cheese strings, formula, a six-pack of Capri-Sun, Play-Doh, knickers. You name it, I have it.'

'Get off the phone!' Mona said.

'I have to get off the phone.'

'Okay. Everything's going to be fine.'

'I know.'

'Oh, James is here.'

Harri's stomach turned. James was at the church. She hung up.

Mona dragged her to the dining-table near the big window that overlooked Nana's favourite rickety old bench and let in lots of light. She'd pulled an eye pencil out of her bulging bag of tricks. 'Are you okay?' she asked.

'I'm fine,' Harri agreed.

Mona pushed her into the chair. 'Look up!' she ordered. Harri looked up. 'Are you sure you're okay? Suddenly you seem pale.'

Harri gave her the thumbs-up, afraid that if she spoke she'd throw up.

Duncan chose that moment to leave the room: he had to pick up Gloria from Shoe World in Sandycove where she'd insisted on going half an hour earlier because the strap of her brand-new sandals had snapped.

'Holy hell, I can't believe it!' she'd cried. 'These shoes cost five hundred euro!'

'What?' Duncan had roared. 'Five hundred euro? Have you lost your mind, woman?'

Gloria hadn't realized he was in earshot and she was in no mood for a price war. 'Darling, we both know you weren't meant to hear that so let's just pretend that you didn't.'

Duncan had grumbled something about five hundred

Jaysusing euro but he could see sense in her suggestion so he let it go. They lived a stone's throw from Sandycove so he had dropped her off, returning home with just enough time to take photos before returning to the village to fetch her. He had made his way to the car mumbling about the cost of everything and wondering how much money had been wasted on these new bloody toe-curlers.

Harri didn't feel like moving or sitting or drinking or even like taking the Valium Mona offered, with the advice that it had worked wonders on her neighbour's daughter, Cliona. Apparently Cliona often suffered with her nerves but, according to Mona, that was because she was a self-centred, ungrateful brat who didn't give a stuff about her hard-working mother, or her father, who often smelt of the chip fat from which he had apparently built an empire. George laughed, and Harri feigned amusement but inside she felt numb.

'Do you feel sick?' George asked, from his mother's favourite antique rocking chair.

'A little,' she admitted. There was no point in lying to him.

'You'll be okay,' Mona said, applying a second coat of ruby-red lipstick. 'Now smack your lips.'

'And breathe!' George instructed, before returning to an article he had been reading on a new species of Sri Lankan tree frog. 'Take a look at those weird staring red eyes. If frogs could kill . . .'

Harri's fiancé James liked frogs, believing them necessary to a well-balanced ecosystem. He had a strange fixation with all amphibians and reptiles; where most saw ick, he saw wonder.

'Did you know that when snakes strike they have a near hundred per cent success rate?' he'd mentioned on their first date.

'I did not,' she'd responded, thinking he was a mental case, and deciding against ordering dessert.

He believed that reptiles were especially marginalized. 'I mean, what have lizards ever done to anyone?'

She didn't reply, hoping he'd change the subject. He didn't. Instead he told her about his pet snake, Ronnie: he'd had him for about three years when Ronnie had died of organ failure. James had blamed himself for not reading the signs. 'He definitely didn't look sick,' he said. 'I loved that snake.' James had a cute wrinkle that appeared just over his eye when he was upset, as it did now.

James worked as an architect. His great love was buildings and he was an artist who strove for perfection. He controlled every aspect of a job, from the foundations to the roof. When he walked around his finished construction he experienced a high akin to that of a rock star playing to a crowd of fifteen thousand at Wembley. James was a builder from a different age, yet he was fierce about the environment, insisting that he only worked on eco-friendly structures.

They had met six years earlier through work. He was building a house; Harri and Susan Shannon, her business partner, were decorating it. On that very day Susan had said she hoped he had a decent IQ because Harri should marry him. Harri had laughed her off and thought no more of it. Susan had always had a keen interest in matchmaking and did so with anyone who would let her. She said it was a replacement for sex. From the outset she was sure Harri and James had chemistry and was decidedly happy when, within weeks of their meeting, they proved her correct.

Susan had recently turned forty-six and for her birthday her husband had bought her a garden hose. It was an expensive garden hose with lots of handy attachments and powerful enough to clean a stone patio, as well as sprinkle the plants, but she had wanted to shove it down his throat.

'James would never buy me a hose,' Harri had said, and she was right. However, he had bought her a shredder after watching a news report on identity fraud.

Susan sighed. 'Whatever happened to romance?'

'I think it's a casualty of feminism.'

'The question was rhetorical and you think too much.'

Over-thinking was probably Harri's biggest problem.

Anyway, two days after Susan had made her little remark about James being marriage material, he had asked Harri out. Although their first date had begun a little strangely, by the end of the evening, while they were sitting outside the Dun Laoghaire apartment she shared with a contemporary dancer called Tina Tingle, things had improved considerably.

When the car had stopped, she had immediately put her hand on the door handle to suggest she was getting out without delay.

'Sorry,' he'd said. 'I'm a little out of practice.'

'It's okay.' She blushed, embarrassed by his frankness.

'Where did I lose you?' he asked.

'Your in-depth description of the texture of Ronnie's scales.'

He laughed. 'I talk utter shit when I'm nervous.'

She smiled. 'My brother does that. After my nana's funeral he talked about belly-button fluff for a whole hour.'

There was silence for a moment or two and James noticed that Harri's hand was no longer on the door handle.

'So you're out of practice?' she said, scratching the back of her neck and facing the windscreen. Out of the corner of her eye she saw him rub his forehead and the crinkles around his eyes suggested a smile.

'It's been a while.'

'Oh,' she said, 'and a while would be what?'

He laughed. 'You're not behind the door, are you?'

'Usually I am,' she admitted. 'Usually I'm behind the door, down the hall and into the boxroom on the left.'

He had a full, dirty laugh.

'So?' she probed. *I can't believe I'm being so pushy.*

'Two years.'

'Can I ask?'

'We were together for four years and she got sick.'

'Oh, my God! I'm so sorry. I'm being way too nosy.'

'No, it's okay. It took time but she got better . . . She got better and decided she wanted a different kind of life so she broke my heart and moved to Australia, where I believe she married a surfer six months later.'

'Right.' Harri was bloody sorry she'd started her interrogation. 'I feel terrible.'

'Why?' His smile had returned.

'Just do.' She shrugged her shoulders.

Harri didn't engage in the lives of those not close to her because sad stories affected her too much. She took them on board and lived them when she was alone. Sadness haunted her.

'What about you?' he asked, noticing that Harri's knees had turned towards him.

'I was going out with a carpenter called Simon for nearly a year. We split up six months ago. It wasn't anything in particular, we just didn't fit.'

'And before Simon?'

'College thing. Ian Grace. He was an engineering student. We were together for just over three years.'

'Trinity?'

'UCD.'

'What happened with you two?'

'He took a job in Saudi. I don't really like the sun.'

'Harri?'

'Yes?'

'If I promise not to talk shit would you agree to see me again?'

'Yes.'

'Good,' he said. 'Harri?'

'Yes?'

'Would you mind terribly if I leaned in for a kiss? I don't mind if you say no.'

'No.'

'Oh, bollocks!'

'Only joking!' And that was it.

They just fitted.

They were both hard workers and both liked to read. Neither of them was particularly into music or TV, preferring a silent room as a background to conversation. They both liked to talk, to cook and to laugh. James could always make Harri laugh.

'Knock, knock?'

'No.'

'Ah, come on! Knock, knock!'

'James.'

'Knock, knock?'

'God almighty, who's there?'

'Gorilla.'

'Gorilla who?'

'Gorilla me a cheese sandwich.'

You know when someone tells you such an utterly stupid unfunny joke that all you can do is laugh at the ridiculousness of it? Well, Harri would laugh and he'd clap his hands, delighting in his hilarity.

'There's something wrong with you.'

'Yeah, there is! I'm hungry so gorilla me a cheese sandwich.'

'Oh, sweet God, don't drag the thing on!'

'You love my jokes.'

She really didn't, but she did love him.

She was gazing out on to a clean street lined with white blossom trees that seemed to herald a time for change. It was while she was adrift in a place beyond the blossom that the awful feeling came in the form of a sweeping wave. Terror rose from within her and threatened to engulf not only her but the entire room. Her head was buzzing. Everything inside her shouted that something was off. *Oh, no, not again!* An overpowering and insane notion crossed her mind that she didn't belong. She had been here before. Her hands were clammy and her heart rate increased. *Just breathe, Harri, like George said.* The clammy hands threatened to shake. *Just calm down, Harri. Don't be a dick, please.* She knew that at any moment she would begin to feel dizzy and then she would disconnect. *Mum is going to kill me.* Her breath shortened and her hands rose to her throat, signalling that she was choking.

Mona was the first to notice. 'Oh, Christ, she's at it again! George, call an ambulance before she goes bloody blue on us!'

1 May 1975 – Thursday

Mam was crying again last night. I heard HIM come in. He was shouting at her calling, 'Deirdre, Deirdre, Deirdre!' Some day he'll wear her name out. I heard him bang at her door. She must have locked it. 'Deirdre, open the door, you miserable bitch!'

'I won't!' she said.

Can you believe she answered him when he'd called her a miserable bitch? What's wrong with her? At least she locked her door. I locked mine too. He's a freak. I hate him. He

16

stormed out screaming that he'd be back, and made his way down the road cursing loud enough for Nosy Crowley in number seven to hear. I saw her curtain twitching as he passed her house, swearing at nothing and everything. You could see she was delighted – that'll keep her talking, the nosy old biddy.

Sometimes I lie awake and wonder why did she have to marry him. Did she really love him or was she just lonely after Dad? I thought we were happy. In fact, I know we were until he came along. She rushed into it – at least, that's what I heard Nosy Crowley say in the chemist when I was hiding behind shelving and she was talking with Mrs Stephens about the last time he left our house cursing. Nosy called her stupid, and to be fair to Nosy, she's not wrong. My mother is a stupid woman. I'd never be stupid enough to fall for a horrible man like him and I'll never marry.

School's a nightmare, can't wait for the holidays. Don't know what I'm going to do – HE says I'll have to get a job. Maybe I will, but not because of him. In two weeks I'll be sixteen. Mam said I might get a bottle of Charlie and a Bay City Rollers tape. I hope it happens. I hope he doesn't drink all the money. I adore the smell of Charlie.

In one year I'll be gone from here. I can't wait. Every day feels like a year and some days feel like ten years. Sheila says she's going to join the bank. Last week she wanted to do hairdressing, and a month ago she was thinking of teaching. I don't know what I want to be. I just know that I want to be anywhere but Wicklow.

I saw that doctor again – he was fishing off the rocks. He looks my age, maybe a year or two older. I'd put him at nineteen. Sheila says he's at least mid-twenties. He always looks sad even when he smiles. He's shy too. It must be hard for him in a new town. I'd hate to be a doctor – people are disgusting. I wonder where he's from.

I had a dream last night. I dreamed I was on a boat that kept returning to shore. Every time the boat inched out to sea it was pulled back. It scared me. I'm obsessing. Sheila says I obsess. She thinks I should relax and enjoy life. Easy for her to say – she doesn't live with a drunk. Her father is getting rich serving all the drunks in town. She's never had to hide in her room. She gets to sit with her dad watching *Morecambe and Wise* on a colour TV so it's easy for her to relax and enjoy life. I miss Sheila. I wish she wasn't with that Dave. What's so great about Dave? He has a Kevin Keegan perm. Sheila thinks it's cool and it's really, really not. He stinks of his dad's Brut and he's always pawing her. Yesterday he kept putting her down trying to be funny, which he wasn't. I wanted to punch him hard. Mam says that sometimes I get a look and it frightens her.

It's after ten and I'm tired. HE's still in the pub. If I go to sleep now maybe I won't hear him. First I'll lock the door. Sheila's dad says that you should never lock a bedroom door in case of fire. It's not fire I'm scared of. I'd rather burn.

I just decided. Tomorrow I'm going to look for a summer job, anything to get me out of this house. It makes me laugh.

The Bay City Rollers

He says I have to get a job but he sits in a pub or leans on the bank wall with his mate all day every day. Mam always makes excuses. She says dockers can only work when the coasters come in, but Anita Shea's dad is a docker and he paints and wallpapers houses, and Tim Healy's dad takes shifts behind the bar in the Pole instead of sitting in front of it drinking all the money he's earned for two days' work in two hours. Anyway, I don't care about that. He can do what he wants. I'm gone from here. One year can feel like for ever or a day.

My dad used to say that. I think I'll sit with him for a while tomorrow. Maybe I'll clean his headstone. Birds seem to think it's a toilet and it's funny because Rita Heneghan is right beside him and her headstone is always clean as a whistle and I've never seen anyone visit her. Once a bird actually did a shit on his one while I was sitting there! My dad would think that was funny. He used to laugh a lot. I miss him. I wish he was here, but he's not so what's the point in wishing? He's gone. Feck him for that.

Oh, and just so I never forget, today in the woods I heard spring. I actually heard it, in the trees and the breeze and the dogs barking along the trails and the sky was so, so blue and the grass was the brightest green. I leaned on brown bark and inhaled fresh air. When all is said and done I'll miss those woods.

2. A&E

Harri woke up lying on a gurney in A&E. Her mother and father were sitting at either side of her. There was no sign of her fiancé. George was standing by the window, commenting on a woman who was clearly making an arse of an attempt to parallel-park. 'Good God, woman, you could fit a small island in there!'

Harri was awake long before she could bring herself to open her eyes. I can't believe I've done it again. Her parents were silent. Eventually she could feign slumber no more.

'There she is,' her father said. 'There's our girl.'

'I'm sorry, Dad.'

'Don't be sorry.'

'I'm sorry, Mum.'

'Ssh, my darling, everything's fine now.'

Within seconds, George was lying with her on the bed, her head resting in the crook of his arm. 'If it's any consolation, you're the most glamorous patient in this place.'

Harri realized she was still in her wedding dress. She fought tears. 'Where's James?'

Duncan's brother, Father Ryan, came into the room with four coffees. Harri's parents relieved him of theirs and Gloria passed George his.

'Do you want a coffee, my darling?'

'No thanks, Mum.'

'She's back,' Gloria said to her brother-in-law.

Father Ryan leaned over the bed. 'Well, hello there,' he said. 'You'll be the death of one of us, Harriet Ryan.'

'Sorry, Uncle Thomas.'

Father Ryan allowed the twins to call him Uncle Thomas but to everyone else, including his brother and sister-in-law, he was Father Ryan. 'Well, they say three times is a charm.' This latest panic attack was Harri's second, the first having occurred on the eve of her first aborted wedding six months previously.

'Where's James?' she asked again.

Gloria's hands fluttered towards her neck, as they always did when she was anxious. Duncan remained silent and Father Ryan was busy drinking his coffee. George spoke up. 'He was here, Harri. He made sure you were okay and then he left.'

'He hates me,' she said, and buried her head in the pillow.

'He doesn't hate you,' said George. 'He's just upset.'

'I've left him at the altar twice, George.'

'You didn't do it on purpose.'

'There's something wrong. I'm obviously mental.'

'No, you're not!' Gloria said, attempting a smile. 'Every bride gets nervous.'

'But they don't end up in A&E!'

'Harri, mind your tone!' her dad warned.

'Sorry, Dad.'

'That's all right, love, we're all a little tense.'

'Where's Melissa?'

'She's settling the kids. She's going to leave them with Gerry and then she'll meet us at my place,' George replied. He drank some coffee and spluttered. 'Awful, just bloody awful!' He was referring to the coffee but it summed up the day beautifully.

Harri lay on the gurney surrounded by her family, yet she was completely and utterly alone. The terror had subsided and in its place were horror and a sinking depression that was turning her brain to glue. *He'll never forgive me. I can't believe I've done it again. What's wrong with me?*

George's apartment was a penthouse in Temple Bar. He loved the bustle of the city centre. He'd bought it four years before, after Nana had died leaving the twins what she described as healthy nest eggs. It was spacious with three large bedrooms; it had two floors and high ceilings. It was painted white throughout and the walls were covered with African and European art collected on many different trips. At night the city lights made for a spectacular view but this evening the blinds were drawn, with a low lamp providing the only break in the darkness.

'Can the patient drink wine?' Melissa asked George, as she poured him a glass while he tucked a blanket around his sister's legs, having insisted she lay on the sofa.

'Her doctor would say no but I, like the man from Del Monte, say yes.' He grinned and patted Harri's flat hair. 'You really need to wash that before something decides to land on it.'

Melissa handed Harri a drink, then made herself comfortable in George's favourite oversized armchair.

'Do I really need this blanket?' Harri asked, pulling at it.

'Yes,' her brother told her.

'I'm so tired,' she said.

Melissa sighed loudly. 'I just don't get it. We all know how you hate to be the centre of attention but this is ridiculous.'

Still at the hospital, after George had told their parents to go home, Harri had broken down, wailing and bawling. She had stopped only when the doctor wondered aloud as to whether or not she required sectioning. Then and there she had pledged no more tears and she was determined to uphold her promise.

'I understand,' George said, his wine swirling around his glass, checking its colour and clarity.

'And?' Melissa said, almost irritated by what she often described as the bullshit tasting techniques he'd learned in his bullshit wine-tasting course.

'She's not ready for marriage.'

'What do you mean she's not ready? She's thirty. They've been going out for six years. They've got an apartment together, a rundown cottage in Wexford and a tank full of exotic fish.'

'So what's your point?' George asked, swishing his wine vigorously enough to cause a minor spillage.

'My point is that she committed three years ago on the day she signed for the apartment. She committed again two years ago when, against my advice, they bought that shithole in Wexford, and once again when they inherited his great-auntie Edna's freaky fish and – Will you please stop swishing and just drink the stuffing wine?'

'That's ownership. Ownership and commitment are two totally different things – and it's my apartment so I'll swish if I want to swish.'

'Homo!'

'Witch!'

'Could you both shut up?' Harri said, and drained her glass.

'Sorry,' George said.

'Me too,' Melissa echoed.

Melissa had been Harri's best friend since they were both aged five. She had been George's first and only girlfriend aged sixteen. He'd broken up with her exactly two weeks and one kiss into their short-lived affair. Six months later he came out to his mother while she was putting out the washing. She pretended to have gone momentarily deaf and it was another four years before George's sexuality was mentioned in the house again.

Suddenly Harri felt the need to throw up. Melissa got her to the bathroom and held her flattened hair away from her face while she vomited red wine. Afterwards Melissa took her to George's spare room and tucked her into bed.

'Melissa, do you ever wonder why things happen?' Harri asked.

'All the time,' Melissa said.

'Do you think George is right?'

'Well, he never has been before.' Melissa laughed a little.

'I don't know what's going on.'

'I know but give it time.'

'James won't talk to me.' She was crying again.

'Give him a little space.'

'How much space? A day, a week, a year?'

'Harri, in the church . . . well, he was devastated too.'

'I didn't mean to hurt him.'

'I know. We'll get to the bottom of it, Harri. I promise.' Melissa turned out the light and closed the door.

'Too late,' Harri whispered, 'I've lost him.'

Melissa sat outside the door, listening to her best friend's sobs. She cried too. She couldn't help it. In James's face she had seen something break. There was no going back. Harri was right, she had lost him, and it felt like a death and a time to grieve.

George had another glass of wine waiting for Melissa when at last she returned. They sat opposite one another, comfortable in each other's company, like family. 'Is she okay?' he asked.

Melissa shook her head. George became unusually quiet.

'What?' Melissa asked, after a while.

'James believes it's all about him.'

'Well, he wouldn't be far off. Two attempted weddings, two pretty serious panic attacks.'

'It's not the only time,' George said, rubbing his chin in what appeared to be a demonstration of careful consideration.

'I don't understand.'

'When we were kids it happened a lot, maybe until Harri hit five or six. I can't remember exactly.'

'But she said –'

'She doesn't remember.'

'But your parents, they told the doctor –'

'They lied.'

'Why would they do that?' she whispered, although her friend was a floor away.

'I don't know.'

'And why didn't you say anything?'

'I don't know.'

'All that stuff earlier about Harri not being ready for commitment . . .'

'That could still be the case. I just don't understand why my parents are lying.'

'She needs to know.'

'I agree.'

'So?' she pushed.

'So I'll talk to them, see what they say. Harri's upset enough – I need to understand before I bother her with this.'

'And James?'

'James needs space. I mean, wouldn't you?'

Melissa nodded. 'I just don't get it.'

'Me neither,' George shrugged, 'but something's off.'

Gloria picked at her evening meal. She'd put together a pasta dish with leftovers from the night before. Father Ryan was starving, having travelled from Galway early that morning after snatching half a slice of toast, then barely making it to the church to hear that his niece would not be joining the congregation. There had been no time for lunch because James had driven him from the church to the hospital. *Poor boy.* He had tried to speak words of comfort but James had been silent and too far away to be reached. The journey to St Vincent's had seemed to last an eternity, especially as James had a tendency towards aggressive manoeuvring.

Father Ryan favoured travelling by bike. His parish was a small one just outside Galway city. He only used the car when he had to travel between parishes to say Mass. 'Nothing like a bit of fresh air,' he'd say. Father Ryan wasn't afraid of the cold – in fact, he welcomed it. He couldn't stand his brother's central heating, which brought him out in a rash, but, of course, he'd never say so, even going as far as to thank Gloria for remembering to put on the electric blanket – he'd discovered this when he had taken his suitcase upstairs. *It's spring! What on earth is the woman thinking?* He'd switched it off.

He was looking forward to going home on the train the next day. He'd sit and eat some lunch, watch the country-side pass him by and attempt to quell his fears and any associated guilt. *I did it for you, Harri. Mostly I did it for you.*

Duncan watched his wife picking at her food, afraid that she might break. He was ever mindful that at any moment he could lose her to the deep depression that had once all but stolen her away. Days like this one were test-ing. He was determined to protect her, he just wasn't sure how. 'Are you still with me, Glory?'

She looked up absent-mindedly. 'I'm cold,' she said.

Bloody hell, Father Ryan thought.

'Maybe you'd like to go to bed,' Duncan offered. 'It's been a long day.'

'No,' she said. 'I wouldn't sleep.'

'I'll turn up the heat.' Duncan got up and went out, leaving his wife and brother alone.

'Is this our fault?' Gloria muttered.

'Don't think that,' he said. 'How could it be?'

'I'm scared,' she said. 'I can't lose her again.' Tears welled in her dark eyes.

'You've never lost her,' he reminded his sister-in-law, squeezing her hand.

'You know what I mean,' she said, allowing a tear escape. 'I can't lose my child again.'

Duncan came back in time to see his wife wipe away a second tear. 'Glory?'

'I'm fine,' she lied. She stood up as he sat down and kissed the top of his head. 'Maybe I will have an early night.'

Duncan again rose to his feet.

'No.' She was adamant. 'I'm fine. Stay here with Father Ryan. Finish your dinner.'

'Goodnight, my love,' he said, from his chair.

'Goodnight, my darling,' she responded, from the door.

Father Ryan sat quietly by the thankfully empty fire-place, staring into his glass. Duncan sat in the chair opposite. Their spirits were somewhere else. After a time Father Ryan broached Gloria's fears with his younger brother.

'Harri's scared of something unseen, something unknown,' he said.

'She shouldn't be.'

'You're still so sure she doesn't deserve the truth? That,

somewhere inside her, she doesn't already know?' he asked, unafraid of his brother's wrath.

'There's nothing to know!' Duncan said, slamming his glass down on the table.

'Today –'

'Today has nothing to do with anything!'

'Duncan –'

'Thomas.'

Father Ryan knew that when his brother called him by his given name he meant business. 'Maybe her panic attacks have nothing to do with anything and maybe they do – all I know is that in the end the truth will out,' he warned. 'No matter what, the truth will out.' He headed up the stairs to his bed, leaving his brother alone to contemplate.

Duncan drank two more glasses of whiskey, then went up to his attic office, to the drawer that held the copy of the file he hadn't had reason to look at for many years.

He opened it and a picture fell out. He picked it up and turned on his desk light. The girl's hair was long and dark, her staring eyes deep green, her skin pale and her lips part purple, part blue. She was seventeen and she was dead.

10 May 1975 – Saturday

It's the tenth of May already. Today I am sixteen! Sixteen! Can you believe it? I can't. Sixteen years ago my mother gave birth to me. It was a warm spring afternoon in 1959. Mam said that my dad nearly crashed the car trying to get her to the hospital. She said it was a miracle that we all survived the drive. He nearly crashed into a tree, a wall and an old man in a cart. He had borrowed his boss's Ford Fairlane and Mam said that he wasn't a practised driver at the time and all she could think about was, how would they pay for a replacement fancy car if they survived the crash? Thinking of him driving like a madman, with Mam roaring at him, makes me laugh. I can hear him. 'Hang on, Deirdre! We're nearly there, girly girl!' He always called her 'girly girl'.

I can hear her too. 'Hang on? I'm hanging on for dear life! Slow down, you maniac!' She used to be so strong. She never let my dad get away with anything. What happened to her?

I'm sixteen. It's so weird. I used to think I'd never make it to sixteen. When I was ten, sixteen seemed so far away, and after Dad died I was convinced I'd die too. I don't know why but for the longest time I had a sense I'd die young. I still do but only sometimes and, anyway, now I'm sixteen and that's not so young. This time next year I'll be seventeen and, let's face it, seventeen is practically ancient.

Mam actually lived up to her promise. She said she might get me a bottle of Charlie and a Bay City Rollers tape and she did. Wonders will never cease. Now that I think of it, she used to always keep her promises before he came along and now . . . well, I know it's not really her fault. She's doing her best. I had a good day. We had cake for tea. Sheila came and it was nice, even if she did bring stupid Dave. Still, he gave me a bunch of flowers. He'd picked them himself and they were mucky but they're nice. He didn't have to do that. Even

Sheila seemed surprised. It made me feel mean for thinking he's a thick even though I still do.

HE was nowhere to be seen, TG. Mam says he hasn't been drinking for over a week now. He's been quiet, no banging doors, no shouting, no nothing. He still can't look me in the eye but I'm glad. Let him keep his eyes on the floor. Let him rot.

Today after school I went to sit by the painting of the *Eliana* cargo vessel on the pier wall. I love looking out across the water and far away. On a clear day you can see Wales. Well, not really, but kind of. The doctor was fishing again. He hasn't been there for a few days. I tripped and hurt my ankle. He came over to help so I pretended it was worse than it was. I don't know why, I just wanted to talk to him. Sheila thinks I like him. She's wrong. It's nothing like that. I mean I do like him but not the way she likes Dave. He helped me up and he sat me on one of the flatter rocks. I said I was okay and asked him his name. He told me Brendan. He's from Cork. I like his accent – it's sing-songy. He's only in town until Dr Anderson gets better. Dr Anderson is about 107 and has had four heart attacks. I told him the old man should stay at home and let him keep the job. He laughed but he says he belongs somewhere else. I know the feeling.

Henry from Delamere's riding school phoned and told Mam that there was a summer job if I wanted it. I'm not sure. Cleaning stables is pretty low – horse manure morning, noon and night. PUKE!!!!!!! Still, there's nothing else out there. I've tried every coffee place in town, and the restaurants and the shops. Henry is the manager. He seems nice, and the owner is never really there. He's a horse trainer and spends a lot of time away. Good. I've heard he's a bit of a bastard from Jessica Harney, whose brother is a jockey. He's twenty-five and half my size so I suppose it's a good thing he can ride. It's a nice place. I'd never been there before the interview. The house is huge!!!!! I wasn't inside it, though. Henry walked me around the stables and the paddocks while we talked. The horses were lovely. A brown one called Betsy really took to me – well, she made lots of noise, tried to butt me and dribbled on my shoulder, but Henry said that's a good sign. WEIRD. Maybe I'll take it and then if something else comes up I can always leave.

HE's working since yesterday and the job will run on till tomorrow. The load is spirits so he'll sneak some to sell or to drink, and either way he'll be delighted with himself – that is, until he gets so drunk that he wants to do nothing but hurt someone. First he'll come home with flowers and a box of Milk Tray and Mam will wear her best dress – and she could really do with a new best dress – and they'll dance in the sitting room and he'll whisper to her and kiss her neck even if I'm in the room. And when I leave I'll hear her laugh, and although she's laughing I know that she knows that in another few hours it's likely she'll be crying and I just don't understand.

I might be knee deep in horseshit but I'll do my best to make the most out of working at Delamere's. The summer holiday is just around the corner and I'm going to do my best to make it a good one. I'm sitting in my room listening to the Bay City Rollers and I smell great. My flowers are in one of Mam's vases. Happy birthday to me!

3. Broken

It was after two when Harri unlocked the door to the apartment she shared with James. When they had first decided to buy, she had insisted that any property purchased would be south-side and by the sea. She didn't want to move far from her parents, and although James was initially reluctant, when they eventually found a two-bed apartment in Monkstown he had been the first to fall in love. Now it was empty as she had suspected it would be. Unopened post lay on the hall floor. The plant on the table across from the door was in desperate need of hydration. The full-length gilt-edged mirror revealed Harri to be a shadow of the girl who had left three days earlier. She hadn't slept one wink in two nights. James was still not speaking to her. His phone was permanently off. George had insisted that if she was intent on going to the apartment he would accompany her.

'No,' she had said firmly.

'But –'

'No.' Harri needed to go home – and she needed to wait there until James returned. She had to see him, to explain, possibly to beg. 'I need to see him . . . to explain . . .'

'Explain what?'

'I don't know,' she admitted.

'Stay one more day.'

She shook her head. 'Thanks for minding me, George, but it's time I left.'

He stepped aside to allow her out of the door. 'I'm always going to be here.'

'I know.' She smiled at her brother. *I know.*

She hung her coat on the rack and opened the door to the kitchen. Healthy plants stood on the windowsill over the sink. She opened the window behind them, allowing sea air to circulate. She put the kettle on and ventured from kitchen to sitting room. Boxes sat in the middle of the floor. They contained belongings, specifically James's belongings. The realization smacked her with the force of a bus. Her legs felt weak and she sat down quickly on the sofa. She stared at the boxes for the longest time, digesting their meaning. *He's leaving me.* In the large tank, James's auntie Edna's exotic fish swam about, unperturbed by the boxes or indeed the woman crying.

It was after six when she heard the key in the lock. She hadn't stirred for a few hours and was afraid to move for fear of stabbing pins and needles. It was a few minutes before he appeared. She was gazing at the door, waiting for it to open. His face betrayed slight shock, making it clear that he hadn't noticed her coat hanging in the hall.

'Harri,' he said quietly.

'James,' she replied.

'How are you feeling?' he asked politely.

'Fine. Better. No, actually I'm worse. With every passing moment I feel a little worse.'

'I'm sorry,' he said, still standing by the door, both arms hanging limply by his sides.

'Why are you sorry? I'm the one who did this,' she said, looking from him to the boxes.

'It's not your fault,' he said, glancing at his exotic fish, swimming and carefree.

'So forgive me.'

'It's not about forgiveness.'

'Don't leave.'

'I have to.'

'Why?'

'I can't do this again.'

'Well, let's just not get married – let's stay as we are. I love the way we are.'

'I can't,' he whispered, and his big grey eyes filled. He shook his head. 'I just can't.'

'It's not you!' Harri cried.

'How can it not be?' he asked.

Harri's head hung low. She was dissolving and James fought the urge to hold her.

'James.'

'Yes?'

'I should go. You should stay.'

'I won't have that. I'll be staying with Malcolm until I find a place.'

'What about the apartment?' she asked dully.

'In a few months when we're settled we can think about selling this place and the house in Wexford.'

'Okay. And the fish?'

'I'll come and get them when I find somewhere to live.'

'Okay.' Her eyes were leaking fiercely. 'I really hate those fish – they freak me out.'

'I know. I'll pick them up as soon as –'

'I'm sorry – I'm just not a fish person,' she interrupted.

'I know. It's okay.'

'I'll take care of them. I won't let you down. I mean, not again.'

'Thanks. Now I should go,' he said, backing away.

'Please don't,' she begged, hands clasped.

'I have to.'

He almost ran from the place, forgetting his boxes. The door slammed and she was alone once more, the last grains of her dignity pooling on the floor. All the while the indifference of the fish taunted her. *Bastards.* Soon she would be hollow and then she wouldn't care. *Is this what it's like to want to die?*

A couple of days later, George had spent a good part of his Saturday morning on the phone to a number of Italian winemakers. His latest venture was a wine shop in Clontarf and he was determined to supply only the finest *vino* – *sans* the middle man – and he was on a charm offensive. During his flitting from here to there he'd become fluent in a number of languages, French and Italian included – languages came easily to him. He'd laugh and tell Harri that talk was cheap in any dialect. He was also good at accents. He could be funny as a Texan or an Italian, a Mexican, an Englishman, a German or a Frenchman. He could do each and every Dublin accent, Cork, Galway, Kerry, Belfast and so on. He understood nuance. He heard it and remembered it. His mum said he could have been an actor, to which he had once retorted that he was gay but not that gay. He was due in Italy on Monday and he thought about taking Harri. He figured she could do with getting away but first he had a dinner to attend.

Gloria had spent most of the day with her daughter. She had arrived at Harri's early with a basket of food. Harri had let her in after Gloria had spent a few minutes knocking furiously. Her daughter looked terrible. It was clear that she hadn't eaten: she was drawn and seemed almost vacant.

'He'll be back,' Gloria had said.

'No, he won't,' Harri had replied, blinking in an attempt to relieve tired eyes.

'He will,' Gloria had repeated. 'He'll be back.'

Harri had ignored her.

'George is coming for dinner. Won't you join us?' Gloria had asked.

'No.'

'Please.'

'I'm drained.'

'Okay,' her mother had said.

Now Harri was silent. Her head hurt. She felt so lost and alone, yet craved her mother's departure. *You can't help me, Mum. I wish I knew what was going on.*

'Last night I dreamed that your father was Mel Gibson – *Mad Max* Mel.' Gloria laughed. 'He was driving a Ford Capri and complaining about the Jaysusing brakes.'

'Last night I slept for maybe an hour,' said Harri, 'and during that hour I dreamed I was lying on cold ground, dying.'

'Oh, I'm sure it's just exhaustion, my darling,' her

mother soothed her, somewhat paler than she had been mere seconds before.

Soon after that, Gloria left and drove into the Super-quinn supermarket car park. There she switched off the engine and cried. Five minutes later she emerged, makeup flawless, in time to catch up with Mona, who was heading towards the butcher.

'Have you time for a coffee?' Gloria asked.

'Of course.' Mona smiled.

Sitting in the coffee shop, Gloria told her friend about her damaged daughter.

'Of course she's upset. She should be on honeymoon. Instead she's alone in a flat with those bearded fish.'

'Mona!'

'Well, they may be exotic but they're bloody ugly.'

'There's one in particular that makes my stomach turn,' Gloria confessed.

'She'll get over it,' Mona said, after a minute or two's contemplation.

'I don't know.' Gloria sighed. 'She loves him. If I had lost Duncan I would have died.'

'She's not you,' Mona said kindly.

'No,' Gloria agreed. *She's definitely not me.*

'Gloria, worse things happen. I don't want to sound cold but it's true. Your Duncan knows all about that.'

'I've never seen her so down.'

'She's bound to be.'

'I think it's more.'

'More than the second wedding that never was?' Mona's voice carried a hint of sarcasm.

Gloria clammed up. 'You're probably right.'

'Of course I'm right. I'm always right when it comes to other people.'

Gloria managed a smile.

After they had parted, Gloria procured the required shopping to entertain her son. He was home before her, and Duncan arrived soon after. George helped his mother prepare dinner while Duncan read the newspaper. He had called in to see his daughter an hour after her mother had left. He had found her listless. She had taken something to sleep. He carried her to bed and tucked her in, the way he had when she was a child.

'Dad.'

'Yes, dear?'

'Have you ever felt that you were a piece from another jigsaw?'

'Everything will be fine,' he said, but his heart was beating wildly.

'I have this creepy feeling.'

'Go to sleep,' he said, fearing to hear any more. 'Go to sleep now.'

He closed the door and leaned heavily against it. His brother's words rang in his ears. *The truth will out. No matter what, the truth will out.*

Duncan was quiet at dinner. Gloria talked about her *Mad Max* Mel dream, making her son laugh.

'I find it hard to imagine Mel Gibson saying "Jaysus-ing".'

'As hard as I find it to imagine your dad in a wife-beater and driving a Ford Capri. That, my son, is the beauty of

REM.' Gloria smiled at her son. She was desperate to leave the image of her tattered daughter behind her.

It was only during dessert that George found the necessary courage to tackle his parents on a subject he knew they would do their utmost to avoid.

'Do you remember when Harri and I were kids?'

'Of course,' his mother said. 'It seems like only yesterday.'

'Do you remember Harri's panic attacks?' He felt it was best not to dick around.

'Excuse me?' Duncan said sternly.

'You had her checked for epilepsy. I remember it. And she always put her hands to her throat as though she was choking – like Mum does when she's nervous.'

By coincidence, Gloria's hands were fluttering towards her neck.

'You don't know what you're talking about,' Duncan said firmly.

'So explain it,' George challenged.

'I don't have to explain anything to you,' Duncan said, standing.

'Sit down, Duncan.' Gloria was alarmed by his tone.

He sat as instructed, eyeing his son dangerously.

George was not cowed. 'Why did you lie to the doctor?'

'We did not lie,' Duncan said, his voice hoarse.

'Why are you lying to me?'

Gloria was suddenly crying. 'We didn't want to.'

George looked at his mother. Duncan rested his head in his hands.

'What the hell?' said George.

'We just didn't want to open a can of worms,' said Gloria. 'They ask so many questions – question after question. It gets so hard to keep everything straight.'

Duncan's eyes darted from his crying wife to his son. He remembered his daughter's earlier disturbing question and, deep down, he knew that the time for avoidance was past. *The truth will out.*

'Dad?'

'We love you both so much,' Duncan said, all trace of his anger now gone.

'I know,' George said. His insides squirmed.

'You are my twins,' Gloria said, pale and shaking. 'My babies.'

Duncan's attention was drawn to his wife. 'Glory?'

'I won't lose her again,' she said, breathing deeply.

'I know. I know, my love. You have to calm down now. Okay?'

'I can't lose her, Duncan. Oh, God help us!'

George was alarmed at the state his mother was getting herself into. He had grown up being careful around her, warned of her delicacy, but he had never seen her break down before.

The conversation was abandoned. Duncan took his wife upstairs to bed and spent an hour settling her. By the time he returned George was on his third glass of wine.

'She hasn't been like that since –'

'Since when, Dad?'

'Well, it's been a long time.'

George had never seen his dad so rattled. It was deeply

disquieting. Duncan poured himself a whiskey and sat in his favourite chair by the empty fireplace.

'Does Mum have some sort of mental condition? Has it been passed on to Harri?'

'No.' Duncan shook his head. 'Well, yes. Your mother has suffered with her nerves in the past but it was as a result of something terrible. She's been fine all these years. And Harri, well, no, your mother hasn't passed anything down to her.'

'Something terrible?' George pushed.

'I can't say.'

'You can't not say.'

'You're right, but not tonight. Your sister has a right to know what you know so I'm asking you to wait. Give me one week. Give your mother and your sister one week.'

'I'm going to Italy on Monday.'

'Cancel it.'

George didn't argue. 'Okay,' he said.

'Thank you, son.' Duncan drained his glass and made his way upstairs to his attic office.

George finished his glass of wine and left his child-hood home. He stood on the street lined with white blossom trees, waiting for a taxi to pass. He looked back at the house and felt like a stranger to the people inside. *What the hell is going on?*

Susan left her fourth message that day. 'Harri, it's me again. I'm desperate to talk to you. I just want to hear that you're okay. Please call me. I swear I won't talk. I won't say a word. Just phone me, just talk to me. I love you. It's Susan by the way.'

Susan always identified herself. It was as if a part of her felt she was invisible to those around her, making it necessary to remind the people she cared for who she was. She hung up and sipped some coffee, sitting at her kitchen counter. She was listening to Moby's album *Play*.

Beth, her sixteen-year-old daughter, smiled to herself. *Bloody* Play*! There are other albums in the world, Mother.* Suddenly she was sitting in front of Susan, clicking her fingers. 'Where were you?'

Susan sighed and smiled. 'Far from here.'

'You heard from Harri?'

'No.'

'You okay?'

'I wish she'd call.'

'She will, Mum.'

'Are you hungry?'

'No.'

'Are you sure?'

'I'm sure.'

'I feel like crying,' Susan admitted.

'So cry.'

'I can't. I'm too old for that.'

'No, you're not.'

'How did you get to be so sensible?'

'Good parenting.'

'Smooth. You're going to ask me for money in the next five minutes, aren't you?'

'No, but I might do in the morning.'

'Beth?'

'What?'

'Are we close?'

Beth's face reddened. 'Of course.'

Susan pretended not to notice the blush. 'Good.'

'Mum, sometimes I worry about you.'

'Don't be silly.'

'I'm not being silly. Sometimes I wish you were happier.'

'I am happy.'

'You're being silly if you think I don't notice. I notice.'

Susan smiled, her eyes filling. 'Okay, I stand corrected. I did not raise a fool.'

'So leave him.'

Susan laughed. 'It's not that easy.'

'It is.'

'No, Beth, it's really not.'

'I love my dad but he's an arsehole to you and it makes me not like him.'

'He does his best.'

'No, Mum, you do your best – he does everyone else.'

'Beth!' Shock brought stinging tears to her eyes.

'I'm sorry, Mum, I shouldn't have said that.' She kissed her mother's forehead. 'I love you, Mum. Goodnight.'

'Goodnight, sweetheart.'

Susan was alone and wide awake in her large and empty marital bed.

It was after midnight when Harri rang. 'I'm so sorry. I was asleep most of the evening. I just picked up your messages.'

'I don't mind. I'm just glad to hear your voice.'

'Is everything okay with work?'

'Don't ask about that. Everything's fine.'

'Me too. I'm fine.'

'Liar.'

'You're right. I'm lying.'

'Tell me what you're thinking.'

'Can't, too fuzzy.'

'Try.'

'I'm sure you said you weren't going to talk and talking includes asking questions.'

'So we're both liars.' Susan laughed, then fell silent, waiting for Harri to speak.

After a moment or two Harri obliged. 'I think I'm losing my mind. I think I've been fighting this meltdown for a really, really long time. I think there's something eating me from inside out. My head hurts, my body aches, I'm perpetually scared. I'm teetering on the edge, Susan, and any minute now if I let go or if I just give in and allow gravity to take over I think I could disappear.'

Susan sighed and closed her eyes, then opened them and focused. 'Well, the good news is that you're not depressive.'

'Excuse me?'

'Depression runs in my family. You, my friend, are far too self-aware to be clinically depressed. That's good news, trust me.'

'So?' Harri asked.

'So, whatever is going on, you have control. You can control it.'

'I don't know.'

'You can.'

'Susan.'

'Yes?'

'I'm still really tired.'

'So sleep.'

'Okay.'

'I'll call you tomorrow and you will pick up the phone!' Susan ordered.

'Okay.'

'Okay.' Susan hung up.

It was close to twenty past twelve and still her husband had not returned from work – no phone call, no explanation, no nothing. Beth was right, it was simple, but she was also wrong. After all, what does a sixteen-year-old know about the world?

30 May 1975 – Friday

Today was the last day of school for eight whole weeks. Wha-hay! I don't know how to write wha-hay properly but it's how I feel. Mr Murphy let us out early. Sheila, Dave and I headed for the woods. He's not so bad, Dave. I mean, he's still a complete thick but I like him a little more every time I see him. He's kind, annoying but kind. He tries to be a man and when it doesn't work he reverts to being a little boy – mostly he's a little boy. Sheila doesn't see that. She sees something else. People are funny. Life is funny. Dave smokes so now Sheila smokes. She smells nasty and coughs a lot but she says it's cool and she likes it. Dave said when he smokes he feels like Steve McQueen. Maybe he does but he sure as hell doesn't look like him. Sheila asked me to try a smoke but life is hard enough without coughing and smelling nasty and my Charlie is reaching its end. I need to earn money to smell good.

I'm starting my new job on Monday. I'm looking forward to it. Henry said I was a natural with horses last Saturday when I went for orientation. I'm not really sure what that means but I do like them. I like their eyes, especially Betsy's – it's as though she sees my soul. It sounds weird and maybe it is but she does. I really like her. She's old. Learners ride Betsy – she's slow and careful and wise enough to know that really she's the one in control. Betsy's kind. She makes me unafraid. She makes me want to ride. Henry said I can if I want to. It's a perk of the job. A few weeks ago I would have thought bollocks to that but now I'd like to. I'd like to canter with Betsy.

I saw the doctor today. He was walking through town with Father Ryan. They were deep in conversation. I didn't like to intrude. Father Ryan's fairly strict and he wouldn't have appreciated teenage interruption. I wonder what they were talking about. What do they have to say to one another? Maybe someone had died or was dying – or something else, something terrible. Dr Brendan smiled at me, that sad smile of his. I wish I knew what's wrong. I feel like I know him but I don't. Sheila is still teasing me about liking him but she hasn't a clue. The doctor is broken. I know broken. My dad was broken before he died. My mam is broken now and me, well, I'm on the way. I'm not there yet, though.

Mam was crying again last night, not because HE was here but because he wasn't. I don't understand her. He was quiet for a while and now he's gone. I think that's good. I love that he's gone but all she can do is cry. He was working and coming home and being normal – well, as normal as he can be. He wasn't drinking. He wasn't being loud and Mr Funny or mean and moody. He wasn't doing much of anything. Mostly he just sat around looking sad. The other night he tried to apologize to me when Mam was asleep and I told him it was fine. He knew I was lying. He put his hand on my shoulder and I flinched. I wanted to punch him in his face. He knew it. He kept saying sorry. Sorry doesn't mean anything. It doesn't take away the fear. He can be sorry but I can be vigilant. My mam is sad. She doesn't see or maybe she doesn't want to see. She married a loser. She married a weirdo. He can be sorry. We can all be sorry. He asked me if I hated him. I said nothing but I suppose I gave him one of those 'I could kill you' looks that my mam talks about. He was gone the next day. He hasn't been home in ten days.

I hope he never comes back.

4. Crabs

It was almost week since Harri had failed to turn up to her wedding. It was four days since she'd ventured further than her own bedroom and two since she'd bothered to shower. Gloria arrived early. She looked as bad as Harri felt.

'Mum, you look terrible.'

Gloria surveyed her daughter, whose pyjama bottoms and string-vest top belonged to different sets; her hair was standing on end and the dark circles once confined to her eye area were threatening to take over her entire face. 'That makes two of us, my darling.'

Harri caught a glimpse of herself in the long gilt-edged mirror in the hallway. *I really need to bin that mirror.* She followed her mother into the kitchen.

'I'm cooking,' Gloria warned, 'and you are eating.'

'I feel hungry.'

'You do?' Her voice held hope.

'Yeah.'

'You're feeling better?'

'Well, I'm not feeling worse.'

'Good,' Gloria was encouraged, 'that's good.'

Harri sat at the counter nursing a mug of tea while her mother made her favourite risotto. Gloria was quieter than usual. They chatted a little and then lapsed into silence.

Harri, while glad of the silence, was also perturbed by it. 'What's going on with you, Mum?' she said at last.

'Oh, nothing, nothing at all!' Her mother was shaking her head too rapidly and was clearly flustered, her hands fluttering to her neck. She was lying.

When Duncan had made it clear that they had no option but to tell Harri the truth, she had fought him.

'Tell George, but we can't tell Harri.'

'Oh, Glory,' he said, 'we can't do that, love.'

'George will torture us but eventually he'll forgive us.'

'And Harri won't?'

'She might not.'

'I don't believe that.' He was resolute.

She had cried more in the preceding few days than she had in many years, only endeavouring to pull herself together when it became evident that her delicate state was tearing a hole in her husband and her son. *Buck up, Gloria. She'll understand. She's your daughter. She loves you.*

'Well, I think I might be coming down with something,' Gloria said, after a moment or two. 'I doubt it's catching, though.'

'Right.' Harri nodded, unsure.

'You could do with a wash but you do seem a little better,' Gloria observed.

'I promised Susan I'd go to her house for dinner tomorrow.'

'Good for you.'

'Melissa's going.'

'A girls' night?'

'No, Aidan will be there but George can't make it. Have you spoken to him lately?'

'No, darling.' *He's calling every five minutes.*

'Huh, he's being weird.'

'Really?'

'Maybe it's just me.'

'You're still coming to dinner on Wednesday?'

'Yes.'

'George will be there.'

Harri spun on her stool. 'He left a message – he said I should be there.'

'Don't spin, Harri.'

'Sorry.'

Gloria put a plate of risotto in front of her daughter. 'Darling, you know I would die for you, don't you?'

The fork stopped short of Harri's mouth. 'What?'

'I would, you know. I'd gladly die for you both. You, George and your dad are my world. You know that, don't you?'

Are mental breakdowns contagious? Have I infected my entire family? 'I hadn't ever thought about you dying for anyone and I seriously hope it never becomes an issue – but thank you. I love you too.'

Her mother smiled. 'Good girl.' She seemed relieved. 'I should go.'

Harri walked her mother to the front door. They embraced and her mother held her for the longest time.

'I'll see you on Wednesday?' Gloria said.

'I promise.'

'Good girl.'

Gloria was gone, leaving her daughter in a state of suspicion. *This is not just me losing it – something's going on.* And as her brother was intent on avoiding her she knew who to pressure for information.

Susan checked the lamb – it was cooking nicely. Beth had abandoned ship, creeping upstairs as soon as her mother's back was turned, even though she had promised to prepare the starter. *Beth's so jumpy this evening.*

Melissa was the first to arrive, thrilled to bits to have an excuse to leave her home, her husband and their two children. 'I can't believe you managed to talk her into this,' she said, referring to Harri, while pouring two large glasses of wine.

'I was pretty surprised myself.'

'Is George coming?'

'Apparently he's busy. He sounded odd.'

'He and Aidan haven't split up again?'

'No,' she said, handing Melissa a knife. 'Start chopping.'

'Will do, boss.'

Aidan was next to arrive. He was in and pouring wine before the door was closed. 'Kisses,' he said, as usual – the word replaced the gesture.

'What's up with George?' Susan asked.

'Can't say.'

'So there *is* something up with him,' said Melissa.

'I can't say.'

'What is it?'

'Allow me to refer you to my previous statement.'

'Don't be ridiculous, Aidan. You've never kept a secret in your life,' said Susan, covering a bowl of salad with way too much clingfilm.

'It's not my secret.'

'So there *is* a secret!' Melissa said, nodding to herself in a manner not too distant from that of Sherlock Holmes's good friend Watson.

'I can't say.'

'Of course you can,' said Susan. 'That is, of course you can if you ever want another referral.'

'Below the belt, Susan, and no, I can't. George doesn't know what's going on. A dinner will be held in the Ryan household on Wednesday night and all will be revealed.'

'Does this have to do with Harri's panic attacks?' Melissa said, remembering her conversation with George.

'Maybe. Then again, maybe not.'

The two women looked at one another, then back to Aidan. It was all terribly dramatic. Aidan loved drama so he hammed it up as much as possible. The doorbell rang.

'That's Harri,' Susan said, in a whisper.

'Say nothing,' Aidan warned.

'There's nothing to say. We don't actually know anything,' Melissa reminded him.

'A good reason to say nothing,' Aidan said.

The doorbell rang again. 'Oh, for God's sake, answer the door, Susan!'

Harri had washed and put on something respectable.

Susan welcomed her warmly. 'It's so good to see you. You've lost weight. Bitch!'

'Thanks.' Harri felt awkward. She had considered backing out but had had second thoughts, fearing the wrath of her well-meaning friends.

Melissa greeted her with a freshly poured drink.

'I'm driving.'

'Oh, well, all the more for me!' Melissa seemed a little too jovial but, then, she didn't get out much.

Aidan hadn't seen Harri since she'd failed to turn up at her own wedding. 'I'm really sorry, Hars.'

'Thanks. What's going on with George?'

Aidan paled a little. Melissa and Susan were left a little dumbfounded, allowing Harri time to assess the situation. *They all know. Bastards.* 'Well?'

'No idea,' Aidan said unconvincingly.

'Susan?'

'How would I know?'

Susan lied almost as badly as Aidan.

'Melissa?'

'I can't say,' she faltered.

Harri nodded. 'Okay. I was beginning to think I was going mad, I mean really mad, but I'm not, am I? Something's going on. What is it, Aidan?'

'Okay, you're right.' He seemed relieved to be forced to capitulate. 'Your parents are going to make some sort of announcement on Wednesday.'

'What kind of announcement?'

'I swear I don't know. They wouldn't say.'

'Try again.'

'It's about you.'

Harri felt the breath leave her. Her knees shook a little.

Susan gently assisted her towards a chair. 'I'm sure it's nothing.'

'George doesn't know what it is?'

'They want to tell you together. If he knew I'd said anything he'd kill me. He didn't want to upset you.'

'I won't say a word,' Harri promised.

During dinner she was quiet. *What could it be? What could it be?*

Aidan, Melissa and Susan managed to get through three bottles of wine and were on another planet. Harri figured she'd stayed long enough to be polite. She went to the bathroom before she said goodbye. When she came out she bumped into Beth.

'Beth, you scared me!'

'Sorry, Harri.'

'It's okay, I was dreaming.'

'Harri?'

'Yes.'

'I'm sorry about the whole wedding fiasco.'

Harri laughed a little. Beth was the first person with enough balls to call a spade a spade. 'Thanks.'

'Harri?'

'Yes?'

'Can I talk to you?'

'Oh. Okay,' she said.

They went into Beth's room and sat down. It was cosy and clean with a desk, a computer, TV, DVD and a sound system with speakers mounted on the wall. 'God, we could be in Dixons!' said Harri.

'Yeah. Listen, I'm in a bit of trouble.' Beth seemed a little jumpy.

'Shouldn't you be talking to your mother?' Harri was beginning to panic.

'I really don't want to.'

'Why me?'

'Well, you're Mum's business partner and friend, I've known you most of my life and I've kind of messed up and – well – you tend to mess up so I thought you might understand.'

Good argument.

'No offence.'

'None taken.'

They sat in silence for a moment or two. 'So what's the problem?' *Please don't be pregnant.*

Beth laughed. 'I'm not pregnant.'

Thank you, God. 'I never said you were.'

'You were thinking it.'

'Yes, I was.'

Beth laughed again. She liked Harri. 'I've got crabs.'

'Oh.' Harri stood up.

'Will you take me to a clinic in town? I couldn't bear to tell my GP.'

'You're sure?'

'Positive. I've been tearing the fanny off myself all day and you can actually see them.'

'Oh, God.'

'I know. Have you ever had them?'

'No.'

'You're lucky.'

Harri sat on the hard chair by the computer. She contemplated wiping it but feared it would be impolite. 'Can I ask how you caught crabs?'

'I'm not a slut.'

'I didn't say you were.'

'But you were thinking it.'

'I certainly was not.'

'Okay.' Beth smiled.

'So?'

'So I was going out with a guy with for six months. We started doing it two months ago and we were being careful. His parents took him skiing last month. He met a slut, slutted with the slut and, long story short, I've got an ice pack shoved down my knickers.'

'I'm sorry.'

'I don't care. He's a slut.'

'You care.'

'Yeah, I do, but I'm all cried out.'

'I know the feeling.' Harri stood up. 'I'll make an appointment tomorrow.'

Beth handed Harri her card. 'Call me directly, okay?'

'You have a card? Sixteen-year-olds have cards?'

'It's easy. Anyone can do it with a computer and colour printer.'

'When I was your age we really didn't have a clue.'

'Yeah, well, think about my poor mother – she has sixteen years on you. Can you imagine how green she was?'

'Green but very likely crab-free.' Harri smiled and Beth laughed.

'You won't say anything?' she asked, and Harri promised to remain silent for the second time that night.

Later, in bed, Harri remained wide awake. Her head was full and yet empty, so many questions and no answers.

What's going on? I don't know. What could it be? I have no idea. Is it about me alone or George and me? I should have pushed Aidan more. Is it my health? I'm thirty years old – surely I'd know more about the state of my health than my parents. Wouldn't I? Why did Mum say she'd die for me? Why does George feel like he has to avoid me? What could be so bad? How upset does he think I'm going to be? Surely this week couldn't get any bloody worse. I should be on honeymoon, for God's sake. God, I ache for James. Please come home! Please forgive me. I'm lost without you. And what about Beth having crabs? Jesus, I didn't see that coming. Should I tell Susan? No, I shouldn't break Beth's trust. It's good that she came to me. I'm an adult. It was responsible of her. Why didn't she tell Susan? They're so close – maybe that's why. Oh, God, maybe should I tell Susan. Definitely not. I'd love to hunt that dirty little bastard down. I wish I could talk to James. He'd think this was funny – the crabs, not the secret. The secret would freak him out. I feel like tea but I'd better not – I'll end up pouring it all over myself. Why do I always become awkward and accident-prone when I'm upset? Holy hell, Susan's baby has crabs! Well, now, what do I really think about that . . .

It was after three when Harri finally dozed off.

2 June 1975 – Monday

HE came home last night. I knew it couldn't last. He was out of his mind. He hit Mam over and over. I ran to Nosy Crowley's but she was on the phone to the police before I knocked on the door. Good for her. She was on her own and was too afraid of him to help. I was too scared to go back. I feel terrible but the police and Nosy Crowley said I was right to stay out of harm's way. Easy for them to say, they weren't getting their faces punched in. They locked him up and I went with Mam in the ambulance. She kept saying she was fine, and she didn't look as bad as I thought she would. She's been worse. Her lip is in bits, though. She's staying in again tonight. Of course he was let out this morning. Typical. She said that was the end of it. He wasn't welcome at home again. I'll believe it when I see it. Why is she so weak?

Dr B – that's what I'm calling Brendan now. It has a nice ring to it. Anyway, Dr B was in the hospital last night. He was visiting one of his patients. She's eighty-eight and dying. He's so nice. I saw her. She's bonkers and he could have easily got away without visiting but he did anyway. He asked after Mam. I told him straight out, and he seemed shocked. He tried to talk to her but she wasn't having any of it. He bought me a coffee later after she'd kicked us out of her room. He said I was strong. I'm not strong. If I was strong HE would be pushing up daisies. It was nice to hear, though, in that sing-songy voice. He said he wasn't used to people being so open. He said it was a nice change. I don't know what he means. I'm hardly in a position to pretend. The whole town knows what HE's like. Well, most of it. What am I supposed to do – bury my head in the sand along with my mam? No thanks.

I started work today. Mam insisted. I'm glad. I hate sitting around hospitals. Besides, I was actually starting to look forward to cleaning up horseshit. So how great is my life? Henry was nice. He showed me around again and introduced me to the people I'll be working with. Delamere's son Matthew will be home all summer. He's working in the stables too. He's my age but I don't really know him, only to see. He goes to a boarding-school in Dublin. He's tall and cute, really cute, but I think he's a bit stuck-up or maybe he's shy. I haven't made my mind up yet. He was mucking out in the stable next to me and didn't say a word – well, not to me. He talked to the horse a lot, though. WEIRDO. It wasn't a bad day, actually. I even got to ride Betsy. I was ready to wee my pants but I thought, why not? It was scary. I felt so high up but it was fun. Matthew was flying around the place on his horse, Nero – he was jumping over fences and everything. I was being led around by Henry. I felt a bit of a twit but Henry says I'll be galloping in no time. I don't know whether I like that idea. I'll see.

It's weird being home alone. Father Ryan called earlier to check on me. He told me Dr B had filled him in and asked if I was all right. What is it with Dr B and the priest? I said I was fine but I offered him tea. We hadn't much to talk about but it felt better having him in the house. He said I could stop by the parish house any time. Why would I do that??? He said he'd called in to Mam but she was sedated. Sedated my eye, she was pretending. Oh, and just to note: Matthew

Delamere looks really, REALLY like Starsky from *Starsky & Hutch* – or maybe it's Hutch. I always get them confused. He looks like the blond one, except he has brown hair. He has a black cord jacket with patches on the sleeves and I know it sounds nerdy but it looks really good. I think I'll talk to him tomorrow.

5. Ms Know-it-all

The following morning, a horribly hung-over Melissa woke up to the sound of crying. Gerry turned over and snored a little for effect. *I know you're awake, wanker.* It was just after five and the fifth morning in a row that Carrie, the baby, had woken for no apparent rhyme or reason. Melissa dragged herself into a sitting position and then stood up. *I'm coming, I'm coming.* Carrie stopped crying as soon as she was picked up. In the week just past she had decided that it suited her to be walked between the hours of five and seven a.m. As soon as Jacob, Melissa's four-year-old, and Gerry awoke to get ready for playschool and work, Carrie wanted a snooze.

The night before, Gerry had promised he'd get up: Melissa had been so tired that she'd threatened to pull out of dinner at Susan's, even though she was desperate for a night out, not to mention being the designated shoulder for her newly separated best friend to cry upon. He had looked her in the eye and told her emphatically that he would take his turn without word or grumble. He had lied. Carrie had started crying and he had ignored her. Melissa had nudged him gently and he had turned over stiffly. She had poked him and he had huffed. The child was near hysterical by the time Melissa reached her. She could have shouted but what would have been the point? Gerry was a nightmare in the mornings.

With the baby in the crook of her arm, she went about securing headache tablets and a badly needed pint of any available liquid. With medication ingested, she sat on the loo with the baby in her arms staring at the ceiling with an intensity that made Melissa wonder if Carrie could see something that she could not. Carrie didn't like it if her mother sat for long so the business in the loo was concluded quickly. Melissa felt sick and hoped to God her system wouldn't require purging. *How can I walk, hold the baby and vomit? Can't hold baby and basin at the same time but maybe I could manage a pot. God almighty, please just let me get through the morning.* Of course, there was no rest for Melissa once the men of the house got up. There was breakfast to make and lunches to pack, necessary items to find.

'Mum, where's my Bart T-shirt?'

'Melissa, have you seen my phone?'

'Mum, where's my runners?'

'I could have sworn I put my briefcase by the sofa in the sitting room. Have you seen it?'

'Mum, where's my lunchbox?'

'My keys. My keys! Have you seen my poxy keys?'

'Mum, where's my pencil with the picture of Captain Jack Sparrow and the rubber on top?'

She'd have to shower, iron clothes, make her child's lunch, steam bottles, drink a coffee, fix her hair and apply enough makeup to hide the fact that she was haggard and ready to give up. *I might just need a roller to plaster my makeup on.*

Gerry was bright as a button and pretending he hadn't let her down. 'Good morning, good wench.'

'Don't good-wench me!'

After acquiring his briefcase and keys he kissed her forehead and she momentarily contemplated head-butting him. She didn't for fear of mentally scarring her eldest child so instead she stormed out of the room, banging the door for effect.

'Jacob, is Mummy in bad humour?' Gerry asked, ruffling his son's hair.

'She told me to shove my Captain Jack Sparrow pencil with the rubber on top where the sun don't shine,' he said, between mouthfuls of cereal.

'Well, I'm sure Captain Jack has no business going there,' he said, and drank out of the orange-juice carton.

'Dad?'

'Uh-huh?'

'Where doesn't the sun shine?'

'In the shade, son.'

'Oh. I don't think he'd really mind so.'

Melissa packed her son's lunch into his schoolbag, then pulled the Captain Jack pencil from her pocket and handed it to him.

'Where'd you find it?'

'In the treasure trove that resides under your bed.'

'Thanks, Mum,' he said, and ran outside to the car.

Gerry pretended he hadn't noticed she was annoyed. 'Where's my kiss?'

'Go fuck yourself, Gerry.'

'That's nice.'

'Not as nice as being a lone parent.'

'Oh, for God's sake!' he said, sighing dramatically.

'Get out! Get out before I knife you.'

It struck him that she meant it. 'Melissa, you seriously need help,' he said, shaking his head as though her outburst had been somehow irrational.

'Yes, Gerry, I do. I need your help – but it looks like I'm not going to get it so fuck off out before I do you in, okay?'

Gerry left quickly. Mrs Rafferty, the babyminder, arrived just in time to give Melissa half an hour to get to a budget meeting that would start in ten minutes and last the next four hours. She would eat a sandwich at her desk before enduring a further sales meeting that would last another four hours, forcing her to take her paperwork home. She'd feed her baby, work on her sales figures, burp her baby, work on graphs, and rock her baby to sleep while printing off her sales proposals. The baby would sleep. Jacob would need help with homework, then he and Melissa would fight over the TV and what he wanted to watch as opposed to what he was allowed to watch. She'd shout; he'd sulk. She'd all but force-feed him his dinner, negotiations breaking down early in the proceedings. 'Just eat the food, Jacob. Eat the bloody food!'

Gerry would get home a little after seven thirty. He'd dish his meal from the oven, take it into the sitting room and there he would sit with a tray and his four-year-old, now jaded from his campaign to break his overworked mother, and together they would vegetate in front of the sports channel. *I hate my life. I can't do this any more.* Melissa had been unable to take any longer than six weeks' maternity leave because of her position as team leader on a massive account that required her constant supervision.

'If it was last year or next year, Melissa, we could have accommodated you but this year you're killing us.'

Melissa had made the sacrifice for the sake of the team because she was a team player. She was suffering from a mild case of post-natal depression when she went back, and although that had passed, it felt like a lifetime since she had been able to breathe. She had broached the subject of leaving work with Gerry on a number of occasions, but he was adamant that they couldn't afford it. She had broached the subject of working part time with her boss but he was adamant that they needed her full time and working longer rather than shorter hours. She spent her time juggling her work and home life and all she seemed to be doing was apologizing to all and sundry for her inability to split herself in two while battling exhaustion. She was on a never-ending treadmill going nowhere fast. *I'm so, so tired.*

It was just before nine and both kids were in bed when she eventually had time to sit down and phone Harri. 'Hi,' she opened the conversation wearily.

'Hi, yourself.'

'Are you okay?' Melissa asked.

'Can't wait for Wednesday!' Harri said airily, as though it was a joke.

She wasn't fooling anyone, never mind her best friend. 'I don't know what to say to you except that I'm sorry for getting so drunk last night.'

'You needed to blow off some steam,' Harri said knowingly.

'I did.'

'How are you feeling?'

'Like crying.' Melissa laughed but she wasn't capable of fooling anyone either, and especially not her best friend.

'We're a fine pair.'

'Undeniably.'

'Melissa?'

'Yes?'

'We'll get over it, okay?'

'Yeah, we will.'

'Promise?'

'I promise.'

After that they talked about a book Harri had been trying to read, a show Melissa had been watching and a song that a girl in Melissa's office had been humming that went *la la la la la la la la*. Harri said it definitely sounded familiar but couldn't pinpoint it, and Melissa maintained it was at the tip of her tongue and driving her insane and she couldn't stop humming it all the time.

'Just ask her,' Harri said.

'She'll think I'm nuts.'

'She's the hummer.'

'She *is* the hummer.'

'Hummers are notoriously unstable,' Harri said, clearly confident that her friend was too tired to delve into her reasoning.

'You're right. I'll just ask her.'

'You'll have to wait until tomorrow.'

'Oh, Mother of God!'

*

It was a little before eleven. The clinic was busy enough. Harri took a number and pointed Beth to a chair in the corner and away from a man who looked like a stalker. Beth was quiet and determined to keep her head down. She didn't talk for a little while. Instead she buried her head in *InStyle* magazine. Harri picked up *Time*. A woman in a nice suit sat next to Beth, who made a face at Harri. Harri pretended not to notice. They returned to their magazines. The woman got up and walked down the hall, possibly towards a coffee shop.

'I wonder what's wrong with her,' Beth whispered from behind her magazine.

'I have no idea,' Harri replied, in an undertone.

'I hope it's not catching,' Beth said, making the face again.

'You mean like crabs?'

'Ouch!'

'Just reminding you that you are in no position to judge.'

'Fair enough. I do like her suit.'

Minutes passed. Harri was reading about the environment and how we were all pretty much dead because of toxic water. Beth was looking at nice shoes. She raised her magazine to just below her eyes. 'Harri?'

'Hmm?'

'Do you think I'll be with a woman doctor?'

'I don't know.'

'I don't want a man.'

'You'll be fine.'

'Do you think I'll have to take anything off?'

'I'm not sure but probably.'

Tears welled in Beth's eyes. 'I don't want to.'

Harri smiled at her. It was easy to forget she was only sixteen. She acted so grown-up but when she cried, she was, as Bob Dylan had once so beautifully put it, just like a little girl. 'They see this every day,' she said, nudging Beth the way George often nudged her.

'They don't see me every day,' Beth said, tears dripping from her chin.

'I know it's embarrassing,' Harri said. 'Wait until you're my age and have to go for a smear test every three years!' She raised her eyes to heaven.

Beth's eyes dried slightly. 'Is that sore?'

'Just embarrassing.'

'You get embarrassed?'

'I lose the power of speech. I used to live with a girl once called Tina Tingle.'

'Tina Tingle?' Beth asked, in a voice that suggested she didn't believe it.

'Tina Tingle,' Harri confirmed. 'During Tina's first smear test she farted.' She smiled at Beth. 'Loudly. It was no real surprise as the woman lived on Indian takeaways.'

Beth dropped her magazine to just under her nose and laughed.

'You'll be fine,' Harri said.

'I suppose if I'm old enough to have sex I should be old enough to handle the consequences.'

Harri leaned back in her chair, sighing. 'How did you get to be so emotionally intelligent at sixteen? Compared to you I was a dribbling dope.'

'All of life's bigger questions are asked and answered in

teen dramas,' Beth said, 'especially *Dawson's Creek*. It's a cliché-ridden classic. I have seasons one to three on DVD if you're interested.'

Harri giggled. 'I think I'm past teen dramas but thanks for the offer.'

Beth's name was called. Harri gave her the thumbs-up. Her young friend had gone pale but she went in regardless. *Good for you. I would have been scratching for years.*

Later, after Harri had paid the bill and purchased the required medicine, and Beth had spent an inordinate amount of time in the Ladies at the Elephant and Castle restaurant in Temple Bar, which was close to George's apartment, they ate lunch in a seat by a large window.

'You're staring out,' Beth observed.

'So I am.'

'You're looking for George.'

'He comes here a lot,' Harri said, as though to herself.

'I heard the drunkards talk last night after you left. They're worried about you and about the secret.'

'Do you know about it?' Harri asked, betraying a little alarm.

'I know there is a secret.'

Harri looked back towards the window. 'He's avoiding me.'

'He thinks he's shielding you.'

Harri laughed. 'Is that what you reckon?'

'No – it's what Aidan said after you left.'

'Oh. So what do you think about all of this? Any *Daniel's Peak*-related light to shed on the matter?' She was amused by Beth's supposed clarity.

'It's *Dawson's Creek* and this secret, well, it's probably nothing.' Beth nodded. 'Adults tend to overcomplicate things.'

Harri smiled. 'I'll bear that in mind.'

They had finished their buffalo wings and Beth was waiting on an ice-cream-based dessert. 'Harri?'

'Yes.'

'What do you think about my dad?'

Harri shook her head. 'I don't know what to say about that.' She had a habit of speaking her mind, which was probably why the sixteen-year-old warmed to her.

'He's a dick,' Beth said categorically.

'Beth!'

'Don't defend him. He's been missing in action for over six months. He's treating my mum like crap. I see how she suffers.'

'Life isn't that simple.'

'That's what she says and it's bull because I'm the one listening to her cry.'

'It's a bad time but they might recover,' Harri said cautiously, knowing she was treading on dangerous ground.

'He's obviously having an affair. God, for all we know he could have a whole other family.'

'You watch too much TV.'

'Yeah, well, you don't watch enough.'

Harri took her statement on board. *Maybe she's right.* 'Beth, sometimes what we see isn't all it seems. I know you love your mum and you're fiercely protective and that's great – but you know she's capable, right?'

'I used to think so.'

'She is, so I'm asking you to back off and give them a chance. They need to work it out themselves.'

Beth's dessert appeared, and silence reigned for three or four minutes.

'Harri?'

'Yes?'

'Do you miss James?'

'Yes.'

'Do you want him back?'

Tears stung Harri's eyes. 'Yes.'

'Does he want you?'

'I don't know. Probably not.'

'I'm sorry. I really am.'

'Thanks.' Harri pressed her eyes before the tears gained enough weight to fall. 'What about you?'

'What about me?' Beth asked, between spoonfuls of ice-cream.

'Do you miss your boyfriend? What was his name?'

'Mark.'

'Do you miss Mark?'

'Mark is a slutty slut-riding slut machine.'

'That's not what I asked.'

Beth sighed and allowed a moment to pass. 'I do.'

'You really liked him.'

'I thought I loved him.' Beth's eyes were now focused on her feet. 'I might still.'

'I understand.'

'I don't. I've cried more than I've ever cried before – and that includes when Mr Bo Jangles died when I was

74

nine. That dog was my life but I've shed more tears over a boy who gave me crabs. I feel sick about that.'

'Hang in there, kiddo!'

'You too.'

Harri dropped Beth to the Dart station. Beth had hugged and thanked her and Harri told her that their day spent in a VD clinic had been a pleasure.

9 June 1975 – Monday

Okay, it's been a full week but at last today I talked to Matthew. I was cleaning a stable door, which was covered in God knows what but whatever it was it was hard to get off. He was passing, taking Lovely Lucinda for a trot, when his dad, the Dreaded Delamere, shouted to him. He had come down from the posh part of the grounds where they train the posh horses and where the rich people helicopter in. I'm not allowed over there – it's a whole courtyard and field over. It even has its own entrance. He was wearing wellies. I don't know him but he looked weird in wellies, as though it was a wrong fit. Matthew froze. I could see his back straighten the way mine does when I hear HIM come in.

Anyway, Dreaded Delamere started shouting about Nero, the horse Matthew exercises. He said he was lame and it was Matthew's fault. Matthew didn't defend himself. I wanted to say, 'It's not his fault,' and 'How dare you?' but I don't know if it is and I don't want to get fired. I really like this job. Dreaded Delamere stormed off leaving Matthew stand-ing in front of me, upset and embarrassed. I said all dads were dicks. He agreed. I said mine was dead and he apologized, which I thought was nice. I told him I had a stepdad who made his dad look like a saint. He disagreed. He said my stepdad would have to go a long way to beat his dad. I know the man only shouted at him and I know I don't know him or his dad but I think deep down he has a case. I don't trust the Dreaded Delamere. He makes me feel weird. I don't care how rich he is.

Sheila had a fight with Dave. She said he doesn't understand her, whatever that means. Sheila's losing it. I think it's because Dave keeps dropping the hand and she said the other night that last week he shoved his fingers up her privates. Apparently that's not comfortable.

Mam's bruises are going down. Her lip is still cut but it's not as fat. HE's moved out. She left his stuff in the garden and he picked it up with a friend from the docks. Maybe this time it's for good. I really hope so. Father Ryan was back around. He and Mam sat in the sitting room alone for over an hour. I tried to listen at the door but Father Ryan is an awful man for whispering. Dr B called too. He was checking in on Mam. I didn't know her rib was broken. He was making sure it was healing well. He said it was. I made him tea and put out a plate of custard creams which I didn't realize had gone soft. NIGHTMARE.

Mam was way nicer to him than she had been in the hospital – she even apologized. He said there was no need. That's just like him. We walked out together. He asked me about my new job and I told him about Matthew. He teased me about liking him and I blushed!!! What a SPAZ. I told him later that he had sad eyes and I swear I saw a tear although it disappeared quickly, but I know what I saw.

The other evening when I left Delamere's I walked home through Devil's Glen. I was surrounded by tall leafy trees, the waterfall, the bending, trickling river, the well-worn closeted trails, and I felt full, as though my heart was bursting, and I don't know why, but it felt warm. In Devil's Glen I can breathe, slow and hard, my head and heart full of the whole world. For that short time I'm in love with this life, no matter how horrible it can be.

I had a dream last night: I was riding Betsy and she was galloping faster and faster through the woods and every now and then I'd have to duck to miss a branch and my heart was beating wildly and I could feel the saddle under me and the reins pulled tight. We emerged from the wood and suddenly we were on the Head, speeding towards the two lighthouses and then down the steep pathway that zigzagged towards the cliffs and to the third lighthouse that seems like it belongs in another country – somewhere that's never without sun.

Just as we passed it and before we reached the cliff edge I saw Matthew and he waved and I let go of the reins so that I could wave back – and then we were falling through the air, Betsy and I, and I didn't care. I was happy to fall. There was silence, no screaming or neighing. I woke up before we hit the water, and although I was sweating I wasn't scared. It sounds strange but it was a good dream.

6. I'm not scared

James arrived a little after ten on Wednesday morning. He brought Malcolm. His former best man was now reduced to labourer and possible buffer.

'Coffee?' Harri asked, as nonchalantly as possible under the circumstances. James was non-committal but Malcolm was gasping. 'I thought you were going to wait until you found a place before you picked up the fish,' she said, although the sooner they were gone the better.

'I know you hate them.' He tried to smile.

You're a gentleman and too good for me. 'I wouldn't have minded. Besides, it's really only three of them. The others are fine.'

Malcolm took one look at the tank. 'It's him, him and him, isn't it?' he said, pointing.

She nodded.

'If they were people they'd be warlords,' he concluded.

Harri had no idea where that notion had come from but it instantly made sense to her. 'You're right.'

James sighed. Obviously he didn't see it. He got busy with the tank. Malcolm followed Harri into the kitchen, where she made the coffee. 'So?' he said aggressively.

'So?'

'How many times do you plan on breaking my best friend's heart?'

'I think I'm done,' she said, and poured the coffee.

'I hope so,' he replied, accepting a mug. 'What now?'

'I haven't a clue.'

'He will always love you.'

'You sound like Whitney Houston.'

'Don't joke – he's devastated.'

'Sorry.' Suddenly Harri was crying. *Stop it, you fool!*

Malcolm's anger disappeared and they found themselves hugging. 'I'll miss you, Harri Ryan.'

Harri couldn't respond, so busy was she sobbing on her ex-fiancé's best friend's shoulder. When eventually she managed to halt the torrent of tears, they pulled apart, and Malcolm gratefully left the kitchen, taking his coffee and a mugful for his best and equally devastated friend, who was deliberating on the most feasible way to dismantle an extremely large fish tank without risking the life of its occupants.

This is going to be a long day.

They were gone before three hours had passed.

Harri searched the apartment but all trace of James had disappeared so she curled up on the sofa and didn't move for hours.

George buzzed Harri's apartment at a little after six. She made her way out to the front where he was parked and settled into the passenger seat.

'Aidan admitted he blurted,' he said, with a sigh.

'Aidan's as spreadable as butter.' She attempted a laugh. Harri hated tension.

'In so many ways,' he joked, before returning to serious. 'I'm sorry for the silence.'

'Don't be.'

'I saw Mum freak out and I couldn't handle it.' George was not used to witnessing his mother's outbursts. She had seemed so unstable it had terrified him.

'Mum freaked out?'

'Don't you freak out, Harri, okay?'

'Okay,' she said, slowing her breathing.

'I don't know what's going on,' he said.

'Okay,' she said again.

'But I know one thing – whatever it is we'll get through it.'

'We will.'

'Agreed,' he confirmed. 'And it could be nothing.'

'Agreed,' she repeated. 'But, George?'

'Yeah?'

'Everything in me is screaming that life will never be the same again.'

'Drama queen!' he teased, but somehow he knew she was right. They drove the rest of the way in silence.

Two days earlier, Father Ryan had just come out of Mass when the call came.

'We need you in Dublin.'

'Why?'

'We're telling them.'

'You're doing the right thing.'

'We have no choice.'

'You're doing the right thing.'

'I wish I had your confidence.'

'She has to know.'

'There could be repercussions for both of us.'

'Duncan, it was a different time. Church and state had a lot more power then. Besides, Harri is your daughter.'

'She'll hate us.'

'Maybe for a time, but in the end she's a Ryan.'

'We can't lose her.'

'You won't.'

'So you'll definitely be there?'

'Of course.'

'Thank you, Father Ryan.'

'You're welcome, brother.'

George used his key. Harri followed him, holding on to his coat-tails like a peasant from another time and place. *Can I have more cheese, sir?*

They sat at the dining-table. Duncan was opening wine. Gloria was nowhere to be seen. Father Ryan's presence was a surprise. He was smoking in the back garden.

George looked at him longingly through the window. 'Do you mind if I join him?' he asked Harri.

'Okay.' She smiled.

'I'll be back in a minute.'

'Okay,' she agreed. *Stop saying okay, Harri.*

Outside Father Ryan greeted his nephew. 'George.'

'Uncle Thomas.'

'You look well.'

'I feel well.'

'Good for you.'

'So you're in on it too.' George was never one to dilly-dally.

'It's not for me to talk on this occasion,' Father Ryan said, and took a deep drag.

George followed suit. 'Yet you're here.'

They were silent for a few moments.

'George?'

'Uncle Thomas?'

'No matter what happens here tonight, your parents – my brother and his wife – and I . . . well, we did what we all believed to be best. I want you to know that.'

Before George could respond Father Ryan had stubbed out his cigarette and gone indoors.

The meal passed in silence. Gloria had been last to join the table. She was pale and, although smiling and pleasant, her hands were rarely away from her neck. They all picked at their food. No one pretended to be in the humour for small-talk. Harri and George remained silent, although their minds were swimming with questions. They waited. Everyone seemed to be waiting.

Eventually it was Duncan who spoke. He stood as though he was giving a speech. 'I'm not sure what to say,' he opened. 'Harri, I'm not sure what to say,' he repeated, looking directly at his daughter.

Her eyes filled. George held her hand, wondering what the hell was going on. Gloria was crying while feigning a smile, and it was frightening.

'You need to understand that you are,' Duncan faltered, 'you are our miracle.'

Suddenly Harri was back in time to when she was barely ten and sharing a seat with Nana on Nana's bench.

'Harri,' Nana had said, 'did I ever tell you that you are a little miracle?'

'Why, Nana?'

'Because you were sent from Heaven when we needed you most.'

Harri controlled her breathing. *I'm not going to panic. I'm fine. I'm perfectly fine.* Duncan continued. 'Thirty years ago Glory and I were pregnant with twins.' He smiled at Gloria and she bowed her head to signal that he could continue. 'It was one of those times,' he smiled at the memory, 'a great time.'

Father Ryan scratched his hand, momentarily distracting everyone. 'Sorry,' he said, slightly embarrassed. *Bloody central heating will be the death of me.*

Duncan continued: 'The pregnancy went perfectly. No problems.' He was nodding to himself. 'It was just perfect.'

Harri's stomach was turning, George's too. *Just say it.*

'Glory went into labour around three o'clock on the thirtieth of April. I was working on a murder case. They were rare then. Your mother was seven weeks early and I was in Kildare. Nana got her to the hospital.' He smiled at his wife. 'Don't forget this was before the mobile phone. I didn't even know Glory was in hospital until nine that night when I called home and Nana was waiting. It was another hour before I made it to the hospital. Harri had been born and George was coming. Glory was near dead.' His eyes filled and Gloria closed hers and bowed her head.

'She was bleeding badly and screaming.' He stopped. 'She was screaming that she was gone. I thought she was telling me that she was tired and giving up. The doctors and nurses didn't speak – they were too busy trying to save George. And then you came,' he turned to George, 'and I held you and I don't know if it was moments or minutes before I asked about Harri.' He looked at his daughter, eyes brimming. 'Your mum's womb was so damaged it was a miracle that George survived. They had to operate. They had to take it.' Again he looked at his wife.

He stopped talking. He just stopped. Moments passed – it seemed like hours.

Father Ryan stared him down. 'Duncan.'

'Yes,' he said. He looked weak for the first time in his life. His stature was diminishing before them. His mighty hands, which his wife had once described as shovels, betrayed fear in the form of a slight tremor. He clasped them together so tightly that the fingers on his left hand went white.

'Tell them.'

'I will,' he said, teetering on the edge of a new reality. *No turning back now.*

Harri's heart was beating so hard her chest wall threatened to crumble.

'Dad?' George encouraged, feeling the same pain.

'Harri was dead,' Duncan said. 'She had died a few minutes after delivery.'

Harri instantly disappeared into numbness, as though she had been switched off.

George looked from his sister, who was staring blankly

at the wall opposite her, to his mother, who was staring at the floor, to his father, who was staring at his daughter, and on to his uncle, who was staring at him and appeared to be silently praying.

'Harri's here, Dad,' George heard himself say.

'Harri died soon after birth. We buried her, son, and your mother, well …'

'They let me hold her,' Gloria said out of nowhere. 'I got to hold her just that once.'

'She's right here,' George pleaded.

But Harri knew what her father had meant because suddenly everything made sense, all those feelings of dislocation she'd experienced over the years. *I don't belong here.*

'Harri?' her father said. 'Harri?'

'Just talk,' she heard herself order.

'I couldn't live with it,' Gloria said.

'Mum!' George cried.

'I wanted to disappear. I so desperately wanted to die. I can't describe it. I was lost, George. I loved you, but I was so lost without her.'

She stopped talking and everyone at the table stared at Harri, but Harri was gone: she was in another place, untouchable.

George was still clawing through this new reality. 'Mum?'

'I had to stay in hospital for weeks, and then I came home to you, George, but I still wasn't right.'

'Several weeks after you were born and your sister died I investigated a death in Wicklow,' Duncan said, taking over from his wife. He looked at Father Ryan, who nodded

86

to him. 'Your uncle Thomas called. He had requested that I be sent. It was a young girl. She was seventeen. She'd given birth in a wood. She'd died, but against all odds her baby girl survived. The baby was you, Harri.'

Harri shot to her feet and passed out.

George remained static. His twin sister was on the floor and yet he couldn't move. *Get up, George. Move.* But he couldn't because suddenly she wasn't his twin and it was all too incredible for feet or legs to function as normal. Gloria broke down. Duncan moved quickly towards Harri but he was further away than Father Ryan, who got down on the floor, held Harri in his arms and whispered words that were inaudible to those around. *Damn him and his whisperings.*

She woke after a few seconds or maybe it was a minute: for those observing her collapse, time had stood still.

'Uncle Thomas?'

'Yes, Harri?'

'I knew. It sounds insane but deep down I've always known!' She was crying.

'Shush now, angel,' he said. 'You are loved. You were always loved.' He held her tight, and in the background, Duncan, Gloria and George disappeared, if only for a moment.

13 June 1975 – Friday

They say Friday the 13th is unlucky and maybe it is, but not for me. Today has been amazing. First of all HE has moved into a place outside town with his bank-wall-leaning friend, the one who helped him take his stuff from the garden before. Mam is still determined not to let him in the house no matter what Father Ryan says about the sanctity of marriage. She's got a cleaning job at the Crow's Nest, and I told her I could help out with the bills now that I'm working. She's sad but I've seen her a lot sadder. Mostly I think she misses my dad. I know I do. He was sick for so long that sometimes I forget what he was like as a normal dad, but then every now and then out of nowhere I see him and he's healthy and strong and smiling and hugging me. I think he really loved me and I think he loved my mam. It's nice to have that. It's nice to hold on to.

Matthew took me riding today. It was weird without Henry leading me around but he promised I'd be okay. Betsy knew I was a spaz so she took care of me. We rode far away from the arena and the trails. I had no idea how big the Delamere property was. It's huge, like their big stone house, which is like a castle without the turrets. I'd say it gets really cold in winter. We rode for ages and then we stopped and settled the horses and sat together under a tree. Matthew told me about boarding-school. He doesn't really like it much but it's better than being ignored at home. His mam is dead. She died when he was two. She fell from a horse and broke her neck, not exactly encouraging when I had to ride Betsy back to the yard. He's lovely and he's not stuck-up at all. He's just not used to attention. He goes to an all-boys school. He has a few friends but he's not a rugby player and unless you're a rugby player you're no one. I couldn't imagine him being no one. It's impossible.

Sheila and Dave are back together after being off for nearly a whole week. He promised not to shove his fingers up her

88

privates and she promised to let him lie under her duvet with her. They haven't met up yet but as soon as they do she's going to call or come over with an update.

I met Dr B down by the pier this evening. I was sitting by the *Eliana* and he sat beside me. He was quiet, much quieter than usual. I asked what was wrong and he told me it was nothing. He was lying so I asked him again. He shouted at me to go away, which was funny because I was there first. I pointed this fact out and asked him what was wrong again. He said I was a kid and wouldn't understand, and he got up to walk away. I told him I would. He stopped dead and looked at me like I was some kind of alien. I reminded him that honesty was refreshing. He sat down again and he cried. I sat with him in silence for the longest time looking out over the sea towards where Wales should be.

When he stopped crying I asked him what was wrong again. He told me I was too young. I told him that maybe I was old enough. He said that he had left Cork because he had fallen in love. So? I said. He said it was with a man!!!!!!! I didn't see that coming. I nearly fell off the bench. I don't know about much but I know he's a really good person and I don't warm to many but I warmed to him. I told him that. He thanked me but I know my words mean little. Dr B hates himself. He thinks there is something wrong with him. I don't. I think he's lovely. I wish he could see that. I don't care who he loves and I promised I'd never tell. I'll keep his secret. Oh, I've just thought of something – is Father Ryan telling him he's wrong to love a man the way he's telling my mam she's wrong to leave my stepfather? FATHER RYAN, PLEASE SHUT UP!

7. Gone

Harri was lying face down on the pillow, her mobile phone resting beside her. *Go away. Go away. Go away.* She picked it up with the intention of throwing it against her hotel-bedroom wall, risking damage to the expensive wallpaper. She needed to aim correctly so as to risk minimum damage because even in the most terrible turmoil Harri appreciated good décor. She used to think she was like her mother that way. Before she took aim she realized it was a call from George.

'Harri?'

'George.'

'I'm sorry for running.'

'It's okay.'

'You were on the floor. First I couldn't move and then all I could do was run.'

'You left your car in the driveway,' she said, as though it was important.

'I don't know what to say.'

'Me neither.'

'I don't know how to be.'

'Me neither. We need some time away, George,' she said, knowing his feelings mirrored her own.

'I'm going to Italy.' He had rebooked his flight an hour earlier.

'Good idea.'

'You sound far away.'

That was odd: Harri was staying in the Clarence Hotel, which was only around the corner from her brother's apartment. She was closer than ever, at least geographically, but then being close has nothing to do with geography: being close is a state of mind so Harri *was* far away and moving further with each passing moment.

'George?' She sounded fuzzy, as if she was drugged but she wasn't – she was just numb to her very core.

'Yes?'

'You're the eldest now.'

'I suppose so,' he said, bringing the phone back to his ear.

'By more than two months,' she whispered. 'You're older by at least two months and a lifetime.'

George allowed the tears to fall. He was alone and it was okay to cry because their world had ended and his twin sister had died.

'Let's not talk for a while,' she said.

'No, Harri.'

'Don't call me that.'

'It's your name.'

'It's someone else's name.'

'Please.'

'George, I can't breathe. Let me be, I'm begging you.'

'Whatever you want.'

She turned off her phone, lay down and disappeared.

George woke to a blinding light. He batted the sun-bleached white shutter back in place while shielding his tired eyes. The required level of dullness restored, he slumped back on his bed. On the pillow next to him lay his phone. Seven missed calls. *Go away, Dad.* The unreliable shutter attempted once more to creep away from the window. He slapped it back into place. *Don't make me break you.*

He checked his watch on the pretty white faux-antique locker. It was after two. He had missed a meeting in a local vineyard, a meeting he had been attempting to arrange for weeks, yet he couldn't bring himself to care. The previous night he had sat alone in the local village bar while locals spoke about him, muttering aloud about the drunken Irishman and debating why he looked so shattered. They had assumed he didn't speak the language so he had listened to them comment on his sadness, his floppy hair, his expensive suit, and even managed to enjoy two women arguing over who had the best chance with him. He had given them a smile of encouragement. He liked it when women were attracted to him – it appealed to his masculinity and vanity.

However, he had remained where he was at the bar and all the while continued to drink. He drank until he could no longer feel his legs. A stranger who disliked his hair but coveted his suit was forced to carry him to the entrance of his hotel. He had attempted to tip the guy but he was polite and refused, even though earlier he had asserted that the Irishman was a waster.

Now in the cold light of day George's head hurt and he was in no mood to talk business. He stood up – and stepped into vomit. *Oh, nice, George, very nice.* He cleaned

93

the floor after which, exhausted, he returned to his bed. He must have drifted off into the deepest sleep. He didn't hear Aidan arrive; he didn't even hear him when he banged his suitcase against the door frame, then against his bad knee. 'Oh, bollocks, that hurt!' He didn't hear the kettle being boiled for a badly needed coffee. 'Bloody Ryanair! How do you manage to run out of coffee?' Nor did he hear the shower run or Aidan dancing under it. 'Hot, hot, hot!'

When George eventually woke up, he saw the back of a head. *What the hell?* He was about to panic when he noticed a familiar tattoo. 'Aidan?'

'Five more minutes,' he mumbled sleepily.

'Aidan.' He nudged him.

'Three more minutes.'

'Aidan!' he roared into his ear.

Aidan shot up in the bed. He took a second or two to orient himself. 'What?'

'What are you doing here?'

'I'm your boyfriend. You've had some bad news. I'm here for you.'

'You're calling what happened "bad news"?' George asked incredulously.

'Well, dear, it's not good news.'

'You shouldn't have come.'

'Of course I should.'

'I don't want you here.'

'Of course you don't.'

George sat at the side of the bed with his head in his hands. 'Aidan, I can't do homotastic witty repartee today.'

'I'm not asking you to, mostly because you're not very good at it.' He smiled at George who allowed himself a grin. 'Good. Let's take a walk.'

'I don't feel like walking.'

'Fine. I'll hire you a wheelchair.'

It was early evening and the sun was still warm. The little cobbled streets were busy with people walking dogs, couples strolling and some with kids in buggies. The old were holding hands and taking it slow, breathing in fresh air.

George and Aidan sat just inside an empty café watching the world go by. George had been quiet.

'Have you seen Harri?' he asked, after careful consideration.

'No,' Aidan said. 'She checked into the Clarence for two days, checked out and she hasn't gone home.'

'What about Melissa or Susan?'

'They've heard nothing either.'

'She can't talk. She can't think. She needs to be gone for a while.'

'Like you?'

'But she's not like me. Is she?'

'George . . .'

'I always knew we were different but still we were the same.' He paused to collect himself. 'I've lost the part of myself that I liked most.'

'You haven't lost her.'

George shook his head. 'Did I tell you that she said she knew? She told Uncle Thomas that deep down she'd always known.' He bit his lower lip, remembering. It had been at that very second he had regained the use of his legs and run. 'You know what I knew? I knew I had a twin sister. What I didn't know was that she was dead.'

'Harri is not –'

'Harri is dead, Aidan. They didn't even give her replacement a different name. How fucked up is that?'

'It's pretty fucked up,' Aidan was forced to agree.

'I keep trying to get my head around it but I can't. My whole life has been a gigantic and pretty fucking mesmerizing lie.'

'Okay, I'm the drama queen in this relationship and it just won't work with two.'

'You think I'm being dramatic?'

'I think that you and Harri may not have shared a womb but you have shared a life, every memory and every milestone. You grew up in one another's pockets, finished one another's sentences. You speak in code, for God's sake. No one gets you the way she does, not even me, and no one gets her like you. So history has been rewritten but history is just a list of facts. You and Harri are real and who and what you are together has not changed.'

'Nice speech,' George said.

'Thanks. I practised on the flight.'

'It's not that simple.'

'I know. It will take time to get your head around it but after that it really is up to you, both of you,' Aidan said, taking his lover's hand and kissing it.

He didn't mind that George pulled away quickly. George hated public displays of affection. It made him uncomfortable. Aidan was tactile, and although mostly he kept his affection in check, sometimes he slipped. Often this would end in a fight but tonight George was too tired for that so instead he pulled his hand away slowly and stared at the passers-by without another word. Later they walked back through the old stone village to the hotel, where they ordered room service and ate dinner in bed before making love. Afterwards they turned away happily. Aidan was out cold in no time. George lay awake, having slept away most of the day.

I can't talk to her. She doesn't want me to. What can either of us say? If nothing has changed why does nothing feel the same?

Gloria was a surprise. She had managed to hold it together exceedingly well and beyond her husband's wildest expectations. She cried, of course, but the deep, dark depression that had once all but consumed her was absent. She was upset but not clinically so. Duncan was grateful for that. His kids were in chaos and so they should be. He understood. He knew it was something they had to be allowed to go through. He just wished he could fast-forward time so that they would understand and see that all was well and they were loved. Then the Ryans could be a happy family again.

To Duncan it seemed odd that Harri hadn't asked any questions. She had sat silently in the aftermath of her brother's flat-footed flight.

Harri had all but disappeared inside herself. After an hour of silence she'd asked for a taxi. Further silence ensued, the taxi had arrived and her mother kissed her tearfully.

Duncan had hugged her so tightly she'd thought her arms would snap. Father Ryan had said he was sorry for all the pain she was about to feel. He reminded her that she was viewed as a miracle and that she was held dear. Harri hadn't stopped to ask any questions. Her mind was too full to accept answers. She'd just wanted out.

The taxi man had talked about the cost of concert tickets. 'A hundred-odd euro for George Michael, me hole, do you know what I mean, love? Don't get me wrong, he's good, but he's not that bleedin' good. I could get seen to for half that, no offence, love. I mean to say, tickets to a gig or a good seeing-to? A seeing-to wins every time. No offence, love. After all, a reality is a reality. Of course George Michael knows all about that. Are you with me?' He had laughed away to himself and hadn't even noticed that the girl in his back seat was crying.

On the night of revelation George had run all the way home and screamed the truth to Aidan. Aidan had waited until his boyfriend was calm enough before calling Susan, who, after an hour of oohing and ahing and oh-my-Goding, phoned Melissa.

'I've known them since they were kids,' she'd said weakly.

'I know you have.'

'No,' Melissa had gone on. 'No way. This is Dublin, not Hollywood.'

'It's true.'

'Harri's not Harri?'

'Harri is Harri. She's just Harri Two: The Return.' In other circumstances Susan's comment would have been funny, but neither woman laughed.

'It's just not possible!' Melissa exclaimed.

'It is.'

'It's impossible.'

'Maybe today – but in 1970s Ireland . . .' Susan said, remembering the time well.

'It's just so macabre.'

'You know what's really weird?' Susan wondered.

'What?'

'I could be my business partner's mother.'

'Excuse me?'

'I've just turned forty-six, Harri's thirty, the dead girl in the woods was seventeen.'

'Oh, that's so . . . that poor girl.'

Soon after that the phone call ended. Neither party slept well, disturbed by their friend's tragedy.

Harri didn't answer her phone except that one time to George. She left the Clarence when Aidan managed to track her down. When the coast was clear she returned to her apartment, packed, locked up and drove to the cottage in Wexford she had bought with James, the one that Melissa had deemed a moth-eaten money pit. Melissa was right, but that was okay because for the first time in seventy-two hours Harri could breathe. She was cold and uncomfortable but she could inhale and exhale easily and, for now, that was good enough.

21 June 1975 – Saturday

Dr B is avoiding me. I can't believe it. He hasn't been fishing at the pier, and yesterday in town he crossed the road when he saw me. I don't understand. If he keeps it up I'm not sure what I'll do but I'll do something because he needs to cop on. Having said that, I haven't a clue what to do. I'll think about it.

HE's still living somewhere else. I don't know exactly where and I don't care. Mam seems to be doing okay. Her face has healed nicely and she's enjoying working in the Crow's Nest. She says the staff are good fun. I'm glad. Cleaning is a spaz of a job and I swear I'd hate it, but if she's happy I'm happy. Just please, God, make sure she doesn't break and bring him back home.

Sheila is fighting with me. I can't believe it. She says I've been flirting with Dave. She's obviously gone a bit bell-jar – in other words, she's a mental case. I don't flirt with Dave – I interact with him more kindly now than before because I feel sorry for him. I pity him. Poor Dave is not my idea of the ideal man. But Sheila is going nuts. I really don't get it. She says I lean a lot when I'm around him. What does that mean? Maybe I lean because I'm taller than him. Sheila is getting weirder and more annoying by the day.

I've been spending more time with Matthew. We talk a lot, and he keeps finding reasons to touch me – my hand, my elbow, my shoulder, my face. Every time he does I feel like throwing up but in a good way. Stupid, I know, but true. Yesterday after we'd finished work he walked me home through

Devil's Glen. We talked about the things we loved. I told him about my inexplicable desire to leave this place even though, when I think about it, I love it. He talked about wanting to be heard. I asked him what he meant but he said he didn't know and he was sick of living in the shadows. Children should be seen and not heard!!! That's what his dad always says.

Poor Matthew, he's been silent for so long. In school he says a lot of it is silence. He makes me weak. When we talk I feel weak. What's that about? When I'm with him the most mundane incident seems almost magical, and when he's not there, what I would have thought interesting is now dull. I crave him. What's that about? Maybe I'm going mental. He talks, and I listen like I've never listened before. He smiles and I light up. PUKE. I know I sound like an idiot but it's true, I can't help it. Sometimes I disgust myself and I want to run away, but then I wouldn't see him and that would be bad, really bad. I look at him and my stomach flip-flops. Sometimes that's uncomfortable depending on what I've eaten.

Matthew asked me to meet him in Devil's Glen after nine tonight. I'm scared. I want to go but I'm really stomach-flipping scared. I feel stupid like a kid. I want to go but what's going to happen? Is he going to kiss me? What else? Will it be weird? I really, REALLY like him. I can't stop thinking about him. What he likes, what he says, what he eats, even what he drinks and, of course, what he listens to. Just to note he hates the Bay City Rollers. He's into David Bowie. I still like the Bay City Rollers but not as much as I did and that bothers me. Am I one of THOSE girls???? I want to go but I don't want to go. When I'm with him I don't feel myself and it's nice but it's not nice. I like alone-me and I'm not sure I like the me that's me when I'm with him. Mam said once, 'You can't choose love. Love chooses you.' I thought she was full of it. I might have been wrong.

Dave found me sitting by the *Eliana* today. He said he'd come to apologize about Sheila fighting with me. That was nice of him. I told him it didn't matter and she'd get over it. Sheila's always been moody. I was reading and he asked if it was all right if he sat for a while. The pier is a public place and it's a free country, so I said fine. I just continued reading and he stayed sitting beside me for the longest time. Just before he left he told me that he really did like Sheila but sometimes the things she said and did made him feel horrible. I told him that I think that's what happens when you love someone – after all, look what happened to my mam when she met HIM. It made me kind of sad and now I'm not sure if I'll meet Matthew. I really want to but what if it turns out badly? Then again I'm no coward. But I'm not a fool for anyone either. Oh, I don't know.

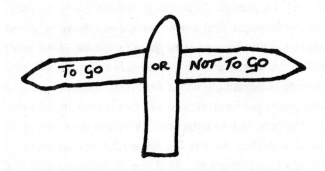

8. All to forget

Susan usually liked to spend Saturday lunchtime in the Avoca shop in Ashford. It was only a spin away in the car, the food was great and so was the shopping. She could stock up in the speciality supermarket, she could browse the cookbooks, the clothes, the novelties, but mostly she could salivate over the utensils. Susan loved utensils – can and jar openers, colanders, strainers, graters, thermometers, whisks and spatulas – of all of which she had multiples. She had a propensity to buy pastry and cake-decorating tools, too, despite her aversion to baking.

Today's the day, she had thought, on silencing her alarm clock. *Time for a clear out.* She got busy emptying over-stuffed drawers. Susan liked to clear cupboards, clean toilets, hand-wash clothes, grout tiles or prune hedges when burdened by unwanted thoughts. She hadn't engaged in a proper conversation with her husband Andrew in more than a week. Mostly he was gone before she got up and he didn't come home until he was sure she would be asleep. Susan needed her eight hours – she couldn't function without them. She'd usually be comatose by eleven thirty with the TV blaring or her glasses halfway down her nose and a book on her chest.

Thank heaven for small mercies, he'd think, passing their room in favour of the guest room. He was tired and the game of avoidance was becoming more trying. Maybe that was why he'd overslept. *Bollocks*. He could hear the kitchen drawers rattling despite the staircase and wide hall that separated him from his wife. She was being loud on purpose, making a point or maybe attempting to remind him that she was still alive.

Dying of thirst, he entered the kitchen quietly. Susan was sitting in the middle of the floor surrounded by utensils. Neither spoke. Andrew poured himself a coffee. Susan continued to sort whisks from spatulas and colanders from strainers. Sunlight was streaming through the windows and it was warm enough to open the french doors, which led to a carefully kept garden. Andrew took his coffee and the newspaper out to the patio.

The radio was on low, the disc jockeys debating their favourite version of Leonard Cohen's 'Hallelujah'. Jeff Buckley won. They spoke of the young man himself in rapturous terms, declaring him remarkable, and agreed that his voice was best described as poignant. A girl used the word 'evocative', to which the others said nothing, but Susan could imagine them nodding in the studio. After that they spoke of Jeff's untimely death and of the music world's great loss. Suddenly Susan found herself crying for a dead rock star she'd never before heard of. *I must Google him.*

It had been one full week since the revelation and although Harri had escaped to her modest Wexford crumbling cottage it was impossible to flee her new reality, no matter how hard she tried. Anxiety had become a staple part of her existence. It didn't come on her fast and from nowhere, rendering her incapable of breathing and tormented by the fear of imminent death. Instead dread crept into her bones insidiously so that although she wasn't blindsided or dizzy, it was constant. Concentration was increasingly difficult. *Where are my keys? In my handbag – so where's my handbag? I'm sure I left it by the door. Christ, where is it? On my shoulder. Right. Now, where was I going?*

She had gone out and filled a shopping-basket with books so that she could dodge irrational thought in her hideaway. *I don't exist. Not only do I not exist but I don't exist in a horrible kip in Wexford.* Reading had often been Harri's escape. The plan was simple. She would read and read and read until she was numb and apart from herself. *Genius.* Unfortunately reading requires concentration. *Ah, crap.* Her inability to concentrate, compounded by a terrible restlessness, made escaping into a book impossible.

Harri's new jumpy disposition manifested itself emotionally and physically in the form of minor tremors and jitters. Once while she was attempting to apply lipstick she noticed her lip twitch. *One twitch, two twitches and here comes the third. Oh, my God, I'm a bottle of vodka away from morphing into Sue Ellen Ewing.* She felt completely shattered and constantly sick. When she did manage to eat, she suffered stomach-crunching cramps. If Harri could have run away from Harri she would have done so. Despite the bad state she was in, despite mounting confusion and anger, she didn't want the people she loved to worry. Each day she would text the man and woman who had pretended to be her parents and her friends the same message. I'm fine. I need more time.

Each day the man and woman who had pretended to be her parents and her friends texted back.

Mum: We're so sorry, darling. We love you.

Dad: It's your dad. We need to talk. Please call soon.

Melissa: Jesus, Harri, where are you? I wish I knew what to say.

Susan: Please come home. I miss you.

Aidan: In Italy with George. What doesn't kill us makes us stronger.

Aidan: Me again. Ignore last text. Talking through my arse. Sorry.

Harri tried to clean the place to keep her mind off things but she was too tired. She tried to sleep but her mind was too restless. She tried to eat but not too much as she was afraid of shitting her pants. *That really would be the icing on the cake.* Her insides were raw and torn. Her eyes burned holes in her head, her skin dried and itched, and each moment that passed she felt a little closer to the edge of reason. *Harri is dead and I'm a* Jerry Springer *guest. Go, Jerry! Go, Jerry!*

She was so tired and so incapable of rational thinking that familiar clumsiness ensued. When she was attempting to make a cup of tea, one twitch, jitter or tremor later the boiling water missed the cup and instead flowed from her hand down her arm to be soaked up by a gathered sleeve. *You are fine. Do not let this get to you. You are better than this.* She turned on the tap and placed her hand under it. Unfortunately it was the hot tap. *You bast— Breathe. It's fine, just turn off the hot tap and turn on the cold. Breathe again.* She pulled at a tea-cloth to douse it in cold water and wrapped it round the scald and knocked a dish off the edge of the counter. It fell on to her foot, bounced and smashed on the tiled floor. *Okay, just limp upstairs, open the bedroom window and fuck yourself out of it.* She could have screamed but she didn't. She could have roared obscenities but that required thought and strength, which she lacked, so she sat quietly on the hard cold tiles, nursed her burned hand and bruised foot and didn't cry. She hadn't cried once in the entire week.

James pulled into the driveway just after seven. Harri had been sitting on the floor since four. She didn't hear him approach. The back door was open and he was standing in front of her.

She blinked. 'James?' she asked, as though she was unsure whether he was a vision or living flesh.

'It's me,' he said, and sat down on the tiles opposite her. He took her hand in his and unwrapped the wet towel. 'What happened?'

'I burned it.'

'Doesn't look too bad.' He smiled.

'No, I suppose it isn't,' she agreed.

'How about standing up?' he suggested. He sensed she'd been on the floor a while. She looked terrible – thin, pallid, drawn.

'My legs are numb,' she said.

'That's okay. I'll lift you.'

'I might fall,' she said. *If I do, I hope I land on my head.*

'I promise I won't let you.'

'It doesn't matter,' she mumbled. Having stubbed her big toe, smacked her face against a press door, jammed a pair of tweezers into her eye and now this latest burned-hand-bruised-foot combo, she was becoming accustomed to short, sharp bouts of pain.

He lifted her up in his arms and took her from the

kitchen into the small sitting room that looked out on to the overgrown back lawn. He placed her on the sofa and closed the tatty curtains to shield himself from the state of the garden.

'I'm making you dinner,' he said, and went into the kitchen, leaving the door open so that they could talk.

'I can't really eat,' she said.

'I'll make something light.'

It would want to be bloody light. Two people, one bathroom, this could be a long night. 'Please don't fuss,' she begged.

He came back into the room. 'Neither of us will. Okay?'

She smiled. 'Susan called you?'

'Susan, George, Aidan, Melissa and your dad. Actually, your dad called about nine times.'

'How did you know I was here?'

'I went to the apartment. Your passport was in the kitchen drawer so I took a chance.'

'Melissa's right – this place is a shithole,' she said, looking at the crumbling plaster.

'Yes, but it had potential.'

Harri was tired but she noted that he had used the past tense. 'I suppose it had.' *Just like we once had.*

Later he insisted that she ate propped up on the sofa. She managed a good few spoonfuls, seemed grateful, then went to the bathroom and stayed there for some time.

'Harri, let me in.'

'No.'

'Please.'

'You really don't want to be in here.'

'You're scaring me.'

Oh, my God, he thinks I'm trying to kill myself. 'Do you think I'm trying to kill myself?'

'No.'

Silence.

'Yes.'

Silence.

'No. Well, maybe. Jesus, Harri, I don't know. Are you?'

She sighed, her head in her hands. 'I have the runs.'

'Oh.'

'So do you still want to come in?'

'No. No, no. I'm fine. I'll be in the sitting room.' James suffered from a weak stomach.

Twenty minutes later Harri returned and slumped on the sofa.

'Sorry,' James said.

'Do you really think I'd hurt myself?'

'I don't know,' he answered honestly. 'Would you?'

'I don't know. Earlier I considered throwing myself out of a window.'

James smiled at her. 'So why didn't you?'

'I was too tired.'

'I'm so sorry about the whole bloody lot of it,' he said.

Harri nodded. 'Me too.'

Just after the word 'me' and exactly on the word 'too', Harri's carefully constructed dam burst and she was crying loud and hard with streaming eyes, nose and mouth. But mostly she leaked grief. She grieved for the dead girl who had given birth to her. She grieved for the mother she'd always known and for that woman's dead baby girl. She grieved for her father, the stranger, the one she thought she knew, and the architect of this most terrible deceit, who felt somehow lost to her. She grieved for her twin, who was now no relation. She grieved for the man she'd loved and lost, even though he was rocking her. She grieved for all that she used to be and for all that she never was. Harri Ryan cried in her ex-fiancé's arms for hours that night and when she was spent, completely and utterly drained, she fell asleep so soundly that she didn't wake when he lifted her awkwardly, nearly dropping her, or when he placed her on the bed, moving her roughly so that he could wrangle the duvet from under her. She didn't wake for another fourteen hours but when she did the man she'd lost was waiting for her.

Melissa hadn't really had time to talk to Gerry until he had surprised her with a babysitter and a meal out. The babysitter was a fifteen-year-old neighbour who, four weeks previously, had been caught sleeping with her boyfriend by her mother, whom Melissa had befriended while on maternity leave. Melissa didn't worry about what would happen when she left the house. *Hey, kid, use our bed. I don't give a stuff. I'm going out.* She dressed quickly, left the girl with a stash of biscuits and some DVDs and hightailed it out the door to the restaurant where her husband was waiting.

Once they were sitting and he was pouring wine, she couldn't help but query his intention. 'Gerry?'

'What?'

'What's going on?'

He grinned. 'Nothing.'

'I don't believe you.'

'I'm just sorry about the other night.'

'You say it like it was a one-off,' she reminded him.

'I don't want to fight.'

'Me neither.'

'So let's not.'

'Okay, let's not.'

'But?'

'But I really need help with the kids.'

'Fine. Now are you done?'

She grinned. 'I am.'

They clinked glasses and drank.

They had ordered and were awaiting starters before she got around to telling him about Harri and her implausible predicament.

'Whoa!' he said, hands up. Gerry was all hands. 'I know you said they adopted her but . . .'

'I didn't say they adopted her – I said they replaced her.'

'Excuse me?'

'Put down your hands, Gerry. You look like you're attempting the Mexican wave.'

'What are you saying?'

'I'm saying they had a daughter who was born alive.'

'Okay.'

'Therefore there was a birth cert.'

'Okay.'

'She died a few minutes after birth.'

'So there was a death cert?'

'Never completed.'

'Excuse me?'

'Gerry, don't be dense. A couple of months or so after the child was born and died, Harri, our Harri, was born in some field or barn or ditch in Wicklow. Duncan somehow got his hands on her and then he collected his twins' birth certs.'

'What about the death cert?'

'I don't know.'

'So the birth cert became Harri's – our Harri's? Is that really possible?'

'Well, it happened so it must be,' she said.

'It's true, stranger things have happened. After all, who ever thought the Terminator would become an American state governor or Steve Irwin, the Crocodile Man, would get killed by a fish? The world is mad!' Gerry laughed, then shoved a large piece of bread into his mouth.

The waiter put a plate in front of him. When he had finished serving, Gerry looked at his wife. 'Duncan and Gloria Ryan are dark horses,' he said.

Melissa thought about it for a moment or two. 'Yes, I suppose they are.'

'What are the chances of us having a little rough-and-tumble later?'

'Very low.'

'Fair enough. I'll have dessert.'

'Well, maybe,' she said, thinking aloud.

'Look, we either are or we aren't. You know I hate having sex on a full stomach.'

'I'm tired.'

'Fine, I'll have the banoffi.'

'But it's been a while.'

'The waiter's on his way over,' he pressed.

'Have the banoffi!' She hated being pressed.

'Fine,' he said, smiling at the waiter.

'You don't have to look so bloody pleased,' she huffed.

He ignored her. Gerry loved a good banoffi.

22 June 1975 – Sunday

All through Mass the only thing I could think of was Matthew, Matthew, Matthew! Father Ryan seemed to go on for ever. I've no clue what he said but no doubt he was sitting atop an invisible high horse. I saw Dr B standing at the back. He looked uncomfortable, as though he was loitering and didn't belong. Maybe he doesn't, but he has a right to bore himself to death as much as anyone else. When I leave home I'm never going to Mass again. I'm never going to Mass and I'm eating cake for breakfast. I can't wait.

I saw HIM standing left of Dr B. I can't believe he has the neck to come to church. He had his hat in his hands and they were clasped. What a creep. I hate him. I hate him. I hate him. He took Communion but Dr B didn't. That says it all. This world is a sad, sad place. How can obviously good people be made to feel abnormal and those full of badness allowed to feel they fit in? Is it normal to be twisted? Is it normal to cause torment? Maybe, but I can't decide where God is supposed to fit in.

Father Ryan has almost taken up residence in the house. He was back again this afternoon. Mam has agreed to go to prayer meetings. She feels bad about her marriage falling apart. She feels bad that she's let God down by protecting herself and me against the bastard from Hell. That's what Matthew called him when I told him what he did to my mam. I never said what he tried to do to me. It doesn't matter. I stopped him. It really doesn't matter. Father Ryan has spoken to HIM and he told Father Ryan he wouldn't hurt her again.

Father Ryan believes him. Father Ryan is a fool. So far she's praying for forgiveness but she hasn't allowed him back. All I can do is wait. I hate it. I hate it. I hate it.

Last night, in Devil's Glen with Matthew, it had all seemed so far away. He'd brought a blanket from the stables – it smelt weird – and he'd stolen three cans of beer from his dad's fridge. I had one, he had two. I hate the taste of beer but it felt nice afterwards. We sat by the waterfall but not close enough to fall in, like that stupid couple six months back – she nearly died. They're both fine now, but they broke up soon after it.

The sky was black, not a star to be seen, and the moon was big and bright. Matthew put on a deep voice and said, "'Man's colony on the Moon – a whole new generation has been born and is living there a quarter-million miles from Earth.'" It sounds rubbish now but it was funny when he said it. He's a massive *2001: A Space Odyssey* fan. He said people either love or hate that film. He's right. I think it's a pile of shit.

He'd brought a flashlight so we wouldn't trip on roots while trailing home. We sat and talked and I told him about Mam and about school and about my teacher saying I had a great command of the English language but no self-discipline, I didn't apply myself, and she wished I could learn to shut up in class. He told me about his mam and her death, and his dad and his dad's girlfriends, boarding-school and a beating he'd once got with a cane. He showed me the scar on his hand. It was small but that's probably because it happened a long time ago. Mostly he keeps his head down. He just tries to get by until he leaves school and home. He's going to America. Why does everyone go to America? He says his dad will never let him ride the way he wants to. He's too tall to be a jockey, he's at least six foot. He says he doesn't want to be a jockey but his dad won't even let him near the bred horses. He wants to break them the way his dad does and like his mam did. He says he'll find a way to do it in America.

I don't know why his dad won't let him – he's brilliant with the horses. Even Henry says so. Matthew's a natural, not like me. I'm still a bit scared but every day I like them more. He kissed me with tongue and he tasted of beer but it was way nicer than drinking the stuff. It was brilliant. We kissed and we kissed and we kissed until we were tired and sore. And still I would have kissed him some more. I'm running out of diary space again.

Just to note: horses have their own personalities. It's weird. Betsy is old and wise, calm and strong. Nero is young and foolhardy and excitable. Lovely Lucinda is a lady – she likes to be petted and she bows her head a lot. Paddyman joke-looks at you out of the corner of his eye and he likes his ears scratched but only for a minute or two. He's randy too. He likes the ladies!!! At least, that's what Matthew says. I really love my job. I can't wait for tomorrow.

9. Every time we say goodbye

James rose at seven. He could never sleep after that and the idea of lying in bed staring at a ceiling never appealed, especially when it was apparent that this particular ceiling was all but coming down. He used the old shower, which had very little power. He finished up using a facecloth in the sink. He sighed as he looked around the old place, with the plaster crumbling and damp stains the size of a fat man's jocks. He traced the black cracks in the Shires porcelain washbasin. The arched sash window would have been beautiful once but now the wood was rotten and the glass was on the verge of falling out.

Within a minute the broken-down images faded and instead he saw a lost future and all that the bathroom could have been. He glimpsed the arched sash window restored to its former glory, a laminated warm wood washbasin with natural graining instead of black cracks. He saw a matching wooden bath in the centre of the room, big enough for two. A Raindance Rainmaker shower-head was perched above him, with its mood lights – and jets for an intense massage. *Christ, I wanted that Raindance Rainmaker.* Very few cottage bathrooms were big enough to carry it off but this one was. *One in a million.* When he had finished shaving and returned to the present he mourned the Raindance Rainmaker for some minutes more. *Two feet in diameter, pressure assisted, it literally creates rain. Ah, well.* Mourning a shower was better than mourning his soul-mate. At least, he had believed Harri was his soul-mate. After the two aborted weddings he was sure that her mind and body had sabotaged them for a reason and, aside from the recent revelation, it was still possible that the reason was she didn't love him enough. Once again a woman he loved had abandoned him. He couldn't go through it all again, that was for sure. He couldn't let her steal the last shred of his dignity.

Malcolm had been kind in letting him camp with him. Thankfully, his friend was resolutely single, which meant James wasn't playing gooseberry. Yet sitting alone in his friend's apartment he had mourned Harri every minute since he'd picked up his aunt's fish. He hadn't returned to work, having booked holidays for his honeymoon. Instead he slept, walked aimlessly and visited showrooms test-driving cars he would never in a million years have dreamed of buying.

'She's lovely.' He'd point to a Mini Cooper. 'I'll try her.'

The salesman would look at him oddly, judging him to be at least six foot three maybe even six foot four. Then he'd look at the tiny car before them. 'Are you sure you wouldn't like to try something a little larger?'

'No, I'll be happy in the Mini,' James would say firmly, then get in, push the seat back as far as it would go and drive off with his knees in his mouth and an over-enthusiastic wave.

That had kept him humoured for a few days but it didn't dull the pain. He didn't dare drink because he knew if he did he'd cry, like his dad did every Christmas when he talked about how he had been a laggard when he'd met James's mother, then lamented over how she'd saved and made something out of him. He had a pride in himself that he accredited to her. James felt that way about Harri, not that she had changed him but that she had accepted him for the man he was. It made him feel the same immense and combustible pride his dad cried over each year. But that was gone. He was raw and sore and so empty he thought it possible that he'd never again know what it was to be full.

But then, from nowhere, the phone had started to ring.

First it was Susan. 'I have to tell you . . .'

Then Aidan. 'You need to know . . .'

After that it was Duncan. 'Please, James. She loves you. She needs you . . .'

Melissa was last. 'I know the others have called and I know it's a lot to ask . . .'

Duncan again. 'James, even if you phoned her . . .' And Duncan over and over until he was forced to switch off his phone.

How was he supposed to respond? What were these people trying to tell him? That his weddings had been aborted for a reason other than lack of love? Were they trying to link his fiancée's panic over marrying him to a dead girl in the Wicklow woods and a life based on a lie? Did their argument hold water? And poor, poor Harri, how she must be suffering – what a nightmare she had found herself embroiled in! Incidents came back to him in flashes. Her nightmares: once they had made no sense and they still made little, but now they resonated. Her awkwardness, the jagged sense of misplacement that had forced her into corners but ensured she stood out, now made sense. Her charming inability to lie, even though she had come from a home built on obfuscation. In James's mind she had always stood apart from her family: from her brother who, though he had the fortitude to be who he was despite encircling homophobia, was desperate to hide the part of himself that agreed with his detractors; from the mother who allowed herself to be treated as a fragile maiden when she ruled those around her; from the father who had long ago halved himself into the detective, who dealt with hate, intolerance, anger, violence, victims, death and dismemberment, and the husband, who wiped his day on the mat to play king in his wife's castle. To James, Harri had stood out from her family because she had always been straightforward.

He had discussed it with a fascinated Malcolm. Was this because she wasn't really a Ryan? Were her strands of DNA so powerful that nature beat nurture hands down? Had a part of her always known? Was he talking bollocks? Did it have anything to do with him?

The final question was the only one that he and the ever-patient Malcolm agreed on over a super-sized pizza. It did have something to do with James because he loved her. He would search until he found her, and he would ensure she was on her own two feet before he left again. Maybe her fear of marriage was connected to the lie she had unwittingly lived and maybe it wasn't, but this was no time for her to deal with their relationship. She had to find herself before she could find him or even them – if there was a them, and he hoped and prayed there was. James would wait for her. At least, that was what he told himself, because it was the only way he could say goodbye to the devastated, vulnerable, beautiful Harri.

James never ate fried food in Dublin – his father had been a bacon-egg-and-chips junkie: he had had high cholesterol, two heart attacks and a bypass because of it – but in Wexford James did like to cook a fried breakfast from scratch. The local butcher sold good-quality herb sausages, delicious black pudding and lean bacon that emitted a hickory-based aroma that made him dribble. He had forgone his luxury breakfast for the three mornings since his arrival. Harri had been too ill to endure the smell of fried pig's blood, but yesterday he felt there had been a breakthrough: he had managed to get her out of bed, out of the house and into the fresh warm air. They had gone over the grassy hill that led to sand dunes and a beach. The tide was far out, so they had walked towards the water rather than beside it. Fresh air blasted their faces, turning them pink, and entered their lungs. When the tide turned they quickened their steps back towards the grassy hill, where they sat and looked far out across the Irish Sea towards Wales.

'I'm sorry,' Harri said. 'I've been sleeping since you came.'

'That's a good thing. You needed it. You resembled the walking dead.'

'I felt like it.'

'And now?'

'Now I feel better. I think I've regained the power of cognitive thought.'

'Good.' He laughed. 'Cognitive thought is pretty important.'

'Yeah.' She smiled and even laughed a little.

'You'll be fine,' he said. 'Better than fine.'

'The second I saw you I felt better. I know it didn't look like it but I did.'

He detected wistfulness, which unnerved him slightly. He didn't want his determination to help the woman he loved confused with an attempt at reconciliation. He was also desperate not to disappoint her – she was in enough pain. He needed to clarify his intentions.

'You are probably the kindest and best woman I've known. It's your habit to put others before yourself sometimes to your own detriment. You really listen. You speak your mind and you care about the people around you even when they disappoint. You have strength. You don't know that about yourself. You see George as the strong one but he's not – he leans on you.'

Harri's smile faded and the fresh light in her eye dimmed. All these compliments could only mean one thing: goodbye. *Bollocks.* She huddled into herself, waiting for him to finish.

'And ever since we first met, I knew that a part of you was a little lost.'

She raised her head and looked quizzically at him, directly into his eyes.

'And you know what I mean. Don't get me wrong. I liked it that you stood out. It was as though you were making a guest appearance in your own life but now I understand. I understand why you never seemed comfortable enough in your skin to fit right in. I understand why you couldn't marry me. You need to find out who you are, Harriet Ryan. You need to do it alone and it'll be fine.'

Harri didn't speak. Instead she smiled and kissed James on his forehead. Then she got up and led the way home.

After they'd had supper, when Harri had eaten most of her meal, they played dirty-word Scrabble into the small hours of the morning.

'"Gap" is not a dirty word!' James argued.

'Not at first glance but it certainly has potential!' Harri retorted.

'Potential?' James wasn't convinced.

'Okay.' She sighed – and then she grinned, which made him grin too. She shook her hair and winked. 'Why don't you come on over here and play "find the gap" . . .'

James turned his head away, laughing. He was also blushing. This blush was born of heat rather than embarrassment and if she'd had the gumption to look she would have noticed his trousers had become a little tighter. But she didn't. Instead she bit her lip and nodded. *Score.*

'You win! "Gap" is a filthy, filthy word!' He laughed, turning to face her, and for a moment they shared a look. Then it was gone.

And although Harri felt like crying she didn't because it wasn't fair on James, who had come to save her after everything.

I love you. I love you. I love you. Don't leave.

They wouldn't speak about it again. Instead she would

agree that it was time to return to their individual lives. It was appropriate: the very next day would signal the end of the honeymoon that had never been.

James called up the stairs to Harri that her fried breakfast was on the table. She arrived moments later and joined him. Her hair was wet: she had plunged it into the stupid washbasin because the stupid shower hadn't been powerful enough to wash out the shampoo.

'I've only given you a small plate but there's plenty more in the oven.'

'Thanks.'

'It's probably better to get an early start,' he said.

'You should do that. I'm going to leave later.'

'Are you sure?'

'Yes.'

'Okay.' He proceeded to enjoy the sinfully delicious black pudding. Harri drank coffee while checking her texts.

Dad: When can we see you? Have you heard from George?

Soon. He's fine, Dad, just give us time.

James moaned on introducing crispy bacon into his mouth. 'You have got to try this.'

She smiled at him. The pure joy he extracted from a simple breakfast had always entertained her.

She was still angry with her parents but she couldn't hurt them. George was ignoring them so she couldn't ignore them too. They were as lost as she was. She felt she could manage her relationship with her father better by text: if she was with him, she might succumb to the urge

123

to punch him. Either that or she'd fall at his feet and cry until she was nothing more than a puddle. She needed more time.

The phone beeped.

Dad: Thanks for talking to me. We miss you.

Now she wanted to hug him tight and tell him everything would be okay – but she wasn't sure that was true. Every moment her feelings towards him changed so she didn't write back. She didn't know what to say.

George was easier. Initially there had been no contact but for the past four days she had sent him a text when she'd woken.

I love you.

It was simple and to the point and each morning, seconds later, her phone would beep. George: I love you too. That was it. Nothing more and nothing less but it was enough for now.

'Are you going to eat that?' James said, pointing to her black pudding.

'No,' she said, dishing it on to his plate.

'I'll really miss this,' he said to her, and she saw his lip quiver ever so slightly.

She wanted to beg him to stay with her and to put his lovely little speech aside. She did need him. She couldn't do this alone. She was only functioning because he was beside her. If he left her, she would be desperate once more. 'Please don't leave me,' she said.

James lowered his fork. 'Harri,' he said.

'Please don't leave me,' she repeated, tears gathering and waiting to fall.

'Don't,' he warned.

'I love you. You love me,' she begged.

'I can't,' he said.

'Why not?' she said, and her tone suggested a simmering rage that she could hold back no longer.

'You know why not.' He tried to stay calm.

'Bullshit!' she heard herself scream. *Oops! Rational has left the building. Fuck it, I'm on a roll.* 'If you really loved me you'd stay with me!'

'I've done this before,' he said, and cleared his throat.

'I don't understand.'

'I can't be your nursemaid. I can't be the one you lean on while you find what you're looking for. I've been there, I've done that, and some surfer in Australia benefited.'

'I'm not her,' she said.

'I know. You mean more to me than she ever did so another disappointment at your hands would kill me.' He laughed but his eyes were leaking. 'Maybe some day when you're whole again we might bump into each other – and then who knows?'

'I can't call you after today, can I?' she asked, finally resigned to heartbreak.

'No,' he said. 'Not for a while.'

'Okay,' she agreed, tears burning holes into her cheeks. *How long is a while? A week? A month? A year? Should I mention a specific timeframe? No. Damn it. Say something. Stop him.*

'I should go,' he said, getting up and leaving the rest of his breakfast.

'Okay,' she replied. *Oh, God.*

His bag was in the hall. She shadowed him to the door.

She could see he wanted to break but he wouldn't, not in front of her. She grabbed him and hugged him tight and her tears dampened his shoulder. *Break. Please break. Break and stay. Break and stay.* He squeezed her and her head disappeared into his chest, wetting the front of his shirt. *He's not breaking.* They stood in silence until he let go. *He's not staying.*

He opened the door and walked out, leaving his longed-for fry, determinedly making his way through the chaotic front garden to his car. He got in and drove.

Harri sat on the step of their holiday home in Wexford shedding tears until there were no more left to shed.

Hours later, while night descended outside, Harri Ryan was doing something that was quite contrary to anything anyone would have expected of her. She was wrecking the place with her ex-fiancé's five-iron. *Fuck strong. Fuck kind. Fuck listening. Fuck lost. Fuck alone. Fuck James. Fuck my father. Fuck my mother. Fuck Father Ryan. Fuck everything and fuck everyone!* She stopped at pulling the sink off the wall. *Fuck me, I've lost it again.*

She vacated the once-tattered, now completely vandalized cottage a little after one, suitcase in hand, and it didn't occur to her to look back. *No more tears.*

George was asleep in the passenger seat of the open-top rented car under a bright rich velvet blue sky. Aidan had graciously agreed to drive most of the way through northwest Italy as his partner was spent from negotiating, finagling and swaggering. George always injected just a hint of swagger into his demeanour when he was in a business situation. He felt it was important in the sales game. No one could carry off swagger quite like George Ryan. Aidan had often said it was one of the things that had first attracted him: George swaggered with James Dean cool. Unfortunately, when Aidan attempted to emulate him he appeared to be in need of a hip replacement. 'Too light on my feet,' he complained. 'No weight in my gait.'

George had agreed but he was quick to point out that it made him a better dancer. Aidan agreed he was most definitely a better dancer – and so he should have been after clocking up thousands of teenage hours in front of 'Footloose' practising the moves. To this day his 'Footloose' and 'Let's Hear It For The Boy' were step perfect. George didn't dance. George didn't do anything he wasn't good at.

They would soon be taking their leave of Piedmont, having secured a deal to ship and sell Barolo, which, according to George, was the greatest of all Italian red wines. Aidan didn't know or care much about that – he was just glad to see a smile on his partner's face. The map on George's lap revealed that their destination was not so far, which was a good thing because the Barolo meeting had run on and they had less than an hour to make the second and, according to George, all-important Barbaresco rendezvous to secure the high-quality yet more affordable wine of choice.

Aidan was glad George had this new venture to take his mind from his family troubles. However, with each passing day he was becoming more concerned about George's determination to ignore his parents and the problems confronting them. 'They deserve it,' he had declared, the evening before, at dinner. Aidan disagreed. George clammed up. Aidan changed the subject so he didn't have to endure George's insufferable huffy silence. He was relieved that George was not taking his anger out on Harri. At least he was texting her. *Poor Harri.* Aidan was very fond of her, and in times of relationship crisis he would often turn to her to help him find a road back to the difficult man he loved. Harri knew George better than anyone else on this planet. That wouldn't change, Aidan was sure, but everything else hung in the balance. He wanted to see Harri to find out where her head was at. He wanted to hear her voice to know she was okay, but he wouldn't call until he was home, which would be the following day. George couldn't bear to speak to his sister until he had worked out what to say. It wouldn't be fair for him to overhear a call between Harri and Aidan. At least, that was what Aidan told himself. Maybe deep down, as much as he missed his pal, he was as unsure of what to say as George was. After all, although George had been deceived he was still a Ryan. Who the hell was Harri?

Later, while he was waiting for George, Aidan enjoyed a glass of wine in the sun, looking out from the villa's stone patio to the tree-lined path that led to the vineyard. Colourful foliage danced in the faint breeze, catching his eye, and the time passed quickly.

Eventually George emerged triumphant from the cellar. He made his way towards Aidan, loosening his tie and swinging his briefcase. He reminded his partner of a schoolboy on the last day of term.

*

On the train that would take them to Verona, they sat opposite one another, soaking up the view and relaxing. They would spend the night in a quaint little hotel before George talked to a man about sparkling wine. Then, after a leisurely lunch, they would head to the airport and home. At least, that was the plan.

It was at dinner that evening, outdoors under a roaring orange sky, that George admitted his intention to remain in Italy.

'I don't understand,' Aidan said, in some alarm. 'The plan is –'

'The plan was. I've decided to head to Tuscany and pick up some decent Chiantis, then go on south.'

'Hold on! You said that southern Italy had nothing to offer but offensive glugging wines.'

'No – I said it had little more than offensive glugging wines. It's the "little" that I'm looking for.'

'You're just avoiding.'

'Don't start.'

'So come home. It's time.'

'I'm trying to get a business running here in case you haven't noticed.'

'You can pick up a few decent Chiantis over the phone.'

'Aidan, I really appreciate you coming on this trip but I'd also appreciate it if you'd allow me to live my own life.'

'You're so selfish. Your parents are going through hell and your sister needs you.'

'My parents deserve to go through hell and Harri – well, she understands me and she wouldn't change me.'

'Not like me,' Aidan said. 'It always comes back to that, doesn't it?'

'Yes, I suppose it does,' George said, and sipped some wine.

'Sometimes I really hate you.'

'So go home!' George spat, and with that, he disappeared down the road. He didn't come back to the room that night, choosing instead to book into a single.

Aidan spent a restless night alone before he made his way to the airport. *You really are an arsehole, George, and I don't know how much more I can take.*

Harri woke up to her doorbell. She steadied herself, knowing instinctively it was her mother – or, at any rate, the woman who had pretended to be her mother. She opened the door to reveal Gloria, pale, thin and frail.

'Hello, my darling,' she said.

'Hello, M-Mum,' Harri stumbled over the word.

Her mother flinched. 'Any chance of a coffee?' she asked, clearly trying to keep her hands away from her neck.

Gloria followed her into the kitchen and sat at the counter while Harri put on a pot of coffee. 'How was Wexford?' she asked then.

'Hell.'

'Right. I suppose it would be.'

Harri couldn't seem to sit still. Instead she was watering the plants on the windowsill, cleaning the counter or fixing her stool.

After a long silence Gloria said, 'You must have questions.'

'Millions,' Harri agreed, 'but I'm not sure I'm prepared for the answers.' She poured coffee that really wasn't ready to be poured and handed her mother a mug.

Gloria didn't complain. 'Will you allow me to explain my part in this?' she said.

Harri nodded. Her mother seemed so vulnerable and scared and she knew Gloria's heart was drenched in her own pain.

Gloria took a breath. She closed her eyes for a moment or two. When she opened them she spoke. 'I was mad with grief. Not only grief. I plunged headlong into sudden menopause because of the hysterectomy. In the 1970s there wasn't the same understanding that there is now. There weren't the same therapies, and God forbid that you'd talk about your feelings or answer that you were anything other than fine.' She took another breath and a slug of horrible coffee. 'Those first few weeks I was sectioned – they felt I was a risk to myself and maybe to George. Maybe I was – I don't remember much about that. I remember the wards, though. They were filled with women. Some were older, some were like me in their thirties, and then there was a teenager – her name was Sheena. I remember thinking it was a terribly exotic name.' She took another breath before she fixed her skirt and wiped her mouth.

Harri stood by the counter silently.

'Poor Sheena had attempted suicide nine times. She was only eighteen. She was a sweet thing but consumed by a terrible darkness that you have to experience to explain so I won't even try. She and I took walks together in the corridors. Sometimes we'd chat and sometimes we'd walk in silence. I'd known her three weeks when her mother brought her some items from the local shop – chocolate, toothpaste, a magazine. An hour after her mother had left Sheena was found dead in the bathroom having suffocated herself with the plastic bag.'

'My God!'

'I left the next day,' Gloria continued. 'I couldn't stay there, not after that. Duncan took me home to George and Nana, but I wasn't right. I lived on prescription pills while Nana was mother to George, and Duncan stayed out working late. Then one day that call came. Soon after, Duncan brought you home and laid you on my knee. I don't remember what he said. I do remember I didn't want to look at you or touch you. I was horrified that he would try to replace my baby girl but then you smiled at me and your hand rose towards mine and you grabbed my finger – you had such strength for a little one. I fell in love. There and then I knew that you had been sent to me. It took me a while to get back on my feet but that day I knew I could.' Gloria smiled at her daughter sadly. 'We should have told you and we were going to when you got older but time passed and it just got harder and harder, until we convinced ourselves that it really wasn't important. We were wrong. We know we were wrong and we are so, so sorry, my darling.'

'Mum,' Harri said.

'Yes, my darling.'

'I'm glad you think I saved you. I just wish you'd thought to do the same for me.'

Gloria's smile faded. 'I don't understand.'

Harri shook her head. 'You knew I felt like I didn't fit in all these years, yet you let me think that there was something wrong with me.'

'No, darling, I swear I didn't.'

'Yeah, you did. I deserved the truth, and you should have been honest. Maybe if you had been I'd be married today, and maybe not, but at least I'd know who I was and why I was such a mental case.'

'You are Harriet Ryan. You're not a mental case and you are my daughter.'

'And yet you seem like a stranger.'

'Oh, Harri!' her mother cried.

'I'm sorry, Mum, but I need to be alone now.'

Her mother rose from her chair. 'I understand,' she said, and without another word she left.

After that Harri put on the electric fire because, despite the fine night, she was cold in her bones. She opened a bottle of red wine, one that George would have described as cheap glugging crap, and turned on the TV. She stared at the screen, show after show. Goodbye, old life. Hello, couch-potato existence.

26 June 1975 – Thursday

It's been a long week. Betsy got sick with colic and I swear I thought she was going to die. Matthew and me stayed with her. (The correct grammar is 'Matthew and I' but I think 'Matthew and me' sounds better.)

But, hold on, I should start with Monday. Matthew was wearing a new leather jacket his dad had brought him from Monte

Carlo. It's really cool – he looks like the Fonz but way better-looking. Anyway, along with the jacket came a blonde woman, Giselle something (I think she's French or maybe German or Dutch). She looks our age but Matthew says she's twenty-six. His dad has moved her into the house. They look weird together. Matthew's not really interested in talking about it. He says she is one in a long line and soon she'll be gone. She's really beautiful, though. I wish I looked like her. So along came Tuesday and after work I called in to see Sheila, who wasn't at home and her mam was really awkward about telling me where she was and she even went red in the face and her dad told me to go home, which was weird because usually he's as sweet as pie.

I was on my way home when I met Dave, who said that she was in the hospital being pumped out. I didn't know what that meant so he told me she'd stolen vodka from the bar and she and Dave went to the castle drinking. Sheila did more drinking than Dave so she got really sick and he ended up carrying her to the hospital!!!!! He says he's in big trouble at home and Sheila's parents have refused to let him see Sheila again. I felt sorry for him. I mean, she robbed the booze, she drank most of it and he got her to the hospital – they should be thanking him. Adults are spazzes. Matthew called down to me later (I always get embarrassed when he sees my house – I'm such a peasant compared to him) and we went to visit her when the coast was clear. It was fun sneaking around and, let's face it, I know the place well enough to be able to.

Once Sheila's mother had left the building Matthew and me went in and Sheila started crying. I felt really sorry for her.

There was black stuff, mascara, maybe, all over her face and she said her mother wouldn't let her wash it off and had told the nurses to leave it. She was stuck in bed with a needle in her hand. I told her I'd walk her to the bathroom and help her wash her face. I don't care what her mam says. She didn't want to – she said she felt too sick. She had the shakes like old man Jeffers except Mam says he has Parkinson's and he's expected to die soon. Sad. I like him.

Sheila was let out of the hospital on Wednesday but she hasn't been seen since. I've gone up to the telephone box in town a few times to ring her but her mam says she's not allowed talk on the phone. It must feel like jail to be grounded in the summer. I wish we had a phone because going up town every time I want to call someone is a nightmare.

Anyway, back to Betsy. Last night Matthew came to tell me that she had colic and she was bad with it. I went to the stables with him straight away. Poor Betsy was really sick. Henry said she had an increased heart rate, which is bad. She was obviously in a lot of pain, sweating and rolling around. I wanted to cry but I didn't because I didn't want to be a spaz about it. Henry gave her paraffin oil, which he said would act as a laxative which basically means that she would shit all over the place. He gave her a sedative too but it didn't seem to help the pain. Matthew and I stayed with her, even though it was after eleven and Mam had warned me to be home by then. I didn't care. I wasn't going to leave Betsy. Just after midnight shit came pouring out of her like nothing I'd ever seen. Matthew and I got out of the stable just in time. She shat straight for an hour and then she seemed to improve.

I got home after one and I thought Mam would kill me but she didn't notice!!!!! She must have gone to bed early. Thank you, God. Matthew and I didn't kiss while Betsy was sick but we kissed all the way home. I think I could fall in love with him. I think maybe I already have. Tomorrow night we're going to the carnival. God, I love the carnival especially the bumpers. Sometimes when I'm behind the wheel of a bumper car I feel like I'm driving a real car and I'm an adult and I'm heading off into the sunset and free to find my own way in the world. I can't wait to really be able to drive. I can't wait to really live. We're going to try to help Dave sneak Sheila out. Matthew is bringing the ladder! I can't wait.

10. Tension Towers

The waiting area was empty save for Susan and her decidedly distant husband, Andrew. He chose to sit on the other side of the room, camped beside a table piled high with magazines that he pretended to flick through. *Christ, Andrew, I'm not contagious.* It had taken weeks of persuasion and every ounce of guile she could muster to talk him into accompanying her. Although he had remained stubbornly and steadfastly silent in her presence for six months, bar the odd monosyllable, and it was obvious that he agreed to counselling to get her to shut up, she was relieved when he had finally acquiesced. However, she didn't hold out much hope. Susan was just tired of talking to a wall and desperate for a conclusion to their misery one way or another.

She wished he would sit next to her but didn't dwell on it. Instead she focused on the painting, large and looming, on the wall above her defiant husband's head. In it a man and a woman sat on the remote ends of a bench both facing forward, both forlorn. At first they seemed completely apart, strangers even, but then it became apparent that while the man's hand was tight by his side his index finger was lifted and poised as though it was about to creep towards the woman, whose hand lay open and waiting. Susan looked from the painting to her husband's face. *If I left my hand open he'd slap it.* He hated being in her presence so much that he appeared distracted, irritated, itchy, even. She wondered why he hadn't left her. *Why don't you just go?* Why had he sworn her to secrecy? He didn't want Beth to know what was going on. That was only one of the things she hoped a visit to therapy could help answer. *She'll hate me, not you.* He was adamant. It was all he had said that night six months and four days before.

'Don't you dare involve our daughter in this!'

'But can you forgive me?' she'd begged.

That was the moment when he had stopped speaking and the moment that their relationship had truly ended. What was left was an illusion. They were stuck in some sort of torment-ridden limbo. *Can't you just forgive me?*

The door opened and a couple came out of the consulting room, the man leading the woman, both staring blankly ahead, neither their faces nor their posture revealing what might be waiting inside. The door closed. Minutes passed. The door opened. A man in his early fifties with wavy salt-and-pepper hair smiled at Susan and Andrew.

They stood.

'Mr and Mrs Shannon?' he clarified pleasantly.

'Yes,' Susan replied.

'Good. Come in.'

They followed him inside. The room was larger than she had expected but then again the rooms in Georgian houses often were. It occurred to her that the Georgians might not be known for their propensity towards personal hygiene but they did have the luxury of space. She smiled to herself. Andrew gave her a filthy look that suggested he would not tolerate anything that approached optimism. There wasn't any sign of a couch. Instead two comfortable chairs were positioned in front of an antique mahogany desk accompanied by an ox-blood leather and mahogany captain's chair. *At least he has good taste.*

Andrew noted that the chairs were far enough apart to negate the necessity for physical contact. *Good.*

The man sat and smiled.

Susan attempted the same but her lip stuck to her upper front teeth giving her, she was sure, a pretty frightening appearance.

'Let me introduce myself. I'm Vincent Mayers.'

'Hello, Vincent,' Susan said, trying to work saliva into a desert-dry mouth.

Andrew said nothing. Instead he focused on the framed document indicating that the man before him had a PhD. *It will take more than that.*

'So let's cut to the chase. Why are you here, folks?' Vincent asked.

Silence.

'How about we start with you, Susan? Why are you here?'

Susan's eyes widened in shock. She hadn't expected to be put on the spot immediately. She'd thought he would start off slowly, maybe get to know them through a little chit-chat. He would ask how they'd met. That was a great story. Or enquire as to whether or not they had kids, and they could talk about Beth and how well she was doing in school and what a lovely voice she had, or how long they'd been together. A lot happens in twenty-six years – they could have talked for a while about the passage of time. Or even a more basic introductory subject such as the weather, especially as it was unseasonably hot for late May, or the fact that the Kirov Ballet would be performing at the Point the very next night.

Why am I here? Oh, God, I feel sick. Her insides were drying, possibly terminally, and the PhD's question had the effect of wiping her once busy mind clean. Another silence.

'Andrew?'

Andrew didn't even pretend to engage. Instead he stared blankly ahead.

Vincent sat back. The silence extended. Andrew gazed out of the window, acting as though he was calm, but his hands clasped in his lap suggested he was not as comfortable as he pretended. His wife was clearly agitated, her hands moving excessively as though she was seeking a suitable place to rest them. She was sweating and, judging by her involuntary lip-curl, her mouth was dry. Vincent offered her water, then sat back and resumed watching them.

Susan desperately wanted to cry.

After the thirty-third minute had passed, Andrew looked her way but a little to the left and beyond her. 'Are you ready to go home now?' he asked.

She nodded sadly and they left without another word. *I don't suppose there's any chance of a refund.* They travelled in separate cars. Susan wasn't ready to return to the house of silence so she drove around the city, directionless, guided only by the one-way systems those around her found

infuriating. T...
she was remen...
returned to the S...
on the second flo...

It was mid-after...
bling, charged with ...
she was capable of...
approached her, handin...
cured from a well-stocke...
one and he had laughed at...
with him, embarrassed that ...

'I'm sick with nerves and c... ...g to
be nervous of,' she had said. *I'm* ... ...*a schoolgirl.*

'I promise.' He made a scou... ...ur sign with his
hand. 'Peanut?' he had ventured, holding out a packet,
making her laugh again.

*Hardly champagne and strawberries but, my God, I'm desperate
for you.* 'Thanks, I'll pass.'

He had drained his glass, placed it on the dresser, then
taken hers from her hand. Her heart was beating so wildly
that her insides reverberated. 'Did I tell you how stunning
you are?' he'd said.

You lying bastard. I love it. 'I remember you mentioning it
once or twice.'

'Did I tell you how you make me feel?'

Please stop talking. 'You don't have to.'

'You are the best part of my day.'

Okay, seriously, stop talking. 'Thanks.'

He'd touched her hand and pulled her close, and every
hair had stood on end. He'd leaned in for an electric kiss

...he kept an extra pair of
...er handbag . . .

...horn, bringing her back to the
...erotic reality.

...you're going, ya thick!' a faceless man
...he passed her.

...m sorry,' she mumbled.

She was on Baggot Street so she parked the car and
headed to Searson's Bar, which had been the venue for her
last dangerous liaison. She hadn't wanted it to be and neither had he. They had just got lazy or maybe miscalculated.
Maybe Fate had intervened or it might have been simple
bad luck. They had been kissing across the table in a
seductively dim corner when she had heard Andrew's
voice. She'd leaked a little wee and turned from the kiss
towards the voice. *Please, God, make me be hearing things.*

He had been standing in front of her in his business
suit holding his briefcase, another man beside him, a colleague or business associate, someone she didn't know.

'Susan?'

Every inch of her had frozen. Andrew had looked
from his wife to his colleague; Tony was the name she
remembered him using.

'Tony, this is my wife, Susan.'

Tony's look of shock had said it all.

'And I'm not sure who this is,' Andrew had said, staring
pointedly at Keith.

Keith had stood up. At six foot five, and broad, he had
an overpowering presence but Andrew, who was shorter
and slighter, had punched him hard in the face anyway.

Keith had taken the punch with the good grace of a guilty man. Andrew hadn't waited for an argument, tears or even apologies. He'd turned and walked away, his colleague following two steps behind. Keith had sat and drained his drink, fingering his swelling eye.

Susan had been in shock.

'Susan?'

She'd nodded.

'Susan?'

'Swords,' she'd mumbled, after a moment or two.

'Excuse me?'

'Swords. He said he would be in Swords.'

Keith had sighed, then signalled to the barman that he wanted another drink. The man had complied and Susan had thought that it was nice of him not to kick them out after what had just happened. She'd felt as if she'd received a whack from which there might be no recovery.

The barman had brought over Keith's drink.

'Thanks,' said Keith.

'Sorry,' Susan said. The man had smiled at her and walked away. *At least he's got a good story for the regulars.*

Keith had drunk deeply, almost inhaling the glass. 'What now?'

'Now I go home and face my husband,' she'd said.

'And me?'

'You go home, glad it was my husband who caught us and not your wife.'

'It's over, isn't it?'

'Oh, yeah,' she had almost laughed, 'it's definitely over.'

'I'm sorry.'

'That makes two of us.'

'I'll walk you to your car,' he'd offered.

'No.'

The excitement was gone. Everything she had felt for him minutes before had disappeared in an instant to be quickly and nauseatingly replaced with a mixture of dread, self-loathing and terror. *What have I done?* She had picked up her handbag and walked away. At the door of the bar she had turned to take one last look at the builder named Keith, who was not looking back. Instead he had been staring into the bottom of his empty glass, more than likely contemplating his lucky escape.

That had been six months and four days ago. She had gone home to an empty house, her husband having packed a bag of essentials and left without a word or note, only to return one week later, the day before their daughter was due home from a school skiing trip. He had told her he had returned for their daughter's sake and, although she had begged and pleaded, he had remained cold, uninterested, stoic. He didn't want reasons, explanations or excuses; he didn't want times, dates or details. In fact, he didn't want anything but silence, a torturing silence that had run on for months.

Searson's was quiet and she was grateful that the barman who had witnessed her scandal didn't appear to be working. Instead a woman served her a badly needed vodka and tonic. She retreated to a booth, deliberately passing the one that had been the scene of the beginning of the end of her marriage. She sat and put her bag under her feet. She stroked her glass before tipping its contents down her throat. She was on her second drink before she called Melissa and asked her to meet her. Her friend hesitated but Susan must have sounded so desperate and tear-soaked that Melissa told her she'd be there in an hour. Susan didn't want to make a fool of herself by getting drunk so she ordered food. By the time she had finished her meal Melissa was sitting opposite her.

'I'm sorry about the short notice.'

'What's wrong?'

'I think my marriage is well and truly over,' Susan admitted.

'I take it the counselling didn't go as hoped.'

'It didn't go at all,' Susan said, sighing. 'I couldn't talk. I couldn't admit what I'd done.'

'And Andrew?'

'He didn't want to be there anyway. He's never going to forgive me.'

'And now you're sure?' Melissa said wearily. She couldn't understand how Susan had allowed her husband to punish her for so long. *Either get over it or get out of it.*

'I know him. We've been married twenty-six years.' She shook her head. 'Twenty-six years, and now when I look at him all I see is anger and hate. He'll never give me the chance to explain. Sometimes I don't think he'll be happy until it's torn me inside out. He doesn't want it to get better. I just want it to end.'

Melissa put her hand through her hair. 'I don't know what to say.' She was glad her friend was hinting towards saving herself. But Susan had often talked about having had enough. *I wish I could believe you this time.*

'There's nothing *to* say.' Susan laughed bitterly. 'I wanted excitement and drama in my life and, well, I certainly got that.' She downed another vodka before shaking the glass at the barwoman, who nodded. 'My husband is determined that I suffer, and I do, but apparently not enough.'

After that final drink she agreed to allow Melissa to drive her home. When they reached the house Melissa went inside with her. *Poor Susan, she's aged six years in six months. She's suffered more than enough. Andrew, you wanker!*

Beth was at the cinema with a friend. Andrew was sitting at the kitchen table reading the paper.

Melissa was first to enter the room. Andrew stood.

'Melissa.'

'Andrew.'

'I didn't expect to see you.'

'Susan needed me to bring her home. She's in the loo.'

'Oh.'

They fell silent.

'Coffee?' he said, after a moment or two.

'No, thanks.'

'Tea?'

'No, thanks.'

'Water?' He smiled at her.

'Nothing,' she said, annoyed that he could find a smile for her while being so cold to the woman who had given him twenty-six years of her life. *We all make mistakes, Andrew. I'm sure you're no angel either.*

'Sit,' he ordered.

She did so out of habit rather than any desire to please. 'Andrew,' she said.

146

'Yes.' Again he smiled.

Stop smiling or I'll murder you. 'I don't believe in meddling in other people's marriages – God knows, I've enough trouble dealing with my own – but what you're doing to Susan is deliberate and cruel.'

'What do you suggest?' he asked calmly.

'I suggest you either attempt to work it out or leave.'

He laughed. 'It's all so easy!'

'Just talk to her.'

'And what would you like me to say?' He was still laughing, which annoyed her even more.

'Okay, fine. Be a baby – but how about doing it somewhere else?'

'This is my house,' he reasoned, with a grin.

'So let her go. Do something, Andrew, because your silence is destroying her!'

'Thanks for your input, Melissa, I'll definitely consider it,' he replied, with the grin firmly fixed to his face.

He might as well have found and flicked the switch marked 'lunatic' on the back of Melissa's neck because she flipped. 'You know, Andrew, it's no frigging wonder Susan had an affair because you are one of the most selfish, self-centred and annoying fuckers I know. You're a cold-hearted, money-oriented bullshit artist who has never had any time for his wife. So you'll keep on punishing her until you decide to call time – but when you do, I honestly hope she hates you enough to really stick it to you. And if you think all of this is her fault you're more stupid than I ever gave you credit for!'

Andrew had stopped grinning.

Melissa's heart was racing. *Oh, shit, I may have said too much.*

The downstairs loo flushed and a moment later Susan came into the kitchen.

'Tea?' she asked Melissa, ignoring her husband and the dense atmosphere in the room.

'No, thanks. I'm leaving.'

'Oh. Okay.' Susan nodded.

'Thanks for calling,' Andrew said.

You smug bastard. 'Go fuck yourself, Andrew!' Melissa retorted – to Susan's shock and, happily, her amusement too.

Susan laughed all the way to the hall door.

'Sorry,' Melissa said sheepishly.

'I don't know what happened in there but I'm glad you said what you did. I'll live on that for weeks.'

'It's like he knows exactly which button to push.'

'It's his gift.' Susan smiled.

'I really hope you've had enough.'

'Me too.'

Melissa and Susan hugged before she closed the door.

Susan didn't attempt to engage her husband and she was still laughing at Melissa as she filled her bath. *Okay, Andrew, have it your way. I give up.*

29 June 1975 – Sunday

HE's back in the house. He was there on Friday morning when I woke. I heard him downstairs making breakfast. They were laughing together. I felt sick. I didn't want to leave my room.

Mam kept calling to me but all I wanted to do was cry. I didn't go to work. I locked my door and hid under my blankets. I can't believe she's let him back. I hate her for it. I wish Dad was here. I wish she had died and left me my dad. HE hasn't come near me. He knows. Mam told him to give me time. I heard her talk to him about me like I'm the trouble-maker. She said something I couldn't hear and he laughed. I hate them.

I didn't want to go to the carnival but Matthew had brought his ladder for Sheila so he used it to climb to my bedroom. I let him in but only because I can't say no to him. I really just wanted to be left alone – besides I hadn't even had a wash so I'm sure I smelt. He knew there was something wrong. I don't like lying to him so I just said, 'HE's back.' That was enough. I didn't have to say any more. He hugged me for the longest time. I wish we could run away. I told him that too. He said maybe one day we would. I hope so. I hope it's soon.

He talked me into going to the carnival. I'm glad he did. It was brilliant. We met Dave at the top of the town and when Sheila climbed down the ladder we all caught a glimpse of her knickers. Dave and Matthew laughed at her because there was a bunny on them. I said nothing 'cause there was a frog on mine. She was like a bird released from a cage. She was dancing her way down the town. Dave kept running after her, trying to hold her hand, but after being confined to her room for nearly a week she needed to be free. It was after nine when we eventually got to Harrington's field. It's usually so bare and muddy, empty and depressing, but when we turned the corner it was full of people and lights, red, green, yellow and blue, all flashing in time to loud, pounding music. Everywhere you looked there were bumper cars, boat swings, carousels, aeroplanes, shooting galleries, ring-throwing tents, chip vans, ice-cream vans – there was even a Waltzer! The smell of candyfloss made Sheila feel sick. I think she's still suffering from all the drink.

Dave won a Scooby-Doo cuddly toy for Sheila. Matthew won me a fish but it died in the passenger seat of a bumper car ten minutes later. RIP. Still he was a brilliant bumper-car driver – we hardly got bumped at all, even though Dave nearly killed himself and Sheila trying to get at us. Matthew drove with one hand and had his other arm around me the whole time. The queue for the chip van was massive so we had ice-cream. Then we went on the Waltzer. I nearly died it was so fast. I thought we were going to spin right out of the field. Sheila puked. She missed Matthew and me but she managed to get most of it on Dave's crotch. He seemed really pissed off and he cleaned it up with Scooby-Doo so Sheila wasn't too pleased either. Dave took her home before eleven because she was scared if she left it any later she'd be caught.

I didn't want to go home so Matthew and I went and sat by the castle overlooking dark water. There was a car parked far behind us with its headlights on, lighting the water up in just one spot. We sat there for ages talking about where we wanted to go and what we wanted to be. I asked him, if we were still together in a year's time, could I go to America with him? He seemed really pleased and started making plans. He's even going to ring the American embassy!!! Then he told me stories about the places he'd been there, describing New York as bustling, crowded, heaving and electric, remembering in Boston the Harvard grounds, red-brick terraces and orange sunsets, and smiling about San Francisco, hills, cable cars, the famous Wharf and the almighty Alcatraz. It sounds so amazing. Matthew's been to America lots of times and he said it's way better than here. He said I could be anything I wanted over there, which is great as I'm not really sure what I want but he said I'll know it when I see it.

It was after twelve and I still didn't want to go home. Matthew was worried that my mam would kill me but I didn't care so I went home with him. His dad is away with 'his bit' – that's what Matthew calls her. 'His bit'! We walked through Devil's Glen and it was pitch dark under the trees and only lit by a perfect half-moon in the rare moments of open ground. It's weird but I didn't notice the moon over the water earlier by the castle! Anyway, it was not a bit scary, even though we could hear little animals rustle in the undergrowth. I don't even want to think about what they were. Actually, aside from tripping on a root and nearly breaking my knee, it was romantic.

Matthew's house is unbelievable. You could fit my entire house in his living room. His room is painted a dark blue with a white ceiling and white wooden door and window frames. He's got four massive stacks of albums, piled so high the top one is hard to reach, and a really cool record player on his floor. The lamp by his bed shines a red light!!! Like the carnival. His bed is huge – it's even bigger than my mam's – and mine is definitely less than half the size. It was good, though – we both had loads of room to spread out. We talked for ages under the red light and he played a band I didn't recognize. The record was scratched so he kept getting up to sort it out but other than that they were really good. We kissed for a while and we hugged and then we went to sleep. It was really nice. I feel safe with him. I hope we make it to America. God bless America!!!!

Okay, now I'm running on to Wednesday of the next week in my diary. I have to get a bigger one but this is important. I forgot to say on Friday night that Sheila and Dave had sex behind the bush where we'd hidden the ladder!!! She said it wasn't planned, which was pretty obvious seeing as it was in a bush. She said she doesn't know what came over them. One minute they were fighting over her puking on Dave and Dave cleaning up the puke with her Scooby-Doo. Then they were kissing, which was the usual, and then she doesn't know – she felt something, something new. I asked her to explain but she went red and said she couldn't and that some day I'd understand, which was pretty condescending for someone who wears bunny knickers. Anyway, she said that after that she couldn't help herself and this is coming from a girl who swore she'd never do it until she left home because if she got pregnant her mother had warned her she'd be out on her ear. And she means it. Sheila's mam is very religious and she has always maintained that she will not live under the same roof as a sinner, which is funny because she's quite happy to serve them booze. Now Sheila is terrified she's pregnant even though she did a lot of jumping afterwards and thinks she got most of his stuff out. Not a pleasant thought and something I could have done without hearing. I don't know if I'll be able to look at Dave in the same way. I'll see. She also managed to cut her knee on a sharp rock and she tore her bunny knickers. She still made it home by eleven because it only took five minutes. She doesn't think she'll do it again unless she is pregnant – then she can do it all day long every day at the side of the road where she'll be living! Even if she does do it again I doubt it will be outdoors. She's been stuck in bed for the past two days with a really bad cold.

11. I am I and you are you

Harri's headache began with a taxi ride to Dublin airport. This was followed by a mad dash through Customs and fourteen miles of airport lounges. In Harri's case, any exercise, most especially running, caused profuse sweating combined with a disturbing inability to control her breathing. Her gasping entrance to the plane was met with several dirty looks from the other passengers, who had had the decency to embark on time. The familiar pain in her frontal lobe was exacerbated by a nasty bump on the head when an overhead locker mysteriously shot open as she passed it. *Arse.*

A man with a beer belly stood between her and her seat. His loud tuts suggested he was displeased at having to get up to allow the shaken and terribly apologetic Harri to gain access to her cramped seat. Sometimes Harri's headaches induced vomiting and, while squeezing past him, she decided that if she was to vomit she would do so on him. Once seated, she congratulated herself. *Bloody hell, I made it. I can't believe I made it.* It had been just three hours since she'd received George's SOS call, and the Ryanair flight to Bergamo was the only one that would get her to Sirmione that day.

The flight was uncomfortable, mostly because of the mind-numbing headache but also because she'd only had enough time to throw a few items into a case, grab her passport and leave in the clothes she was wearing. Unfortunately, as she had earlier attended a new-business meeting with Susan, she had on stilettos and, having run far enough to qualify for the Olympic Games, they were now embedded so far into her feet that they would probably have to be surgically removed.

Three hours later, she navigated her way to the airport's nearest exit and found the small, air-conditioned bus to Sirmione. She handed the driver the exact fare – *Thank you, God, for the euro*. She was now heading towards Lake Garda and the tiny island of Sirmione without having had to engage with one Italian. She sighed. *Okay. I'm fine. Everything's fine*. Harri was not a happy traveller. The few times she'd bothered to leave her own country, to travel into the abyss she considered abroad to be, had been mostly either to join or rescue the man she had until recently believed to be her twin brother.

George had insisted they share their twenty-first birthday together although he refused to leave Cape Cod, so Harri and their parents had travelled to him. Before that, aged eighteen, she had caught a flight to Biarritz, where he was participating in a surfing contest even though his parents had banned him from attending due to upcoming exams. He'd broken his ankle and needed his sister's savings to pay the hospital bill and her shoulder to lean on when hopping on and off the planes. She'd once gone to Venice at his behest because he had broken up with his first love and was desperate over the whole thing. There had been a few trips after that but, thankfully, they had been to English-speaking countries so not as stressful for the girl who was pathologically afraid of anything or anyone she didn't understand.

And now once more Harri was travelling to George. He had called, slightly panicked because he had woken up with what he believed to be a broken nose. Clearly he was still drunk as he had started the conversation in harassed Italian. She had had to remind him that she didn't speak it and asked if he could manage English. He conceded that English was possible. He was slurring and it became slowly apparent that he had gone on a three-day drinking binge that had culminated in a punch to the face.

It was after ten when she reached his hotel. He was sleeping soundly when she knocked.

'*Chi c'è?*' came his groggy response.

'George?'

'*Chi c'è?*' he reiterated.

'George, it's me, Harri.'

'*Harri? Sei tu?*' Clearly he was still not properly awake.

'It's Harri. Your –' The word 'sister' caught in her throat. 'Let me in for the love of God.'

The prayer seemed to work. George opened the door, sweeping back a fringe that needed cutting, revealing two black eyes and a swollen nose. 'What are you doing here?' he asked, in a tone that suggested he didn't remember their earlier conversation but that he was glad to see her. He was smiling.

'Good God, George. Look at the state of you!' She followed him inside.

He glanced into the mirror. 'Oh, that's why my face is

hurting,' he said. 'I called you, didn't I?' he added sheepishly.

She nodded.

'Old habits die hard,' he said, sitting on the side of his bed. He looked at his watch. 'Still, you must have made serious time.'

'You've no idea.' The familiarity of their situation was comforting. She sat on the single bed opposite his. 'You'll need to see a doctor.'

'No, it's fine,' he protested.

'No, it's not,' she argued.

'I'm sorry I called. I was drunk.'

'Don't be and I know.'

'I've really missed you, sister.'

'I've really missed you too.'

'You're still the one I call,' he said, smiling to himself. 'When I'm down and out, you're still the one I call.'

She grinned. 'Lucky me.' *I haven't lost him. He hasn't lost me. He's a pain in the arse but he's still my pain in the arse.*

'What are you thinking?' he asked suspiciously.

'That you're a pain in the arse and I'm really glad you called me.'

'Aside from the bender, street fighting, broken nose and black eyes, I'm glad too.' He laughed but that hurt so he stopped.

'I'm calling the hotel doctor,' she said, lifting the phone.

A woman on Reception answered in Italian and she froze. *I have no idea what she's saying. What the hell is she saying?* George grabbed the phone and one medical

157

examination two showers and a number of painkillers later, he and Harri were sitting in a nice restaurant close enough to the imposing Rocca Scalgera and far enough away from the scene of the unfortunate fracas that had occurred the night before. The castle was lit up in all its Gothic glory.

Harri stared at her menu.

'Do you want me to choose for you?' he said.

'Great.'

The waiter approached. Harri dropped her gaze to the floor. George ordered a number of items with which she was completely unfamiliar. He smiled warmly at the waiter, who smiled back despite George's fearsome appearance. George turned to Harri. His eyes rested on her but he said nothing.

'What?'

'You really need to get over your fear of foreigners,' he said, with authority.

'Why?' she asked, like a child chastised.

'Because it's weird, not to mention rude,' he said, wagging his finger.

'I'll tell you what weird is. Weird is when you wrap a T-shirt around your feet and hop across a room rather than stand barefoot on a tiled floor.'

'Tiles are cold and hard,' he protested. 'I have very sensitive feet.'

'And as for rude. If rude was an Olympic event you'd take the gold.'

'Bullshit!'

'What about the time that Tina made a pass at you and

you informed her that even if you weren't gay you wouldn't stick someone else's dick in her?'

George sat back in his chair to contemplate. 'Tina Tingle, your old flatmate?'

'How many Tinas have you said that to?' Harri grinned.

Laughing, George put up his hands in surrender. 'That was years ago and I sincerely hope my behaviour has altered for the better since then.'

'Well, my guess is that last night you weren't punched hard in the face for nothing.'

'There is that,' he said. 'I just wish I knew what I'd said so I could avoid any future battering.'

The food came and, both ravenous, the Ryans tucked in.

Afterwards they strolled together arm in arm by the lake. George liked to have an arm around a woman in public. It made him feel masculine and virile and especially so with his diminutive sister, who, when abroad, clung to him like a child afraid of getting lost. They sat on a bench, staring at the moon, both quiet and tired after the events of the past few weeks.

'How's Susan?'

'Aidan's fine.'

'I didn't ask about Aidan.'

She looked towards her brother.

'Okay,' he agreed, holding his gaze on the bright moon. 'How's Aidan?'

'He's annoyed and frustrated and fine.'

'He won't take my calls.'

'He's punishing you.'

'Any idea how long it'll last?'

'Until you come home.'

'Oh.'

'You'll come home with me?' Harri asked.

He sulked. 'It's only been a few days.'

'It's been more than a few days. You have a new business to run, a boyfriend waiting for you and a life back home.'

'You didn't mention Mum and Dad.'

She shrugged.

'Have you seen them?' he asked.

'Mum,' she said quietly.

'How is she?'

'Contrite.' She sniffed a little.

'And Dad?'

'We've texted but I can't face him yet.'

'Why?'

'You've a neck to ask.' She laughed.

'Oh, I know why I can't face him but tell me why you can't.' The answer might seem obvious but George needed to know exactly what Harri was thinking. He needed to feel he knew her as well now, on the Sirmione shoreline, as he had nearly a month previously when he had thought they shared a birthday.

'Because he'll take me into his office and he'll sit me down and he'll get out a file and he'll open it and he'll tell me and show me things I'm not ready for. Don't forget I was once one of his cases.'

George was silent for a few minutes, absorbing his sister's words. In his outrage and contempt for his parents'

lie, he had forgotten something important. He had forgotten that Harri, once lost, might soon be found, with all
the frightening implications that that entailed. *She has
another family somewhere. That really should have occurred to me
before now. God, I'm such a selfish sod.*

'What are you thinking?' she asked, after a minute or
two.

'That I'm a dick.'

'Oh.'

'Harri?' he said, after another moment or two.

'Yeah.'

'Are you scared?'

'Not any more.' She smiled at him. 'Maybe a little nervous but definitely not scared.'

'Are you curious?'

'Yeah,' she admitted. 'I am.'

'Are you still my twin sister?'

She nodded. 'I am.'

'But?'

'But,' she sighed, 'I'm also someone else.'

'I can forgive them but only if you can.'

'The parents?'

'Yeah.'

'So we'll forgive them.'

He stood up and took her hand and together they
walked away from the shore and towards their hotel room
where, twenty minutes later, George would make an ill-
conceived joke implying that as they were not now
technically related she should probably turn her back so
she didn't get too aroused by his muscle-bound body. He

didn't duck in time. The pillow hit his face and, because of the previous night's injury, it felt like a brick. *I really need to learn to shut up.*

5 July 1975 – Saturday

I can't believe it. Dr B has moved into Matthew's gate lodge! Henry asked us to help him unload boxes from his car. I carried the light stuff and he was really strict about us bending our knees before picking anything up. When Matthew went out to get stuff for sandwiches, Dr B mentioned he'd seen us at the carnival. I asked him why he hadn't said hello and he said we were in a mammoth bumper-car battle at the time. He made me laugh. He was right – it was a mammoth battle, Matthew against Dave, who took it a little too seriously for my liking. Anyway, he said that, out of my school uniform and with makeup, I looked a lot older than my years. Sheila's Dave said I'd definitely pass for twenty-three! I suppose looking in the mirror at my old face all the time makes me think that others like Dr B are really young when they're not. He's probably twenty-six but he only looks about twenty. It's weird. I hope I don't always look older. That would be terrible – I'll look like my granny at twenty-five. Dr B said he almost didn't recognize me with makeup on. I told him I'd been able to buy beer since I was thirteen. He frowned at that, crinkling his face, but I said that if he can tell me he likes men I can tell him I buy beer. I didn't tell him I don't like the taste. He conceded that I had made a good argument after going very red and shuffling a bit. He's very sorry he let his secret slip and I don't think he's really sure how or why it happened. I think he was just like a bubble on the verge of bursting and I just happened to be there at the time.

Anyway, I had Tuesday off so I thumbed to Bray and headed to the bookshop and spent half the day looking for the perfect moving-in present. In the end I came across it by accident. I was looking through some second-hand books in the corner and came across *A Passage to India*, which had been a present I'd received from my granny the year before last. I nearly had a fit. I thought it was a travel book and I really don't think I'd like to go there. I mean, I wouldn't even know what they were saying and that's just weird.

I was wrong. It was a brilliant story about a poor Indian doctor who lives under British rule, which means they probably do speak English or at least they did. I don't know. God, I'm sooooo ignorant. Anyway he's falsely accused of touching up some stupidly named English woman during a day out at the caves and all hell breaks loose. It's really good. I was glued. Anyway I was looking through the writer's other stuff – *Howards End* looked kind of boring and *A Room with a View* looked like it could be a bit sexy. Then I came across a book called *Maurice* and it's only a story about homosexuality! Unbelievable! So I *bought A Room with a View* and *Maurice* and the man behind the counter gave me a dirty look when he saw what I was buying but he didn't ask my age because I wasn't in my uniform and I was wearing makeup. Last night I started reading *Maurice* (Dr B will never know it's a second-hand book). Holy Mother of God, I think there'll be parts I'll have to read with one hand over my eyes!!!!! I'm only at the start of it but already I really feel sorry for Maurice and Clive. I'll give Dr B the book when I'm finished. I hope he likes it. I hope it has a happy ending. If it doesn't have a happy ending maybe I won't give it to him. I don't know. I'll have to think about that.

HE's keeping his head down. He hasn't said a word to me and I haven't said a word to him. Mam is pretending not to notice. Father Ryan has visited twice and the other day the three of them knelt in the sitting room and said the rosary before they had tea and biscuits in the kitchen. It makes me sick to my stomach. Father Ryan asked if I would pray with them but I said no way and Mam said later that I gave him that look, the one that would frighten the devil himself. Tough! If Father Ryan thinks a rosary or two, a few cups of tea and some biscuits will make any difference he's a fool. If he thinks by talking my mam into letting HIM back into our house that he's done a good thing he's wrong.

I haven't seen Matthew in three days. His dad came home without his bit and took Matthew to somewhere in Spain with him. He didn't say why he wanted Matthew to go with him, but he doesn't really talk to him, just kind of orders him around. They won't be back until mid next week. I really miss him. I wish he was home. I haven't seen Sheila either – she's still locked in her room. Dave has been up and down Matthew's dad's ladder like nobody's business. Her parents are too busy in the bar to check on her so she and Dave have her room all to themselves. Little do her parents know she's been having the time of her life just above them!!! Having said that, once she found out she wasn't pregnant she told Dave they

164

couldn't have full sex for a good while as she didn't want to risk it, so they're doing other things that she says are private. Suddenly Sheila is private. I've heard it all now.

Henry said I'm getting to be a much better rider. I'm not a natural, though, not like Matthew. Betsy is good to me. She'd want to be after she almost shat all over me. That will be hard to forget. Anyway, although the days are a little longer without Matthew, I still love working with the horses. Maybe I'll go into horse training. Maybe I should be nicer to Matthew's dad. I'll think about that. The door is locked. I'm tired. Going to sleep now.

12. Limbo's just a stopgap

In the weeks after Harri had returned from Wexford and before she went to Italy she had allowed disillusionment to consume her. As Aidan had put it one afternoon, if she was a taste she'd be described as tart with a hint of bitter. He had appeared the day after his own return from Italy. When she'd opened the door to his annoying rap, he'd bustled past her, tanned, wearing white and smelling of a combination of Paco Rabanne and Lynx, which he insisted on spraying down his pants in what her brother had once described as an OCD-type manner.

'Is that the TV I hear?' he asked, trailing into the sitting room just to be sure. 'Wow, I didn't think that thing actually worked!'

Since returning from her holiday home in Wexford, Harri had done little except work and watch TV. Television was the greatest thought-antidote imaginable. She could remain awake and free from contemplation, consideration or deliberation for hours on end. Instead she was free to live someone else's joy or misery, fear or fortitude. She could stare blankly at the screen and become embroiled in another's nightmare without having to consider or ponder her own. She found that she liked crime shows best. *CSI* was particularly fascinating and conveniently seemed to be showing every time she turned the TV on. It had such an impact on her that when her dad had told her about her origins, in the attic, one of the few thoughts that had passed through her paralysed mind was *They'd never have got away with that in Nevada*, not to mention *Jesus Christ, Jesus Christ, Jesus Christ, this stuff only happens in films.*

Aidan made himself tea while cursing her brother. 'He's a pig'; 'I'm sick to death of him'; 'Selfish selfish selfish!'; 'Where are the teabags?'; 'I've reached my limit with him, I really have'; 'Are you going to say anything?'

'He wants a few days on his own, that's all,' she reasoned, squeezing her teabag: Aidan had a phobia about squeezing other people's – 'It just feels so wrong,' he'd once explained. Teabag removed, she handed him her mug so that he could pour in the milk and pass it back to her.

'Excuse me, Harri, but this is your nightmare, not his. Okay, your parents lied to you both and his real twin is dead but, boo-hoo-hoo, get over it already. You're the one who is the outsider in your own family. You're the one who doesn't know who she is or where she belongs. You, my friend, are the square peg in the round hole.'

'Thanks for reminding me and putting it so beautifully.'

Aidan always could make her laugh, most especially when he was at his inconsiderate best.

'I'm only saying it like it is,' he said, and drank some tea. 'Christ, the milk's off!' He made a gagging sound and poured both mugfuls into the sink. He opened the fridge and took out two cans of beer. 'How's work?'

'Busy. We've a few projects going. Susan's in Howth

working on a penthouse and I'm in Dalkey, fixing up a really nice little café for a couple from Cork. I hope it does well for them.'

'Any work going?' he asked.

'Susan will need you in Howth next week. I think the client wants the place painted top to bottom. They're still at the decision-making stage but give her a call.'

'Will do,' he said. 'And you? Still avoiding your parents?'

'As much as possible. I've seen Mum but I'm keeping clear of Dad for a while.'

'Why?'

'I'm not ready.'

'Are you angry?'

'Yes.'

'You want to punish him?'

'No. Yes. Maybe. I don't know. Mostly I just want to be left alone.'

'And why wouldn't you? People are bastards.'

They sat back and contemplated that fact.

'Still, what a shock. It's all so fucking shocking,' he said, after a minute.

Harri took a large gulp of beer. 'If I grew a mini-mickey I'd be less shocked,' she said contemplatively, making her pal laugh.

'Interesting,' he mused, and was relieved that the pre-wedding Harri was making a return. Shock and grief had all but stolen her away and one month on he was really missing his friend. Harri was in freefall and it was hard to do anything but hold your hands out, yell and hope for the best while you were freefalling. Hitting the ground would hurt but he counted on her to do so running. *Come back, Miss Harri, we miss you down here.*

'Aidan?'

'What?'

'I think I do want him to suffer.'

'Your dad?'

'Yeah – and Mum too.'

'That's okay.'

'I feel sick about it.'

'Don't be. You can wallow a while longer but soon, my friend, you'll have to change that gloomy tune and return to us the effervescent little do-gooder that you are.'

One beer later he was leaving to meet a friend for a pint. 'What's the point in getting a tan if you can't go out and sicken a freckled white Paddy or two?' he said. Then he kissed her cheek and headed for the door. 'You'll be all right. Everyone thinks George is the strong one, but they're wrong.'

He had a point because the very next day she was on a plane heading to Italy to bring her battered brother home.

Susan cornered her in the office whenever she could. 'Do you want to talk about it?'

'No.'

'Are you sure?'

'Yes.'

'Sometimes it's best to just let it all out.'

'Sometimes it's best not to.'

'You're having a really, really terrible time. First ending it with James and now this unbelievable revelation.'

'I'm fine.'

'Of course you're not. Just let me know if there's anything I can do.'

'You can shut up.'

'Say no more,' Susan said, and zipped her lip.

Melissa would phone five times a day. 'What are you doing?'

'Working.'

'I hear noise.'

'I'm in an antiques shop.'

'Anything nice?'

'I'm fine.'

'I didn't ask, smartarse!'

'I'm fine.'

'Any news?'

'No.'

'Are you going to your parents for dinner any time soon?'

'No.'

'You have to go some time.'

'So you've said.'

'Well, I'm right.'

'Is that it? Can I go now?'

'Fine. Go.'

Two or three hours would pass.

Melissa again. 'Jacob is being kicked out of his playschool for biting some kid with big ears.'

'Oh, my God, what are you going to do?'

'Sit him on the bold step, threaten his life and then find another nursery.'

'Why did he bite the kid?'

'Apparently it was a mission of mercy. He thought if he bit the tops off the kid would have normal-sized ears.'

Harri laughed.

'It's not funny.'

'I know, I'm sorry.' *It bloody is funny.*

'I was in a meeting with a new client and now I'm on my way to collect him because fucking Gerry is too busy. And didn't you know his job is far more important than mine?'

'I wish I could help but I'm in a traffic jam on the M50.'

'It's fine. Don't worry. So, have you spoken to your parents?'

'No.'

'Are you going to?'

'Not today.'

'Right. I'll call you later.'

Another few hours would pass.

'Jacob and Gerry had a screaming match. I swear the man is as bad as the child. Jacob threw the tantrum to end all tantrums and eventually cried himself to sleep. Gerry's in the bath in a sulk. They woke Carrie, who now thinks it's first thing in the morning and wants to play. Don't eat that, darling. No, darling. Please do not put that in your mouth. Just a second. Carrie, ta ta! Right, where was I?'

'Jacob cried himself to sleep, Gerry's in the bath and Carrie thinks it's morning,' Harri summarized.

'I hate my life.' Melissa sighed.

Harri laughed. 'I'm watching my third *CSI* in a row and I saw this particular episode yesterday and possibly the day before too.'

'Oh.'

'Yeah.'

'Have you talked to your parents?'

'You're relentless.'

When Harri returned from Italy with George in tow and summoned the courage to face her parents, it was a relief to all.

6 July 1975 – Sunday

I was sitting by the *Eliana* and just staring out to sea thinking about nothing. I didn't notice HIM sit beside me. I suppose I was daydreaming and far away. It was early. Nine or maybe nine thirty. I felt his arm on my shoulders. I moved, but too slowly. He held me in place. He must have been out drinking all night. I could smell the drink on his breath and when he leaned in for a kiss I stamped on his foot. He cried out and let go a little. I ran. I could hear him shouting that I was waiting for him and I wanted it.

I don't know how I didn't see him. I don't know how I managed to let him get so close. I don't know if he was right. He was so drunk he couldn't have been quiet in his approach – he would have been stumbling. And the smell of him alone! Where was I in my head that I didn't see or hear? What's wrong with me? I can't tell Matthew because he'll do something and then we'll end up in trouble and it doesn't make sense that HE can get away with it but he can. HE can do what he wants because he has a marriage licence and that's a licence to do anything. I didn't want to come home so I walked and walked, past the castle and the Strand and on to the head and around by the lighthouses and down to the cliffs. I sat at the edge and I'm not saying I would ever kill myself but for the first time ever I thought how easy it would be. It was only fleeting and I could never leave Matthew, but that's it. I realized that he is the only one I have to stay around for.

Coming back here was hard. Putting my key in the door and turning it was harder. I used to love this little house on Castle Street. I loved that we were in town and beside the pier. I loved my little room that looked on to Mam's well-kept garden and the way the light streamed into the sitting room on a sunny day. I loved the smell of cooking that hit you the second you opened the door. Mam used to cook all the time. She would start the dinner at one to serve it at six. She loved to bake apple tarts, rhubarb tarts, fairy and queen cakes. She doesn't do that any more. The house doesn't smell of cooking any more. The sitting room seems duller, older, and tatty, even. The garden is overgrown and my room isn't my room any more. He's taken everything – and every day he makes me a little more scared.

13. It's been a month but it feels like a year

The trip up the stairs to the study seemed to take longer than ever before. Three floors plus the converted attic made four flights, and the combination of expectation, fear, silence and creeping dread encouraged Harri to believe that she might never reach her destination. *I might have a heart attack. I could easily have one – it's beating too fast. Don't panic, Harri. Don't be* My Left Foot *about it and, for Christ's sake, don't die on the stairs.* At the top, her father turned to her and took the key from his pocket.

Duncan had aged ten years in one month. When Harri had pulled up in her parents' driveway she had found her father sitting on Nana's bench, and when her eyes met his, the anger she had felt all but disappeared. He was old now, his face lined, his brow furrowed, and when he stood up, unsure and eyes watering, he seemed smaller. The hulking gravel-voiced hero of her youth had turned into a stranger. He was lonely, scared and at sea in uncharted waters. *I know how that feels.* Resentment trickled away and pity filled her. His head hung low, and although he met her eyes, the man she knew wasn't looking back at her. She couldn't bear his pain, so she smiled and hugging him tightly.

'I just needed time, Dad.'

He wrapped his arms around her and, by Nana's bench,

her dad the warrior had cried for the love of his daughter Harri.

Gloria was waiting by the stove, having just checked on the shepherd's pie. She was wringing her hands so that they wouldn't flutter. 'There you are, darling,' she said, clearly happy that her daughter was arm in arm with her broken husband.

It seemed so odd that, in the Ryan household, it had been Gloria's mental state that had long been cause for concern. Gloria had been upset by the events that had led them to this appalling place. She had worried for her daughter and son, for how the truth had affected them and how it would affect them in the future. She worried that she would lose them and specifically Harri. *Will she run off now? Will she find a family somewhere else? Will she no longer need or want us?* But deep down there was a calm she couldn't explain. *We'll be okay. We have each other and we'll be okay.* She had felt sad and had cried because deeply buried memories had been exhumed: she had seen once more the face of the baby girl she had lost as vividly as though she was pictured on the wall before her. She recalled the contours of her little button nose and her discoloured rosebud lips. She had had floppy dark hair like her twin brother's. Her nails were so long they needed cutting and the thumb on her left hand curled towards the palm while the fingers were stretched out. When Gloria had held her that one and only time thirty years before she had decided that her daughter might have been a concert pianist – her elegant fingers looked like those of a piano player. She knew, too, that she would have been athletic – as her twin had turned out to be. That night, when the doctor and nurses had all but pulled her little girl out of her arms, something inside her had broken. It had healed long ago, and although the scars remained, she had always known she would never break like that again.

Gloria had been the strong one and Duncan had fallen apart.

His kids hated him. He was full of regret, and for the first time self-doubt had seeped in, threatening to fill the unseen fissure that had begun to creep through him the day his lost daughter was born. Thirty years ago his wife had leaned on him and now he would lean on her.

'You see? She's texting,' she had said, when his daughter couldn't bring herself to talk to her father but still couldn't be unkind enough to ignore him. 'Don't mind George – we both know he's a selfish sod.' She had smiled and squeezed his hand tight before pulling him out of his bed and into a standing position. 'We've had thirty years to get used to this – surely you can give them thirty days.'

'It'll never be the same,' he had mumbled, head in hands.

'No, darling, it won't,' she had said, stroking his hair. 'But that's okay.'

He had kissed her hand. 'What would I do without you, Glory?'

'Well, darling, right now you'd probably lose ten pounds and smell.'

He had laughed.

'Now get in the shower and I'll make you a breakfast fit

for a lord!' She had left him to sit on the side of his bed but his mind was already elsewhere.

He was back in that Wicklow wood, pulling his brother's coat away from a dead teenage girl's face. His brother was standing beside him. 'I knew her,' he'd said. 'I know her mother.'

'Where's the baby?' Duncan had asked.

'She's with the local GP,' Father Ryan replied, still staring at the dead girl.

'She has a black eye,' Duncan had said.

'It's not related.'

'Have you contacted her family?'

'No.'

'Why not?'

'I want you to come back with me to the GP's house,' he had said. 'Now and before it's too late.'

Did we do the right thing? What did we do?

During the last month, Duncan reflected now, he had relied on his wife more than he would ever have thought possible. A change of balance had occurred in the Ryan household.

The key turned in the lock and the door swung open, revealing Harri's dad's office. It always looked the same, dark and dusty, even though Mrs Gallo cleaned it along with the rest of the house once a week on a Tuesday. The floor-to-ceiling shelves filled with endless books and papers gave the place its dusty feel and the dark wooden bookcases, floorboards and office furniture lent themselves to gloom, despite the large triangular roof window, which seemed to be designed to stream light into a corner of the room where a large locked cabinet stood. It held copies of all her father's case files. It was the Ryan household's Holy Grail.

Duncan switched on his desk lamp and slumped into his chair.

Harri sat opposite him.

He didn't need to go to his cabinet: the file was in the drawer beside him. He opened it, pulled out a thick cream file and placed it on the desk before them. The edges were frayed and yellowing. He looked up at her. 'Move around,' he said, as though she was once more a child and he was about to read a story.

She pushed her chair around and sat next to her father. A moment or two passed while they settled themselves.

'Are you ready?' he asked.

'I don't know.'

He put his arm around her shoulders.

'Dad?'

'Yes, love.'

'Why don't you just tell me?'

He told her about the morning of 11 July 1976. He had just been escorted from the psychiatric wing of the hospital that temporarily housed his wife. She had been listless, medicated and a world away from him. He had attempted to discuss her depression with a doctor who didn't seem familiar with her case. An argument had broken out and regrettably he had threatened to break the man's nose.

'It was a very stressful time,' he remembered ruefully.

Nana had been charged with caring for George, who was ten weeks old and suffering from colic. 'Poor Nana! We really landed her in it. George had lost his twin and his mother in a matter of moments.' Duncan sighed. 'And if I'm honest he had lost me too.'

Duncan had returned to work immediately, only taking two days off to attend his brother's Mass for his dead daughter and to bury her.

One week later he took another day off to section his wife, but otherwise he worked longer hours than ever before. 'It kept me going.'

Later that day he returned to the office – he was working on an arson case in West Dublin. A farmer had burned down a shed he couldn't afford to fix in the hopes of an insurance payout. He had no idea that a drunk had taken refuge there and was fast asleep inside. 'That fella did five years for that,' he said. 'We never did identify the corpse and nobody ever came looking.'

Harri felt sorry for the man who had burned to death and for the arsonist, who had become an unwilling murderer. 'That's awful,' she said, and her dad couldn't help but smile.

'Don't you take that home with you, Harri Ryan,' he said, tipping the top of her head. 'It was only an aside and not meant to upset you.'

'I'm not sure I've room, Dad,' she said.

'I remember when you were twelve and you found a bird, almost dead, and took him home. You sang to it and it died in your hands.'

'George says it was my singing that killed it.'

'You cried for that bird. Such a big heart for such a little girl.'

'You're changing the subject.'

'I am.' He proceeded from where he'd left off.

He was back in July 1976 late one night, eating at his desk, which he was doing often at the time. The station was quiet so his feet were up and, exhausted, he fell asleep. The phone woke him.

'Dad?' said Harri.

'What?'

'When I said tell me I didn't mean every detail.'

'Well, I'm telling the story – I should be able to tell it the way I want to.'

'Right, then. I'm sorry I didn't bring a flask.' She sighed and her dad smiled to himself. *She's still my girl.*

The clock on the wall had told him it was after one a.m., the man on the phone was his brother and he was verging on hysteria, which was disconcerting.

'I need you,' Father Ryan had said. 'I need you in Wicklow tonight.'

Duncan asked why, and was told that a girl had given birth in the woods and died. 'There's more to it,' Father Ryan had warned. 'Don't tell anyone and come alone.'

Duncan didn't waste time arguing. He knew that arguing wouldn't get either of them anywhere so he got into his car and just under an hour later he was in a Wicklow wood by his brother's side, standing over a dead girl covered with a priest's black coat. He stood there silently while his brother finished a prayer.

'Dad?' Harri interrupted.

'Yes, love,' he said, again returning to the present.

'What was her name?'

'Olivia,' he said, 'but she was known as Liv.'

'Liv?' Harri repeated, contemplating the irony.

Duncan resumed his tale. 'We left her there,' he said.

Father Ryan had insisted on taking him back to the GP's house where the GP waited with the baby.

'Me,' she clarified, as though there was some need to do so.

'You,' he confirmed.

He remembered how distraught the GP was and that his name was Brendan something – but, of course, all that information was in the file. The three men sat together at the doctor's kitchen table and the doctor outlined the reasons why he wanted the child to be kept away from the girl's mother's house and out of the system. Father Ryan had agreed that it was best for the baby to disappear; he said he would deal with the girl's mother and stepfather, and the boy.

'Her brother?'

'No. The father of . . . the baby.'

Harri stayed silent.

'The doctor knew him well,' Duncan went on. 'In fact, he lived on the boy's father's land. She was trying to make her way to the doctor's house – at least, that's what we believe.'

'And the boy?' Harri's heart began to race – any minute a vein would pop in her neck.

'Staying with his grandparents in Meath.'

'What was his name?' she asked, holding her neck to keep any rogue veins in check.

'Matthew Delamere.'

Silence.

'They were both only kids.'

Silence.

'But when I met him I could tell he really loved her. He was devastated, broken. And, trust me, right about then I understood broken.'

Silence.

'Harri?'

'He knew?' she asked, and for some reason she was filling up as though a kid she didn't know had betrayed her and the mother who hadn't made it past her teens. 'He let you take me?'

Duncan nodded. 'He did, love.'

So, while the girl was cold and the boy was blissfully unaware, asleep in his grandmother's spare room less than two hours away, the priest, the young doctor and the detective had sat up in the doctor's kitchen drinking coffee and smoking cigarettes, and there in the wee hours they had devised a plan. Duncan and Father Ryan would return to the place where the girl was and remove any evidence that she had been found. Duncan would then take the baby girl home. At first light the young doctor would put on his sports kit and go for a run before he'd make a call to the local police station about the girl he'd found dead in the woods. Father Ryan would be summoned and he would insist on his brother, a senior ranking detective, being involved. He'd get his way because the local sergeant not only owed him a favour, he was afraid of him. Besides, he was well and truly out of his depth. Duncan would return and take over the investigation. The young doctor would sign the death cert and the priest would break the news to the girl's mother.

'But how?' Harri asked in something approaching a strangled whisper. 'How did that plan work with no baby?'

'There was a baby,' he said.

And if Harri didn't have heart failure right then and there she was never going to. Holy fuck!

'George wasn't the only twin.'

'Excuse me?'

'You were barely breathing on your mother's belly. Your sister was dead on the ground.'

Harri's hands covered her mouth and she was certain she would throw up. She didn't.

'Take deep breaths,' he ordered.

'I'm fine,' she replied wearily, eyes watering.

'You have that look,' he said, 'the one that frightens people.'

'I'm fine, Dad.'

'Harri, you've gone very pale.'

'Wouldn't you?'

'I suppose so.'

Again they sat in silence.

'But why?' she asked, after ten long minutes.

'Why what?'

'Why would Uncle Thomas and the doctor be so desperate to make sure that I didn't go to my grandmother?'

'There were problems. Your real grandfather was dead and she'd married again. He was a drunk, violent, and your mother was desperate to get away from him. She had some sort of hold over the young doctor – she wasn't just a patient. I think in some ways he loved her.'

'*What?*'

'Not like that, Harri, and besides he was little more than a kid himself – twenty-six maybe. Anyway, in those days the boy, Matthew, wouldn't have had a look in even if he thought he could manage. His family would never have supported him for fear that the scandal would destroy their reputation. His grandfather was a man to be reckoned with – the death was all over the news, and even though the whole town knew Matthew was going out with the girl, his name never made it into the papers. And, well, your grandmother was a weak and unwell woman. Besides, the minute I saw you I fell in love. You were so small, so fragile and still a fighter. You looked at me so fiercely it made me laugh. It was the first time I'd laughed in ages. I knew in my heart that you were for me and I was for you so I took you home. You were never a replacement, not in our hearts.'

Harri was crying, her nose running like a tap. The tissue she had located up her sleeve was sodden. 'What about the boy?' she sobbed.

'Poor kid.' Her father went on to explain that he took Matthew's statement in the young doctor's house. Matthew had told them that he and Liv were planning to run away, that he had money saved and tickets bought and it was only two weeks away. Duncan remembered that the boy

184

had seemed fixated on that fact. 'Only two weeks away.' Matthew had repeated it over and over to himself while gnawing at his knuckles. They had planned to take the boat because of the pregnancy and they would land in Wales. After the baby was born they'd find their way to the States. At least, that was the plan. 'Only two weeks away.' He was confused because the baby wasn't due for at least another month. And he refused to accept that sometimes babies came early. He had constantly looked at the doctor – as though, with words, he could bring her back. 'It was HIM,' was the only other thing he repeated. 'HE did something.'

The boy was right. The stepfather had done something two nights before. He had attacked her just as Father Ryan arrived to visit. He came between them but not before she received a black eye. It was then that the young doctor spoke to the boy about the baby who had lived, and explained that he, Father Ryan and the kind man in front of them wanted to help. At first Matthew had been speechless, but the doctor had talked and talked and talked, and by the end the boy had had only one request.

'What?' Harri asked, as breathless as an asthmatic after a ten-kilometre run.

'He just wanted to meet you once and get a picture. So, one week later, just after midnight, I took you to the pier in Wicklow and we sat on a bench, and on the wall behind was a painting of a Greek ship called the *Eliana*. He held you and kissed you and whispered stories about your mother, and you slept the whole time. Two weeks after that he was gone. The death was ruled accidental and, thanks to the young man's powerful father, his identity was never revealed.'

'Case closed,' Harri said.

'Case closed,' Duncan repeated.

They sat in silence, Duncan recovering from his draining recollection and Harri still absorbing a new and disturbing reality.

'You didn't have to tell him,' she said, after a while.

'I know,' he replied.

'That was really brave of you,' she said.

'Thanks.'

'And really stupid. It all could have blown up in your face.'

'I know.'

'But right.'

'I think so.'

'And he's never called or written or anything?'

'No.'

'Dad?'

'Yes, love?'

'Have you any pictures in there of Liv when she was alive?'

'I do.'

'Maybe you could give me one of those. I don't want to see anything else.'

'Good idea,' he said. 'Tell you what, you go downstairs to your mum and George and I'll fish one out.'

'Okay,' she said, getting up. She kissed her old dad on the forehead. He said nothing but she could feel his relief because she was relieved too.

George was tipsy on Italian wine and was waltzing his mother around the kitchen as though the past weeks had been a collective figment of the Ryan family's imagination. Gloria was playing along, happy to have her two children under her roof. George was good at pretence. He had decided and agreed upon forgiveness so there was nothing more to be said. He didn't want details of the twin who had died or reasons for his parents' actions. He had a twin in Harri, he had parents, a boyfriend and a new business, and that was enough to be dealing with. His sulk had reached its conclusion and he was ready to move on. Time to go through the motions of forgiving and forgetting.

Gloria, like her son, was happy to sidestep anything approaching discomfort in favour of equilibrium.

Harri's mother and brother, dancing around the kitchen, told Harri in no uncertain terms that the time for mourning, reflection or introspection had well and truly passed. In the words of a much-loved drunken homo: build a bridge and get over it.

7 July 1975 – Monday

Yesterday on the cliffs I thought about dying but only for a split second. I left them, walked home and locked my bedroom door. While I was lying on my bed, writing in my diary, a boy two years younger than me from my school fell from the same cliffs. I can't believe it. It's so weird and so awful and he didn't want to die. He was with friends and they were trying to rob the eggs from the gull's nest right on the ledge.

They do it all the time and it's madness. I don't think they'll be doing it again. His name was Shane McCafferty, he was a footballer and he had a girlfriend called Jackie. I don't know her – she's from Rathnew. The boys with him were taken to the local police station to make a statement. Sheila's dad said they were all wailing. Shane's mother was taken to hospital because she went into shock and she suffers with her blood pressure. The coast guard went looking for him and they were trying to be hopeful about finding him but Sheila's dad said that if falling from the cliff hadn't killed him, the rocks would have, and if they hadn't he'd have drowned. Sheila's dad can be very negative. All the same, this time he was probably right. They haven't found the body yet and it's been over twenty-four hours so at this stage they know he's gone. It's so sad I can't stop thinking about it. The poor boy, I wonder where he is now. Is he happy? Is he glad he died or is he sick with himself for risking his life and future over a stupid seagull egg?

Matthew and I called to Dr B. He made tea and told us the search was ongoing and mentioned something about the body surfacing in nine days. I didn't know what he was talking about. He mentioned something about the expulsion of body gases and I switched off – it's just so disgusting. Shane's mam is in a terrible way. It made me feel bad about not considering my own mam when I sat up on those cliffs but, then, she doesn't deserve it. Dr B asked after her. I said she was fine but I was lying. She's acting strange again. She was fine for a while and now she just sits at the table in the kitchen and stares at the wall. She still goes to Mass and she still watches *Coronation Street*, so that's something. I don't know what's wrong with her. Maybe she's scared too. Maybe that's what being scared does to you. HE hasn't come home. I don't think she even notices.

They can't hold a funeral for the boy until they find his body. It's so sad. I wish I could do something to help. Maybe when they find him and he's buried I could ask my mam to bake an apple pie and I'll take it to Shane's mam. I don't think apple pie upsets blood pressure. I'll check with Dr B.

14. I'm Melissa and I Google

In the days following Harri's trip to her father's attic, she made a sincere effort to keep to herself. She just needed a few days to reflect. Of course, that was never going to happen. She was hounded by her friends until eventually she agreed to a meal during which she would discuss the matter once and once only. The whole nightmare would then be laid to rest and she could get back to normal – or, at least, whatever normal would be now that she was single, empty and living alone. *Maybe I'll get a rabbit.*

'You wanker!' Melissa roared at her husband, then slammed the front door behind her. Gerry stood mouth agape, holding his infant daughter Carrie with his son Jacob pulling at his trouser leg.

'What's a wanker, Dad?'

Five minutes earlier Gerry had arrived home to find his wife pacing around the house in one high heel with a considerable dollop of baby food running down the front of her top and a look on her face that suggested he was a dead man walking. He'd been happy enough up to that point, having had a good day at work followed by a pleasant game of squash before partaking in a nice creamy pint or two. Or three. His good humour was destined not to last long.

'What time do you call this?' she had greeted him, in a manner approaching sinister.

'It's a little after eight,' he replied airily, having taken a moment to examine his watch.

'I was supposed to meet Susan and Harri at seven thirty!' she screamed, with the kind of frustration that was nearing the Land of Hysteria.

'Ah, you won't be too late,' he said in a calm voice, hoping it would inspire calm in her.

It did not. She stopped searching under furniture and behind cushions for the other shoe and turned on him, one leg shorter than the other. 'You promised,' she said, seething. 'You promised to be home by seven so that I could go and have a meal with my friends.'

'And you can,' he said, hands in the air. 'You'll only be an hour late.'

If Melissa had a gun she might have used it. 'An hour!' she roared. 'An hour!' She was limping towards him as he backed away from her. 'My top is ruined, Jacob has forgotten where he's hidden my shoe and it's at least forty minutes from here to the restaurant.'

'So sort yourself out, get in the car and go!' He was laughing at her. Maybe it was because he had indulged in three pints rather than the one he'd admit to or because he had vented his own everyday frustration in the squash court – or maybe he really didn't have a clue as to how much he was taking for granted, but Gerry laughed in the face of her fury.

Carrie was on the floor, crying, and Jacob was jumping up and down in the one spot counting to ten.

Melissa stopped to absorb her husband's ill-considered

mirth. *Mental note: buy a gun.* Ten seconds after that thought she picked up her baby, shoved her into her husband's arms and stormed out of the house, wearing one shoe, no makeup and with half of that baby's dinner down her front.

Aidan, Susan and Harri were waiting for Melissa while indulging in a bottle of wine accompanied by a basket of breadsticks.

'So, missus, what's going on?' Aidan asked Harri, as if he didn't know.

'Apart from the dissolution of my relationship with the love of my life, the discovery that I'm the living twin baby of a dead teenage stranger and swapped for another dead baby, not much, thanks for asking.'

Aidan grinned. 'How about you, Susan, any chance you can beat that?'

'Well, my marriage is in the toilet but that's not news, and Beth is in exam frenzy. She's in such a bloody mood that it's like living with Barbra Streisand.'

'I'd love to live with Barbra Streisand,' Aidan said, winking at a smiling Harri. *Nice to see you smile.*

'Homo.' Susan sighed.

'Breeder!' Aidan responded, holding his smile at Harri.

'And two nights ago I bumped into Keith,' Susan said, pretending nonchalance while perusing an upside-down menu.

'Keith the builder?' Harri said.

'Keith the builder,' Susan confirmed. 'He was in Tesco with his wife.'

'Oh,' Harri said.

Aidan was too rapt to talk.

'What did you do?' Harri queried.

'I smiled and walked past them.'

'Good for you,' Harri said.

Aidan knew there was more. *Come on, you dirty bitch, tell us something filthy.*

'Five minutes later he called me, asked if I'd meet him. I did. We had sex in his car. It was great. I've no plans to see him again.'

Aidan made a kind of yelping sound. Harri's mouth fell open.

'I thought I'd feel terrible, but aside from slight back-ache, I actually feel good,' Susan said. 'My husband hates me, so why not?'

'Why not indeed?' Aidan agreed, raising his glass. 'I'm so glad I'm not the only one going to hell! I'll save you a seat.' He patted the empty chair beside him. Harri laughed, which reminded him that if she didn't commit some sort of Vatican-certified Hell-bound sin soon, she might end up in the clouds alone. 'We've got two homos, an adulterer and, let's face it, sooner or later Melissa will be a murderer so what about you, Har? What can you do to hitch a ride on the highway to hell?'

'I'll get back to you,' she said, wondering whether or not the serious diseases, pain and torment she had recently wished upon her substitute parents would be enough. She was trying to forgive them, but their deceit was eating away at her. Perhaps one day in the future the Harri sitting at that table would be gone. *Good riddance, you didn't exist anyway.* She knew George was pretending too. He had danced with his mother and made nice over dinner. He'd toasted their family and had been charming, forgiving and deceiving. She could see it in his eyes, the eyes that refused to meet those of either parent. The Ryan family were doing what the Ryan family did best: they were pretending and hiding and lying and sweeping every irritation, uncomfortable emotion and bad feeling under the carpet. How long the charade would last was anybody's guess.

Melissa entered the restaurant barefoot, holding her handbag tight against her chest. She looked the maître d' in the eye and, with a beaming smile, announced that she had seen her party and would not require help being seated. He didn't seem to notice she had no shoes on – but, then, how many people look down?

Susan was the first to speak. 'Where are your shoes?' she asked, proving that in any situation the saying 'there's always one' has merit.

'Don't ask,' Melissa said, taking her bag away from her stained top.

Harri poured her a large glass of wine.

'Thanks,' said Melissa, and had a long drink.

'Kids are hard work,' Susan said, sighing.

'Husbands are harder!' Melissa said, and had another gulp.

'I hear that,' Susan agreed.

Harri remained silent. The scene before her only served to remind her that she had neither kids nor a husband. James was gone, she missed him more than she would have thought possible, and rabbits were probably banned by the apartment-building committee.

'Are you okay?' Melissa asked her.

'Fine.' She grinned for effect.

'You look constipated.'

'I'm fine.'

'There are prunes on the menu,' Aidan interjected.

'I don't need prunes.'

'I was only saying. It's not often you see prunes on a menu.'

'Where's George?' Melissa enquired.

'He's up to his tits in carpenters, electricians and plumbers,' Aidan said. 'You'd swear he was converting bloody Buckingham Palace. He's had me painting all week and he's a fussy little bastard.'

Aidan was lying. George was up to his eyes in it but not so much that he couldn't stop for a meal. The real truth was that George didn't enjoy nights on the town with the girls, and Aidan was sick of making excuses for him. They'd argued about it earlier when Aidan had begged him to come, especially in light of Harri's latest ordeal. George was adamant he had no intention of wasting time listening to idle bloody gossip, baby talk, marriage talk and Aidan's bitching.

'I don't bitch.'

'Aidan, have you ever met yourself?'

'Your sister needs you.'

'And I'm there for her on our own time.'

'You never come out with us.'

'Three women and you are not my ideal dinner companions. Melissa and Susan are lovely women, my sister is my world, but just because I'm gay doesn't mean I like girly nights.'

'Isn't it funny how you enjoy their company here in our home but not in a restaurant?'

'Don't start, Aidan.'

'Just saying.'

'So don't say. I have my friends and you have yours.' George was annoyed to be having the same stupid argument for the millionth time.

Aidan gave up. What was the point? George's supposed friends were all adrenalin junkies who, when not hurling themselves out of planes or bungee-jumping off buildings, were talking about it or planning it or getting pissed on it. They didn't know George, any more than he knew them. They had nothing in common except their hobbies. When George needed help with his business plan it was Melissa who spent three nights drawing up his proposals for the bank; when he needed décor discounts, it was Susan who ensured he got what he needed. For everything else he relied on Harri. They were his real friends and his real friends wanted to have a night out with him so that together they could move past the recent terrible revelations. But why argue reason with a man like George? He'd made his mind up so that was that.

Aidan had slammed the door to signal his exit.

George had been tired after a long day spent wrangling with an electrician.

'I'm just not comfortable putting the spots there,' the man had said.

'Excuse me?'

'It doesn't feel right to me.'

'It doesn't have to feel right. It's what I want,' George had snapped.

'Yeah, well, that may be the case but I'm the one doing the work and four spots so close together in that particular area does not look right to me.'

'I am the fucking customer.'

'There is no need to swear.'

'I think there is.'

'Really there isn't.'

'Are you going to put the spots where I've asked or not?'

The man sniffed and rubbed his sleeve under his nose. 'It's your funeral.'

'Are you trying to say putting them close together is dangerous?'

'No.'

'Oh, for Christ's sake!'

Days before, in a moment of weakness, he had agreed to go for the meal but that was only to get Aidan off his back. Then he'd forgotten about it so it was an unpleasant shock to find Aidan waiting for him in his best smart casuals reeking of Paco Rabanne and with a big smile plastered across his face.

'You have half an hour to get ready.'

Bollocks. 'Aidan, I'm not going.'

The argument had taken off from there.

After Aidan had gone, George realized he had no food in the place and was sick at the thought of ordering in once more. He knew Aidan was furious with him and that the argument could go on for days. Part of him really needed a good night out and of course he loved all the girls – it was just Aidan around the girls that he didn't like. He became giggly, girly, loud and camper than camp, and George found it embarrassing. Of course, when he brought this up, Aidan called him a homophobe and screamed and shouted, 'You're as bad as them! I am what I am. How dare you judge me?' George had no comeback – at least, none that gained anyone's sympathy. Now he sat alone waiting for the delivery of his third chicken satay that week, simmering and trying to remember why he and Aidan were together in the first place.

Harri had talked about her dad, her mum, the dead twins, the girl in the woods, the dead girl's fragile mother and vicious stepfather, Father Ryan, the young doctor and the boy who'd lost his love.

'I think it's very romantic,' Susan declared, after one too many.

'Your idea of romance must be sharp tacks in your knickers,' Aidan said. 'The girl died alone under a fucking tree with a dead kid between her legs. How is that romantic?'

Harri winced and Melissa kicked him.

'I meant the boy's love for the girl. She was dead and he loved her so much he was willing to let his little girl go just to keep her safe from the stepfather the girl loathed. I swear it's like a Mills & Boon.'

'You're such a sap,' Aidan said.

'It's a nice thought, Susan, but Aidan's right – you are a sap,' Harri concluded.

'Excuse me?' Susan said.

'He was just a kid. He didn't want a baby,' Harri said, swirling the contents of her glass thoughtfully.

'And now?' Melissa asked.

'Now what?' Harri responded.

'And now he's a grown man.'

'My age,' Susan reminded them. *I wonder what he looks like.*

'And now nothing,' Harri asserted.

'You're not the slightest bit curious?' Aidan asked.

'No,' Harri lied.

'Really?' Melissa said. 'That's a pity because I Googled him last night.'

Harri went slightly pale. 'I can't believe you did that,' she whispered.

The other two said nothing.

'Did I step over the line?' Melissa asked, a little alarmed by the silence. Nobody spoke. 'Okay, maybe I shouldn't have but I didn't think. My computer was on and, you know me, I'm a Googler.' Melissa was sweating now. Aidan and Susan shuffled in their seats uncomfortably.

'So what did it say?' Harri asked, after a long pause.

Melissa cleared her throat. 'Well, he's a horse breeder. It turns out he's a very well-known trainer and big with the horsy set. He lives in some mansion in Wicklow. He's not married and, other than you, he doesn't have any kids. Oh and he's minted.'

'My parents have money,' Harri replied, slightly offended that finance had been mentioned.

'Yes, they do, but this guy would make the Ryans look like peasants.'

'And he's single?' Susan clarified.

'Well, he's unmarried. He may have a girlfriend.'

'So he's *very* rich,' said Aidan.

Melissa ignored him. 'I printed off a picture. It's not great – my colour printer is rubbish – but if you want to see him . . .'

Susan's mind buzzed. *Please be good-looking. Oh, Jesus, what am I doing? How desperate am I? Get a grip, Susan.*

Harri sighed. 'Show me,' she said.

'Okay.' Melissa nodded and took the picture out of her handbag. She unfolded it and smoothed it out on the table.

The man before them was dressed in a tuxedo and grinning while holding up a glass of champagne. The caption read: *Matthew Delamere Back on Form.* He had a full head of thick wavy brown hair that matched Harri's, but was shorter. His smile was wide and his eyes had a twinkle in them.

'You have his eyes,' Melissa said.

'He's a ride,' Aidan said.

'He really is,' Susan agreed. *God, I really feel like calling Keith. Don't do it, Susan. You're better than that.*

'He's a rich ride,' Aidan said, and sipped his wine. 'Every cloud . . .' Harri gave him a dig. 'Right,' he agreed with himself. 'Too early to be positive.'

Harri felt weird and decided she needed the loo. She excused herself and sat on the toilet, trying to regain her composure. When it didn't work she cried.

'Are you okay, dear?' a woman asked, from the next stall.

'Yes, thanks,' Harri sobbed.

'Sometimes all you can do is have a good old cry,' the woman said.

'True,' Harri spluttered.

'Good girl,' the woman said, and left her to it.

2 August 1975 – Saturday

It's been a whole month since I wrote in my diary. Damn it, I've missed so much and, no matter what, I won't remember everything. I broke two fingers on my right hand – that's why I couldn't write. Two really bad breaks. I was in bits and they're still really sore. I was racing with Matthew and fell off Betsy. Henry said I was lucky I didn't break my neck, and I seriously don't know how he worked that one out. I landed on my hand, not my head. Dr B gave me a letter for the hospital and Matthew came with me. I didn't bother telling my mam – she'd just have embarrassed me. She's being a psycho at the moment. One minute she's laughing, the next she's crying, then she's laughing again, then she's screaming, then she's apologizing before crying, then laughing, and so on. I swear she's got so mad I even felt sorry for HIM one night last week. It was only for a moment, then I wanted him dead again so that's all right.

I've been able to continue working in the stables although I've been doing more in the office, which I love. The girl on Reception got a job in Dublin and left them stuck so my broken fingers couldn't have been better timed. I've been answering phones mostly and taking notes on a chalkboard because chalk is way thicker and easier to hold with the claw

I have instead of a hand. It was Matthew's idea and seriously genius. I was up in the posh trainer's part of the property and, holy hell, was it posh. At the start Matthew's dad ignored me but then he came into the office one day shouting about a lunch order that hadn't been delivered to him and a Saudi prince!!! Anyway, the girl who'd gone off to Dublin must have forgotten to order from some posh place, ironically in Dublin, so while he was going mental I rang Sheila's dad and asked him to pack up a traditional pub lunch and deliver it and he was only too happy to oblige and the prince loved it. Afterwards Matthew's dad said I was great at thinking on my feet and I'd make a good PA. I've no idea what a PA is or exactly what a PA does but it sounds brilliant.

He's been all over me since. Well, when I say all over me I mean he thinks I'm brill – and if I didn't want to go back to school to do the Leaving Cert in September, I'd say he'd keep me on. I don't think Matthew would like that, though.

Now, what else? Sheila and Dave were off for two weeks but they're now back on and she says they definitely won't break up again. Yeah, right, and my mam isn't bonkers! Dave broke it off because he thought she was being too clingy and she wasn't supportive when he said he wanted to be a rock climber for a living. Dave is a total spasm. A rock climber? Who does that? How does that pay? Why would you do it? What is the point? I wouldn't mind only he's the laziest boy I know. He wouldn't scratch himself if he thought someone else would do it and I'm sure behind closed doors his mam does it for him. She's weird-looking and always has a wet hanky at the ready. Dave still wants to be a rock climber and

Sheila's pretending she's happy with that because her mother told her it's just a phase.

Sheila is now seriously considering becoming a hairdresser and not like before when she was only talking about it. She's even done my hair in an up-style. It wasn't very good – there were loads of lumps and my head hurt but she's a beginner and hasn't had any training yet so you never know.

Dr B! What can I say about Dr B? He's at a crossroads and gone goggle-eyed! We've got closer since I broke my fingers. I forgot to mention he hated my present of the *Maurice* book. He nearly lost his temper when he got around to reading the back of it and we didn't talk for a week. Then when I broke my fingers he admitted he did read it and I didn't say that I'd read it because it was really sexy and I didn't want to go red and he said that he loved it and thanked me and told me it had made him feel normal. I told him I understood, but he laughed and said I couldn't possibly understand what it felt like to be a pariah, and I couldn't answer him back at the time because I didn't know what a pariah was, never mind how it was spelt. Later I looked it up in the dictionary, and now that I know what it is, he's wrong. He may like men but nobody knows that, only him and me, and everyone knows that I'm living in a house of violence, everyone knows my mam is being odd and falling apart and that my stepdad is a drunk, and everybody thinks they know exactly what goes on and they don't.

I hear them talk and whisper and wonder. I watch the world pass me by and just because I'm a teenager it doesn't mean it doesn't affect me. I see the person I want to be and the world I want to live in and it's out of my reach by miles. I'm a stupid kid to be ignored and trodden upon – so if anyone knows what it's like to be an outsider I do. Have a wank, Dr B, and get a clue! Well, that's what I thought but I didn't say it.

At my next bandage appointment I told him I now under-stood the term and explained why I was right and he was wrong. He laughed at first but then he was sad. He said that my frustration and pain were a rite of passage and his was a burden to bear for eternity. That's Father Ryan talking – I can even hear it come out of his mouth. What a load of old shit! I told him as much. He thinks the Church knows what it's talking about and maybe he's right – but maybe he's wrong. I asked if he'd ever considered that and he admitted he hadn't. I told him that my dad's brother (a hippie the family doesn't talk about) once said to me that there was only one rule that applied: treat others as you wish them to treat you. It was New Year's Eve and he was drunk but it made loads of sense. He said anything above or below that was utter bollocks. I think he's right. You are who you are and as long as you live a good life and treat people well, aren't you decent and good and worthy of all that Heaven has to offer?

Dr B didn't talk much after I brought up my drunken uncle but he did say he was glad he'd met me. That was nice. He seemed surprised that I haven't spoken to anyone about him, but why would I? He's my friend. Plus he's really sorted out my fingers.

Father Ryan is being weird. He keeps trying to talk to me, asking about how it is at home. I told him it was shit. Well, I didn't say 'shit' but I told him my mam was going mental and HE would explode any day. He asked me what I meant, as though I was speaking a different language. What do YOU mean? I said, I swear I did, and it was really cheeky, but what does he expect, shoving his nose in people's business when he has no idea? Does he live with someone who swears at him and brutalizes him every day of the week? Has he ever been in hospital so swollen he couldn't speak? Has he ever locked his door and prayed and prayed he wouldn't be attacked? Father Ryan doesn't have a clue and yet he comes into my home and preaches the Lord's word, the same Lord who hung out with whores and thieves and liked them because at the end of the day He was human and they were probably a better laugh than the pious bullshitters that in the end viciously murdered him.

Father Ryan doesn't like it when I say what I think. He twitches and stutters and his neck goes red, and then he quotes and reasons and argues and I switch off because I don't care. If he had left well enough alone my mam wouldn't be so mad that she left the house the other day forgetting to put on a skirt but that's another story.

So much more has happened. Matthew and I are brilliant. When I'm with him the world's a better place. We talk and talk and we never seem to run out of things to say and it's never boring or dull. We talk about everything. I even told him about that night a few months back when Mam was out walking and HE was drunk and came into my room. I told

Matthew everything and I never thought I'd actually say it. He was so angry he wanted to find him and kill him, and it was nice that he was so angry. It was nice not to be the only one angry, and now that he wants him dead too, it makes me feel a little better about things. I was beginning to think I was a bit sick in the head. Anyway, I told him I was fine and I'd be able to fight HIM off but now he worries. He says he's going to put an extra lock on the door for me, a padlock.

I wish he didn't worry. He has enough going on. His dad is being really mean to him. He puts him down all the time and it's getting worse. I don't know why. He'll be back in school in September and I dread it. What will my world be like without him? I can't imagine. I don't want to. He's my world. I won't see him for weeks and weeks because his dad only allows him home for holidays. What a dick! Matthew is the love of my life.

Two weeks ago we lay on the marram grass (which is as soft as any mattress – it's so soft it bounces under your feet – weird) by the castle listening to the sea and watching stars and we put our hands in each other's knickers and it was really, really nice, and today he whispered that he'd save me and he held me so tight it hurt. He'd save me, he said, because he knew I needed saving. I didn't have to ask. I'll love him for ever for that. I'll love him for ever for everything. I love him so much I miss him when he's with me. Maybe I'm mad like my mother!

Okay, one last thing. I'm listening to Elton John and he is so amazing. 'Rocket Man' has been out for ever but for the first time I love it. Matthew has all his singles and I really love 'Candle In The Wind' and 'Don't Let The Sun Go Down On Me'. The Bay City Rollers are over and he's for ever, you can just tell.

Anyway, I'm going out now. My fingers are liberated and Matthew is taking me for a picnic by the Glen strand. I love the water. Maybe some day I'll work in water. I'm a great swimmer. This morning I opened my window and there was the blackest, fattest crow on my ledge. I know everyone hates them but I don't. It was lovely. It sat so still and its neck was arched and it was proudly facing towards the sea. It turned its head my way slowly and it wasn't scary, it was beautiful. I didn't move. I just waited and then it looked me straight in the eye. I swear it looked at me for the longest time and I looked at it, and then it was gone and I needed to sit down. I don't know why it was weird. Would it be crazy if I thought that the bird knew something I didn't? I suppose so and still . . . Matthew will be here soon. We're going to town to meet Sheila and Dave and his English cousin Simon.

15. If only

June had been a long month and, despite good weather and lots of work, Susan was glad to see it end. She had slept with Keith three more times, once in a hotel, once on a king-sized duvet behind some rocks just before dawn on Killiney beach and once in the middle of the day on her own marital bed. It was after that particular fulfilling but guilt-ridden tryst that she had truly admitted to herself that her marriage was over. Keith had left soon after they'd finished, and as the door was closing behind him she had found herself packing a bag. She didn't cry or even think too much, just mechanically packed all that she needed to survive outside her home.

She called Harri from the car. 'Can I stay with you?' she asked, as soon as Harri picked up the phone.

'Of course,' Harri replied, without needing to ask any questions. After all, Susan's last desperate act had been a long time coming.

'I'm on my way,' she'd said. *I'll face Beth when I'm settled. I'll tell her everything. Please, God, don't let her hate me.*

Harri was waiting with fresh sheets on the pull-out sofa, tea, biscuits and a bear-hug. 'I'm so sorry,' she said. She had thought Andrew had thrown his wife out, and was shocked to hear that she had thrown herself out.

'I couldn't do it any more,' Susan said. 'I couldn't bear the silence and the lies.'

'What about Beth?' Harri asked, alarmed when she realized that Susan's escape had been spur-of-the-moment and unplanned.

'She doesn't know.'

Beth was working in a boutique in town and would be home later, although Susan wasn't sure when. Harri instructed her to call her daughter. As a recent victim of lies, Harri was adamant that she needed to be told. Susan left a message on her daughter's mobile phone asking her to come to Harri's after work, adding that it was important.

Beth arrived a little after eight. Harri fussed over her, trying to persuade her to eat some leftover lasagne. Susan remained quiet. Beth said she didn't want food, instantly sensing that something bad had happened. Harri decided to have a bath and leave them to it.

'What's he done?' Beth asked.

'Nothing,' Susan said. 'He's done nothing.'

'I know he has!' Beth said, full of fire.

'It's me,' Susan admitted. 'I'm the one who had the affair. He caught me seven months ago.'

Beth was sitting, yet her legs still managed to go from under her. She visibly sank in the chair. 'You?' she questioned in alarm and disbelief.

'I'm sorry,' her mother said.

'You?'

Her mother nodded. Beth didn't understand. All the

time she had thought her father was the one playing away, that he was destroying their family, the bastard. All that time when she was slagging him off, berating him and comforting her mother, her dad had been the victim. Beth was speechless.

'I'm sorry,' Susan said again.

Beth regained the power of thought, word and movement and suddenly she was standing, then pacing and shouting, 'He didn't say anything! Why didn't he kick you out? Why did he let me talk to him like that? Why did he cover for you?'

All Susan could say was that she didn't know because she didn't know why her husband had insisted that their daughter should not know about her deception. He had made her promise not to say anything to Beth and she had agreed, willing to do anything to get him to forgive her. It had occurred to her that it had been odd that when Beth was spewing her venom at him he had never defended himself and never pointed the finger in the right direction. In the end the lie had imprisoned, demoralized, degraded and trapped her. She had wondered if that had been his intention, but it had seemed too Machiavellian and too cruel. She couldn't explain to her daughter why her father had been so desperate to hide Susan's adultery. It made no sense.

'Who was he? When and for how long? How many times? Why?' Beth had shouted over and over again, while circling Harri's small sitting room.

'A builder. Not long. A few times. Does it really matter? I was lonely.'

Susan didn't want to have to explain her sex life to her daughter. It wasn't right. She wasn't going to tell her daughter that her father had lost interest in sex two whole years before she even dreamed of having an affair. She would never tell her that she had tried everything to entice him – getting a makeover, losing weight, dressing up, dressing down, boots in the bedroom. She'd even attempted to woo him in peep-hole lingerie. He had laughed at her – he had laughed at her a lot. She would cry and he'd storm out. Sex was not something he was interested in having with his wife and she missed it. She wanted to feel attractive and alive and loved, not like an old woman, dried up and waiting for death. She was forty-six and horny. She wanted sex from her husband. She bloody deserved it, and she was angry because he had made her hate herself, and sad because she missed what they had once had, and guilty because it was wrong to do what she had done with Keith. Part of her screamed that she was innocent because Andrew had left her first. He might not have fucked somebody else but he wasn't fucking her either – and he should have been because that was his bloody job. She had friends but what she wanted was her husband and he just wasn't there. But she couldn't say that to Beth. All she could say was that she was sorry – but sorry wasn't good enough.

Beth all but spat at her mother. 'You disgust me!' she said, grabbing her coat.

'Where are you going?' Susan begged.

'Home to see my dad and to apologize for being such a stupid bitch!'

She slammed Harri's front door.

Harri got out of the bath and into her bathrobe. When she entered the sitting room Susan was sitting in the middle of the floor. Susan didn't need to rehash the argument. Harri had heard it all through the thin doors and walls. She didn't have to explain her point of view or excuse herself because Harri knew that Susan's husband had lost interest in her a long time before.

'I'm sorry,' Harri said.

'There's a lot of that going around lately.'

'There is.'

Later, Harri and Susan sat together, drinking cocoa and watching an episode of *CSI Miami*, Harri having exhausted *CSI Las Vegas*.

'You really need to get over *CSI*,' Susan commented, halfway through the show.

'I know. Did I mention there's a *CSI New York*?'

'Oh, sweet Jesus! You do know that it's basically the same bloody show over and over and over again, don't you?'

'That's what I like about it,' Harri said. 'I find it comforting.'

Andrew didn't get home until after eleven. Beth was waiting.

She had cried most of the evening. She had phoned four of her friends, her favourite cousin Jessica and the ex-boyfriend who had given her crabs. He was most sympathetic and offered to come over, but after serious consideration she decided against allowing him access to her home. Her grief would make her weak to his advances and she didn't trust him not to give her another dose of something unpleasant. She waited for her dad in the kitchen, sitting at the table, back hunched, hands clasped and head low.

He seemed a bit shocked when he opened the kitchen door and saw her there. She raised her head slowly. 'Beth?' he said, betraying slight panic.

'I'm sorry, Dad,' she replied.

'Sorry for what, love?' he said, with a tremor in his voice. He sat beside her.

'She told me the truth,' Beth said, and she was crying.

Andrew blanched.

'She told me what she did.'

'Right,' seemed to be the only word he could manage.

'She's gone.'

'Right,' he repeated.

'Why didn't you tell me, Dad?' Beth asked, bewildered. 'All those times I attacked you for being a dick to Mum. It was her all along.'

'And she's gone?' he mumbled.

'Dad?'

'Yes.'

'Why didn't you tell me?'

'Because I wanted space to forgive her.'

'And you couldn't?' she asked, in a tone that suggested she knew the answer.

'No, I suppose I couldn't.'

'Screw her!' Beth said, hugging him. 'You have me, Dad, so screw her.' And with that Beth transposed every ounce of the anger she had felt for her father on to her mother. *I can't believe she's done this to us.*

Andrew hugged his daughter. Although he didn't speak his head was bursting with too many thoughts travelling in too many directions, causing an ache. *She's really gone? She told Beth – the bitch! I begged her not to. Are we over? For how long? For good? What about Beth? Is this what I wanted? I hate her. Where is she? This is my fault. Will I miss her? Twenty-six years. Twenty-six years. Twenty-six years. Why was sex so fucking important to her? Why couldn't she take me as I am? What's wrong with me? Will I be alone now for ever? I should have forgiven her or at least pretended to – but if I'd let her back in she would have worked it out. There's something wrong with me. I'm not a man. Oh, God, my wife is gone!*

Andrew returned to the bedroom he had shared with his wife until seven months before. The dressing-table was void of anything belonging to Susan. Her dresser drawers and her side of the wardrobe were empty. The bedclothes were changed because even though she was leaving him she had been kind enough to ensure he returned to a clean bed. He sat down on his side. It was this bed that had broken their marriage.

For such a long time Susan and Andrew had worked beautifully. They had laughed together, enjoyed each other's company, shared ideas, opinions and an interest in most things. He'd never understood her impulse to buy kitchen utensils but aside from that they were usually in unison. In fact, up to three years ago they would have been seen as the perfect couple – not bad going after twenty-three years. But then it changed. He changed. Andrew had begun to experience difficulty in the bedroom. He had grown up on a farm and was a middle child of six. He had two sisters, both Irish dancers, and three brothers, all strapping lads and none shorter than six feet two. Andrew had been county boxing champion at sixteen. He was as smart as he was big and the first of his brothers to go to university. He had studied law and excelled. When he grew tired of that he bought property and when that no longer satisfied him he had lectured part time and set up an investment-property consultation business, which quickly became a thriving success. He liked to drink, play cards, and enjoyed golf. He had played football well into his forties.

Andrew was a man's man, having come from a long line of men's men, and he wasn't used to failure. Until three years ago when that man, the only one he knew, had begun to ebb away. At first he'd thought he was tired, but after a while he wondered if he had lost interest in his wife – but he hadn't. At least, he didn't think so. She was still beautiful to him, despite a slight middle-age spread, a crude C-section scar and stretch marks. He kind of liked those: they were silvery and told the story of their miracle daughter. He used to trace the lines with his finger, marvelling at how the little girl fast asleep in the next room had come from such a petite woman.

Then he'd wondered if he was stressed – but he didn't feel stressed except when his wife pressured him for sex, and especially when she went to great lengths to titillate him. He had laughed at her and didn't know why. He could only reason that it was panic-induced. He hadn't meant to laugh and he knew how much he had hurt her. He had thought about talking to her but he couldn't. No matter how hard he tried, he couldn't bring himself to admit what was really going on. She had got so angry and he was so embarrassed. It sounds stupid for a grown man to be embarrassed in front of his wife, but he was, and the longer it went on the harder it was to confide in her or anyone else. He'd made an appointment with his GP once and he'd got as far as the car park but no further. As he was parking it occurred to him that he was in the same golf club as his doctor so obviously that wasn't going to work. He had kept hoping the problem would go away – but it didn't.

When he had begun to suffer problems he had tried a number of remedies, such as vigorous masturbation, which had led to a slight penis bleed. *Oh, God, my dick!* He didn't try that again. Instead he had watched porn – soft core and sensual, hard core and downright grab-you-by-the-back-of-the-neck filthy – but nothing had worked. He'd phoned sex lines and talked to women with names like Busty or Pussy Freak. Busty had been nice enough – she'd had a sexy French accent and was a Neil Simon fan. He hadn't stayed on the line with Pussy Freak for too long – she'd come on a little strong and had a voice so deep she could have passed for a man. Of course he'd tried Viagra, which had made him feel dizzy and a little sick.

After he'd found his wife kissing another man he'd got into his car and driven until he'd spotted a whore. She'd jumped in, and ten minutes later he was sitting with his trousers around his ankles and she was sucking and sucking but he just couldn't get hard. 'Here, mister? You'd want to see someone about that.'

And now his wife was gone. His marriage, as pathetic as

it was, was now over and all because of his inability to confess his humiliating impotency. If only he'd had the courage. He hated himself – stupid, stubborn, childish. He had stood by while the woman he loved tore herself in two trying to please him. He wished he'd had the strength to ask for help – but how does a fifty-year-old man who has never asked for or needed help set about it? More importantly, how could a man's man like Andrew admit to impotency?

'Dad, you're crying,' Beth said, and he wiped his tears away. She had knocked on his bedroom door, but he hadn't answered. She put a tray holding a mug of tea and a plate of biscuits on the bed beside him.

'Thanks,' he said.

'She doesn't deserve you,' Beth said, and her father closed his eyes.

'I'm really tired,' he said.

'Me too.'

'I'll see you for breakfast,' he promised.

'Okay.'

She closed the door behind her. He looked around the room and resumed crying because his daughter was right. Susan didn't deserve him. She deserved better than him and now she'd probably go out into the world and find that better man.

3 August 1975 – Sunday

My mam was really weird this morning. I found her sitting in the middle of the front garden. It was raining and she was just sitting there. She was crying, and when she saw me, it was almost as though she didn't recognize me. Tingles went up and down my back. It was eerie. Then she was fine. I picked her up and we walked inside together and I made her some breakfast and she asked after Matthew and it was like nothing had happened. I really think HE's pushing her over the edge but there's nothing I can do about it. I'm going to stay in tonight just to make sure she's okay. There's a programme on about the IRA ceasefire so I'll watch that with her. She'd like that.

Last night was good. Matthew brought me to a really nice restaurant. The prices were huge but he gets a big allowance so he said I could have whatever I wanted. To be honest, it was all a bit too fancy for me. I'd have way preferred a burger and a Coke to calf's liver or duck. Ducks are sweet, and I really don't like the idea of eating them, but I have to admit it was tasty but only if I closed my eyes because it looked weird on the plate.

We went back to his place, and his dad called us into his drawing room. He was watching *The Late Late Show* and Gay Byrne was talking to Minnie Brennan from *The Riordans*. Her hair was lovely. Matthew's dad asked us what we were doing. Matthew told him nothing. His dad told him to tread carefully. Matthew told him to go back to Argentina – and his dad threw a glass at him!!!! Matthew ducked but I never saw it coming and it barely missed me. It smashed right over my head. I've only just got my fingers out of bandages and now my head was nearly split open. Matthew's dad got a shock and started to CRY! Matthew called him a drunk and we went to his bedroom. Matthew put on Elton John and he told me that since his dad split up with his bit he'd been drinking and acting the eejit. That, and it will be Matthew's mam's anniversary the day after tomorrow. I told Matthew we should visit her. He didn't want to but I insisted. I'm going to make a picnic and the weather forecast is good so we can sit and eat with her and it'll be nice. I'm looking forward to it.

I was talking to Christopher Nolan the other day in town. He's a friend of Shane McCafferty's older brother. He said Shane's mam hasn't left the house since he died. I feel bad about not bringing over an apple pie but I asked Mam to make one and she said she was too tired. I should really learn to do it myself. I mean, how hard can it be? Although now it's probably a bit too late – she'd think I was some sort of weirdo if I arrived up at the door with a pie now.

Christopher said Shane's brother Éamonn isn't taking it too great either. He's broken up with his girlfriend Ellen after five years together and he's jacked in the football and he, like Shane, was a great footballer. I was still talking with Christopher when Father Ryan asked me to help him carry his shopping. It was too heavy for his bike as he'd done a big shop. Get a car, Father Ryan!!! Anyway, he carried two bags on the handlebars, one on the back of the bike with the handles wrapped around the seat, and I carried the lightest one, which wasn't so light. He asked about my mam and I said I was worried. He said he'd noticed she was a little off himself. He said he'd found her sleeping in the confession box. I told him she sleeps a lot these days. He asked if HE was hitting her. I wish I could have said yes but he's been too busy staying out drinking to hit her. Suits me. He's at home so rarely it's like he doesn't live there any more. There's a lot of work at the docks and when he's not working he has enough money to keep him in the pub with his stupid tooth-less friend.

Father Ryan thinks that Dr B should take a look at Mam, especially when I told him that sometimes she forgets to put on her skirt. It's strange I didn't think to say anything to Dr B. I knew she was acting weird but everything she does is weird to me. I should have said something. I should have realized something was wrong. My poor mam. What could it be? Father Ryan said it's probably just stress. I hope he's right, and if it is, I hope he takes one long look at himself because if she's stressed she's stressed because she brought that monster back into our house on Father Ryan's say-so. I didn't say that, though, but he's no fool. He knew what I was thinking because I gave him the look.

16. Something old, something new

By the time Harri arrived George was frantic. 'Where were you?'

'Working.'

'Nothing's ready – it's going to be a disaster,' he said.

Harri glanced around the shop. 'It looks great!' She loved the floor-to-ceiling beechwood shelving running nearly the length of the left wall. The space was narrow and the arched ceiling gave it a cavernous feel. The artwork that hung behind the till was bright and bold – and the refrigerated room on the right was inspired and bloody cold.

'George, let me out. Not funny, George.'

'I see nipples.'

'And I'm looking at a very swollen left testicle.'

'Okay, okay!' He let her out – the look on her face meant business. And she'd done some kick-boxing.

She was happy to report that the cold room was beautifully appointed. 'It's a good finish,' she said, following him through the shop.

'What do you think of the spotlights? Are they too close together?'

'No. They're perfect.'

'The painting?'

'I picked it. I love it.'

'What about the flooring?'

'The flooring is exactly like I said it would be. It's fantastic.'

It was as though George had forgotten that Harri had made a serious contribution to the décor but it had been before her ill-fated wedding and she hadn't been on site since. 'It's all worked out beautifully.' She grinned.

'You haven't seen the best bit,' he said, grinning back, and she followed him down the spiral staircase into the cellar, which had been converted into a tasting area. The room wasn't entirely set up. Aidan was sweeping the old flagstone floor, and the boxes were open but the wine was yet to be uncorked. The nibbles were stacked and covered with clingfilm.

'What do you want me to do?' she asked, taking off her jacket.

'The floor,' Aidan said, handing her the broom.

'Aidan!' George exclaimed.

'I'm pissed off sweeping. I'll open the wine.' He flopped down on the bench and grabbed a corkscrew.

George began to lay out the sandwiches and buff the glasses while Harri swept, then dusted around the shelving, which housed yet more wine. Five small round tables with four seats each were scattered around the space. A Ray LeMontagne CD was playing. Once the tablecloths were spread, the floor was clean, the wine open and the food laid out, it was time. Aidan poured himself a glass of wine, and offered Harri water because she was driving. 'Still or sparkling?'

'Still.'

'At least have sparkling.'

'What's the bloody difference?' Harri laughed. George raised his eyebrows.

'Bubbles. Obviously.'

'I don't want bubbles.'

'You've no sense of adventure, you know that?' Aidan said sulkily. He was spoiling for a fight. *Uh-oh.*

George walked around in circles with a double espresso from the place next door. 'No one's coming,' he said.

'It's one minute past eight,' Harri pointed out.

'No one is coming,' he repeated.

'And I'm the drama queen!' Aidan snickered.

'Calm down,' Harri soothed her brother. 'They'll be here.'

They sat in silence while Ray sang 'Can I Stay?'. The doorbell rang just as he was asking someone unseen to whisper to him. George was up the stairs in seconds, leaving Harri with Aidan.

'Everything all right?' she asked.

'Everything's great,' he confirmed, but his demeanour suggested he was lying.

For a while Harri had sensed that all was not well with Aidan and George and wondered how long it would be before they'd split up again. *He's never going to be who you want him to be, Aidan.*

George arrived downstairs with four guests, including the wine critic he had hoped for. After that it was Harri who trudged up and down the attractive but energy-consuming stairs to answer the door.

The night was in full swing. George was talking business

and charming the pants off two middle-aged women, one of whom was the critic he was set to impress.

'Oh, here we fucking go! George Clooney has entered the building,' Aidan sneered.

'Aidan!' Harri warned.

'Well, look at him – all over them. It makes me sick.'

Duncan and Gloria were in a corner talking with Melissa and Gerry. Duncan was thrilled with his son's achievement, and when George arrived at his father's side he told him so rapturously, slapping him on the back. 'I'm proud of you, son!'

George was polite and stayed with his dad for a minute or two, but the encounter was awkward. He had yet to find it in himself to forgive his parents their terrible lie, despite all appearances to the contrary. Gloria didn't notice: she was too busy ignoring her family's new reality and instead devoting herself to catching up with Melissa about the babies, and with Gerry about work.

Harri and Aidan were the designated wine-pourers.

Susan arrived with a partner. 'This is Keith.'

Harri nearly dropped the bottle she was holding. 'Hello, Keith. It's lovely to meet you.'

Aidan was a little tipsy. 'Not bad, Susan, not bad at all.'

Keith just stood there, and Susan went red. Aidan winked at Keith, who, clearly perturbed, downed his wine.

Harri dragged Aidan into the back storeroom. 'What are you doing?'

'Surely you mean what's Susan doing?'

He had a point.

'I don't know – it's a bit weird,' she conceded.

'It's fucking insane. Andrew's on the guest list.'

'He's not coming, is he?'

'Well, he said he might. He said he'd bring Beth.'

'Sweet Jesus! Red alert! Red alert!'

'Calm down,' Aidan said laughing.

Harri was crap in a crisis but always entertaining. There'd been the time when she was caught up in a bank raid on Henry Street. The raiders had told the customers to get on the floor and when they'd asked her why she was still standing she'd said it was because she couldn't remember how to bend her knees. The raiders had had a sense of humour – which her father said was a good thing or she'd have left the place with a bullet in her.

Aidan promised to deal with Susan if Harri would deal with the tasting table. He was getting tired of using the word *soupçon*. Initially he had felt the term lent him a certain air of professionalism but after four glasses of wine and twenty-four *soupçons* he was reaching his limit.

'Waiter, the Barolo. Mmm – I'm tasting tobacco, vanilla, chocolate and . . .'

'A *soupçon* of wild strawberry.'

The man with the large nose smiled and Aidan smirked. *I'm not a waiter, and read the back of the bottle, Dick-nose!*

Dick-nose called Aidan over to him many times so that he could talk at him. 'Now, young man, the Bardolino – I'd say it's light and fruit-filled with a faint cherry flavour and . . .'

'A *soupçon* of spice.' Aidan smiled the sickly smile that, to those who knew him, meant bad things could happen.

'Indeed.' The man smiled back.

I'm not going to do you, you old queen. Aidan was bored. He wanted to get away from all this stuffy wine crap, and he was sick of watching George flirt with the women. *You're gay, okay? You're gay.* He wanted to drink a beer and dance to Kelly Clarkson rather than age to Ray LeMontagne and Peggy bloody Lee.

'Who the hell put on Peggy Lee?' he asked, when he approached Susan.

She shrugged her shoulders.

'Right, come on, get your coat – we're leaving.'

'I've just got here.'

'Andrew and Beth may be coming.'

'Keith, drink up.'

They were gone before the wine had hit the back of the builder's throat.

When George had a minute, Harri explained that Aidan had left with Susan.

'Thank God! If he'd said *soupcon* one more time I was going to murder him.'

Andrew and Beth never appeared. Duncan and Gloria left with Melissa and Gerry, who were running home to have a shag because they had the will and the energy and if they hurried it might just last until they made it into the sack. The tasters and critics left smiling. George closed the shop just after eleven. 'Not bad,' he said. 'Not bad at all.'

Harri agreed. 'It went well.'

'Have a glass of wine with me,' he begged. 'I need to come down from all the excitement.'

'I'm driving.'

'One glass.'

'Half a glass.'

'Good,' he said, leading her downstairs.

The candle in the middle of the table was guttering. Harri and George sat opposite one another in the dim light and clinked glasses.

'I love Paul Weller,' George said, smiling.

'Who the hell is Paul Weller? Does Aidan know? Is that why he's so angry?' Harri asked, alarmed enough to dribble a little wine.

George laughed at his musically retarded sister. 'He's the guy singing on the CD.'

'Oh,' she said. *It could have been Paul Gascoigne for all I know.*

'I asked James,' he said.

Harri nearly choked. 'You didn't.'

'I was hoping he'd come. I know you miss him.'

'Understatement. What's that saying? You never know what you've got till it's gone.' Her brother squeezed her hand. 'I even miss his stupid knock-knock jokes.'

'Don't!' George said, laughing at the memory. 'Knock-knock!'

'George.'

'Knock-knock!'

'Who's there?' Harri said, her head in her hands.

'Wooden.'

'Wooden who?'

'Wooden you like to know!'

He was laughing and Harri joined in.

'He'll come back, Harri,' he said then, 'maybe not tonight but he will be back.'

'Nice dream.' She smiled. 'What about you and Aidan? Why is he so angry?'

'It's hard.'

'I know.'

'We're so different.'

'I know.'

'I do care about him.'

'I know.'

'Stop saying "I know".'

'Okay.'

'Who ever said that opposites attract?' George asked, swirling the contents of his glass.

'Paula Abdul.'

'Well, then, that says it all, doesn't it? You know what Aidan said the other night? He said I hate myself. Can you believe he actually thinks that?'

'I can.'

'What?'

The shock registering on George's face was funny, and Harri grinned – but not for long.

'Excuse me?' George's tone was elevated, suggesting he was getting snotty.

Oh, no – and we were having such a nice time.

'Look, George, everyone who loves you knows that there is part of you that would prefer to be straight.'

'Bullshit.'

'George, you're a modern-day Rock Hudson. In public you're every woman's dream but in private you're . . . yourself.'

'Oh, come on! I can't help it if women find me attractive.'

'No, you can't, but you don't have to encourage them and you do. You want strangers to think you're straight.'

'Because it's easier.'

'Easier to flirt outrageously all night with those two women? That's not easy.'

'It's business.'

'Okay.'

'You don't believe me.'

'You forget I'm the one who found you cutting yourself at sixteen. I'm the one who held you when you cried for two days when you couldn't make yourself shag Grace Fanning.'

'That was one crisis summer and I came out earlier than most of the gay men I know.'

'You came out to Mum, Dad and me. You came out in the Ryan household where nobody talks about anything. You didn't come out to your friends or your classmates or anyone else until you were well into your twenties.'

'Just because I'm not Liberace doesn't mean I'm not content with my lot.'

'I hope so, George, because you've got a lot.'

'And you?' he said, changing the subject – consensus as to whether or not his sister and boyfriend had a point would not be reached that night.

'What about me?'

'Aidan told me about Matthew Delamere.'

'Oh.'

'You're not even curious?'

'I am,' she admitted. 'I'm very curious.'

'So?'

'Tomorrow's my birthday,' she said. 'My real birthday.'

'I hadn't registered the date.'

She sighed.

'You're going down there, aren't you?' he said.

'Yeah.'

'You're sure?'

'Positive.'

'You want me to come with you?'

'No.'

'Thank Christ! I've just opened a business.'

Harri laughed. George was a selfish old sod but at least he was honest about it.

Later that night, when she was tucked up in bed, she wondered what she would have done if James had been there. She missed his face, the crinkle under his eyes, the way he grinned, the way he licked his left incisor just before making a point. She missed his hair, his hands and everything else that began with H. *I miss your hamstrings.* She missed all of him. She wondered about Matthew Delamere and what he must have gone through in the wake of losing his girlfriend. *Did he really love her? Does a seventeen-year-old understand love? Did he ache? Did he bury a part of himself with her? Does he even remember her?*

Harri stared at the picture her dad had given her of a smiling seventeen-year-old Liv stroking an old horse. She had such light in her eyes and a dirty grin. She was tall, much taller than Harri, and lean. They had the same hair and cheekbones but it was hard to see any other similarities when she looked from the girl in the picture to herself in the mirror – but, then, the girl in the photo was just a kid. The very next day, 11 July 2006, was Harri Ryan's actual birthday, and Matthew Delamere's girl-friend Liv would have been dead for thirty years. *I'm so sorry. I wish I could change it for you. I hope you're resting in peace, pretty girl.*

'Harri?' James repeated. 'Harri, I know it's you. Are you going to say something?' A few seconds passed. 'Harri, this is ridiculous.'

'Sorry.'

'At last she speaks.'

'How did you know it was me?'

'No one else calls me in the middle of the night with nothing to say.'

'Sorry.'

'Stop apologizing. What time is it?'

'Just after three.'

'What's wrong?'

'I have a picture of my mum. My real one, not Gloria.'

'Does she look like you?'

'A little. Susan thinks I'm the head cut off her and Melissa said so too but I don't see it.'

'Does she look happy?' he asked.

'Yeah, she does.'

'Good,' he replied, and Harri felt instantly better.

She'd first called him after Melissa had shown her a

picture of her father. She had been silent that night too. She had really only wanted to hear James's voice but then she had changed her mind and pretended there was something wrong with the line.

'Can you hear me now?' she'd asked.

James's turn to be silent.

'Do you mind that I called?'

'No,' he replied. 'Nice to hear your voice.'

She'd told him about her dad.

'Do you want to meet him?' he'd asked.

'No,' she'd said, not really knowing if her answer was true.

'Well, there's plenty of time,' he counselled.

'I haven't had a panic attack,' she said.

'Of course you haven't. They only tend to happen when you're due to marry me.' He said it lightly but she sensed his pain.

'Not true,' she said. 'My parents told me it used to happen a lot when I was a kid.'

'But they said . . .' He trailed off as it occurred to him that her parents had done a lot of lying and, in the general scheme of things, that particular lie was inconsequential.

They had talked on and off since that night. It was always at Harri's instigation, when she was at breaking point, and usually the call began with silence. Except for once, two weeks previously, when she'd seen him in a coffee shop in Bray with Tina Tingle. Tina was leaning in for a kiss and Harri was walking with a client discussing fabric samples – otherwise she would have fallen to her knees right there on the street.

That phone call began with the words 'Tina fucking Tingle!'

James had laughed but Harri wasn't amused.

'How the hell?' he'd asked.

'I saw you,' she'd said, in a tone that dripped disgust.

'Saw us what?'

'Kissing!' she'd said, through gritted teeth.

James had laughed. 'Since when has a peck on the cheek constituted romance – which I presume is what you believe you witnessed?'

'Peck on the cheek?' she'd said, and realized that if anyone had cheek it was her. *Who the hell do I think I am?*

'I'm converting her attic,' he'd told her.

Tina Tingle has her own attic. For some reason Harri had seen Tina Tingle as a permanent renter.

'How is she?' she'd asked, as though the call had just begun and was merely continuing on a pleasant note.

'She's fine. Married.'

'Married,' Harri had repeated, winded.

'To a dentist.'

'A dentist. Jesus!' Harri had never seen Tina Tingle married to a dentist. 'Did she ask about me?'

'No.'

'Oh.'

It was weird. Tina and Harri had lived together for a few years, yet when Harri had moved out their friendship had ended without malice, an ill word or deed. It had just ended. It turned out that Tina and Harri had had nothing more in common than a shared address. So why would she ask about Harri?

233

'Well, I asked after her.'

'No, you didn't,' James reminded her. 'You saw me with her, presumed an affair and called her names!' He was laughing.

She had wondered if he missed her as much or even half as much as she missed him. Either way it wouldn't matter: James had made up his mind to give her space and there was nothing she could say or do that would change his mind. She hoped that he would live up to his promise of waiting for her. She knew if she didn't hurry up and sort herself out he might slip away from her. *What if I never really know who I am? What if the only thing I want is you? What if, while I'm faffing around trying to find myself, you find someone else? Bollocks to this finding-yourself stuff! Is it really necessary? I am what I am, whatever that is, and I want my life back with you and me and our little country kip that's falling down around us, and maybe a house instead of the apartment and a rabbit. I'm seriously thinking about getting a rabbit. Isn't that enough?*

'I should go,' he'd said.

'Right, me too.'

''Bye.'

''Bye,' she'd repeated.

He used to end every call with 'I love you'. If truth be told it had got on her wick a bit because it meant she would have to say, 'I love you too,' and that was okay if she was alone but she felt stupid saying it in front of strangers on public transport or in a shop or in the queue at the bank or, God forbid, a garage where invariably she'd get some crack from an old fart with too much time on his hands: 'Do you love me three, darling? Ha! Do ya see what

I did there? Go on, you good thing!' She had often bitched about it to Aidan but she missed it now that it was gone. She had made a real effort to stop calling when she'd realized she was averaging a call a week. She was scared she'd end up relying on him too much and afraid that if he did find someone new, someone who knew who she was and what she wanted and wasn't verging on being a little bit mental, that he'd ask her not to call any more and that would kill her. Still, that night at three o'clock, with her mother's photo still in her hand and tears falling from her eyes, all she'd wanted to do was talk to James. And, when, after less than three minutes on the phone, he had made her feel considerably better and therefore suitably sleepy, she was glad she'd called, even though talking to him was sometimes more painful than not talking to him.

9 August 1975 – Saturday

I had such a great day with Sheila. It was hot and we spent it on the beach sunning ourselves and catching up. It seemed ages since we were alone together. She said that Dave shoves his knickers up his arse and does a funny walk with a good impression of her mother giving out about the price of a nice slice of ham. She did an impression of him doing an impression of her mam, shoving her bikini bottoms up her own arse, just as Mrs Brown from Brown's bakery was passing. Mrs Brown didn't seem too impressed but I was rolling around. She said her dad's thinking about selling the bar and retiring. He comes from Kerry and he's always wanted to go back.

She says she really doesn't want him to sell. She'd thrown the wobbler to beat all wobblers when he mentioned it. She says if they sell they'll definitely end up in Kerry and where will that leave her? She has one more year of school and where will she come home to if they bugger off to Kerry? After messing up one too many hairstyles she's back to considering nursing now and she's pretty sure that's what she wants to do – when Dave stood on a piece of glass, she pulled it out of his foot, then cleaned and bandaged the wound. He was crying like a baby but she said that even though he was wailing and carrying on she did a really brilliant job. I could see her as a nurse. She's definitely bossy enough. If Sheila told you to drop your drawers you would.

Dr B asked me in for a cup of tea on Wednesday. I was passing the gate lodge on my way to the stables. I still can't believe I'm back in the stables. I bet the only reason Matthew's dad kicked me out of the office is because I saw him cry. Anyway, it's not so bad. I did miss Betsy and Nero and Henry is a nicer boss by far, and it's way nicer to be around Matthew and watch him ride. He looks amazing on a horse. It's a pity he's way too tall to be a jockey but it wouldn't suit him to be short. Anyway, Dr B called me in for a cup of tea. We talked about my hand and he made me flex it a few times and we listened to the radio and the DJ played a song called 'Born To Run' by a guy called Bruce Springsteen and Dr B turned it up and we danced in his kitchen. He was twirling me around and we were laughing, and that man can really sing and it was weird – I really did feel like I wanted to run somewhere. The DJ said it wasn't available to buy and that he had got it in America so I've been listening to his show every night since just to hear it.

I think Dr B is lonely. He tends to stay away from the crowd, keeping himself to himself. It's a pity but I suppose he doesn't like football, drinking and fighting. I told him he should learn to ride. I've got much better and I'd help him out. He could start off on Betsy. Matthew said he'd help him too. So that's what we did. We went riding yesterday. Matthew was on Nero, I took Favourite, she's Henry's best pony, and we put Dr B on Betsy. She was good to him and had him galloping in no time. He really took to it and I'd say he'll keep doing it. He was really happy afterwards.

When he went home Matthew and I went walking in the woods. He looked so handsome in the streaming light and he pulled me in to him and leaned on a tree and kissed me and told me he loved me and I told him I loved him too. Every part of me wanted to burst and it felt so good. Sometimes when I'm alone, sitting in this room behind a locked door, I wish I didn't love anything or anyone because everybody knows that love hurts, but I do so I'll have to live with it. Since I've met him I've never been happier. He makes me smile and feel warm inside, and when he touches me my heart races and my hands sweat and I lose the power of thought and speech and my head buzzes and my heart and stomach dance and spin and I'd die for him. I'd die for him with a smile on my face.

Mam thinks I'm going to Dublin with Sheila and her mother next weekend but I'm not. I'm going camping with Matthew. Mam won't know any different. She has given up her cleaning

I Love you Matthew Delancey

job and I can't remember the last time she bothered to leave the house. Anyway, I don't really think she cares and HE, well, he and I don't speak. He stays well clear, knowing I would kill him as soon as look at him.

I can't wait for next weekend for Matthew and me just to be alone together. Matthew will be going back to school in the first week of September and it seems like ages away but it's not. It'll fly by and then he'll leave me and I'll be broken-hearted, but I can't think about that now. All I can do is live for now and enjoy the time we have together. I'm not going to be miserable. I'm going to be happy and glad and things will work out. I just know they will.

Dr B tried to see Mam but she wouldn't let him in. Father Ryan tried to talk to her but she shut the door on him too. She's not so bad at the moment. She's wearing all her clothes and she's started to cook again and the other day she even did a bit of weeding. We watched *Coronation Street* together and she laughed at Deirdre and Ray. I can't remember the last time I heard my mother laugh.

Yesterday morning I woke up crying. I have no idea why but I felt a terrible darkness and so alone, but that was a dream.

I'm not alone – at least, not any more. I've got Matthew. Father Ryan told me once that no one was alone as long as they had a relationship with God. Well, that's nice for him but give me Matthew over God any day!!!!!!

Today Matthew kissed me by the old stone wall under a light blue warm sky with not a cloud in sight and then, arm in arm, he walked me home. At my door he told me I was the best thing that ever happened to him. I've never been anybody's best thing before. Today was a good day and maybe one of the best.

17. A secret shared

Matthew Delamere woke a little after six. He lay still for a few minutes, listening to the stranger next to him breathe. *What's her name? What's her name? What's her name?* The party the evening before had been an impromptu celebration after the successful purchase of a highly sought-after filly despite strong bidding competition. The hotel had been packed for the auction but there was also a wedding and a ladies' lunch. Somehow all three events had blended. The excitement had become too great for Henry, and after a hearty meal, Alfio had taken him home. Henry was still living in one of the lodges on Delamere land, and although he was pushing eighty-two and officially retired, he still tended the horses and could always be found strolling around the grounds. He loved a good auction, especially when Matt flexed his consider-able financial muscle.

'Oh, she's worth it, son,' he'd said. 'She's worth it all right.'

'Good man.'

'Good man yourself!'

Alfio had returned later to find his boss in the bar chatting up two ladies who had finished lunch and were looking for something more fulfilling. Matt was only too happy to oblige.

'Ladies, this is Alfio.'

Alfio bowed his head. It became obvious instantly that the blonde with the boob job was the object of Matt's desire. The pretty redhead smiled and patted the seat beside her. Tentatively Alfio sat. *Ambushed! Tomorrow he will suffer.*

'Alfio is a champion polo player,' Matt said to the girls, signalling to the barman for more drinks.

'I was,' Alfio said, in a tone not too distant from huffy.

'Once a champ, always a champ.' Matt raised a glass to him. *He's going to kill me. I hope she's worth it.*

'Oh, I loved *The Champ*. I've seen it a hundred times and it still makes me cry,' the blonde said, laying her hand across her considerable breasts.

'Oh, that's the one with the kid from *Silver Spoons* in it.' The redhead shook her head. 'What a little heartbreaker!'

'Some people shouldn't be allowed grow up,' the blonde said, with authority.

Matt nodded, then glanced at Alfio, who responded with a look that suggested he might be considering shoving a polo stick up his boss's arse.

'Yeah,' the redhead said thoughtfully. 'The kid from *Silver Spoons*, the *Uncle Buck/Home Alone* kid and that little spiky-haired one from *Jerry Maguire*.'

'Aaah!' the blonde said, slapping her friend's hand. 'I love him!'

'Remember the bit about the human head?' the redhead squealed.

'It weighs eight pounds!' the blonde almost shouted.

Matthew put his hand up to his face so Alfio couldn't

tell if he was laughing, grinning or reconsidering his need for sex. *Please, please, please, reconsider.*

Matt didn't reconsider so Alfio was forced to listen to twittering and bullshit and bear witness to tentative groping and when it was time to book a room, which no doubt Matt would do, he would be obliged to make an excuse to the redhead because he just wasn't interested. Alfio sat quietly while Matt held court, making the two ladies giggle and squeal. He thought about the girl he'd left at home in Argentina, a brunette beauty with large coffee-brown eyes, mocha skin, full mouth, full bosom, and long, lithe legs. She was intelligent, fiery, strong, athletic and funny. She was everything. *Ah, Maria, you have ruined me.* He smiled kindly at the tiny redhead, who was telling a story that involved traffic.

'Bumper to bumper and no one was going anywhere and I thought, I'll never hold on. So two hours later, with tears in my eyes, I hitched up my skirt and peed at the side of the car while three builders in a Hiace shouted, "Go on, ya good thing!"'

Cue laughter from the blonde and Matt.

Alfio had had enough.

'Oh, no, stay!' the redhead begged.

'I'm really tired,' he explained.

'One more drink!'

'No, thank you.'

'Ah, come on!'

'No.'

'Ah, you will!'

'This is beginning to sound familiar,' laughed the blonde. 'G'wan – g'wan, g'wan!'

The redhead covered her mouth. 'Oh, my God, I'm Mrs Doyle!'

The two women were laughing raucously again. Alfio hadn't a clue what they were talking about. Neither did he care.

'Oh, Alfio, you wouldn't know this but we're quoting from a very funny Irish comedy – it's called *Father Ted*,' the redhead said, with her hand firmly fixed on his arm. *You're going nowhere, mister.*

'Really?' He sighed.

'Poor Dermot Morgan, he was taken too young.' The blonde shook her head.

'RIP,' the redhead said solemnly, and blessed herself, thereby loosening her grip on Alfio. He took his opportunity and, within seconds, was gone.

The disappointed redhead left in a taxi soon after.

Matt and the blonde made their way to his hastily booked suite.

What's her name? What's her name? What's her name?

Now, in the cold light of day and with a headache, Matt was sorry he'd stayed. The blonde was a board in bed. She just lay there with a fixed expression while directing: 'No. Not down there . . . Touch me here . . . I don't like it on top . . . I don't want to move . . . Have you come yet?' She dropped off after twenty minutes and even as a sleeper she was annoying, both restless and loud.

He knew by her breathing that she was still sleeping

heavily so he got up and showered leisurely. She woke when he was shaving.

'Morning, Matt,' she said, standing behind him and looking into the bathroom mirror.

'Morning, sexy.' He grinned from force of habit rather than anything else.

'Will I order breakfast?' She reciprocated his grin.

'If you're hungry, order what you want. I'll take care of the bill.' He winked at her.

'You're not staying?' She sounded disappointed.

'I have an early business meeting. Sorry.'

She smiled. 'Okay.' *I'm going to order everything on the menu and rob anything that isn't nailed down, you using tosser!* 'It was nice while it lasted.'

'It certainly was,' he lied, as the washbasin emptied. He put his clothes on in seconds.

Plenty of practice, no doubt, she thought, watching him from the bed to which she had returned. He was gone in less than five minutes, and five minutes after that she was ordering from the extensive menu.

Alfio was waiting in the car with two takeaway coffees, two Danish pastries and an *Irish Times*.

'You're a lifesaver.'

'*Beso mi culo, boludo!*'

Matt smiled. 'I'll give you that. Last night was not me at my most shining.'

'*Come mierda!*'

'You eat shit!' Matt laughed.

'They say that Argentinians are hot-blooded but I've

never known a man to air his dick as much as you, Matt Delamere,' Alfio said in disgust.

'I'll take that as a compliment.'

'It wasn't meant as one.'

'Doesn't matter.'

It was after eight when Alfio turned into the long, winding driveway and passed the gatehouse, the stables, the training grounds on the way to the house. Matt got out and Alfio drove on to the car park. He had a full day ahead of him, breaking in a Californian thoroughbred stallion.

Matt entered the house by the back door. Patsy Byrne, the housekeeper, was standing on a chair, cleaning out the presses. 'You'd want to watch yourself, Patsy. That's a broken hip waiting to happen,' he said from the doorway.

'Are you trying to say I'm old?'

'No comment.' He chuckled.

'So help me down,' she said.

'I'll get you a proper stepladder. Health and safety and all that. Maybe for your birthday.'

'Charming,' she said, pretending to be annoyed.

An hour had passed before Matt left his home again, dressed in riding gear and with a large bunch of flowers he'd grabbed from the vase in the hall. He rode past the training grounds, the stables and the gate lodge, through Devil's Glen and down the narrow road that took him to the graveyard. He tied up Shadow, his favourite horse, at the entrance and walked the rest of the way. It was just after nine thirty and the place was empty, save for an old lady hunched over a worn headstone.

He made his way to the grave and rested his free hand on the stone that bore her name while clutching the flowers firmly to his chest. 'Hi there, kiddo,' he said. 'It's been a while, maybe even the full year. I was away at Christmas, I would have been here otherwise. I see Henry's been, though, keeping the place tidy and the roses trimmed. He's good, still going strong. I think he'll outlive us all. Brendan's good too. What's that you used to call him – Dr B?' He laughed, put the flowers into the vase on the grave and sat on the grass beside her. 'He's still living in the gate lodge. Can you believe it? He loves that old house and that old house loves him. He's done a lovely refurbishment job on it. The old fella has taste. Look at me calling Brendan old. He's fifty-six. I remember when Henry was fifty-five and we thought he was ancient. I turned forty-seven three months ago. My dad was forty-seven when . . . He was in Monaco, remember? We'd had that massive row before he left. You stopped me punching him. I was so annoyed with you . . . I'm sorry. Hey, remember the nights we spent by the castle looking up at the stars? I'd go back in a second.' He sighed. 'I swear I'd go back in a second.' He held on tight to her stone. 'Hey, Liv, I still love you.' He stood up. 'But don't tell anyone, okay? It's our secret.'

He went to fetch some water for the flowers, then left her resting place as quiet and serene as he'd found it.

Most of his day would be spent on the phone. Many of the calls he made would be transatlantic so he had until after lunch before his workday proper would begin. Brendan was sitting out in his garden when he passed on Shadow.

'Brendan.'

'Matt. Come in. Have coffee with me.'

Matt dismounted and tied Shadow, who shook his head vigorously, to a low branch. He sat down and Brendan poured coffee from the percolator.

'You're expecting company?' Matt asked, referring to the extra cup.

'I was expecting you.' Brendan smiled. 'How's our girl?'

'Still gone, Brendan.'

'Thirty years is a long time.'

Words always seemed to fail Matt when Brendan talked about Liv. He never mentioned the baby; neither of them did. Matthew sat back in his chair. *She's thirty today. Happy thirtieth, Harriet Ryan. I wanted to call you Olivia after your mother. Olivia Delamere. Happy thirtieth, Olivia Delamere.* He was miles away even as Brendan talked about his recent trip to Las Vegas.

'Dusty place. I wouldn't go again.' He had liked San Francisco. In fact, he had liked it so much that he wished it had occurred to him as a younger man to get off his arse and move there, instead of hiding in a wood in Wicklow. *It could have been so different.*

Later when Matt emerged from his haze he talked about his latest acquisition. They toasted it with fresh coffee and Brendan's homemade muffins.

'You could have been a baker.'

'I could have been a lot of things.' Brendan grinned and Matt laughed before they fell into a comfortable silence.

'Are you free for dinner tonight?' Brendan asked.

'I'm seeing Clara.'

'Ah, the lovely Clara! Are you serious about her yet?'

'Jesus, Brendan, it's only been three months.'

'Three months can be a lifetime.'

'We'll see. She's a nice woman. Ticks all the boxes.'

'Such a romantic,' Brendan joked.

'You can talk!' Matt retorted.

'All right, all right,' Brendan said, his hands in the air. 'I give up. I haven't a clue what I'm talking about.'

Matt laughed. 'We're a right pair!'

'We most certainly are. How about tomorrow? I'll do a rack of lamb, we'll break out the cards and make an evening of it.'

'Sounds good,' Matt said, getting up. 'I'll see you around seven.'

Brendan was left alone in his garden. He contemplated life and death and the passage of time. He remembered Liv and her sense, her strength, her stubbornness, her open heart and her inability to lie. He missed his young friend. *What would you be like now? Would you still be a fighter? Would you have held tight to your beliefs? Would the world have worn you down?*

Four miles away, in a care home, Liv's mother Deirdre sat in her chair by the heater under the large window that looked out on to the grounds. The gardens were separated by the long, winding avenue that led to the electric gate and out of the hospital. The gate was too far away to see from her chair, but when she closed her eyes, she could hear in her mind the motor whirr as it opened and closed. Her hands remained clasped in her lap. She didn't have much use for them. She didn't dress herself, or prepare food or drinks; she didn't greet those who passed her, and when she spoke, which wasn't often, she wasn't animated.

A nurse approached with tea, putting it on the window-sill by the old radio she had constantly playing. She liked talk radio. Ryan Tubridy was a great man for chat and in the afternoon she would listen to Joe Duffy. She used her hands to change the radio dial from Ryan to Joe and Joe to Ryan. And she used them to lift her cup so that she could drink her tea.

It was a Tuesday, and Tuesday was hair-wash day. She kept her hair short and even. Although it was grey and she didn't use much conditioner, it was still soft and a little flyaway. She didn't like people touching her head. She didn't like hair-wash day. She didn't struggle or whine or moan, just cried a little. The tears flowed in silence. She wasn't one for making much noise.

'How are you feeling, Deirdre?' Nurse Trisha asked.

'Fine,' she said.

'Are you ready for your medication, love?'

Deirdre nodded. Trisha handed her the pills and Deirdre had them swallowed before the nurse had time to hand her a glass of water.

'I see you got some flowers,' she said, but Deirdre was finished interacting. Instead she was staring out of the window at the gardener pruning a hedge.

'By your bed,' Trisha said, attempting to engage her again, but to no avail.

For Deirdre, Trisha's voice disappeared behind Ryan Tubridy talking with some woman about weddings and bad music and drunken fumbling while she watched the sun redden the back of the gardener's neck.

The nurse made her way down the corridor and towards the staff room. Maisie was making coffee.

'Deirdre just got a serious bunch of flowers.'

'No card,' Maisie said.

'No,' Trisha confirmed.

'He never leaves a card,' Maisie said ominously, piquing Trisha's interest.

'Who?' Trisha asked, intrigued – after all, it had been a slow morning.

'Matt Delamere,' Maisie replied, handing Trisha a coffee.

'The horse trainer?'

'The very one.'

'Why?' she asked – she was new to both the hospital and the area.

'Did you ever hear about that girl who died giving birth in Devil's Glen in the mid-seventies?'

'Yeah. Very sad.'

'Deirdre was the girl's mother. Matt Delamere was the boyfriend.'

'Good God!'

'I know.'

'So where was he when she was bleeding to death?'

'Who knows? That GP, what's his name, found her.'

'Jesus. And no one knew she was pregnant?'

'Well, if they did they certainly didn't make it known.

Anyway, back in those days you'd be sent off somewhere so I'd be surprised.'

'He must have felt awful,' she said.

'Well, he hasn't been paying Deirdre's bills for twenty years for nothing.'

'You're joking me!'

Maisie walked out of the room, leaving Trisha to ponder on a nice piece of gossip. People lived mad lives.

Susan was looking through some catalogues in the front passenger seat of the car. 'There's some great stuff in here,' she said to Harri, who was driving. 'Do you think we could nip in? Bray is on the way.'

Harri sighed. 'All right, all right. Don't get your knickers in a knot.'

Susan had insisted on coming. As soon as Harri had mentioned she was taking the day off, Susan had known something was up and questioned, hounded and annoyed her until eventually she broke. Usually Harri could have escaped Susan but unfortunately, as her friend was camping in her sitting room, avoidance was not an option. They were on the road four hours later than she'd intended. An order of Valbonne distressed furniture had gone astray and Susan had spent most of the morning on the phone with the courier company while Harri had made excuses to the client. *So much for a day off.*

'It will take less than an hour. We'll be in, we'll be out,' Susan said, still flicking.

'Fine,' Harri said, slightly annoyed. *I'm only going to visit my dead mother, no need to make it any kind of priority.*

'Great,' Susan said happily. 'We might stop for a bit of lunch too. I'm starving.'

'You're pushing it!' Harri warned, and, judging by the look on her face, she meant it.

Susan turned on the radio. Ryan Tubridy was talking about wedding bands. She laughed. 'You know what mine was called?'

'No.' Harri sighed.

'Mixed Grill.' Harri couldn't help but giggle. 'Still, they were a ruddy good band.' Susan's smile faded – she'd reminded herself that her marriage was over.

The day was bright and warm. The sun shone in a bright blue sky so Harri and Susan drove with the top down. The new motorway stretched before them and with it the promise of an adventure that neither woman felt fully prepared for. For Harri the questions that swam in her mind were simple. *What lies ahead? Am I doing the right thing? Do I really want to open this can of worms? Could I even turn around if I wanted to?* For Susan there was only one: *What do I do if she falls apart?* The car took the women towards Wicklow with the sun on their backs. They smiled at one another intermittently but mostly they kept their eyes forward and their mouths shut.

Melissa would have loved to be with her friend on the first time she would celebrate her actual birthday – well, celebrate was an exaggeration of what she would do. Mourn was more accurate – or maybe not. After all, although she was visiting her dead mother, in reality she was merely visiting a dead stranger. Gloria was her mother and still very much alive. It was all a little confusing and hard to grasp, so much so that although she wanted to be with Harri during her time of need, she really hadn't a clue what to say to her. 'Chin up' didn't quite cut it, and neither did her other favourite, 'Never mind, it could happen to anyone.' Still, she would have liked to spend the day with Harri, not necessarily because she felt she could help, but because anything – even a trip to the grave of a seventeen-year-old who had bled to death – would be a break from the increasing demands her boss, her colleagues, her husband and her children were putting upon her. She was halfway through a presentation when the phone call came. She had asked not to be disturbed and poor Ellen was incredibly apologetic when she escorted her out of the meeting room and towards the phone at the front desk.

It was Jacob's teacher. 'Jacob has a pain in his tummy.'

'Is he pale?'

'No.'

'Hot?'

'No.'

'Has he been sick?'

'No.'

'Well, then, I'm sure he's fine.'

'He's complaining of pain. I can't ignore it.'

Melissa sighed. 'Sometimes he says he has a pain in his tummy if he's doing something he doesn't like doing.'

'He's doing what he does every day and likes it just fine, plus he didn't eat his lunch and refused a chocolate biscuit.'

'I'm on my way.' Jacob never refused a chocolate biscuit. Why the hell hadn't the woman started with that?

Jim, her boss, met her in the cloakroom. 'Where the hell are you going?'

'Jacob's sick.'

'You're halfway through a presentation.'

'I know and I'm sorry but there's nothing I can do.'

'Where's your husband, your nanny, your mother?'

'Where indeed? On a day off and retired in Spain.'

'Melissa.'

'Jim.'

'This can't go on. I depend on you. This firm depends on you.'

'I'm sorry. I'll sort it.'

'What am I supposed to say to the client?'

'Tell them I'm sorry. I'll reschedule for whenever suits them.'

'Not good enough,' Jim said, shaking his head.

'It's the best I can do,' she said, and left.

She tried to call her husband four times from the car but each time his phone went to voicemail. She arrived at Jacob's school a little after eleven. Jacob was waiting for her at the door.

'I have a pain.'

'I know, buddy. I'm going to take you home, we'll put on *Thomas* and you can lie with Snuggles on the sofa.'

The crèche rang as she was pulling out of Jacob's school. 'Carrie vomited.'

'Oh, God. I'm on the way.'

Carrie was asleep when she picked her up. She decided to bring the kids straight to the doctor. Jacob complained that she had promised him the sofa, *Thomas* and Snuggles, and the doctor's surgery didn't offer any of those. She cajoled him with promises of a new *Thomas* toy when he got better. After she'd spent an hour in the doctor's waiting room, then gone into his surgery to receive his patented dirty look when she couldn't tell him what her children had had for breakfast because she'd left home early this morning, he concluded that the ailment was viral and would have to run its course. One prescription for a kiddie pain reliever and sixty euro later she was back in the car with a now grumpy Carrie and a moaning Jacob. 'My tummy still hurts.'

The shopping-centre car park was jammed but she eventually found a space. Carrie was now crying and Jacob was rubbing his tummy and repeating, in a particularly annoying sing-song voice, 'Sore. Sore. Sore. Sore. Sore.' With Carrie in her arms and Jacob by the hand Melissa navigated the busy shopping centre until she reached the chemist. Despite her daughter's wailing and her son's persistent moaning, she acquired the prescribed medicine and, laden with children, near deafened and suffering from an overloaded bladder, she queued to pay.

Her phone rang. It was her boss and she thought about ignoring the call but she, unlike her husband, whom she was contemplating battering to death, had never been able to ignore a phone. She dropped Jacob's hand and held the phone to her ear. Her boss rather snottily reported on their client's not so favourable response to her leaving mid-meeting.

'Mum!'

'Just a second, Jacob.' Carrie was still crying. 'Can I deal with this tomorrow?'

'Mum!'

'In a minute, Jacob.'

'I need your password. I've promised to send on your presentation notes. It's the least we can do.'

'Can I not send them on first thing?'

'Mum!'

'I'd rather they had them now.'

'I'd prefer to do it myself.'

'Well, we'd all prefer that you do it yourself, Melissa, but unfortunately I'm here and you're not.'

She argued on that she wasn't comfortable with anyone else going through her computer. Jim said he didn't really care what was comfortable, bearing in mind that her abrupt exit could lose them a client. She sighed and absent-mindedly looked down towards where her son had been standing less then a minute before. He was gone. Initially she was not alarmed, but then she looked around and still couldn't see him.

'Jacob!' she shouted into the phone. 'Jacob!' she shouted again. She was out of the queue and moving down the closest aisle.

'Melissa, what's wrong?' Jim asked.

'It's Jacob – he's gone,' she said, now running down the next aisle. 'Jacob!'

She hung up the phone and was yelling so loudly the manager came to her assistance. He and another girl called Jane joined the search, calling Jacob's name, but he wasn't in the shop. He was gone. Melissa joined Carrie in crying. She sat on the floor and cried and cried and the poor manager did his best to calm her and the girl called Jane ran in and out of the shops next door asking if anyone had seen a little boy called Jacob. Security was summoned.

Melissa was now shaking and Carrie was stunned into silence. 'He was here and then he was gone,' Melissa repeated to herself. 'I was holding his hand but then work called.' She was crying again. 'Oh, God, where is he?' She didn't think to try to call her husband. Her mind was a blank and fear had engulfed her. She could do nothing but repeat herself and bite her nails. 'He's not well,' she said, a number of times. In her head were images of missing children, later found dead. *Oh, my God!* Melissa clung to her little girl, praying. *Please be okay, son. Please come back.*

Twenty long minutes had passed before a security guard called Tim arrived with Jacob. When she saw him Melissa burst into tears, accompanied by loud sobs. Jacob, on seeing his mother near hysterical, did likewise, jarring Carrie sufficiently for her to join in. Once they had all calmed down, approximately ten minutes later, Tim the security guard explained that he had found Jacob in the toilets.

'I needed to poo,' Jacob said. 'It was coming.'

Melissa didn't scold him for running off. He had tried to get her attention. The child had the runs and she had ignored him in favour of arguing about a stupid bloody presentation. She gathered herself and thanked the shop manager, Jane and Tim, then left the centre with the pre-scribed medication that the manager had insisted she take for free. At home, when her children were medicated and sleeping, she poured herself a large whiskey and cried again. *I just can't do it any more.*

Melissa's problem was greater than exhaustion and a well-meaning but ultimately unhelpful husband. Her problem was that she was fast becoming a stranger to herself. Once upon a time she had been a dedicated worker and a professional, hailed as a stand-out performer. She had sailed through school, and college was a breeze, and from a very young age she had been destined for the fulfilling career her mother could only have dreamed of. Melissa's professional life was exciting, challenging and rewarding. It afforded her a large bank balance and the comforts associated with that. She was respected and contented. Life was good.

Then she had had Jacob. And, of course, she had had a plan. She was only six months gone when she'd found the perfect babyminder. She would take the minimum maternity leave and return to work. She had known that at first there would be teething problems, as with any new venture. It was impossible to plan for every eventuality but she felt confident that once a routine was established she could do and have it all. Melissa hadn't prepared herself for guilt.

She hadn't known that with motherhood came worry like she'd never known, love that was frankly overwhelming, and the greatest need to be with her baby. The day she returned to work she cried in the toilets for more than an hour. She had thought leaving him would get easier but it didn't. She had thought she'd fight the urge to call home twenty-five times a day but she couldn't. She had thought that if she could just switch off the little part of her brain that constantly reminded her of what she was missing everything would return to normal and she would be the single-minded professional she had been before.

It didn't return to normal and Melissa found herself slightly tortured and very torn. She hadn't spent years in college and working her way to the top of her profession for nothing. She couldn't just throw it all away and, looking around her, lots of women were perfectly happy to leave their babies at home while they worked. Mother of four Denise Green had not only said that working was as fulfilling as it had ever been but it was the saviour of her sanity. Melissa was embarrassed by her perceived inadequacy and lived in denial, quashing the urge to renounce her place in the man's world her sisters before her had fought so valiantly to ensure and return to the kitchen where she yearned to be – baking with her son, playing games, watching him grow, being there, and being his mum.

Eventually she had fallen into a routine and managed her work and home life well. It was only when her perfect babyminder called to tell her that Jacob had clapped or stood or walked or called her 'Mama' that her heart threatened to break and those dark thoughts had first emerged. *What if I stayed at home?* Of course, that was a ridiculous notion. She would have gone insane just like Denise Green had said. She was a professional, not a cookie-cutter. But then Carrie had come along, and with her, double the work and double the heartbreak. Her job was suffering and her kids were suffering and her marriage was suffering and, most of all, she was suffering. She was tired all the time. She was haunted by leaving not one but two children, and the prospect that yet again she would hear of her child's development from someone else.

Melissa needed a break. Melissa needed to stop. Melissa needed to come clean. Since Jacob was born she had pretended to be someone she used to be but wasn't any more and the lie had taken its toll.

18 August 1975 – Monday

We went to Brittas Bay and pitched our tent on the grass overlooking miles of white sand dunes. Well, maybe not miles but it seemed like it. The weather was amazing so when we arrived (we biked there, by the way, which nearly killed me) it was heaving with people. Loads of Dubliners down for the day and kids in colourful togs with ice-creams and shovels and old women with big dark-coloured togs and swaddled in towels even though they were complaining about the heat. The sea was full, as far as the eye could see, with people swimming, wading, walking, floating, splashing, jumping – and there were the sounds of seagulls, and mothers calling for their kids, and kids calling for each other, and men playing football off to the side, and the water lapping and swishing, and heat on our backs and on the soles of our feet. The sun glinted on the water and the air weighed on me like a cosy old jumper, and all the while the DJs played what Matthew called sunny songs. I'll remember my weekend away for ever. Matthew did most of the work. He was a Boy Scout and well used to putting up the two-man tent he had managed to carry on the back of his bike along with the sleeping-bag. He's very strong and fit and I suppose he has good balance too. It must be from riding

Nero. I was half dead and all I'd carried was the radio and our toothbrushes and some knickers and things. The sun was so hot we didn't need too many clothes. Good thing too because there was no way I could have carried them.

When the beach got quiet, just after eight, we snuggled up together and watched the water. That never gets old. You'd think it would but it doesn't and I can't explain why. We ate sandwiches from the shop down the road and drank a few cans of Harp. I still don't like beer but it does make me laugh – well, Matthew makes me laugh but things definitely sound funnier when I've had some beer. There was a man on the beach walking his dog. It was after ten and still bright. The dog was chasing its tail and the man was standing watching and waiting. Eventually the dog got tired of that and jumped up on the man. He gave the dog a hug, the same kind of hug you'd give a person. The dog panted and ran off and the man followed, his dog barking and yelping, high on freedom. He was too far away to see his face but I bet it was a kind one. I bet he's a really nice person. He probably has a good job – maybe he's a doctor or a banker – and he's probably married and he loves his wife and he's probably got kids who don't have to lock their doors at night. In fact, they probably don't even have locks. To say nothing of a great big padlock like Matthew's put on my door for me – he's so handy.

So, we watched the sea and Matthew was quiet and kind of far away. And I knew what he was thinking. Two weeks left. In two weeks he'll be back in boarding-school. We try not to think about it but it's hard when every shop is full of back-to-school stuff. We keep agreeing to live in the moment, but how can we live in the moment when we know that soon our life together as we know it will be over? Am I being too dramatic, like Joanie Flynn three doors down who cries at the drop of a hat and pretends to faint when she's in trouble? It doesn't feel too dramatic. Matthew says he's fine about going back but I know he's not. Last year he was bullied – he only told me that recently. He was embarrassed about it. The school told his dad and his dad had to get involved and he said his dad knowing was worse than the bullying. His dad called him names but the boys were suspended and the bullying stopped. Before, a few people talked to him but no one does now because he's known as a rat. Stupid fools. They'd rather let bullies run riot than put a stop to them and be called names. I told him as much and he said it was easy for me. Everyone says that but I don't think it's easy. I just think I'd rather go down fighting! He laughs at me when I talk like that but I can tell he likes it.

Before this weekend we didn't go the whole way because we were scared about me getting pregnant and it's really hard to get protection. Sheila is using the natural method – she says it's all about the cycle. She talked about fertile days and non-fertile days and egg production, and I just switched off. She got a library book and now she's an expert. She will definitely make a good nurse. Then the other night in our cosy sleeping-bag it just happened, and I'm scared about being pregnant but I'm glad we did it. It was right. Matthew did it before last year with a girl in Boston so I pretended it wasn't a big deal but it really was. I felt like – well, actually, I don't know what I felt like, a grown-up, maybe. I don't know. I didn't think I could love him more this week than I did last but I do. Looking into his eyes when he was moving inside me, something clicked. I can't say what but in that moment I was inspired and everything made sense. It sounds so weird and maybe I'm a spaz but suddenly I found a place in the world. And I don't mean that I'm his and that's enough. I mean for the first time the future became clear and not some distant island. I'm going to be a writer. I'm going to put my heart, my soul, my experience, my lack of experience, my dreams, my hopes and my love – most of all my love – down on paper. Some day when I really have something to say I'm going to write because everyone loves a good story.

We've been talking more about going to America after the Leaving Cert next year and particularly Kentucky. There are universities in Kentucky and I could go to one. My school work is strong even if I do talk all the time. I could get in – at least, that's what Matthew says. I could study English and Matthew could work in Keeneland. Last week he asked his dad if he could organize it and his dad said he would, and then he said he doesn't care if Matthew ever comes back – but that's because Matthew's dad is a shit but his friend Ronnie runs Keeneland and he's a great man. Matthew says he'll take us both in. He has a big family and his wife Marjorie and all the kids (eleven!!!) ride and they have hundreds of stables and stable hands, and the workers are treated like family and they have big barbecues every weekend and a huge porch with a swing and everyone's welcome at the dinner table and it's like a real family, big and loving and fun. Matthew could break and train horses and I could study and we could have a life together. It's so real I can almost touch it. God, I hope I'm not pregnant. Maybe I'll read Sheila's book.

Mam won't talk to me because I let Dr B in the back door. He thinks there's something wrong in her head. He wants to do some tests but she won't go with him. HE came home and she was shouting at Dr B and then, of course, HE started shouting because he just loves to shout. Dr B left but he asked me to keep an eye on her. I don't know how that's going to help but I said I would.

Dr B is getting really good at riding. We've been riding together a lot lately. I'm still a bit nervous but I pretend I'm not, and Dr B and Matthew don't seem to notice. Dr B has nicknamed me Trouble. It makes Matthew laugh so I don't mind. In fact, I like it. Hi, it's nice to meet you! I'm Trouble!!!!

HE hasn't had any work for a few days and he's itching for a fight. She's so quiet and withdrawn all the time, it's even hard for him to pick a fight with her. He's looking my way again but I'm not scared any more. In my head and my heart I'm free. Soon Matthew is going back to boarding-school. He's going to do everything possible to come home at least once a month, no matter what his dad says or does. All we have to do is get through eleven months and we can start our new lives. Eleven months isn't long. Eleven months is nothing. Roll on next July!!!!!

18. I knew I knew you

Aidan always cleaned when he did something his internal moral barometer deemed wrong. He cleaned when he'd told his mother to fuck off after a particularly nasty row about personal insurance. He cleaned when he'd lied to his friends about being sick just because he wanted a day off. Then again that was the problem with working for friends: lies are problematic and guilt-ridden. He cleaned when he'd used George's credit card to buy tickets to Macy Gray after a fight about cheese. He cleaned when he'd stolen a T-shirt from Gap – he was dared to by a guy whose name he couldn't remember. He cleaned when his sister asked him to mind her three kids and he pretended to have flu. Aidan was cleaning his apartment when the phone rang. He took off one Marigold before answering.

'Aidan.'

'Andrew?'

'I know this is coming from nowhere but could we meet some time this week?'

'Look, if it's about Susan and the builder –'

'It's not.'

'Oh. Right.'

'I'd really appreciate it.'

'Okay.' *What the hell does he want? Make up an excuse. Oh, fuck, come on, think of something. He's waiting. Think, you fucking moron.* 'I'm free tomorrow late afternoon, early evening.'

'Good, great. Okay, tomorrow. Brilliant. Thanks. See you then.'

'Andrew?'

'Yeah.'

'When and where?'

'Oh.' Andrew laughed. 'Sorry. Anywhere in town suits me.'

'How about the Westbury around five thirty?' *No one knows me in the Westbury.*

'Perfect.'

'See you then.'

'And, Aidan . . .'

'Yeah?'

'Thank you again.'

Aidan put down the phone and, as Susan and Harri weren't picking up their phones, he called Melissa. She had finished crying fifteen minutes beforehand and was on her second whiskey. She could have told Aidan what had happened but she was too ashamed. She was even considering hiding from Gerry the fact that she'd almost lost their son. She answered the phone brightly: 'What?'

'You're never going to believe who called me.'

'George Michael?'

'No.'

'Damn it, what's the point in hanging around with homos if it doesn't get me closer to George Michael?'

'Are you finished being Dublin's answer to Joan Rivers?'

266

'Okay. Go on.'

'Andrew.'

'Andrew Shannon?'

'The one and only.'

'What the hell did he want?'

'To meet me.'

'You're not going to meet him, are you?'

'Yeah.'

'Aidan.'

'What?'

'He's a prick.'

'Melissa, life is not that simple.'

She sighed because she knew he was right. 'I wonder what he wants.'

'No idea.'

'Maybe he's gay.' She was being sarcastic, yet, judging from Susan's version of their non-existent sex life, it was a one-in-a-million possibility.

Aidan laughed. 'And I'm Tipper Gore's wet dream.'

She laughed. *What the hell had made him think of Tipper Gore?* 'Yeah, I suppose the notion is pretty outlandish. Speaking of which, what the hell was Susan thinking, arriving with that Keith person?'

'She wasn't. She's just a little lost, that's all.'

'That makes all of us. Did you hear where Harri's gone?'

'No.'

'To Wicklow.'

'Jesus. That was quick.'

'I hope not too quick.' She hadn't embraced the idea

when Harri had called her the day before, especially as she couldn't go with her. Then again she had been the Googler so in a way she blamed herself. *It's too soon. Take some time. Google a bit more. Read your dad's file. Have a holiday. Get back with James. Fuck it, get back to your life. I wish I could get back to mine.*

'Melissa.'

'Yeah?'

'Can you keep a secret?'

'No.'

'I'm serious.'

'So am I.'

'I want to tell you something.'

'So tell me, but I cannot guarantee that I won't tell the next person I see.'

'You sound like Harri and it's pissing me off.'

Melissa laughed. 'Just tell me.'

'No, forget it.'

'You're being a baby.'

'You love Gerry, don't you?' he asked, out of nowhere. 'I mean, you bitch and moan but that's what women do. Am I right?'

'Be careful. You may be on the phone but I will find a way to hurt you.'

'Seriously.'

'Of course I love him.' Melissa smiled to herself, remembering earlier that morning her husband's familiar kiss and the warmth when she spooned him. Quite suddenly she felt like crying again. *I nearly lost our son. Jesus Christ, I nearly lost him. Get a grip, Melissa, calm down. He's home, he's in bed, he's safe. You're fine. Drink up. Pretend it's all okay.* 'What's this about?' she asked.

'Nothing,' he said. The moment for truth had been lost. 'Well, anyway, I'll give you a buzz after I've seen Andrew.'

'What the hell does he want?' she repeated.

'I don't know. And tell Harri to call me when she gets back. I can't believe she didn't tell me what she was up to – although I was in one of my moods last night.'

'I noticed, and will do.'

Aidan hung up the phone and sighed to himself. *How the fuck am I supposed to meet Andrew when I've at least a week's worth of cleaning to do?*

By the time Susan had finished looking at furniture in Bray, and by the time they had driven to Wicklow town and stopped for something to eat, it was a little after four. The town was narrow to drive through, bustling with people, and a maze to find parking in. There was nothing by the pier or on the street behind it and the main street was far too busy. Eventually they found a space by the old jail.

'Oh, look, they do night tours!' Susan said, as they headed back to the car.

'Great.' Harri sighed.

'It's not going like you planned, is it?' Susan asked.

'Not really, no.'

'I'm getting in the way.'

Harri felt sorry for her friend. She'd been bedraggled since she'd walked out of her own home and, God love her, she couldn't seem to find her way back to normal. If

Harri was lost, Susan was even more so, and the builder was a symptom of that.

'It's okay. I don't know what I was expecting. Maybe we should take the night tour of Wicklow jail and go home.' She deactivated the car alarm and they sat in.

Susan turned to her friend. 'Look, why don't I check out all that Wicklow town has to offer while you head to the graveyard? You don't want me there.'

Harri smiled. 'You don't mind?'

'No. It looks like there are some half-decent shops around here.' Susan grabbed her bag, pulled her friend to her and kissed her forehead. 'Good luck, Harri. I hope you find what you're looking for.'

'Knowing what I'm looking for would be enough,' Harri admitted, with a slight smile.

Susan got out and waved her off down the street in search of the graveyard.

Brendan completed his afternoon surgery at four on the dot. Despite a rampant vomiting epidemic, all was well with the Wicklow folk and he intended to make good use of the rest of his day. First he would grab a takeaway coffee in Donnali's, then he'd head on over to the graveyard and later he'd take in eighteen holes of golf. The coffee shop was busy with tourists and locals alike.

'There you are, Dr McCabe. I was saying to Sarah we haven't seen you in an age.'

'Keeping the head down, Martina.'

'That vomiting bug is desperate.'

'Yeah. It's knocking people for six.'

'My Malachy is in bits with it – at least, that's what he pretends.'

'Bed rest, Martina. Bed rest and liquids.'

'Unfortunately, Doctor, you've just described his entire life.'

He was on his way out of the door, coffee in hand, when he nearly walked into Sheila Doyle.

'Dr McCabe.'

'Sheila.'

'Are you well?'

'Fine, just heading up to visit Liv.'

Sheila's face fell. *The eleventh!* 'I forgot,' she admitted, embarrassed.

'It's been a long time,' Brendan said, smiling at her.

'I was her best friend. I should have remembered.'

'Don't be silly, Sheila, you've a houseful of kids, a business to run and an insulin-dependent husband with a stubborn streak a mile long.'

'You remembered,' she said quietly.

'The benefit of living alone. How's Patrick, anyway?'

'Good. He's driving me mad but good.'

Brendan squeezed Sheila's shoulder. 'I hope I didn't upset you,' he said.

'No – and thanks for reminding me.' *I can't believe I forgot you. Jesus, Liv, I'm sorry.*

Susan busied herself in the local boutiques, finding a particularly tasteful silk top within three minutes flat. *I believe my Visa will take some battering today.*

She and Harri had not discussed her attending George's

opening with Keith – in fact, they had carefully avoided that conversation. Susan didn't really know what she was doing. The consequences of her actions had only dawned on her when Aidan had explained that her husband and daughter could arrive at any moment. She had all but collapsed, and even after they had left the premises and were heading into the Front Lounge, a bar her husband would never have frequented, she couldn't rid herself of the bitter taste of fear or failure – or something else she couldn't quite put her finger on. She looked at Keith, who was clearly uncomfortable in a gay bar. *What the hell am I doing?* He was uncomfortable with the whole evening, if truth be told. He had never signed up to be a boyfriend and going to a wine-tasting was the remit of a boyfriend, not a casual lover. Susan had pretty much tricked him into it and he hadn't been happy. Neither had she. And it was impossible without serious therapy to even attempt to contemplate why she had done such a thing. Keith had left the bar after one drink.

Aidan had been with some of his friends from the scene. Susan knew one or two but they were on a buzz and didn't have too much time to spend talking to a middle-aged woman with a sad face. Aidan tried to cheer her up with a Sambuca and it was then that she had hailed a taxi back to Harri's.

Alone on the pull-out bed in Harri's sitting room, Susan had tried to make sense of her new life.

Beth wouldn't take her calls. Her husband might as well have relocated to the moon and the married man she was having casual sex with had no interest in leaving his wife or being her boyfriend. She was free but Keith was still married. And even if he wasn't, would she really want him in her life? *He's holding me back.* It was at that moment that Susan Shannon made a pledge to herself that she would not see her married builder friend again. And not because of guilt about the woman whose husband she was shagging, and not because her friends were silently judging her even if they pretended they weren't, and not because she was afraid that her daughter would find out. And just because she wasn't considering a stranger's marriage didn't make her a bad person – a little selfish maybe, but not bad. Susan decided that she was a good person who had just walked out of a dead marriage because she had wanted more, and the married builder Keith was never going to be more.

She lay awake for a long time that night reliving her marriage, the good as well as the bad, remembering her daughter's milestones. She cried and even laughed a little as she said goodbye to her old life and in her mind she let go.

Today was a new day, a new beginning for both Susan and her business partner, Harri. To celebrate she would shop until there was nothing left in Wicklow to buy. *Jesus, I'd love to get my hands on a decent spiral mixer or a hand-painted wooden spoon.*

Harri made her way slowly through the graveyard, as she had no idea where to start. It was only natural to begin at the beginning. *I'm never going to be that lucky.* She was on her knees trying to make out a name and cursing herself for not bringing her glasses when a man passed and she thought about asking him but then reconsidered. It would be rude to assume that everyone in Wicklow knew everyone else, dead or alive, and so she allowed him to pass without a word while coveting his takeaway coffee. *I'm gasping.* She managed to cut herself on a bramble and bruised her knee when she tripped over a stray pot. *This is stupid. I'm never going to find her.* There was an office at the entrance but it was closed and there was no such thing as a map of plots. Harri was tired and emotional and sick of hurting herself. *If I bang into one more bloody gravestone!* But still she walked on, reading each one she passed.

Brendan made himself comfortable on the grass. 'Hi there, Trouble!' he said, looking at Liv's name printed in black. 'Thirty years and I swear it seems like yesterday. I wish you'd written that book. I would have loved to read it. I bet you it would have been a bestseller. It's all about time – you were just out of it, Trouble, and none of us saw it coming. I promise I would have saved you if I could have. But you know that. I had a fling in San Francisco, you'll be delighted to hear. He was forty, so I suppose you could say I'm a cradle-snatcher. He works in design. We didn't do much talking about design, though. You would have liked him. He's the kind of gay man you always wanted me to be. Self-assured, proud and happy. And I am. I'm a different man from the one you knew back then, a lifetime ago. I think you'd be happy with the way I turned out – at least, I hope so. I do miss you, Trouble.'

He was silent, sipping his coffee, when he saw a woman

making her way from gravestone to gravestone. As she got closer she became more familiar. Her hair, her bone structure, her mouth and particularly the look that crossed her face when her ankle gave way on gravel. Brendan stood up. 'You're looking for Liv,' he said.

She stopped dead in front of him. She nodded.

'She's here,' he said.

She made her way over to where he was standing, looked at the name on the stone and the date.

'Happy birthday, Harri,' he said.

'Thank you,' she whispered.

'My name is Brendan McCabe.'

'The doctor,' she managed.

'Yes.'

'I'm not ready for this,' she said, and her legs went from under her.

2 September 1975 – Tuesday

Today I said goodbye to Matthew. I cried until I felt so sick that all I could do was lie in my bed. He cried too. Henry took us to the station because his stupid dad has gone to France. Matthew had enough cases to suggest he'd be gone for ever. I can't stand it. The summer is over and he is gone. Everything in me is aching from my head to my toes and inside I'm screaming. Henry waited for a while and then he said his goodbyes and ruffled Matthew's hair and told him he'd miss him and promised to take good care of Nero. I was already crying because Henry was saying all the things that Matthew's dad should have been there to say and then Henry was gone and we were alone and I was still crying and he was trying to be strong.

On Saturday night Matthew and his dad had the biggest fight. I was there. It started because Matthew asked if he could come home every weekend. Loads of the other boys in his school get to go home every weekend, but his dad said no. Matthew argued with him and said it wasn't as if his dad would notice whether or not he was home. His dad lost it and the things he said were so hurtful and they weren't true either.

Matthew could be anything he wanted to be. He isn't a fool or a waste of time. He could never be a disappointment. The hurt in Matthew's eyes when his dad said those things will stay with me for ever, and later, when he cried, it was like being knifed. I mean it. It felt like a knife slicing through my insides. That has never happened before and I really, really hope it doesn't happen again because it is highly unpleasant. When his dad said he was glad Matthew's mother was dead so she didn't have to see what a loser her son was, Matthew was going to punch him. He raised his arm and made a run at his dad and I held him back by his jumper. I don't know why. It was instinct. Mathew shouted at me afterwards. He said I shouldn't have interfered. He was right. I should have let him punch his dad. I feel really bad about that. I need to learn to mind my own business. Matthew was angry with me for a while and it hurt me almost as much as seeing him cry.

Matthew's dad is so mean. You can see it in his eyes. He's cold through and through. He always seems angry and he likes to hurt people. He was enjoying himself. I think he's a very sad man and I wonder how Matthew and I got so unlucky. If his mam and my dad had lived, our lives could have been so much better.

The train pulled in and nearly took my legs from under me. People were boarding and it seemed like for ever we were standing there looking at each other, desperate. He's off to a cold boarding-school where he doesn't talk to anyone from one week to the next and I'm back in my room with the door locked and eleven long months ahead until we leave here for ever. Sometimes life is too hard. Today I cried so loudly that I actually heard myself as though I was standing outside my own body and witness to its breakdown. I'm worried for him. I'm worried he won't make it another year now he knows what it's like to be loved and to have friends.

Last night Sheila, Dave, Matthew and I went to Keoghs' farm. It was Dave's idea. He wanted to send Matthew off in style. As usual Sheila and Dave started the night with an argument. She maintained that her granny always warned her never to cross the glen after dark. As Keoghs' farm was past the glen, and Dave thought Sheila's granny was full of shit, he stormed off, leaving Matthew, Sheila and me stand-ing there. Eventually he came back and talked Sheila around, especially as he'd gone to a good deal of trouble to leave a picnic basket with snacks and beer at the farm. I'd never been to Keoghs' farm before and I have to admit I wasn't that keen on spending my last night with Matthew by a haunted farmhouse. I mean, what if Sheila's granny was right?

Anyway we went up there and it really did feel weird. The fact that the old farmhouse is big, imposing and derelict doesn't help and there is an eerie vibe to the place, but the weirdest thing is the dead orchard. Every tree is standing there stone dead. It's like something from a film. Dave and Matthew went inside but there was no way I was going in there and Sheila was white in the face and so nervous she kept running behind a dead tree to pee. She says nervous bladders run in the family on her mother's side. We had the picnic in the dead orchard. Dave had gone to a lot of trouble with snacks and beer and cheese sandwiches he had made himself. He even had candles and a flashlight and one of his dad's golf clubs in case of a spiritual encounter. I don't know what he thought a golf club would do in the face of a rest-less spirit but, to be fair, he said he wasn't sure himself. Matthew said he'd read somewhere that you just tell a ghost you'll pray for it and it'll vanish. I really hoped he was right because my hair was standing on end.

Nothing happened. There was not a ghost to be seen and it was nice. We told ghost stories, drank beers and talked about the good times we'd had at the carnival, by the castle and on the strand. Dave apologized to Matthew for thinking he was a stuck-up posh git when he'd first met him, and Matthew took it well. When we had left them, Matthew said it was the first time in his life he'd had friends.

Poor Matthew, he breaks my heart. He's in that place now and he's alone. I wonder if I close my eyes and concentrate really hard can I communicate with him?

No.

Shit.

HE's home. I can hear him shouting. He's drunk and Mam is crying.

I wish I had Dave's golf club.

He's gone now. When I got into the kitchen she was cowering by the sink and he was standing over her, getting ready to pounce. He's lucky his stupid gap-toothed friend called because if he hadn't he would have got a dinner plate over his head. I'm so tired of this. I miss Matthew. Matthew, please come home.

19. One day at a time

Aidan was early. Aidan was always early. He had brought a newspaper and was reading an article on conservation in the Appalachians while munching a plain chicken sandwich. He was having a beer when Andrew appeared. He sat in the comfortable chair opposite and began by shaking Aidan's hand and thanking him for turning up. Within seconds the waitress was beside them. She took Andrew's order.

'So,' Aidan said.

'So,' Andrew repeated.

'Why am I here?' Aidan asked. After all, he was Susan's friend, not Andrew's. They were polite to one another and had spent some time together at various events but they didn't know one another, not really.

'I have a problem,' Andrew heard himself say.

The waitress returned with Andrew's drink and both men fell silent.

When she was gone Andrew continued, 'You're probably wondering why I'm talking to you.' He laughed. 'It's because I don't know who else to talk to.'

Aidan was getting nervous. *What the hell . . .*

'Three years ago I started having problems. I ignored them. They didn't go away. Two years ago the problem got worse. I kept ignoring it, and while I was busy pretending nothing was wrong, my wife had an affair.'

'What are you trying to tell me?' Aidan asked.

'I can't have sex,' Andrew said, his head lowered. 'There, it only took three years to admit it.'

'Why are you telling me?'

'I don't know. Because I couldn't tell anyone else and you're so open and free and –'

'And gay.'

'And gay.'

'Being gay doesn't make me an expert on dicks, you know.'

'I know. I just thought maybe you'd come across it or heard something about the problem,' Andrew said, rubbing his face. 'Oh, I don't know, I thought maybe gay men talk about things.'

'You've tried Viagra?'

'Makes me dizzy – and those other brands too. Nothing works.'

'There's a clinic in James's Street. I'll come with you.'

'I'd really appreciate that.'

'Andrew?'

'What?'

'How could you not tell her?'

Andrew shook his head. 'I suppose I'll have the rest of my life to work that one out,' he said sadly.

'She thought you didn't want her.'

'I know.'

'It nearly destroyed her.'

'I'm sorry.'

'Jesus, Andrew, people like you belong to another time.'

Andrew and Aidan separated on Grafton Street.

Andrew promised he'd call Aidan with the details of his appointment. Aidan had tried to talk him into speaking to his wife but Andrew was adamant that he didn't want her involved.

'Why?'

'Because.'

'Because what?'

'Because she's gone, Aidan.'

'Only because you let her go.'

'I don't want her pity.'

'Oh, balls, Andrew. She's your wife.'

'Yeah. Tell that to the builder.'

A little later Aidan was in Jurassic Park having a drink when he spotted Lorcan, the twenty-four-year-old he'd slept with two nights before. *Balls*. The whole point of going into Jurassic Park was that all those under the age of thirty stayed on the other side of the George, the youthful fun side where every day is Mardi Gras and age is just a number, not indelibly marked on your face.

'I hoped I'd find you here,' Lorcan said, sitting beside him.

'There should be an over-thirties age limit in this bar,' Aidan said, keeping his eyes fixed forward.

'I thought you were going to stop playing hard to get after the other night.'

'I was drunk when I said those things. You're twenty-four and I'm in a relationship.'

'So?'

'So don't start.'

'You like me.'

'I really don't.'

'You do – that's why you can't look at me. It's too painful.'

Aidan laughed.

'I really like you,' Lorcan said, with his head tilted.

'I'm in a relationship.'

'You're not happy.'

'That's none of your business.'

'Aidan, every time you break up with him, you come to me. Every time you fight with him, you come to me. Every time he does something you don't agree with, you come to me. We like the same things, we laugh together, and we're attracted to one another. I'm patient but not infinitely so.'

'I shouldn't have knocked on your door the other night,' Aidan said. 'It's not fair on you.'

'He's never going to get you the way I do,' Lorcan said.

Aidan laughed. 'You don't really know me.'

'I know you better than he does.' Lorcan left Aidan on that note.

Why is it so easy to have the answers for everyone else's relationship and yet be completely and utterly useless about your own?

Melissa was already on the computer when Gerry answered the door to Aidan.

'Jesus, it's coming down out there,' he pointed out.

'Really? I hadn't noticed,' Aidan replied drily, while he dripped on the mat.

'Yeah, yeah. Get in.' Gerry grabbed a towel from the bathroom under the stairs and handed it to Aidan, who wiped his face and patted his hair dry. Gerry took his coat and draped it on the radiator.

'Coffee?'

'I'd love one. Where are the kids?'

'Blissfully in bed.'

Aidan checked his watch. It was getting on for eight thirty. 'So where is she?'

'Upstairs on the computer. She's been printing stuff off since you called. What's going on?'

'Oh, nothing.'

'Right.' Gerry knew better than to interfere – besides, a match was starting. He handed Aidan the coffee. 'You know where to go.'

Melissa was staring at the screen when he went into her makeshift office.

'Well?'

'Well, it could be anything. Listen to this. "Fifty-two per cent of males between the ages of forty and seventy have reported some degree of impotence." Can you believe that?'

'I'd rather not.'

'"Age is one factor in ED" – that's short for erectile dysfunction. "The majority of men with it do not seek or receive adequate advice or treatment."' She was nodding. 'Remind you of anyone we know? Still can't believe it. What a moron. If my Gerry hid something like that from me I'd murder him.'

'There are days that if your Gerry buttered his bread

with the wrong knife you'd murder him. He's still here by the grace of God, the poor bastard.'

'Ha, ha, you should think about going on the road with that kind of material,' she said, without looking away from the screen.

Aidan smiled. She was in her element, glasses at the tip of her nose, clicking away, accessing the fountain of information, regurgitating facts and figures. Although Aidan had promised Andrew he wouldn't say a word about his problem to Susan, he had not made such a promise about mentioning it to anyone else and so, in the wake of his encounter with Lorcan, he had called her from Jurassic Park. Andrew had asked him for his help so he would give it and to do that he had to know a little bit about what he was dealing with. As his laptop had died on him three months previously it was only natural that he should call upon his friend the Googaholic.

'"Psychological reasons account for one third of cases." Do you think it's psychological?'

'I'm not a doctor.'

'Okay. "Physical causes of ED. Erection occurs in response to signals to the brain, erectile tissue, cylinders, sponge-like", blah, blah, blah. "Fibres contract, the sponge is wrung out."'

'Jesus, Melissa.'

'I'm only reading what's there. Okay, where was I? Oh, "draining veins open up".'

'Okay, that's it. Read it in your head.'

They sat in silence, Aidan studying a poster about a stressed housewife on the wall in front of him and

Melissa reading the ins and outs of a flaccid versus hard penis.

'Here we go. "Possible physical causes of ED. Diabetes." He doesn't have that. "High blood pressure." He could have that.'

'Jesus, I have that,' Aidan said. 'It's not outrageously high but at my last check-up my doctor said it was a little high.' He was slightly pale.

'It has to do with hardening of the arteries.'

'Oh, God.'

'Calm down. You're fine. Oh, and smoking.'

'He doesn't smoke.'

'Not now but he did for about twenty years.'

'Oh, God, I smoked.' Aidan was beginning to feel very sorry he'd sought Melissa's Googling expertise. *Sometimes ignorance is bliss.*

'Multiple sclerosis. No. Parkinson's disease. No. Prostate surgery. No. Spinal injury?'

'I think we'd have noticed.'

'Yeah. Okay, how about some cures?' she said, click-clicking.

'Yes, please.' Aidan was still suffering slight shock. *A little high. What does a little high mean? How high does it have to be before your dick stops working?*

'Drugs. He's tried them. They don't work. Okay. "A mechanical vacuum device causes an erection by creating a partial vacuum, which draws blood into the penis."' She looked from the screen to Aidan. 'Not ideal, is it?'

'Not really, no.'

'Oh, look, here's a diagram. Jesus!'

286

'I don't want to see it! I don't want to see it!' Aidan put his hands over his eyes. It was at that point that Gerry walked in.

'What the hell is that?'

'A penis pump.'

'Sorry I asked!' He backed out, closing the door behind him.

'It's not for me!' Aidan shouted after him.

'Oh!' Melissa said, making a face.

'What?' Aidan wasn't sure he wanted to know.

'"Many men achieve stronger erections by injecting drugs into the penis."'

'Oh, no. No. No.'

'Okay, moving on. "Surgery can implant a device, reconstruct arteries or block off veins that allow blood to leak from the penis."'

'Poor Andrew!' Aidan said. 'Poor, poor Andrew.'

Aidan left Melissa's with a heavy heart.

George answered the door in an apron.

'I didn't expect dinner,' Harri said.

'I was cooking anyway.'

'Do you always eat after nine?'

'If I did, I wouldn't be the perfect male specimen you see before you,' he said, with smile.

'Where's Aidan?'

'Off radar.'

'Oh.'

She sat down at the kitchen table and it was only then that she remembered she'd hardly eaten all day – she'd been so wound up at lunchtime that the food had stuck in her throat.. He dished up chilli and opened a bottle of wine – something he said would complement it, but Harri was more interested in water: her brother was known for his fire-alarm chilli.

'Well?'

'I met the doctor,' she said. 'He was there at her grave.'

'The doctor who found you,' he clarified.

'Yeah.'

'Odd.'

'Bloody odd. He knew me.'

'What?'

'He knew me. He knew I was looking for her and he called me by my name.'

'Well, maybe Dad told him what he was calling you.'

'But why would he remember and what was he doing there and why was he involved in the whole thing in the first place?'

'I don't know. Didn't you ask him?'

'I couldn't. I froze. Actually, I thought I was going to have another stupid panic attack but he made me breathe with my head between my legs.' She shook her head. 'My head was between my legs.'

'I think that's the least of your worries. What did he say?'

'Not much. As soon as I could breathe I ran. He called after me but I just wasn't ready. I'd thought, I'll go to Wicklow. I'll look at a gravestone. How hard is that? I didn't expect to have to deal with the living. The living have no business in graveyards.' George nodded.

'He called out that his name was McCabe and he was in the phone book and he'd love to see me again.'

'You want me to come with you?'

'I didn't say I was going.'

'You will.'

'You have a new business to run.'

'So we'll go next Sunday.'

'Are you sure?'

'Positive.'

'Okay, but don't tell Mum or Dad.'

'I promise.'

After that they ate the chilli, and George talked about his business and the write-up the shop had received in the *Independent*. He spoke about Aidan and his inability to reach him. 'He just needs a few days to cool off. It'll be fine.' He spoke about their parents. 'I just can't seem to get past it. I don't know why.'

Harri talked about her concern for Susan. She had hoped that getting away from Andrew would strengthen her, but she seemed to be falling apart. 'She cried herself to sleep last night.'

'It's early days.'

'I know.'

'What about you?'

'Oh, I often cry myself to sleep.' She grinned, but she was telling the truth. *I wonder what James would make of Brendan McCabe.*

Susan worked late. Her day had begun badly and was getting worse by the second. Delay after delay had occurred, leaving her in the middle of a room without silk wallpaper on one side, an unfinished kitchen, because the carpenter had walked out in a huff when the delivery men brought some wrong units, and four extra chairs that nobody would take responsibility for. She had called Aidan, hoping he'd help out with the wallpaper crisis, but he was odd on the phone, saying he had important business to attend to, business he couldn't discuss. That was unusual for Aidan because Aidan would talk about anything. He had hung up before she could push him. *If you want something done, Susan, do it yourself.*

She finished papering at ten and spent another hour removing the boxing around the kitchen cabinets so that they would be ready to install. She left a message with the shop that if their delivery man wasn't there to collect the chairs by ten a.m. she'd put a hold on her client's credit card and burn them. She made it back to Harri's for midnight.

Harri was drinking cocoa and watching another effing episode of *CSI*.

'Oh, Harri!'

'Sorry. Couldn't sleep.'

'I know the feeling,' Susan said, slumping on the sofa.

'Cocoa?'

'No, thanks.'

'Why didn't you call me?'

'Ah, it was fine. I got the job done. How did you know?'

'Aidan rang. He said you needed help but when I called you'd turned your phone off.'

'He was acting weird.'

'He's avoiding George.'

'How did your job in Swords go?' Susan asked.

'Good. He's a nice guy. He knows what he wants. He has good taste and a big budget.'

'That's what I like to hear.' She smiled. 'A few more clients like him and I'll be out of your hair.'

'I like having you here,' Harri admitted.

'Thank you.' Susan's eyes welled.

'Have you heard from Beth?'

'No.'

'She'll come around.'

'I hope so.' Susan wiped away a tear. 'I really hope so.'

Harri went to bed soon afterwards, leaving Susan to her pull-out bed. She made a promise to herself to take her mum out to lunch. She couldn't imagine causing her the pain she saw in her friend's eyes.

26 September 1975 – Friday

Matthew's not coming home. Henry said he got in a fight with some other boy and had all his privileges taken away. Henry said I shouldn't cry, that he's fine, but I know he's not. Matthew's not a fighter, he didn't start it. It's not fair. His stupid dad could have told them he wanted his son home but he didn't. I hate him. Henry said Nero is missing him too. Dr B has been taking him out. Sometimes I ride with him on Betsy but Betsy's seemed tired lately. I know how she feels. I tried to call him on the phone down town but they wouldn't let me talk to him. It's like he's in jail. School isn't supposed to be jail. Everything is wrong. I can't sleep. I've had a headache for the past three days.

I forgot to lock my door last week. I never forget but somehow I did. I woke up and HE was on top of me with his hand over my face. I tried to scream but nothing would come out. It was like I was rendered dumb. I could hear myself screaming in my head but there was no sound. He was grabbing at me and trying to part my legs but I managed to cross them and I held them together, vice-like. He'd have had to break them. His hand slipped and I bit him as hard as I could and when he yelped my mother called out from her room asking who was there. I could hear her shuffling. So he slapped me and got off me and I heard the door close behind him. He'd taken the padlock that Matthew had installed so I asked Dr B for a loan because I was short of money, being back at school, paying for lunches and having to buy a stupid book I'd lost. I need to make the money last that I got working, and besides that, I wanted him to ask me what the money was for. I wanted to tell him. And he did ask and I did tell and he wouldn't let me go home. He told me I was to stay with him in the gate lodge that night and that he would sort something out. He called Father Ryan and he came down just as Dr B was making us some tea. They went into the other room and I couldn't hear what they were saying.

Afterwards Father Ryan said my allegation was very serious and asked me if I was aware that God was always watching. I told him if He was, and as Father Ryan had a direct line, he could just ask Him what happened. I was being cheeky but he didn't respond. Instead he just nodded and said he would deal with it. He agreed it was best for me to stay in Dr B's spare room that night but only if Minnie Jones his housekeeper stayed too. Minnie arrived after eight with a face on her. She had an early night and Dr B and I stayed up talking. He said I wouldn't have to go back if I didn't want to. I told him I had to go back. My mam needed to be taken care of. He said Father Ryan would talk sense into HIM and I laughed. Dr B and poor Father Ryan, they really think you can talk sense into someone like HIM! There's no talking to someone like HIM. Dr B should just have given me the money for the new lock in the first place.

Father Ryan did talk to him and HE denied it and Father Ryan got a punch in the face for his trouble. HE said I was a lying little whore when I eventually did go home. Mam didn't even seem to know what was going on. She was acting like it was just another stupid argument. Dr B called and HE threatened him but Dr B didn't back down. He said he'd be watching and if he even suspected anything he'd call the guards, and if the guards did nothing he'd call some friends who didn't care about the Church or the law and would smash his face in as soon as look at him. He was frightened. I could see it. He looked at me as though I was making everything up and he spat on me after Dr B had left.

Mam was in bed sleeping, but really I think she was just pretending to be asleep. She can't handle any of this stuff. She's not able for it. Dr B has bought me a new padlock and I'll never forget to lock my door again.

I've been writing to Matthew and he's been writing to me. I keep the letters folded in my diary and read and reread them and when I close my eyes I can hear his voice. In his last letter he was so excited about coming home. And now he can't. He must be devastated. I wish I could see him. Ten months to go. Only ten months to go.

19 September

Liv,

Only one week to go. I can't wait. I've been counting down the hours and the days and the minutes and the seconds and, well, you get the point. I miss you. I miss you. I miss you so much it's worse than a kick to the balls. When I get home let's go riding through the woods and we can have a picnic by the waterfall while the weather's still good. Next month will be too cold. How's school? How's Sheila and Dave? Tell them I said hi. I'm studying and keeping to myself and living for the weekend. I've no news, never do, but I love you.

Love, Matt

PS Liv, I used to be lonely but I'm not any more.

20. Men will be men

Dinner started off well. The lamb was delicious and fell off the bone. Matt had brought a decent wine, one of his old friend's favourites. Brendan didn't broach the subject of his chance encounter until the dinner was long over and they were playing poker.

'Dealer shuffles,' Brendan said, handing the cards to Matt. 'How was Clara?'

'Good,' he said, shuffling. 'She's thinking of relocating to the UK.' He dealt five cards each.

Brendan picked up his hand and viewed it before resting it on the table. 'That's come from nowhere.'

'Not really,' Matt said, putting his own cards face down. 'She's been talking about it for a while.'

'You didn't say anything.'

'Nothing to say. What's your bet?'

'One euro.'

'Feeling rich!' Matt laughed, tossed in his own coin. 'How many cards?'

'Two.'

'Dealer takes three.'

'Will you miss her?'

'I don't know. I'll tell you when she's gone.' He took back Brendan's discarded cards.

'I visited Liv yesterday.'

'Good. Are you betting?'

'Another euro.'

'I'll see you.'

'I met Harri there.'

Matt stopped as though something inside him had powered down. He became very still.

Brendan put his cards down. The game was over. He got up, lifted a bottle of brandy from the shelf and wiped two glasses. He placed them in front of his paralysed friend and poured. Brendan drank but Matt didn't move.

'She looked so like her,' Brendan said. 'Not as tall but her face was so familiar.'

Matt remained silent.

'She got a fright – she didn't expect to meet anyone but she knew who I was, Matt. She asked me if I was the doctor.'

Tears leaked from Matt's eyes.

Brendan bowed his head.

'Did she talk to you?'

'Not really. She needed help controlling her breathing and once she recovered she ran, but I called after her. I said I was in the phone book and told her to call. I hope she heard me.'

'She was due to get married last month.'

'What?'

'She didn't make it to the altar. It was the second attempt. Poor guy, James something.'

'How do you know all this?'

'I've been keeping tabs her on since I returned from the States fifteen years ago.'

'You never said.'

'Since that night by the *Eliana*, when I held her, a part of me never let go.' He shrugged. 'How could I? She was all I had left of Liv. I used to wait every year. I'd think, She'll come and find me. I was beginning to think it wouldn't happen. Do you think it will?'

'I don't know,' Brendan said sadly. 'When she saw me she said she wasn't ready.'

'I've waited thirty years. I suppose I can wait a while longer.'

He left his brandy untouched. He went home soon after.

Brendan nursed a second brandy on his sofa. All this time Matthew had never spoken about the child he had given up. Brendan had had no idea he had been following the events in her life.

The appointment had been for half past one. Aidan finished working around twelve, got home in time for a shave, a wash and a change. There were three messages on his machine from George and four missed calls. *I can't deal with you right now.* He met Andrew in the hospital car park. He had decided against making any comment about Melissa's research. As his mother always said, if you've nothing positive to say, say nothing at all. Andrew was shaking visibly.

'Are you all right?'

'Grand.'

'You're shaking.'

'I know.'

Aidan wanted to say it wouldn't be that bad but, judging by what he'd read, it might well be – and maybe Andrew had carried out some research of his own.

'You'll be fine,' he said, when they were sitting, ironically and unwittingly, on the same chairs Harri and Andrew's daughter Beth had been sitting on weeks earlier.

'What do I say?' Andrew gasped.

'"I can't get it up,"' Aidan whispered.

'Right. I feel sick.'

'Hospitals have that effect on people – it's perfectly normal,' Aidan said, patting his arm.

'I don't think I can do it,' Andrew said, standing up.

Aidan pulled him back into his seat. 'Don't be stupid. You can and you will.'

They didn't speak after that. Instead they waited to hear a nurse call his name. If someone had asked Andrew what had eventually driven him to seek help he wouldn't have been able to answer, at least not immediately, but if he thought about it long and hard he would have said he had nothing left to lose. When his name was called, and after a little push from Aidan, he was on his feet and in the doctor's office, listening to the door close behind him.

Aidan waited five minutes, ten minutes, fifteen minutes, twenty minutes, half an hour. *Jesus, how long does this take?* After an hour Andrew appeared but he was on a gurney, his shirt was open and there were patches on his chest.

'Andrew?' Aidan leaped to his feet and joined the hospital staff racing with the gurney.

'Please give us room, sir,' one nurse said.

'What's going on?'

'Your friend is having a heart attack.'
Oh, sweet Jesus!

George was in the cellar doing a stock-take when his phone rang.

'I thought you'd left the country!' he said.

'Andrew's having a heart attack.'

'*What?*'

'Andrew Shannon is having a heart attack as we speak.'

'How do you know?'

'I'm in the hospital with him. He's been having a problem with his dick. I said I'd go with him, hold his hand or whatever. He went into the office and he was fine. He came out of the office on his back having a heart attack.'

'Christ! Why did he ask you?'

'I don't know, George. I hardly think that's what we should be focusing on.'

'Calm down, Aidan.'

'You'll have to tell Susan.'

'Why me?'

'Because I can't do everything. I have to go. We're in James's Street.' He hung up, leaving George dumbfounded.

'Hey, George!' Susan said, into her mobile phone while she was perched precariously on the second-highest step of a ladder.

'Hey, Susan!' George said, a little too airily.

'Are you okay?'

'Are you near a chair?'

'I'm on a ladder. What's up?'

'Get off the ladder.'

'What's going on?'

'Are you off the ladder?'

'George?'

'Just get off the ladder.'

She got off the ladder. 'I'm off the ladder. Are you happy?'

'Andrew's had a heart attack.'

Silence.

'Susan?'

'Yes.'

'He's in James's Street. Aidan's with him.'

'Is he all right?'

'I don't know the details.'

'Did you say Aidan's with him?'

'Yes.'

'What's Aidan doing with him?'

'Long story. I think you should go to the hospital and maybe call Beth.'

'She won't answer me. I'll get Harri to pick her up from work.'

'Okay. Good. Let me know if you need anything.'

'Yeah, okay.' She hung up in a daze. *I should go to James's Street. How do I get there from here? I should just go. I'll remember the way in the car.*

Andrew had had many a nightmare in his day but this one was particularly nasty. He had dreamed he was having his dick examined when an almighty pain took hold of him and it felt like nothing on earth. He grabbed his left arm and chest and slumped, and the doctor whose hand was wrapped around his dick said something and called for someone and suddenly he was on a gurney with Aidan racing behind it.

He woke up to discover it wasn't a dream. That was a kick he could have done without. He was alone. *Where's Aidan? Oh, God, somebody find Aidan. He can't tell anyone I'm here.*

Aidan was outside getting some air and drinking coffee, which was surprisingly good, from a real coffee shop in the hospital concourse, which was more like a shopping mall than part of a hospital. *Shops, restaurants, a feckin' juice bar. Since when have you been able to eat and drink healthily in a hospital?* He held his phone close to his ear and spoke loudly to combat the level of noise and bustle around him.

Harri was in the car and on the way to pick up Beth from the boutique she was working in. She had him on speaker. 'I'm going through the park so if we get cut off I'll call you back.'

'Okay,' he said. 'What are you going to say to Beth?'

'I'm going to tell her the truth.'

'You can't.'

'Why not?'

'Because you can't tell her that her dad had a heart attack while having his dick inspected.'

'She's not a child and I've no intention of saying that. I'll just say he was in the hospital having a check-up when

301

he had a heart attack, which is exactly what happened without the graphics.'

'Fine. I wonder when it would be appropriate for me to leave?'

'Is Susan there yet?'

'No.'

'When she gets there.'

Aidan sighed. 'Right. I'd better go back.'

'Okay. I'll see you if you're still there.'

Aidan hung up and walked back to where Andrew was lying awake, alert and deeply embarrassed. Aidan steadied himself outside his friend's husband's cubicle. He pulled back the curtain with a smile plastered on his face.

'Well, Andrew Shannon, you certainly know how to give a man a scare.'

'You called Susan, didn't you?' Andrew was clammy, weak, nauseous, tired, with all kinds of liquids flowing through his veins and the memory of torturous pain still fresh in his mind.

'No,' Aidan said.

'Thank you,' Andrew said, his hands clasped in simulated prayer.

This exposed the two cannulas, one sticking out of each hand, that allowed the administration of the required intravenous fluids, making Aidan feel a little light-headed. He fixed his gaze on a white locker with a missing handle.

'I called George,' Aidan told the locker. 'George called Susan.'

Andrew sighed.

Aidan was on a roll. 'I also called Harri, who is collecting Beth from work and bringing her here.'

Andrew was silent for approximately seventy-five seconds while he absorbed this information. If he wasn't knocking on Heaven's door he could have got up and out of the bed, marched Aidan to the nearest window and thrown him out of it. *When I get out of here, you'd better run.*

After those seventy-five seconds, Aidan explained to Andrew that although it was highly likely that his reason for being in the hospital would come to light, relatively speaking, his dick was the least of his problems. Aidan had not come to this conclusion quickly. He had spent the previous night awake and worried for the health and safety of his own dick. *I wonder if I asked, would someone here check my blood pressure?* But Aidan was sure, having feared he was watching his friend's husband breathe his last, that when it came to a dick and a heart, the heart wins. While he had been contemplating life and death on a hard hospital chair, imbibing a non-fat latte, he had surmised that the heart-beating-dick theory was an analogy appropriate to the state of Andrew's marriage. This epiphany was one he could not but share with his weary new friend, and whether it was Aidan's utter belief in his own reasoning or the fact that Andrew's heart had momentarily failed or just the drugs, it made sense to Andrew.

Aidan sat back in his chair, content. *My work here is done. Susan, hurry the fuck up.*

Susan drove at forty kilometres per hour the entire way to the hospital. She couldn't manage to push on the pedal.

Instead her foot rested, almost hovered. She didn't actively drive into the James's Street car park; the car seemed to take her there. So many questions clouded her mind. She parked, and when she took her hands off the steering-wheel, she saw that she was shaking. She had a little cry before she got out and was grateful for the rain that came from nowhere and soaked her. Others ran with news-papers or handbags over their heads, but she couldn't break into a jog, never mind a run. She had come off a ladder and her world had switched into slow motion.

She stuttered at the desk when she asked the woman for directions to Accident and Emergency. There, she asked a nurse, stumbling over 'wife' as opposed to stutter-ing 'Andrew' but the effect was the same in that it made her want to bawl.

Like Aidan before her, she spent a short time collecting herself outside the cubicle that held the heart patient who used to be her husband.

When Andrew saw her it occurred to him that she looked worse than he did. *She still cares after everything.* He noticed the shake in her hand despite her attempt at con-cealing it behind an oversized handbag. *What is it with women and large bags?*

She was attempting to smile but that annoying dry-mouth syndrome had returned, ensuring her lip stuck to her gum.

Aidan stood up and guided her to the chair he'd been sitting on. She sat without a word. He leaned in. 'Would you like some coffee?' he asked, speaking slowly and enun-ciating each word as if he was speaking to a deaf mute. 'I can get you some coffee. There is a lovely coffee shop. Seriously, it tastes great.'

'I'm fine,' she said, and even through the haze she could sense her friend had lost it a little.

'I'm going to get a juice. Do you want a juice?'

'No.'

'Right.'

'Aidan?' she asked.

'Yeah?'

'What are you doing here?'

Aidan looked at Andrew, who shook his head and sighed. Aidan raised his hand in farewell and left them.

Harri entered the shop and looked around. She couldn't see Beth anywhere. She walked up to the counter and was annoyed when the woman fixing the till roll pretended not to notice her. 'I'm looking for Beth Shannon.'

'She's on a break,' the woman said, without removing her gaze from the till.

'Do you know where she's taking her break?' Harri asked, in a tone that suggested she was ready to kung-fu fight.

'No,' the woman responded, in an equally frosty tone.

'You must have some idea.'

'Well, I don't own the girl and I left my divining stick at home so you're out of luck.'

'Her dad's just had a heart attack.'

The woman's eyes met Harri's now and it was instantly apparent that she was sorry she'd been such a bitch. 'She's in Burger King.'

'Thank you,' Harri said, and left.

Burger King was jammed and Beth was still queuing when Harri found her.

On the trip to the car Harri explained what had happened. The information stopped Beth in her tracks so Harri gently guided her into the car.

'Buckle up,' Harri said, as she started the car. 'Everything will be fine.' She was quite pleased that she wasn't freaking out, driving into walls and forgetting her own name. *I don't know what people are talking about. I'm great in a crisis.*

She accelerated and the car felt spongy.

'Harri.'

'Yeah.'

'It might work better if you take off the handbrake.'

'Right. Will do.'

Beth went from shock to anger in record speed. She decided that her father's heart attack was her mother's fault. 'I hate her. I hope she burns.'

'Beth!' Harri warned.

'She could have killed him!' Beth pouted.

'Oh, Beth, seriously, no, don't do that.'

'Do what?'

'Don't make this about blame.'

'Why not?'

'Because you don't know what you're talking about.'

'I know she had an affair and broke his heart, today being the physical manifestation of same.'

Today being the physical manifestation of same! Who talks like that?

'Beth, you do not know the full story of your parents' break-up.'

'So tell me.'

'Do you really want to know everything?'

'I have a right to know.'

'Really?'

'It's my family too.'

'Okay. Fine. Do me a favour. Close your eyes.'

Beth sighed loudly before doing as she was told.

'Now, picture your parents having sex. Better still picture your mother on her knees.'

Beth's eyes and mouth shot open at the same time. 'Harri, what is wrong with you?' she almost shouted.

'So, do you want to know everything now?' Harri asked.

'*Noooo!*' Beth shouted.

'I believe I've made my point.'

Beth was silent.

'Your parents are people. People are fallible. Your parents have their problems and you wading in with only half of the information will not help anyone. You judged your dad and gave him a hard time but you didn't know the whole story. So now I'm asking you to learn from that, to realize that you don't know the full story and you shouldn't judge. Stop judging and forgive her. Forgive them both.'

'Have you stopped judging your parents? Have you forgiven them?' Beth asked.

Harri bit her lip. She recalled the stilted lunch she had shared with her mother and her last monosyllabic conversation with her dad. 'No.'

'Well, then!'

'Look, Beth, adults are really good at giving other people advice. Unfortunately we're not so good at taking either our own or anybody else's, which begs the question as to why, after millennia, we bother giving advice at all. The thing is, we all make mistakes and we know we're making mistakes because we're looking at the people around us making the same mistakes. The human race has an extraordinary capacity for stupidity. But, bearing that in mind, I'm asking you to listen to my advice and take it. Break the cycle, Beth.'

Beth sat back in her chair. *An extraordinary capacity for stupidity! Who talks like that?* 'You're really weird, you know that?'

'I wasn't aware of that, no, but I'm listening and I'm taking what you've said on board.' Harri turned into the hospital grounds.

Beth grinned. 'Okay. I'll follow your advice but on one condition.'

'What's that?' Harri asked.

'You take your advice too.'

Harri smiled. 'I'll try.'

9 October 1975 – Thursday

Matthew's dad is dead! Oh, my God. Oh, my God. Oh, my God.

10 October 1975 – Friday

I was waiting with Henry when Matthew arrived. He looked weird. His face was grey and strange. He hugged me and held on for ages. I was grateful. I can't explain how grateful I was. Henry took him home and the housekeeper made him something to eat and she was crying and Henry was saying the nicest things and Matthew was being really strong. Even though he hated his dad it was very sad. Even though I hated him it really was very sad. His grandparents arrived and his granddad said we should all go and that he wanted some time alone with his grandson. So I left. It was after ten so Henry drove me home. He said that Matthew's dad was driving in Monaco when he had an accident. He was with a woman. She was dead too. I asked him what will happen to Matthew. It was only when I saw his grandparents that I started to worry. What if they take him away? They live in Meath. They can't. Please, God, don't let them take him.

11 October 1975 – Saturday

Matthew said his grandparents haven't discussed anything with him other than arrangements. The body isn't coming home until next week! Matthew can stay at home until after the funeral and then he has to go back to school. His grandparents asked him what his dad had been doing in Monaco but he didn't even know he was there. He's holding up well, seeing as he's worried about what's going to happen too. He cried because he remembered that the last time he saw his dad they'd fought and said horrible things. I told him I thought his dad was just really sad that his wife had died, and for some reason he couldn't let her go, and over the years it kind of made him bitter and that maybe looking at Matthew was too sad for him. Matthew thought about that and said it made sense. Now he thinks I'm really wise. I'm not.

I told Dr B about the fight and he said those things. I would never have thought of that. But I can't say anything to Matthew about Dr B because he'd go mad if he knew I'd told anyone. Anyway, it seems to have helped and that's what counts. I still can't believe Matthew's dad is dead.

18 October 1975 – Saturday

Matthew's dad came home on Thursday morning. The removal was Thursday night and the funeral was yesterday. Matthew's been doing really well all week and he hasn't cried since last Saturday. It seemed like the whole town was at the funeral. Matthew's dad knew so many people. Sheila and Dave came and they bought a wreath between them, which was really nice and made me feel a bit sick because I didn't think of buying one but I don't have the money and I don't think Matthew noticed. Still I feel bad about that. Dr B told Matthew he would always be there for him, which was really nice. Father Ryan said the Mass and talked about all Matthew's dad's achievements. I knew he was rich but I hadn't realized he was so good at what he did. He's done a lot. I suppose that's stupid of me but I just never really thought about it. Matthew's gran cried a lot. His granddad didn't. He just sat there with her hand in his.

Henry helped Matthew carry the coffin. Aside from Matthew's grandfather I didn't know the others. Sheila said one of them was an Abbey actor. I've never been to the Abbey so I wouldn't know. Matthew's quiet. He just lies in his bed and listens to sad music, mostly Carole King's 'So Far Away' and T-Rex's 'Cosmic Dancer'. He listened to those two songs for hours. It started off being really sad and then it got so boring I switched it off. He doesn't want to talk but that's okay. He doesn't want to touch and I understand that. He doesn't really want to do anything. He reminds me of my mam a bit. I hope he'll be okay. I hope nothing has to change but then everything changes. He's going back to school tomorrow night and his grandparents still haven't said any-thing to him about his future. That family is really strange.

19 October 1975 – Sunday

Matthew's gone back to school. I can't believe it. I missed him. His grandparents wanted to take him out for a meal and then drive him to Dublin. Henry said it was all very last minute and he couldn't call me because I don't have a stupid phone. He's gone. I don't know when he'll be back. I don't even know if he's coming back. I don't know anything. I never got to say goodbye. I just can't believe it.

21 October

Liv,

I'm so sorry I missed you but my granddad wouldn't let me call in to say goodbye. I don't want you to worry. He talked to me and he agreed that I'm old enough to stay in my own home on breaks from school. He was running a business at fourteen so I have no business acting like a child. He's spoken to Henry, who's happy to supervise, and this is the best bit – I can come home every weekend if I want. Henry said he'd have me home anytime and Granddad thinks it's a good idea for me to be around the horses more and learn the business. Can you believe it? I'm coming home on Friday night. Today is Tuesday (sorry I couldn't write yesterday, I had to go on a school trip to a stupid cave) so by the time you get this letter I might be on my way home.

Love Matt

PS Everything is going to be fine.

21. I know what I said before but this time it's true

Harri stood up and looked at her parents.

'What are you doing, my darling?' Gloria asked.

'I forgive you,' she said.

Gloria looked at Duncan, who looked back at Gloria and then rested his eyes on Harri.

'I know you thought you were doing the right thing. I know that if you hadn't taken me in I would probably have gone into care, and I've had a very good life as a Ryan. I'm glad I'm a Ryan.'

Duncan smiled. 'Well,' he said. 'Well,' he repeated. 'What?' he asked someone unseen.

Gloria smiled and her eyes filled. 'We're so happy you feel that way, Harri. We love you so much.'

'I know,' she said. 'I know you do and I love you and so does George, even though he's intent on holding it against you for at least another month or two.'

'Oh, darling, that's just George,' Gloria said, with a wave of her hand.

Harri sat down. 'I'm going to be having dinner with Matthew Delamere tomorrow.' Her parents' faces fell.

'I phoned Dr McCabe. I met him at Liv's grave and he told me I could call him and I did. He asked me to dinner and he said that Matthew would like to meet me.' She gulped. 'At first I hung up on him but then I called him back and agreed.'

She waited for a response. Both parents remained quiet.

'I just want to meet him,' she said.

'Of course you do.' Duncan nodded. 'It's only natural.'

Gloria remained quiet.

'Mum?'

She nodded and smiled, then stood up. 'Can you hand me your plate, darling? These dishes won't wash themselves!' The conversation was over.

When she had discovered her husband's blood pressure was off the charts and that this was responsible for both his erectile dysfunction and heart attack, Susan had been stunned. 'Erectile dysfunction?'

'Yes,' the doctor had said.

'Erectile dysfunction,' she repeated.

'Mrs Shannon, I take it you are aware that your husband has suffered with ED for going on' – he looked at his chart – 'three years now but we're taking steps to control his BP and obviously we'll have to discuss diet, exercise, et cetera. We'll get the heart healthy and then we'll deal with the ED.'

'Erectile dysfunction,' she said again. 'Right. Thank you.'

She walked away from the doctor, who hadn't finished his medical update. *It takes all sorts.*

It would be unusual for a wife to want to punch her husband while he was attached to a heart monitor but that was exactly what Susan wanted to do. The instant the doctor had told her that her husband was suffering from erectile dysfunction their problems fell into place. *How could I have been so stupid? Wait a minute! How could he have been so stupid? And so cruel. I thought he didn't want me any more.*

She drank a glass of celery, apple and carrot juice that the girl behind the counter in the juice bar swore had a calming effect. She hadn't lied because by the time she was sitting by Andrew's side the desire to punch him had disappeared, leaving only a terrible sadness in its wake.

'I'm sorry,' he said. 'I'm so sorry.'

'You killed our marriage because you were embarrassed,' she said, her voice drenched with tears.

'I know,' he said. 'I know what I've done.'

'I thought it was me,' she said. 'I thought you didn't want me.'

'I was a very stupid man.'

'A stupid, vain, arrogant and ridiculous man,' she said.

He nodded, and smiled a little: if she was calling him names maybe they had hope. 'Susan.'

'You had your chance, a million of them. I said good-bye to you.'

'But you're still here,' he pointed out.

'For Beth.'

'Beth is at home in bed.'

'And Keith?' she said, and saw him shudder.

'I'll forgive you if you forgive me.'

'That's big of you,' she said angrily. *This is your entire fault. The whole ruddy lot of it. None of it had to happen this way. Fuck you, Andrew!*

'I know you're angry.'

'Quick alert MENSA, there's a genius in the room.'

Andrew loved it when his wife was sarcastic – and he hadn't given her the opportunity for that in such a long time.

'Don't laugh.'

'Sorry.'

Suddenly it dawned on her that, despite the anger and recriminations, for the first time in a long time she and Andrew were on a level playing field. They were both at fault and they were both victims. *Interesting*.

What was also interesting was that their daughter was behaving in a manner approaching kind, considerate and benevolent almost. 'Are you hungry, Mum? I got you a sandwich just in case'; 'You look tired, do you want me to take over?'; 'Are you okay for a coffee?'; 'Dad need anything, anything at all?'; 'Mum, you look like you could do with a hug.' Beth's turnaround was miraculous and had an effect on both her parents.

On the third day of Andrew's internment in James's Street hospital he reached for his wife's open hand, reminding her of the painting on the couple counsellor's wall. *It will take time and work but we might just be okay.*

When Harri got home she found Susan packing.

'Well?'

'I'm going home.'

'Good.'

'Baby steps,' she said. But she was smiling and seemed happier than she had in a while.

Harri was delighted.

'It might not work.'

'I know.'

'We still have a huge amount of stuff to work through.'

'I know.'

'There's a lot of pain there.'

'I know.'

'Will you stop saying, "I know"?'

'Okay.' *What is everyone's problem with me saying, 'I know,' when I do know?*

Harri helped her move her stuff to the car.

'Thank you for everything,' Susan said gratefully.

'It was really good to have you.' Harri meant it. Susan's presence had helped ease her loneliness and it might even have broken her *CSI* habit.

'I will not watch one more second of that bloody show.'

'Ah, please!'

'No.'

'It's my apartment.'

'No.'

'That is so unfair.'

'Live with it.'

Harri waved her friend off and took a bath. *Tomorrow is a very big day. Do not mess it up. Do not have a panic attack. Do not end up in hospital.*

They took Harri's car but George drove. He would never in a million years agree to be driven by Harri.

'Why?'

'Because you're crap.'

He seemed obsessed with the fact that she didn't keep a map in her car.

'We don't need a map. It's a straight run on the motorway.'

'That is not the point.'

This is going to be a long drive.

George was airing grievances so that he could talk and he wanted to talk because he was nervous. George always talked when he was nervous. 'Look at that. What is the government thinking? How many more fucking flats are they going to build? You know, in ten years Irish people won't know what a piece of grass looks like'; 'I am sick to death of people overtaking without indicating. What is so hard about indicating? Indicate, you pissing moron!'; 'You know what kills me about NASA? They kept going back to the moon. There's nothing there, move on!'

Harri was happy to listen and smile and nod when appropriate because it was helping to keep her mind off the impending appointment. The gate lodge was easy to find: it was stuck out in front of a property that seemed to go on for several miles.

'So this is what a peasant feels like,' George said, turning into the driveway.

Harri was silent.

'It's fine, Harri. Everything is fine.'

She nodded.

'Breathe. And keep breathing.'

Brendan opened the door and waved to them both. George got out of the car and shook his hand. 'George Ryan.'

'Brendan McCabe.'

'Nice to meet you.'

'Nice to meet you.' Brendan turned to Harri. 'It's good to see you again, Harri.'

'She's a little overwhelmed,' George said, guiding his sister around the car.

'Of course – come in,' Brendan said, smiling.

Harri's legs felt like lead and she was all but dragged in by George.

'Glass of wine?' Brendan asked. 'Dinner will be ready in half an hour.'

Both Ryans decided against wine. Harri was busy wondering where Matthew Delamere was.

'Matt shouldn't be too long.'

When Matt opened Brendan's front door to let himself in, he heard Brendan talking to another man – must be George Ryan – about Harri's fear of travel and foreigners.

'It's not exactly fear, it's more a sense of discomfort,' a woman's voice – Harri's, it must be – said.

'You've cried over it.'

'He's exaggerating and, besides, he has a fear of tiled floors.'

'It's not a fear, it's a sense of discomfort,' George said, and Brendan laughed.

Matthew listened at the door, afraid to go in.

'George speaks four languages,' Harri said proudly.

'Harri works with tiles,' George said, emulating his sister's pride.

Brendan laughed. 'What do you do?'

'I'm an interior designer,' Harri said.

'Impressive.'

'Not really but I like it.'

The door opened and Brendan smiled. 'Matt.'

George jumped up to shake Matt's hand.

'George.'

'Matt.'

'Nice to meet you.'

'Nice to meet you too.'

Harri stood and faced him. 'Hi.'

'Hi.'

The room was silent and tense.

'Who's hungry?' Brendan asked, in an attempt to break the stare-off.

Dinner was an extraordinary affair in that it wasn't extraordinary at all. Brendan and George behaved as if they'd known each other a lifetime and Matt and Harri, while quieter, still found things to say.

'The last time I broke my leg. Which leg was it?' George turned to Harri.

'The right.'

'The last time I broke my right leg I swore I would never snowboard again. People think skiing is harder but I don't find that to be the case.'

'How many times have you broken your right leg?' Brendan asked, amused.

George thought for a second or two before looking at Harri.

'Once. You broke your left twice.'

'I thought I broke it three times.'

'No, two breaks and a torn ligament.'

'Jesus, that was sore!' He involuntarily rubbed the back of his leg. 'So, Matt, you must have fallen off a horse once or twice.'

Matt nodded. 'Once or twice.'

Brendan, clearly sensing a lull in the conversation, decided to ask George to help him with dessert. They got up, leaving Matt and Harri alone.

'You're smaller than she was,' Matt said.

Harri wasn't sure how to respond so she didn't.

'You have the same hair – you even wear it the same way.'

'I was thinking of getting it cut,' she said. *Change the subject, you're freaking me out.*

'Do you ride?'

'No. George does.'

'Would you like to ride?'

'No, but thanks.'

He was staring.

'You're being weird,' she said, and he laughed.

'I'm sorry.' He was staring again. 'I expected you to be more athletic.'

'Do you say everything that comes into your head?' she asked, in wonder.

'A lot of it.'

'It's very annoying,' she concluded.

'You're exactly like her.' He shook his head. 'That's the kind of thing she would have said.'

Happily it wasn't long before Brendan and George

returned from the kitchen with home-made cheesecake. Afterwards Brendan insisted that Matt take Harri up to the stables.

'It's a ten-minute walk and Henry's dying to meet you,' Brendan said.

'He's like my second father,' Matt said. 'I promise you'll be back in half an hour.'

The walk was nice and quiet.

'It's beautiful here,' Harri said, taken by the hundred plus shades of green, the old trees, the dirt path, the sounds, the fresh-smelling air and the general weight of passing time in the air.

Matt nodded and walked on, remembering when he was younger and the girl walking beside him was the girl he loved.

'You're thinking of her, aren't you?' she asked.

'If I'd had a choice I wouldn't have let you go,' he said.

'Oh.'

'I'm sorry,' he said. 'Usually I'm good with women.'

'Lovely,' she said.

'I shouldn't have said that – I'm sorry. I don't know how to be around you.'

'Be yourself.'

'You don't seem to like me being myself.'

'True.' She laughed.

Henry was cleaning out Derby Girl's stall.

'Henry!' Matt called.

Henry walked into the courtyard and stood still a second before putting his hand up to his forehead. 'There you are,' he said, his old eyes watering. 'There she is,

Matty,' he said, sniffing. 'You're smaller,' he said, with a single tear flowing down his cheek, 'but that's all right.'

Now Harri felt like crying too.

Matt was steadfastly stoic. 'She's a smasher, Henry,' he said to the old man.

'Ah, well, she comes from good stock.'

After they had walked Henry back to his house, Matt told Harri about how Henry had taken care of him after his own father died. 'He's a good man,' he said.

'Did he know she was pregnant?'

'Oh, no. Nobody did.'

'Can I ask you something?'

'Of course.'

'How did you think you could keep it a secret?'

He shrugged. 'We were kids.'

25 December 1975 – Thursday

My last period came on 30 October. I think I'm in trouble. I've been throwing up and my chest is so sore that last night it woke me. I haven't said anything to Matthew because he's still trying to get over his dad and, anyway, there might be nothing wrong. I'll wait another few days. No, I'll wait till the New Year. If I haven't got it by the New Year I'll tell Matthew. The first week of the New Year. He's spending Christmas with his grandparents in Meath, leaving poor Henry all alone. I'd never thought about Henry being alone before, not until he was asked to watch over Matthew. Now every weekend they're like two peas in a pod. It's nice. We all muck in together with the horses and we ride and Dr B comes up and he helps too, and it's like we've got our own family, which is good because I might as well have no family here.

HE took a job in Galway for the month – at least that was what he told my mam. I don't think she cares much about anything any more. Today we had chicken for Christmas dinner. I cooked it. Mostly we just watched TV. She gave me a pendant – it had been my granny's. It's nice. I'd bought her a bottle of perfume and a book but she didn't even look at them. Not really, anyway. We just sat on the sofa, time passed, and now I'm up here writing it all down, not that there's much to write. Matthew will be home the day after tomorrow so everything will be back to normal. Well, at least I hope so. Maybe I'll talk to Dr B, maybe not. No. I'll just wait and see. It's probably fine. Sheila and Dave have been having sex for ages and she hasn't got pregnant. Everything will be fine. Happy Christmas to me.

22. If I could change . . .

Harri and George had a lot to talk about on the way home from Wicklow.

'Brendan's nice,' George said.

'He seems it,' she replied.

'Do you know what he told me when you and Matt were at the stables? He said that the first person he came out to was Liv.'

'No!'

'I swear.'

'That's so strange,' she said.

'Funny old world.'

They talked about Matt a lot.

'I like him!' George laughed.

'But didn't it freak you out when he kept talking about the way I looked?'

'Natural.'

'What about the way he says everything that comes into his head?'

'You do that.'

'But I have to be asked.'

'True,' he agreed.

'He thinks I don't like him.'

'Do you?'

'Yes. No. I don't know.'

'I'd say lots of women like him.' George was smiling.

'Oh, seriously, George, don't do that.'

He laughed. 'He's a looker.'

'George, please, I get car sick at the best of times.'

'Henry sounds like a nice man.'

'He made me want to cry.'

'You know what I think?'

'What?'

'I think the girl who died in the woods in 1976 was really loved.'

'Me too.' She smiled. 'Me too.'

Deirdre was sitting in her chair by the heater under the large window that looked out on to the grounds. Matt rested his hand on her shoulder.

'Hi, Deirdre.'

'Hi, Matt.'

'Sorry it's been so long.' He sat in the spare chair next to her.

She shrugged her shoulders. 'Has it?'

'Deirdre.'

She blinked at him.

'Remember I told you a secret a few years ago.'

She nodded. 'About the girl who looks like my Liv.'

'That's right.'

She blinked at him.

'I met her today. It was awkward. I think I made a bit of a tit out of myself.' He waited for a reaction but there was none. 'You'd really like her, Deirdre. She has that look, the one that puts you in your place the moment you say something she doesn't like.'

'It'd frighten the devil,' Deirdre said, with a little giggle that seemed to come from a faraway place.

'That's the one. Maybe some day I could bring her to meet you. Not today or tomorrow, and maybe not for a while. I don't know when I'll see her again and things are very up in the air but maybe some day I could bring her here. Would you like that?'

She blinked at him.

'Deirdre?'

But Deirdre's mind had moved on.

'Well,' he said, getting up. 'Maybe one day.'

Doctors would often discuss and debate Deirdre's depression and associated altered behaviour, which had been diagnosed soon after her daughter's death. For thirty years she had been in and out of mental institutions, where she had received any number of treatments. Unfortunately it was only following an EEG test in the mid-nineties that it had become clear that the cause of Deirdre's mental condition was a brain injury, no doubt a result of the abuse she had suffered throughout the 1970s. The diagnosis had come too late for surgery so they were forced to continue her medication: it had long ago become clear that Deirdre would not find her way back.

Deirdre had returned to her little home in Castle Street many times over the years but never for long, and during her times of internment the tiny mortgage payments had mounted. When it became obvious to all those around that she was unable to take care of herself, Matt had moved her to a care home and paid all her bills because that was what Liv would have wanted.

Seeing Deirdre always made him sad because in that last week Liv had been so sure that her mam was going to be all right – but that was Liv, determined to look on the bright side no matter what. *We were only kids.*

George only realized how tired he was when he opened his front door. It had been a hectic week at work, and driving to and from Wicklow in a day was no joke, especially when there was a bloody two-hour traffic jam on the way because of two broken-down lorries.

'How the hell does that happen? Look at them side by side, taking up the whole fucking road!'

Aidan was waiting on the sofa. He was quiet. The TV was off. George knew it was time so he sat down.

'We don't work,' Aidan said.

George nodded.

'We keep trying. I'll give us that.' Aidan smiled. 'And I don't want to hate you but if we keep going . . .'

'Me neither,' George said.

'I'll really miss you,' said Aidan.

'You'll really be missed,' George replied sadly.

'You're selfish and have issues that you may never resolve but you're fascinating and worldly and fun and passionate, and you're kind and I wouldn't take back one minute of our four years together,' Aidan said, tears threatening.

'Maybe the minute we had a gun stuck in our faces after

you mooned out of a bus window in Egypt.' George grinned.

'Yeah, okay, I'd take back that minute.' Aidan laughed.

'You're camper than Christmas and sometimes I know you're just doing it to annoy me.'

Aidan nodded.

'You're loud, you're bitchy, you're patient – you've been very patient. You're funnier than most people I know and when I said I loved you I meant it.'

Aidan sighed and stood up. 'Goodbye, George.'

'Goodbye, Aidan.'

They hugged,and Aidan left quietly. George sat alone and heartsick in his apartment in the centre of Dublin. *If I could change I would have changed for you.*

It had been a long week and, between George and Aidan, Harri and her new dad, Susan, Andrew and the whole bloody lot of them, Melissa was ready for a quiet uneventful night with her husband.

She took Jacob up to bed.

'One more *Scooby-Doo*,' he begged.

'No.'

'Half one.'

'No.'

'One more Maha-maha-maha-mammy!' he wailed.

'Jacob, you can maha-maha-maha-mammy me all you want, love. You can scream, you can shout, you can roar, you can do that kicking thing you do on the floor, but you are not watching another *Scooby-Doo*.'

Jacob thought about this for a second or two, then

screamed, shouted, roared and did the kicking thing on the floor until, exhausted, he fell asleep.

Gerry was downstairs rocking Carrie, who had a cold.

'Is she all right?'

'She's still stuffy, poor little mite,' he said, looking down into her face.

'She picks up everything that's going round.'

'She's a person and people get sick.'

'Not that often!'

'Okay, okay! Anyway, Mrs Rafferty has the worst of it, minding her while we're at work.'

'Look,' she said, 'I've been doing some figures and if we get rid of the two cars and maybe buy one a few years old, and if we cut out a family holiday for a few years and tighten our belts, I could leave work.'

'No.'

'Gerry!'

'Melissa, we can't afford it.'

'But we'd save on childcare.'

'No!' he said, wiping Carrie's nose.

'You know what? Fine. Fine. Fine. I'll just die standing, will I?'

'I have no idea what that's supposed to mean,' he said. *Jesus, here we go again.* The door slammed. *Looks like it's just you and me, kid.*

Harri opened the door in her dressing-gown, with a big smile on her face.

Melissa held up a bottle of wine. 'Can I stay?'

'Why not? I've just got rid of Susan.'

Melissa flopped on to the sofa while Harri opened the wine.

'I still can't believe you met your dad.'

'I know.'

'I still can't believe Susan and Andrew are giving it another go.'

'I know.'

'I still can't believe George and Aidan have split up.'

'I know.'

'Everybody else is moving forward and I seem to be stuck in the same old rut.' She clinked Harri's glass.

'He's still not budging, then?'

'He won't even discuss it.'

'Still, you've worked so hard to get where you are.'

'I know.'

'You might hate being at home all the time.'

'I know.'

'But then something's got to give.'

'I know.' Melissa smiled.

'If only you could go part time.'

'It's just not an option – the firm is too small and my job is too big.'

'What are you going do?'

Melissa picked up her glass. 'Have you taken Matt up on his offer yet?'

'No.'

'If you do, how would you feel about company?'

'But it's midweek.'

'Exactly. I think it's time Gerry got a taste of my life.'

'Oh, you wouldn't!'

'Oh, I bloody would!'

'I'll make the call.'

Melissa clapped her hands. 'Road trip, road trip!'

It had been a week since Matt had met his daughter for the first time in Brendan's kitchen. He'd waited until Wednesday before he'd made the call inviting her to attend a horse show in Seville. He sold it on the basis that she'd get to see what he did and it would be a nice break – and maybe it would be easier to get to know one another on neutral ground. He'd sounded nervous on the phone and like he wasn't used to sounding nervous.

'I don't know,' she'd said.

'Think about it.'

'Okay. I will.'

'Good.'

There was an uncomfortable silence and then the phone call ended. When she rang him on the Saturday morning to confirm she would go, along with her friend Melissa, he was delighted. 'Fantastic! I'll show you a great time.'

Later she went to her parents' house. Her dad was sunning himself on Nana's bench. She kissed his furry cheek and sat beside him.

'A good day,' he said, looking up at the bright sky.

'It is,' she agreed.

'Last Sunday was nice too.'

'It was.' She laughed.

'How was he?'

'Fine. Nice. Weird.'

'I suppose that's to be expected.'

'Dad?'

'Yes, love.'

'No matter what, he's not you.'

Duncan rubbed his beard on her face the way he had done when she was a child. She pushed him off, laughing.

'Your brother is inside with your mother,' he said conspiratorially. 'He's been here most nights this week.'

'Still missing Aidan.'

'It's early days. And what about you?'

'Me? Well, I'm going to get James back.'

He turned his head to look at her. 'Good for you!' He slapped his thigh. 'That's the best news I've had in a long time.'

She listened to the phone ringing and thought about hanging up, but it was too late.

'Hello?'

'James.'

'Harri.'

'Is it okay that I'm calling you?'

'I was just thinking about you.'

'Ha. How funny.'

'Are you okay?'

'I'm good,' she said. 'I'm really pretty good.'

'Great.'

'James, the last time we were together you said I needed to find myself or something – well, I'm doing that. I've visited my mother, which, granted, is just standing in front of a stone, but I've had dinner with Matt, my father, and his doctor friend, and I met old Henry – you would just love him – and I'm going away to some horse show in Seville with them next week, and it's weird but it's not weird and I miss you. Every day. And I know it's not much and I've a way to go but can I ask you to hold on?'

'Yes.'

She laughed. 'Okay. And, James?'

'Yes.'

'I was thinking of a Christmas wedding.'

'Don't push it.'

'Understood.'

'Call me when you get back from Seville.'

'I will.' *I love you, you knock-knock-joke-telling weirdo.*

30 January 1976 – Friday

Okay, slightly panicked. My period has still not come and I decided to wait before upsetting Matthew because it might have been a false alarm – he had a hard Christmas with his grandparents, school is difficult and I only get to see him on weekends. I'm making excuses. I'm a coward. I'm a pregnant coward. I'm so sick all the time and tired. I fell asleep in the biology class today. The teacher was doing the reproductive organs, which was ironic. I keep puking and puking and puking. If puking was an art form I'd be Leonardo da Vinci. I think I've lost weight too – my school shirt is swimming on me. I wonder how long that will last.

I was riding with Dr B on Monday evening and it was freezing. Betsy was not one bit happy and I don't blame her. I wasn't too happy myself but I'd promised him I'd go with him.

I was thinking about talking to him and maybe I would have but then I thought, I don't know if he has a duty to report it, like he had a duty to report HIM coming into my room, not that the police did anything about it, but what if he has a duty to report me and they do something about me? Pamela Whelan's older sister Pauline (there are four girls in that family and they all begin with P!) got pregnant two years ago and she was sent to a convent in the midlands and when she came back she had no baby and she's been a bit weird ever since. And Dave told Sheila about his cousin Loretta. She got pregnant and was sent to England and that was four years ago and the family never speak of her. He doesn't know what happened to her. I'm in big trouble.

Anyway, I was thinking of telling Dr B and then I thought I wouldn't and then he told me that he had met someone. I nearly died. Dr B has found someone. I'm happy for him. They met at some dance in Dublin and he's only seen him three times but they get on great. They both like cards and chess. He has a car and a full-time job as a factory manager. It's brilliant. I told him I was so happy for him and I wasn't lying. I even forgot that I was pregnant for a while. I have to tell Matthew this weekend and I'm dreading it. He keeps talking about Kentucky being only six months away. I thought after his dad died that our plans would have to change but Matthew won't inherit until he's twenty-one and his dad's friend still wants him to come and Henry thinks it's a great idea and now I've gone and ruined everything. He's going to hate me.

Please Forgive me I Should have read Sheila's book

1 February 1976 – Sunday

Matthew and I had a huge fight. He said I had lied to him and that I should have told him and that all this time he's been making plans and now they're all messed up. He was so angry. I said I thought it would go away. He said I was like my mother. That hurt but he was right. I stuck my head in the sand just like she does and now I don't know what to do. He wouldn't talk to me. He said he couldn't look at me and I'm desperate. I know I was wrong and I know I've hurt him but I just want him to hug me and tell me it will be okay. I don't want to go to a convent and come out with no baby and a bit mental. I don't want to go to England and disappear. And what if HE finds out? I'm in big trouble. Matthew, where are you?

2 February

Liv,

All I could think of on the train was you. I shouldn't have said those things. I sounded like my dad and I didn't mean to

336

*make you cry. I know you weren't lying. I know you were try-
ing to make the best of things the way you always do. I want
you to know that we'll be okay. Maybe we can still go to
America and even if we can't I'll marry you. I'd marry you
tomorrow. Maybe Henry could talk to my granddad and we
could get married as soon as the exams are over, we'll see. I
just don't want you to worry. I think you were right not to tell
Dr B. I think it's better if we keep it to ourselves for a while.
My grandparents are very old-fashioned and your mother
isn't very well so we'll say nothing at least for a while. Please
don't worry and please don't cry any more. I'm so sorry. I
love you. I'll see you at the weekend.*

Love Matt

23. No, no, no, no and no

Susan and Harri met Aidan in Paddy Cullen's bar. The place was jammed as usual but they found a seat at the very back. Aidan looked well, having just returned from a week-long getaway to Playa del Ingles. He was tanned, relaxed, fresh-faced and happier than the girls had seen him for a long time.

'I always thought Playa del Ingles was a horrible kip,' Susan said.

'Oh, it is, but it's a gaytastic horrible kip – besides, if you spend a few quid it's not so bad.'

'I'm not going to ask what you got up to.' Harri grinned.

'Better not,' he said, curling his lip the way he always did when he was thinking something filthy. 'And George?' he asked, as if it was better to get it out of the way.

'He's good.'

'Still hanging out with his mother?' Aidan asked, smiling.

Harri gave Susan a dirty look, before returning Aidan's gaze. 'Yes, he is but he's fine.'

'I'm glad. And you, Miss Harri. I hear you're heading to Seville.'

'Next week.'

'And Melissa . . .'

'. . . is still planning on walking out on her husband and

two kids for three days midweek. We're calling it Operation Fuck You Gerry.'

Aidan laughed. 'A bold move.'

'Desperate times and all that,' Harri observed.

Susan was quiet.

'Susan?' Aidan said, and she smiled at him. 'How are things with Andrew?'

'Difficult,' she said honestly. 'Sometimes it feels like we're strangers.' She bowed her head. 'But we're working on it and at least Beth is being a moody cow again so we're back to some normality!' She laughed a little.

'And how's his dick?' Aidan said.

'Surgery soon, maybe before Christmas.'

'Say no more!' Aidan said, with his hand up. 'I'm sorry I asked.'

They spent a very pleasant night catching up, so Aidan waited until the end of the night to reveal to his two friends that he was leaving.

'Leaving where?' Susan asked.

'Ireland,' he said.

'Bollocks!' Harri laughed.

'Remember my friend from California?'

'The one with the electric car?' Susan guessed.

'No, he lives in California but he's from Berlin. I'm talking about the guy from California living in London.'

'Oh, the one who cries when he sings that song from *The Lion King*?' Harri said, with her finger in the air.

'Yes.'

'Well?' Susan pushed.

'He's been contracted to do a massive refurbishment

job in Kent. It's a stately home, a listed building. I'd get back into conservation plastering, pargeting, lime washing, lime plastering and all the interesting stuff. The stuff I'm good at. I'm sick of painting and decorating brand-new builds. I worked hard to get good at what I do and in the past two years I've got lazy. I took work because it was there and it was easy but I want more than that.'

Susan raised her glass. 'That's great.'

'Don't go!' Harri said, with moist eyes.

'It's not for ever,' he said, smiling.

'You don't know that,' she said.

'I'll miss you, ladies.' He raised his glass to meet Susan's.

'Ah, there's plenty more fag-hags where we came from!' Susan said, laughing.

Harri leaned over and kissed his cheek. 'I love you,' she said, and he knew she meant it.

'I love you too,' he answered.

Melissa didn't get to say goodbye. Carrie was still sick, Gerry had a conference, and Aidan was leaving the next day.

George wasn't used to working all day or, indeed, most evenings. In fact, George wasn't used to working much at all. He'd managed to avoid any real work until this his thirtieth year and, although he had realized a long-held dream, he was beginning to recognize the value of hard-earned money. He was tired most evenings yet, without Aidan, his apartment was nothing more than an empty space. As Aidan had never formally lived there and had had a place of his own, George hadn't grasped how much time they'd actually spent together in the apartment. He wasn't used to being alone. He didn't like it. He tried to make the best of it but when that failed he drove to his mother's house, where she would fuss and cook and pour him wine, and they'd laugh about things that not very many other people would find funny, including his father. As soon as Aidan had left George, Gloria and Duncan were forgiven. George's forgiveness, although born of necessity, was gratefully received in the Ryan household.

'Oh, darling,' said Gloria, 'I haven't told you Mona's jumping out of a plane for charity.'

'Moaning is jumping out of a plane?'

'For the paraplegics.'

'Does she know a paraplegic?'

'No, darling, but, as I said to her, she's only a jump away.'

George and his mother cracked up laughing while Duncan mumbled that they weren't as funny as they'd like to think. *Being a paraplegic is no bleedin' joke.*

When at last George returned to his own abode Harri was on the phone before he'd put his coat down.

'How did you know I was home?'

'I had a feeling. Did you know Aidan's moving to London?'

'Oh.'

'Are you all right?'

'I'm fine.'

'Are you sure?'

'Positive.'

'Okay. I just wanted you to know.'

'Thanks,' he said, in a tone that suggested he was light, happy, even.

'What?' she asked suspiciously.

'Nothing.'

'Do not lie to me.'

'Okay. Okay. Calm down, put away the axe.'

'So.'

'Brendan called me.'

'Brendan who?'

'Brendan McCabe.'

'And?'

'And we're going for a drink.'

Silence.

'Harri?'

'No way.'

'He's nice. He's attractive. I like him.'

'He's more than fifty years of age.'

'So?'

'So it's mad. It's madder than mad. It's mental.'

'I like him.'

'No. No. No. No. No. No. And no!' She hung up. George put the phone down. *I like him.*

27 March 1976 – Saturday

If my last period was on 30 October we think I'm about four and a half months. If we leave Ireland straight after the exams nobody will know until we get to Kentucky. It's a risk but I'm still small, probably because I puke the minute I smell food. I can't remember the last time I ate anything

342

other than a carrot stick. I really love carrot sticks and I hated them before. My tummy is rock-hard. Matthew said it's like a boxer's. You can't see anything when I'm dressed but the last night when he came home and we were in his room I took off my clothes and my belly was huge. He kept laughing and touching it and making me do poses in front of the mirror. It's not so big this morning. It sounds mad but it gets way bigger at night. I hope it stays that way. I don't mind if it's big at night as long as it's small during the day.

Sheila's suspicious – it must be the nurse in her. She keeps asking me about what I've had to eat. I need to be careful of her. I love Sheila but she has a really big mouth. My mam hasn't a clue. She just does her own thing, which is nothing, really. HE's been back a few weeks but he's busy unloading paper at the docks. Mam has really let herself go. She used to dye her hair but it's grey now. Long grey hair looks weird. I can see why people think she's scary. Dr B is still trying to get her to do some tests but you might as well be talking to the wall.

I'm also trying to steer well clear of Father Ryan but for some reason every time I turn around he's there. Always asking questions, always trying to talk about patience and love and God and I don't know what else. I switch off. I think he still feels bad about talking Mam into letting HIM back only for Dr B to tell him that he tried to have sex with me. Poor Father Ryan, he's trying his best. He was visiting the school the other day and we sat together at lunch. Sheila ran off – she didn't want to be seen with a priest – but I don't care. He's nice, really, and sometimes he's even funny. He

343

doesn't like cars and he gives out about them a lot and he doesn't like the heat. Who doesn't like the heat? He said it makes him itch. He likes it cool. I said he should move to Poland. He said he'd think about that. He ruffled my hair just before he left, like Henry ruffles Matthew's. It's nice to have someone look out for you even if it is a priest who would shove you in a convent as soon as look at you if he knew you were pregnant. I hope I stay small. I hope they don't know.

Sometimes I get hungry and I'm not sick but I try not to eat because if they find out it could all be over, everything we've worked for. Matthew said no matter what we'll get to Kentucky. He'll make sure of it. I know we'll get there. I can't wait. Four months to go!!!

24. Reality bites

Harri's phone rang in tandem with her alarm clock. The clock screamed beep-beep, shortly followed by her phone singing the Pussycat Dolls' 'Loosen Up My Buttons'. She shot up in her bed. *George, will you stop messing with my ring tone!* She turned off the alarm and picked up the phone. 'Up.'

'Good. Synchronize your watch because Operation Fuck You Gerry is a go,' Melissa whispered in her kitchen, while Gerry and Carrie slept soundly above her head. Jacob was ensconced in front of *Scooby-Doo* with a bowl of cereal.

She'd made Jacob's lunch, packed his schoolbag and left it by the front door. The day before she had ensured that the kitchen was well stocked with food and that Mrs Rafferty would be turning up at eight thirty to take care of Carrie (who had recovered from her cold but still 'had a few sniffles' – or so Melissa had told Gerry). But for three days after that Melissa's family were officially on their own.

She retrieved the suitcase she'd hidden under the stairs and was waiting outside for the taxi when it pulled up. *Seville, here we come!*

Harri was queuing by the check-in desk. She wasn't talking. She just handed her ticket and passport to Melissa and walked off. Melissa took no notice of this as Harri was clinically unable to communicate before eight a.m. As it was only six, Melissa was not only prepared for silence but only too happy to bask in it. She was nearly at the top of the queue when Harri returned with two coffees. She handed one to Melissa in silence, Melissa received it, and together they stood sipping until called to cross the yellow line.

The plane wasn't full. Melissa liked to sit by the window. Harri liked the aisle seat. The middle one was free and became a place for newspapers, magazines, a makeup bag, and some bonbons for Melissa to suck while ascending and descending. The plane took off at eight fifteen and talking was allowed.

'My dad's sister Noreen's ear started to bleed on one of these flights,' Melissa said, tipping her head to the side and scrunching her mouth into an O shape. 'Can you imagine? Blood poured from it. My father always said it would never have happened if she'd been sucking.'

Harri thought of a dirty joke but it was too early to bother delivering it.

'So, are you nervous?' asked Melissa.

'A lot of Spanish people speak excellent English.'

'Not about that.'

'Oh. Yeah, it will be weird but we have our own room and it's not like we'll be joined to him at the hip. Plus he's working, you know, horse trading or whatever so . . .' She shrugged.

'Are you excited?' Melissa asked, with a grin.

'Is nervous the same as excited?'

Melissa thought about that for a minute. 'Not sure – it might be. I'm excited. I can't wait to meet him.'

'Don't flirt. If you flirt I'll die.'

'Of course I'm not going to flirt! I'm a married woman and he's your father.'

'He's only five years older than Gerry.'

'It's mad, isn't it?'

'Yeah, it's mad.'

Melissa sniffed. 'Do you feel a change in pressure?'

'No.'

Melissa popped a bonbon just to be sure. 'I wonder how the kids are?' she said, and looked out at the white fluffy clouds beneath her.

Gerry turned off his alarm at seven a.m. and reached across the bed to find an empty space. This wasn't unusual. Melissa was probably walking the floor with Carrie but if that was the case why was Carrie crying? When the crying didn't stop and instead became louder and more intense he got up.

'Melissa?' he called.

'She made my breakfast and left,' Jacob said, from the bottom of the stairs.

Gerry looked down at him. 'What are you doing, son?'

'Watching *Scooby-Doo*.'

'Okay.' He walked into Carrie's bedroom, where he found a very distressed little girl. 'Don't cry, Daddy's here. Don't cry!' She wasn't complying. So he walked with her. 'Shush . . .' She bawled. He introduced a bounce into his step. 'Shush . . .' She bawled louder. He bounced his little girl in his arms while attempting to reach his wife on her mobile phone. It was turned off. *Blast it! She said nothing about having an early meeting.* It was only when he went to the kitchen that he noticed the note on the fridge door.

Dear Gerry,
You say we can't manage without two wages. You say that we both work hard. You say that most of the time I make a fuss about nothing – after all, Jacob goes to playschool and Mrs Rafferty minds Carrie. You say it's not so hard and maybe you are right but to be sure I think we should test this theory. I'm in Seville and won't be back until Friday morning. Mrs Rafferty will be here at 8.30 and Jacob will have to be in playschool by 9.00.
Good luck,
Your loving wife,
Melissa
xxx

He laughed a little. *This is a joke. She's joking.* 'Melissa! Ha ha, very funny!' Silence. 'Melissa!' *She's not joking. Oh, my God, she's not joking.*
'Dad, I'm hungry.'
'I thought your mother fed you.'
'She did but I'm still hungry.'
'Okay.'
'Dad, get Carrie to stop crying.'
'Okay.'
'Dad!'
'What?'
'I'm cold.'

It was at this point that Gerry realized his son was naked. *Jesus. Okay.* 'Where are your pyjamas?'

'I took them off.'

'Why?'

'I wanted to.'

'Right, let's go upstairs.'

They trudged upstairs.

'I want Spiderman.'

Gerry put the Batman boxers back in the drawer. 'Here we go – Spiderman!' His son stepped into the boxers and he pulled them up. 'Right – jeans.'

'I want cargo pants.'

'Can't see them.'

'Okay. I want –'

'Jacob, see these jeans in my hand? You're wearing them.'

Jacob shrugged as he wasn't too pushed either way.

Getting the child's top on was hardest, especially with a weeping Carrie in his arms. When his son was fully dressed Gerry sighed, happy to have achieved a remarkable feat.

'Dad!'

'What?'

'My Spiderman boxers feel tight.'

'What?'

'I think they're too small.'

Oh, God, kill me.

With Jacob in his Batmans and dressed once more, they trooped to the kitchen. *Maybe she's hungry.* He put Carrie into her chair. She roared. He picked her up and sniffed her. *Oh, dirty nappy alert!* He walked back up the stairs to his daughter's room and changing table.

'Dad, where's my breakfast?' Jacob called from downstairs.

'In a minute!' he shouted down.

'But, Dad!'

'Jacob, give me a minute.' *Where're the nappies? Where the hell are the nappies? Oh, okay, here they are. Right, nappy wipes. Where are the wipes?*

'Oh, sorry, Carrie, Daddy didn't mean to put you down on the cold wipes.' *Okay, clothes, she needs clothes. Anything will do.* 'Carrie, if you just stop crying Daddy will finish dressing you and then you can have a lovely bottle.'

'She eats food in the morning like me. I eat food in the morning,' Jacob said, suddenly standing by his father's side.

'Okay, okay,' Gerry said, leaving his daughter in a fresh nappy and a T-shirt. 'Let's go.'

'Dad, you can't leave her with no pants.'

'Jacob, are you hungry or not?'

'I told you I was.'

In the kitchen Carrie threw her food around but she had stopped crying. Gerry was happy if one spoonful in four made it into her mouth. Jacob was eating his breakfast in front of another episode of *Scooby-Doo*.

Just as Gerry was about to take a bite out of a slice of toast he heard Jacob crying. 'What's wrong?' He ran into the sitting room to find Jacob's upturned bowl on the floor and his breakfast all over him.

'Back upstairs.' *Melissa, this is not funny.*

Mrs Rafferty arrived at eight thirty on the dot.

'Mrs Rafferty.' Gerry smiled. 'Welcome.'

'Thanks,' she said, looking at him strangely. 'Where's Melissa?'

'Seville.'

'She never told me.'

'That makes two of us.'

'Oh,' Mrs Rafferty said, nodding, before giving a little wink. *Oh, yeah, I've seen this before. She's blown a gasket, and he'll be lucky if she doesn't bankrupt him.*

Gerry handed her Carrie, who was covered in orange gunk. 'I'm sorry, I know she's supposed to be dressed but if I don't leave now Jacob will be late for playschool and I'm never going to make it into work.'

Mrs Rafferty nodded. 'No problem.'

'Right, Jacob, get your schoolbag – come on, let's go.'

'Gerry.'

'Yes.'

'Maybe you should get dressed first.'

Gerry looked down at himself. *I'm standing in front of Mrs Rafferty in a pair of jocks. Sweet loving Jesus!*

There was a car waiting for them at the airport. A man with a sign reading *Harri Ryan* was standing by the gate. Melissa went ahead and conversed with him until they reached the car. It was a limo.

'Fancy!' Melissa said, grinning.

The driver opened the door and the ladies stepped inside. Within seconds they were on their way.

'He speaks English,' she said. 'Nice man, he used to be in the army.'

'You were only talking to him for two minutes.'

'I have a gift,' she said, playing around with the remote control. 'Some TV?'

The Hotel Hacienda Benazura's white walls climbed from deep green grounds into an azure sky.

'Wow!' Melissa was looking out of the limo window with her guidebook in her hand. 'It says here it's a tenth-century farmhouse. Stunning, isn't it?'

Harri smiled and agreed. 'It's beautiful.'

The car stopped at the hotel entrance. The driver got out and opened the door.

'You're a gentleman, Dario,' Melissa said.

Harri smiled at him. 'Thank you.'

'You're welcome.'

'You see? Dario doesn't bite.' Melissa giggled.

'Well, you did make me promise,' he said to her, and they both laughed.

Jesus, they were only talking for two minutes.

Matt spent a lot of the morning in his hotel room walking around in circles. Alfio sat contentedly on the patio reading a Spanish newspaper.

'Just sit,' he said.

Matt appeared and leaned on the balcony. 'Do you think it's too soon for this trip?'

Alfio smiled. 'She isn't a new girlfriend.'

'Aware.'

Alfio laughed. 'It'll be great.'

'We've only had a few hours together and now I'm dragging her to Seville.'

'She wanted to come.'

'I just want her to like me.'

'She'll like you.'

He sighed. Alfio smiled to himself. He wasn't used to his boss being out of control, especially with women. It was interesting to watch.

Matt disappeared into his room and returned having changed his jacket.

'Is this better?'

'She won't care about your jacket.'

'Alfio!'

'It's better. Can I get back to reading now?'

'If you don't want to be disturbed, read in your own room.'

There was a knock on the door.

'She's here,' Matt said, clapping his hands together and exhaling in a manner reminiscent of a fighter about to enter the ring.

Alfio got up and came into the room.

Matt opened the door, revealing Harri and Melissa.

'You must be Melissa,' he said, shaking her hand. 'Welcome to Seville!'

'Thank you, Matt.'

Do not flirt with him.

'Harri.'

'Hi,' she said.

He turned to Alfio, then back to the girls. 'This is my sidekick, Alfio.'

Alfio approached to shake their hands. 'Don't be scared,' he said to Harri. 'I speak English.'

Harri's confusion was written clearly on her face. *How does he know?*

'Brendan mentioned something,' Matt said, laughing.

Melissa was busy staring out the window. 'Would you look at that view!' She walked out on to the balcony. 'Can anyone else smell orange?'

Alfio followed her and they had a discussion about the local orange blossoms.

Matt sighed. 'Is this okay?'

'What do you mean?'

'Being here. Is it okay?'

'It's nice,' she said. 'As long as you don't point out how short I am, that I have an evil look or that it's really weird I'm not athletic.'

He laughed. 'I'm so sorry.'

'Apology accepted.'

The hotel had won some food awards, and as it was early evening and the bar had a beautiful outside area, they ate there.

'I could live on tapas,' Melissa declared, and looked at her watch. 'What time is it in Ireland?'

Gerry's secretary knocked on his door and entered. He pointed to the phone to show he was on a call. She knew he was. He'd been on the same call for forty-five minutes and his nanny had been on the phone three times. She held up a sign.

YOUR BABYSITTER IS LEAVING YOUR HOUSE IN 15 MINUTES.

'What?' Gerry shouted into the phone. 'No, sorry. No.

Ah, Ernest, could I get back to you with those figures? Something's just come up here and, ah, it needs my immediate attention. Okay. Great. Great. Great. Okay. Great.' He hung up and looked at his watch. 'No. No. She should stay until five.'

'Not on a Wednesday,' Lorraine said. She pointed to the phone. 'She's on hold.'

'Oh, God, it's Wednesday. Shit!' He grabbed the phone. 'Mrs Rafferty, I'm so sorry! I forgot it was Wednesday . . . No, I understand your time is precious. Yoga is very important.' He sighed. 'The best I can do is forty-five minutes . . . Well, maybe there's a later class . . . Okay, I'm leaving now.'

'So I'll cancel your meeting with Noel?' Lorraine queried.

'Fuck!' Gerry cried. 'Yes, fuck it!'

He was met at his front door by a very pissed-off Mrs Rafferty.

'I'm sorry! I hit prime-time traffic.'

'I've missed my class. I might as well have stayed on.'

Well, why didn't you, then, you old witch?

She left after he'd apologized some more.

Carrie had a tooth coming through, which, Mrs Rafferty pointed out, accounted for her bad humour. Jacob was bored with *Scooby-Doo*, it was raining and he wanted to go swimming. Gerry was stressed out past the point of no return from sitting in traffic and needed a drink. He poured himself a gin and tonic and sat on the sofa, undoing his tie. Carrie started to cry when Jacob hugged her too tightly.

'Jacob!' he shouted, frightening Jacob, who was only being nice.

His son started to cry. Gerry considered joining his children. Not even one day down, but Melissa had made her point.

George was led to his table by the maître d'. He shook Brendan's hand and sat.

'I ordered a glass of house red while I was waiting. I hope you don't mind,' Brendan said.

'Not at all.' George smiled. *But we're not drinking house with our meal.* It was odd that neither man felt awkward and idle chat was unnecessary. It was odd that, although they had only met once, they felt like old friends. *I know you.*

Brendan laughed when George talked about his youth, growing up with Harri as his twin and the way they still were now. 'When we were five I jumped out of a tree.'

'One of your broken legs?'

'An arm. Harri ran into the kitchen and instead of telling Mum that I was in a heap in the garden she punched her in the knee.'

Brendan laughed. 'Punched her?'

'She thought if she punched her and ran out that Mum would follow her and that was exactly what happened. Mum chased her, screaming about her knee, until she stopped at my feet with Harri pointing. She's never been good in a crisis but somehow she always muddles through.'

'Seeing her brings Liv back and it's hard,' Brendan said.

'I'm sorry.'

'Oh, don't be!' He shook his head. 'The best things in life are hard won.'

'I don't get it.'

'Seeing Liv in Harri hurts but it also brings great joy.'

'She must have been a good friend.'

'She was only seventeen but I think she was the best friend I ever had.'

'I don't know what I'd do if I lost Harri.'

'You'd mourn her and then you'd move on.'

'I wouldn't want to.'

'No, you wouldn't.'

'And Matt, has he moved on?'

Brendan grinned. 'Matt's dad lost his wife when Matt was a kid. He never got over it. He became bitter and twisted. Matt swore he'd never be his dad and he's not. He's a good man, kind, and he loves life. He also loves women!' He laughed. 'Maybe a bit too much and, yeah, he still loves her but he'll find his way.'

Brendan got into a taxi outside the restaurant and rolled down the window. 'We should do this again.'

'Absolutely.'

'Good night.'

'Good night.'

George watched the car disappear down the road. *Oh, crap, I really like you, and Harri's going to kill me.*

25 April 1976 – Sunday

At the start of the month my tummy was sticking out and staying out and it was getting way too hard to cover up so now that I've stopped being sick I've decided the best thing to do is to eat all around me so that I'll look fat. Skinny arms and legs and a big belly is too obvious but fat arms and legs and a fat tummy and a big jumper just might get me through. I've been eating and eating and eating. Mam even made a joke about it the other day. I couldn't believe it. We were in the kitchen and she said that if I ate any more I'd burst and she thought it was funny because she laughed and that was really good to see. HE was there too but he was hung-over and listening to something on the radio.

Dave called in the other night. He said he had something to tell me and he was very serious. He asked me to go on a walk so we went around the town. He said he'd seen HIM with another woman and they were kissing outside the Pole. I told him I didn't care and I hoped he'd go off with whoever she was and leave us. I pity her, though. She hasn't a clue what she's getting herself into. He thought it was a bit weird that I didn't care but then he doesn't know the half of it. He said he liked me with a bit of weight on. I nearly died. He said Sheila thought I should know and that he was glad he'd told me. Sheila's so funny – she's in school with me every day, she's my best friend and she gets Dave to tell me. People are odd. I mean she knows I hate HIM. In fact, that news really has cheered me up. I feel like celebrating. I think I'll have a bun.

I was over in Dr B's the other evening playing chess. He thinks if we keep playing I'll discover I really do like it. WRONG. Anyway, we were playing and I was giving out about some stupid annoying rule involving a basic pawn strategy or some other shit and out of nowhere he was crying!!!!! The man he'd been going out with didn't want to see him any more. He'd said Dr B was messed up and told him he should get help. Dr B is not messed up. I told him I'd love to find that man and give him a good talking-to. That made Dr B laugh. I asked him why his friend said those mean things.

He said he'd talked to him about his fear of going to Hell. Father Ryan has been adamant that if he acts on his desires that's where he'll end up. I told him not to worry, that Father Ryan says that to everyone, even married people if they use contraception. So if he is in Hell he'll be there with the rest of us. He laughed again but you could see he was worried. I get worried too sometimes. Maybe I will end up in Hell and if it's half as painful as double science on a Friday afternoon it'll be pretty bad. Anyway, I told him that if he wants to debate good and evil and whether or not he's either, he should stick to doing it with Father Ryan, not when he's in bed with another man. He went red and said he never mentioned where the conversation took place but I could tell. He told me that life would be very dull without me, which was a really nice thing to hear.

Seeing as he was so open with me I was desperate to tell him that I was pregnant but I'd promised Matthew so I didn't. I hope he forgives me.

25. It's my trip to Seville and I'll cry if I want to

The Palace of Exhibitions and Conferences with its gold-domed roof looked like something you'd see in *Star Wars*. There was a little man-made lake outside, reflecting its grandeur and beauty. The place was packed with people, horses and livestock. Harri felt a bustling energy come from the floor and fill her from her feet up. Every inch of the place was draped in colour. The arenas were spectacular, lined with red earth, and on display were Spain's most beautiful horses. Some were pure white and stood out against the colourful background. Matt, Harri and Melissa had watched the show-jumping, driving and dressage, moving from arena to arena, part of an ever-increasing throng.

Matt was busy explaining to Melissa the difference between Pintabians and Arabians so they walked off together, leaving Harri and Alfio by the ringside where judges were viewing stallions from a particularly successful stud farm in northern Spain.

Alfio leaned in to stare at one particular horse. 'You see his natural ease of disposition?'

'I see him standing there.'

He laughed.

'I think they're beautiful, though. I was always so afraid of actually having to get up on a horse that I never really took the time to look at them,' she added.

'Is that how you feel about foreigners too?'

'Ah!' she squealed, and he chuckled. She joined in. 'Maybe.'

She asked him about himself and he told her about his background growing up on a stud farm in Argentina, then about his champion polo days and about the accident that had ended his career. He told her about his love of training and how he'd met Matt in Uruguay and that when Alfio had called him a year later, heartbroken and in need of work, Matt had flown him to Ireland straight away. 'He's a good friend,' he said.

Harri was more interested in his story of heartbreak, and after a few protestations he told her about Maria, the love of his life, who had left Santa Cruz for a physiotherapy job in Buenos Aires. When Harri asked him why he hadn't gone with her, he replied that his whole life was in Santa Cruz.

'So why are you living in Wicklow?'

'Because after she left, I couldn't stay there.'

'So why didn't you follow her to Buenos Aires?'

'I did,' he admitted, 'but it was too late. She had found someone else.'

Harri established that Maria had been really annoyed with Alfio for not supporting her in her dream after she had invested many years in supporting him and his polo playing. She also confirmed that he had waited eight months before following her, so realistically a girl who looked half as good as he had described would be dating by then. What she didn't understand was why, if Maria was the love of his life, he didn't just go for it.

'Go for it?' he repeated.

'Call her, tell her you still love her, you were stupid and you'd move to the end of the world for her.'

'It's been two years.'

'So what have you got to lose?'

She allowed him to think about what she'd said. *That's what I'm doing. James, batten down the hatches, I'm coming to get you.*

Melissa and Matt were seated at the bar in the hotel.

She was charmed by him and yet she had started to fret a little about the family she'd abandoned.

'Call them,' he counselled.

'If I call, Gerry will tell me something terrible. I'll freak out, get on a plane and that will defeat the purpose.'

'But you can't relax,' he pointed out.

'Matt, this isn't about relaxing – this is about proving a point.'

'Right.'

They remained seated in the bar in silence.

It had not gone unnoticed by either party that Harri had done everything in her power to avoid Matt.

'She's just freaked out,' Melissa said, after a while.

'Me too,' he replied. 'She didn't want to come, did she?'

'Not really. I suppose I made her.'

'I shouldn't have asked. I made such an arse of myself when we met I just wanted to make it up to her.'

Melissa laughed. 'She doesn't think you're an arse.'

'What does she think?'

'She's confused.'

'Well, I know what that's like,' he admitted. 'I shouldn't have rushed things.'

When it became apparent that Harri would not be joining them, Matt and Melissa made their way to the hotel restaurant and ordered some food.

Over dinner Melissa talked about her problem. 'You see, Gerry thinks it's just a phase. He thinks sooner or later I'll be back to myself, but I'll never be back to myself because that was the old me and this is the new me' – she waved her hand, spilling a little wine – 'the stay-at-home-with-the-kids me.' There were tears in her eyes. 'I mean, I don't like that notion either. I didn't get a degree and work my arse off for the past twenty years for nothing. But, Matt, I'm a mother first. That's it. That is the reality. I am a mother.'

That night Matt did a lot of nodding. Melissa wasn't really looking for his opinion or even advice, she just needed someone to listen.

'You're such a good listener,' she said, a little tearful since she had drunk three glasses of wine too many. 'Harri's lucky to have you.'

Matt smiled. *It's a pity she doesn't think so.*

Alfio spotted Harri in the garden. 'I thought you were dining with Matt?'

'Don't feel like it,' she said, and sat on the bench.

He joined her. 'It's all a little much?'

'I shouldn't have come. I'm not ready for this.'

'Matt never does things by halves.'

'I came for Melissa, really. I thought it would be easy but every time I look at him I feel weird.'

'Weird how?'

'I can't explain. I have so many questions but I'm not sure if I want the answers. He's a stranger and yet when he looks at me it's with such great expectation. I can't handle that. He keeps talking about the way I look and I know he thinks I resemble her and it's creepy. He seems like a nice man but I'm not sure that he's the kind of man I want to know. I don't like horses – I don't care how pretty they are. I don't like country estates, welly boots and fleece jackets. I don't like the way he looks at me so intensely when I talk. I don't like him knowing so much about me, or that he's been watching me from afar. I don't like that he can't seem to let go of a girl who died thirty years ago. I don't like that he keeps texting me. I hate texting.'

Alfio laughed. 'Have you finished?'

She smiled a little. 'I don't like that he's flirting with my best friend. There, now I'm done.'

'He's been waiting for this for thirty years.'

'I know.'

'He's missed you for thirty years.'

'I know.'

'He just wants to get to know you.'

'I know.'

'He's not just some stranger who wants something from you and he's not just about riding horses, welly boots and fleece jackets. He's smart and funny and kind and, yes, he's a womanizer and flirt but he's also a gentleman and, like you, he's just a little lost.'

'I'm scared,' she said. 'He's been waiting for this for so long. What if I'm a disappointment?'

'You're not.'

Matt escorted Melissa to her room. 'I had a lovely night,' he said.

'Liar.'

Harri opened the bedroom door and Melissa passed her silently, leaving her standing face to face with Matt. 'Sorry I disappeared,' she said.

'It's okay. Sorry I pushed you to come here.'

'You didn't. Melissa did.'

'I shouldn't have asked.'

'I shouldn't have accepted.'

He laughed, and she smiled. 'We sound pathetic.'

Matt nodded. 'I have an idea. Why don't we just have breakfast tomorrow? All I ask is one hour.'

'Okay,' she agreed. 'One hour.'

Breakfast was stilted and, although both of them made an effort, for a large part of their hour together they sat in an uncomfortable silence.

'Do you ski?'

'No. George does.'

'Oh. I love to ski.'

'Yeah, so does he.'

Silence.

'Ever lived abroad?'

'No. You?'

'America. Kentucky.'

'Nice?'

'Beautiful.'

'Oh.'

Silence.

'The eggs are really good,' he tried again.

'Yes, they're lovely.'

'I love eggs.'

'Me too.' *This feels like a really bad date. Oh, my God, I'm feeling panicked. Silence. Breathe. It's all fine. Breathe in and out. In and out. Not too quickly. In. Wait. Out. Wait.*

'Are you okay?'

'Fine.' *In. Out. In. Out. I have no idea what to say to this man.*

Harri managed to regain her composure but lost it once more following an embarrassing misunderstanding with the waiter, which seemed to confound both of them.

Matt valiantly attempted to recover.

'How about we ask each other a question?' he suggested hopefully.

'Okay, you go first.'

'Is your dad a good man?'

'Yes,' she smiled, 'he's better than good.'

'I sensed that. I'm glad I was right.'

'Did you want to keep me?'

'I was seventeen.'

'That's not what I asked.'

'Yes and no. I'd just lost Liv. I was turned inside out. I was a mess.'

'I understand.'

'It still hurt to let you go.'

366

She smiled. 'This has been nice.' She got up and left, having given him fifty-five minutes of her time.

Back in the room, Melissa was attempting to sleep off a hangover. She woke to her friend crying at the end of the bed.

'What's wrong?'

'It's never going to be like it used to be,' she sobbed.

'I know,' Melissa soothed. She got up and joined Harri. 'But that doesn't mean it's the end of the world.'

'It fucking feels like it!' Harri said, making Melissa smile. 'The waiter thought we were a couple.'

Melissa laughed so heartily Harri was forced to join in.

Gerry was on red alert. 'Okay, Melissa, you want to play games. Fine.' He decided that the previous day had been a nightmare only because he wasn't prepared. That would not happen today. The alarm went off at five, approximately two minutes before his daughter awoke crying. He walked around in circles before attempting to take her into the shower. She didn't like the shower so he got out quickly and without washing. He tried to get dressed but she really did not like it when he stopped moving. After tripping over his trousers, he wrapped himself in a towel and gave up.

He laid Jacob's clothes out on his bed so that when he awoke they were ready.

'That's what you're wearing,' he said, pointing to the clothes. Jacob started crying. 'I'm not listening. I'm not listening.' *Oh, God, I sound like Melissa.*

He put Carrie into her chair with a jar of food she

could throw around and while she did that he made Jacob some toast.

'I don't want toast.'

'You're having toast.'

'But –'

'It's one day – just eat the toast.'

And while Jacob ate toast Gerry dressed. He ate the end of Jacob's toast and took Carrie upstairs to wash and dress her.

'Don't forget my lunch.'

He made Jacob's lunch.

'I can't find my bag.'

'Where did you put it?'

Jacob shrugged.

Gerry spent fifteen minutes looking for the bag, which he eventually found in the hot press.

At eight thirty on the dot Mrs Rafferty arrived. He handed her the baby.

'Jacob, let's go.'

Jacob arrived into the hallway. 'Hi, Mrs Rafferty.'

'Hi, sweet man.' She looked him up and down. 'That top looks huge on you.'

'Dad said he doesn't care.'

'Right.'

''Bye, Mrs Rafferty,' Gerry said, pushing his son out the door.

He had to take Jacob inside the playschool personally as it was a rule. Then the teacher wanted a word with him.

'I don't have time.'

'Excuse me?'

'Seriously, I'm not a bad parent, I just don't have time!'

He ran out of the door and got into the car before she could follow him.

The traffic was back to back. He called Lorraine. 'I'm going to be fifteen minutes late.'

'They're already here.'

'Christ.'

'I could entertain them if you want – maybe a medley from *Grease*?'

'Lorraine.'

'What?'

'This is not the time for funny.'

Gerry was twenty-five minutes late for his meeting and his fellow attendees were not too impressed.

As Mrs Rafferty would be with the kids until five, he filled his briefcase with work he could take home and left the office at four fifteen, making it home for four fifty-nine. Mrs Rafferty had her coat on. From five o'clock until eight, he ran around the house after Jacob playing cow-boys and Indians, cooked, fed his two kids and cleaned the kitchen as Mrs Rafferty had made it clear that she was not a cleaner. He then dressed Jacob and Carrie for bed, changed his daughter's nappy three times, read his son three stories and attempted to drink two coffees, neither endeavour successful. At five past eight he opened his briefcase and by eight twenty-five he was face down on the table and fast asleep. He woke at ten.

'Susan?'

'Hi, Gerry.'

'I need you.'

She laughed.

'She told you what she was doing to me, didn't she?' he said.

Susan admitted that she had.

He sighed. 'I give up.'

'What can I do?'

'I have to be in work for a conference call at eight.'

'I'll be in your place by six forty-five.'

'Oh, thank you! Thank you, Susan. Thank you. Thank you so much.'

The next morning she arrived at six forty-five just as she had promised. She took over handling the kids while Gerry got dressed, reviewed key figures for his conference call and ate an actual breakfast. He was gone by seven fifteen. At eight thirty Mrs Rafferty arrived and Susan took Jacob to playschool. After spending the afternoon picking up fabrics for a client, she returned in time for Mrs Rafferty to leave at five. Gerry got home just before six. Both kids were fed and sitting in front of *SpongeBob SquarePants*. Susan served Gerry his dinner and sat drinking coffee while he ate.

'I had no idea,' he said. 'I mean, I lived here and it's not like I didn't pitch in but I had no fucking idea.'

Susan laughed. 'When I had Beth, women didn't really work.'

'Well, now I can see why.'

'It will be tight,' she said.

'You've no idea.'

'But it will work out.' She smiled.

'I just worry that she'll leave her job and realize she

hates being home. I tell you, I think I'd rather die painfully.'

'You're exaggerating.'

'No. I'm really not.'

'I think she will miss it. She's loves her job but she just can't do it all and, as it turns out, she just wants to be there for her kids. Who'd have guessed?' Susan smiled.

'She can always go back,' he said, rubbing his forehead.

'Or she might want to do something else.'

'When the kids go to bed I'll play around with some figures.'

'Tell you what? I'll put them to bed and you start right now.'

'Thanks, Susan,' he said, kissing her cheek. 'You're a star. Andrew's a lucky man.'

'Yes, he ruddy is,' she said, with a grin.

9 July 1976 – Friday

HE was drunk and bumped into me. I lost my balance and he grabbed me. His hand must have felt my hard stomach because he knew. The minute he touched me he knew it was more than fat. He'd been calling me names and I didn't care. I said to Matthew he could call me anything he wanted, I don't even hear him any more, but when he touched me and he looked at me I knew it was going to be bad. He hit me in the face with a closed fist. I thought my eye was going to come out of the back of my head. It knocked me down. It was so loud even Mam heard it and she came running and then he screamed that I was a slut and he was pulling at my clothes and she jumped on his back and wrapped her hands around his neck and she looked like a woman possessed and she screamed that she would never let him touch me and he was choking she was holding his neck so tight, and I swear – no matter how hard he tried – he couldn't shake her. He fell to his knees before she let go and then she kicked him and told him to get out and he did. He just left. And afterwards she put ice on my eye and when it wouldn't go down she took me to Dr B.

We walked together through Devil's Glen and if she realized I was pregnant she didn't say anything. Instead she just breathed in the fresh air as though she'd forgotten what fresh air smelt like. She didn't really talk but when I said, 'Thanks for helping me,' she stopped. She kissed me and told me she loved me with all her heart and then we walked on in silence and all I wanted to do was cry but it hurt too much. Dr B took away the scrunched-up knickers filled with ice that I was holding up to my eye and he said it was nasty but I'd be fine. Mam waited in his sitting room and watched *Coronation Street*. He asked me what had happened and I told him, 'Nothing,' but he knew I was lying and then he asked me straight out if I was pregnant and I said yes and asked him how he knew and he said he'd guessed and instead of being annoyed he apologized for not noticing sooner. I told him not to worry, that I'd gone to a great deal of trouble so that people wouldn't notice. He checked me out and said he was worried I might go sooner than we thought. I told him I couldn't because Matthew and I were going to Kentucky in a fortnight. He asked how and I told him Matthew was doing everything.

That was when he rang Matthew's house and told him to come down, and then everything went a bit weird and basically he said that our plan was rubbish, not in those terms but that was what he meant. By the end I was crying, Matthew was crying, Dr B was pacing and Mam was still watching the TV, even though *Coronation Street* was long over. And then some time after that it was agreed that Matthew would go to his grandfather and seek his permission to marry me. It has something to do with money and the estate or something – I don't know. I switched off.

Anyway, Matthew said he would and then we were engaged and we hugged and Dr B made tea and we clinked our mugs, and Mam was still watching TV. Dr B said if she wouldn't listen to reason he might have to put her into hospital forcibly. I asked if he could really do that and he said he could. I told him about how she'd saved me and that I really thought she was improving and I do, I really do. He said he'd keep an eye on her but our priority was Matthew going to his grandparents. He's leaving the day after tomorrow. I can't wait.

26. The treasure in Castle Street

'Okay. I have a question,' Harri said, holding the phone to her ear and sighing into the receiver.

'Go on,' Matt prompted.

'When did you fall for Liv?'

'Oh, that's easy. One day in the stables my father came out of nowhere screaming about one of the horses being lame. I'd exercised the horse so of course it was my fault. He called me every name under the sun and all the while she was standing in the stable behind me. I knew she was there and I liked her so I was really embarrassed.'

'So what happened?'

'After he stormed off she walked up to me and nudged me. I was so red I didn't want to look at her but she smiled and told me not to worry, that all dads were dicks.' He laughed at the memory. 'I fell in love then and there.'

Harriet laughed. 'All dads are dicks! What a beautiful story.' She was making her way around the market with Melissa, who was tired and hungry. 'I should go.'

'Okay.'

'Enjoy the horse show.'

'I will.'

She hung up.

Melissa turned to her. 'So let me get this straight. He

brought you to Seville so that you could communicate on the phone?'

'It works better like this.'

'To each his own, my friend. To each his own. Now let's eat. I'm starving.'

Alfio knocked on Harri's door at a little after six. 'I called my ex-girlfriend.'

Harri opened the door and allowed him in. 'Well?'

'She's married.'

'Oh. Shite. Sorry.'

'No. It's good. I've been holding on to what was for too long.'

'You look like you might cry.'

'That is because I might.'

Oh, Jesus. 'Well, what does Matt say?'

'He says what he always says. Get laid.'

Charming.

'But, you know, this time I think he's right.'

'Good for you.'

'Thank you, Harri. You've opened my eyes. It's been painful but necessary.'

'You're very welcome.'

He left just before Melissa made it back from the pool. 'Are we meeting Matt for dinner or what?' she asked.

'No, drinks afterwards.'

'Great.'

'With Alfio.'

'Nice guy.'

'Looking to get laid.'

'Not that bloody nice. I've a husband and two kids to get back to.'

Harriet smiled. *And I've got James, whether he likes it or not.*

Gerry was waiting at the airport for Melissa with flowers and a large apology. She was just glad to be home. She hugged him tightly and asked after their kids – Susan was kindly minding them. All the way home they talked about how they could manage and what they would do, and even after they'd arrived, they sat in their driveway talking.

'You're sure?' Gerry said.

'I'm just so tired,' Melissa said.

'I know,' he confessed.

'It won't be for ever.'

Gerry kissed his wife. 'Rather you than me.'

'It won't be for ever,' she repeated.

Melissa would be sad to leave the company and her friends, and she knew she'd miss the gossip and the jokes, the work, the money and the benefits, but her job was demanding and so were her kids, and she knew she just couldn't do it all any more. She handed in her notice two weeks later, and that night she had the first good night's sleep she'd had in more than a year. *Hello, world, I'm back.*

Matt insisted on walking Harri to her car in the long-term car park.

'So is it okay if I call you?' he said.

Harri smiled. 'It's fine.'

'Good,' he said. 'I suppose you know Alfio is going home.'

'Well, he couldn't hide out in Wicklow for ever.'

'He was the best trainer I had.'

She laughed. 'That's tough shit.' She got into her car and he waved her off – it was too early in their relationship for a hug.

She drove out of the airport and straight to Malcolm's, where James was still staying. He opened the door.

'Hi,' she said, beaming at him.

'Hi,' he replied.

'I've come back from Seville and while I was there I told an Argentinian guy to take a chance on the woman he loved and it didn't really work out – but fuck it, because now I'm here asking you to take a chance on me. I love you. I want to marry you, and you know what they say – third time lucky.'

'How romantic of you.' He laughed.

'Yeah, well, I'm a big romantic.'

'No, you're not.'

'No, I'm not . . . but I could change.'

'No, you couldn't.'

'No, I couldn't. So, are you in or out?'

Malcolm arrived home with two bags of chips, a kebab and a battered burger only to find his flatmate's tongue down his ex-fiancée's throat. *Ah, well, all the more for me.*

In the month following Harri's trip to Seville she spoke with Matt Delamere often. The phone was so much easier than face to face. She felt calmer and she thought he did too.

'You know what I don't get?' Harri said, into the phone, while propping up her pillow to make herself comfortable.

'What?' Matt asked, sipping a glass of wine in his conservatory.

'Brendan found her. But what the hell was he doing out in the wood in the middle of the night?'

'He said he was going for a run.'

'And you believe him?'

'At the time he was a celibate gay man so I suppose anything is possible.'

'Poor Brendan.'

'You know, once, years ago and when he was very drunk, he told me he heard her calling him.'

'Telepathically?'

'That's what he said.'

'Impossible.'

'That's what I thought but then I remembered something.'

'What?'

'Liv used to try to contact me telepathically when I was at boarding-school. She always got so pissed off when it didn't work.'

'Bloody hell.'

Matt laughed. 'I'm sure he was just running off some frustration.'

'Yeah.'

Harri said goodnight, then thought about what Matt had said. She wondered whether or not she'd mention it to James, who was in the other room halfway through a box-set of *CSI*. *I'll just sleep on that one.*

*

378

One morning, not long after that conversation, Brendan was sitting at his kitchen table reading the newspaper and indulging in his second cup of coffee.

'Brendan?'

'Harri?'

'Yes.'

'Well, hello.'

'I hope you don't mind me calling this early in the morning.'

'Of course not.'

'Do you mind if I ask you a question?' She was holding the phone between her ear and her shoulder to facilitate making toast.

'Go ahead.'

'On the night Liv died, why did you call Uncle Thomas?'

'Who the hell is Uncle Thomas?'

'Oh, I'm sorry – Father Ryan. Why him?'

'Because Liv's mother wasn't well. Her stepfather was an animal who had just been escorted out of town – and poor Matt, well, he was only a boy. I promised Liv I'd take care of her and I failed. After all the business with her stepfather, Father Ryan felt he'd failed her too. I knew he'd help and he did.'

'Brendan?'

'Yes?'

'That night in the wood, did she really call out to you telepathically?'

Brendan was slightly shocked by the question. He was silent for a moment. 'Call me crazy, but I think she did.'

'Wow,' Harri said.

After that they chatted for a little while – long enough for Harri to burn four slices of toast – but the end of the call was the most intriguing part.

'Harri?'

'Yes?'

'How's George?'

It was a month before her wedding. The Shelbourne was jammed but Harri could spot Matt a mile away. She waved and he smiled at her. She rose and he kissed her cheek. They sat.

'How's Clara?'

'Good.'

'I'm glad.'

'James?'

'Great.'

He grinned. 'I broke up with Clara.'

'So when you said she's good you meant she's better off without you.'

'Thanks a lot. I'm going to remain single for a while.'

'Single or celibate?'

'I haven't decided.'

It had been about four months since they had first met and, although it was still new and sometimes strange, Matt and Harri had formed a nice little friendship. It turned out that although they had not many common interests they were alike in that they valued honesty over propriety.

'Nervous?' he asked, surveying the menu.

'Not a jot.'

'You've no plans on stuffing up a third wedding, then?'

'Nope.'

'Good for you.'

'Thanks.'

The waitress was a blonde in her late twenties. 'What can I get you?' she asked.

'Well, my dear, that depends on what you're offering,' he said, arching an eyebrow.

'Don't you dare!' Harri warned.

It was never going to be a traditional father-and-daughter relationship but Harri already had that kind of dad in Duncan Ryan. She found she quite enjoyed her time with Matt on a completely different level, which was new and interesting.

Before they left, he mentioned Liv's old house on Castle Street. He told her he'd bought it a few years beforehand and that it was hers if she wanted it. 'A wedding present,' he said.

'It's too much.'

'No. It's not. It's rightfully yours and, besides, there's a huge amount of work to be done. I was thinking it might make a nice little holiday home.'

'We have a place in Wexford.'

'George says it's a dive.'

She laughed. 'It's a complete dive.'

'Well, the house on Castle Street is probably not much better but I think, in its time, that place saw a little happiness. Go and see it. Think about it.' He handed her the keys. 'You don't have to take it if you don't want to.'

'Thanks,' she said. 'I don't know what to say.'

'Don't say anything. Just go there. I think you'll like it.'

'I will.'

'One more thing. Liv's mum, Deirdre, left her room exactly as it was on the night she died. It's untouched, like going back in time.'

'Thank you,' she said, and suddenly her eyes were welling. 'Thanks.'

He nodded and they said their goodbyes.

George had been seeing Brendan for several months before he had the courage to tell Harri. 'I really like him.'

'La la la!'

'Harri, I really like him.'

'La la la!'

'Are you going to stop that?'

Harri took her hands away from her ears. 'As I've already pointed out, he's twenty-six years older than you.'

'I know.'

'He was my dead mother's friend.'

'I know.'

'He's my brand-new father's best friend.'

'I know.'

'Stop saying, "I know."' For the first time Harri realized how annoying it was. 'Do you really think you have a future with this man?'

'I do. I really, really do.'

He had spoken in earnest. *Bloody hell.* 'Fine, then.'

'Really?'

She nodded. 'It's not like you'll do anything but what you want to do anyway.'

'That's true. After all, I am known for being selfish,' he acknowledged. 'Thank you, Harri.'

'You're welcome, George.'

After just a short time together, it seemed as if Brendan and George had never been apart. They shared the same interests, dressed similarly, enjoyed the finer things in life and, most noticeably, they were comfortable together, as though they really and truly fitted. The gap in each of them had closed.

Harri enjoyed spending time with her brother and his boyfriend, but to Brendan, the presence of George and his old best friend's daughter in his life meant the world. 'I'm really happy,' he told George one night, lying in bed, warm and relaxed. 'I can't remember being this content.'

'Me too,' George said.

'I was so lonely,' Brendan went on, 'for so long.'

'And the romantic in you likes to believe that your friend Liv had a hand in us meeting.'

Brendan's smile widened. 'You know me so well.'

George laughed. 'Well, whether it was Liv or Fate or just bloody good luck, I'm grateful.'

It was two weeks before the wedding. Harri rang Susan from the car.

Beth picked up.

'Well?' Harri asked.

'He's still in surgery. Do you know what they're actually doing to him?'

'I don't want to know.'

'They're reconstructing –'

'Beth, I do not want to know.'

'Mum keeps making dick jokes. Like, why did the dick cross the road? Because it could.'

'That's not funny.'

'I didn't say they were funny. Dad's laughing, though, so that's good. Oh, she's back from the loo – I'll put you on to her. See ya, Harri.'

'See ya, Beth.'

'Hi,' Susan said.

'Well?' Harri asked.

'He should be out shortly. I'm starving.'

'Me too.'

'I'd love a chicken tandoori.'

'Exactly what I was thinking.' Harri looked at James, who was driving. 'We'll have to stop for a chicken tandoori.'

'Are you in the car?' Susan asked.

'On the way to Wicklow.'

'You're going into that house, aren't you?'

'Yeah,' she said.

'Best of luck.'

'Thanks.'

'Right, I'd better go,' said Susan.

'Tell Andrew I said hi.'

'Will do. Love to James.'

She hung up and Harri looked at James. She sighed.

'What?'

'Nothing.'

*

They stood outside the house for less than a minute. Harri put the key into the door and opened it. They walked around the downstairs, the tiny hall with the steep staircase, the back kitchen that led to an overgrown garden. The front sitting room was small but full of light. They made their way upstairs, with Harri leading. The first stop was the bathroom, which was surprisingly large.

'Are you thinking what I'm thinking?' James asked.

'This room is perfectly proportioned to house a Raindance Rainmaker shower.' She sighed.

'Bingo!'

Liv's bedroom had her name on the door. Harri stood outside looking at it for a moment or two. The name 'Olivia' was faded, almost gone. She opened the door to reveal a small room with a small bed, a locker stuffed with girls' magazines, nail varnish and creams. The wardrobe housed her clothes: jeans, tops and a smock or two.

'Jesus, people are wearing them again now,' James pointed out.

Her school uniform hung there, but was pushed to the side and on its own. The desk by the window was tiny and there was engraving in its soft wood.

Liv loves Matthew
One day at a time
Kentucky

James found a big padlock in her top drawer. 'What the hell is this for?' he said, raising it high.

Harri sat on the bed, a little overwhelmed.

'Are you okay? You look pale.'

'I'm fine.'

'Sure?'

'Can you feel her presence here?' she asked.

'No,' he admitted. *And if I could I'd run out of here like my arse was on fire.* 'Me neither and I'm glad. I'm glad she left this place.'

It was James who noticed the slight bump in the mattress.

'Well, it's old.'

He lifted it. 'I've found something.' He held up a thick book.

'It's a diary,' she said, eyes glistening.

A few letters fell out. Harri picked them up. 'They're from Matt.'

She opened the first page and read aloud, '"January 1975. And so starts another year. God, I hope it's better than last year. Sheila said it has to be because everyone knows that every year ending in five is a good one. Sheila really is a SPAZ!!"'

She laughed and hugged the diary tight. 'It's her,' she said, tears falling.

'Who knew we'd find treasure?' he said, holding her close to him.

11 July 1976 – Sunday

I woke up feeling sore and all day I'm getting cramps. I was making Mam some breakfast and had to bend over with the pain but then it went. She seems brighter since HE left. He collected his clothes yesterday and it was Father Ryan who drove him to the station. I don't know where he's going and I don't care, but Sheila said her dad told her that one of the lads that normally drink in the Pole was in his bar last night and he said HE's going to London. It's so great that he's gone. I swear even when I've got cramps I'm smiling. I really think, after a few months away from him, Mam will be back to her old self . My eye is healing well, which is good if I'm going to be getting married soon. Matthew left to go and see his granddad this morning and before he left he slipped a letter through my door only because I said since he'd finished school I really missed his letters. He is so romantic.

It's late and the pain is much worse. Mam's in bed asleep. It's raining. If I go now and take the short-cut through Devil's Glen I'll get to Dr B's in half an hour. It's probably nothing but better to be safe than sorry. I'm so sick of not having a phone!!! Maybe if I close my eyes and concentrate really hard I can communicate with him so that he can meet me halfway.

No.

Shit.

Before I go. Today I took a walk in the afternoon because I thought it might help with the pains. I haven't really spent much time by the *Eliana* since HE grabbed me there, but today I stayed for a whole hour just looking out to sea. I know I'm always saying I can't wait to leave Wicklow but I love it here too. Wicklow's in my bones so, no matter where

I go, I'll never leave it and that's okay by me. I'd better go before the rain gets any worse.

One last thing! I'M GETTING MARRIED!!!!!!!! Hello, I'm Liv Delamere!!!!

10 July

Liv,

Tomorrow morning I'll be on a train to visit my granddad to get him to agree to me making you my wife. Dr B is right. It's the right thing to do, but, more than that, it's the only thing I want to do. I want to call you my wife. I love you more than I knew it was possible to love. My heart is full and it's full of you. Henry says angels exist and I think he's right because I'm going to marry one. (Don't puke, I'm serious!) I can't wait to come home to you. I can't wait to make you my wife. See you soon, Liv Delamere.

Love

Matt

27. The wedding – take three

The date was 27 December 2006, and it was the third time Harri was set to marry.

She'd slept like a log the night before, with her fiancé beside her.

'I'm not doing it unless we go to the church together,' he had said.

'But it's unlucky.'

'Could it possibly be any more unlucky than being left at the altar twice?'

'Good point.'

Now James was in George's room. Malcolm and Brendan were helping him with his tie, his vows and her nerves.

'What did you say? Honour, protect and what?' Malcolm said, through a mouthful of toast.

'He said honour, protect and cherish,' Brendan said. 'That's lovely.'

'I'd speak up, though, if I was you – I thought you said honour, protect and banish.'

'Big day.' Harri's dad had greeted her with a wink on the landing.

'Big day, Dad,' she agreed, grinning.

'Three times a charm,' he said.

'Fingers crossed,' she said, kissing his hairy cheek as

he passed with his paper heading for his en-suite bathroom.

Her mother was calling her from her own bedroom.

'Darling, there you are. The aquamarine outfit or the
pale pink?'

'Those are from my last weddings. It's not like you to
recycle.'

'Well, I've promised your father I'll reduce my carbon
footprint and my Visa bill, and seeing I didn't get to wear
them to anywhere other than A and E . . .'

Harri laughed. 'The aquamarine.'

'Good choice. Now get going. Mona will be here in
half an hour, and ever since Desmond dropped out of
school she has a face on her like a donkey's hole.'

Harri burst out laughing. 'I love you, Mum.'

'I love you too, my darling.'

Back in her room she had a long shower, then made her
way over to the chair that looked down on the pretty stone
patio and across to the ancient oak tree. The rain poured
down from a heavy grey sky.

'I couldn't give a stuff,' she said, hugging herself in the
comfortable towelling dressing-gown her mother had
given her six years before when she'd first left home to
move twenty minutes down the road to the UCD campus.
She sat there and thought about Liv for a while. *You would
have been a lovely bride, Liv.*

There was a knock on the door and George was lying
on the bed before Harri managed to say, 'Come in.'

'Moaning's here. Mum's making her a coffee so you have
five minutes before the all-important hair and makeup.'

'Thanks.'

'You look incredibly relaxed. Have we met before?' he asked, in jest.

'Ha ha.'

'Are you all right?' he said seriously.

'Never better.'

'It's pissing rain out.'

'Let it rain.'

'Dad and Matt have cracked open a vintage bottle of brandy and they're halfway through it.'

'I hope they drink it all.'

'James is planning on singing "Unchained Melody" at the reception.'

She laughed. 'He bloody will not!'

'My God, I think we may actually be going to a wedding today.'

'You can count on it,' she said.

Duncan and Harri stood under an umbrella by the church door. She stepped inside and he closed the umbrella, shook it and laid it on the floor. Inside she could see all the people she loved: Melissa and Gerry with Jacob and Carrie, Susan, Andrew and Beth, who was holding hands with the boy who had given her crabs, George and Brendan, Matt and her mother, Aidan, who had travelled from London with his boyfriend Quan, and all the other people who had been kind enough to turn up a third time.

And on the altar was her uncle Thomas, known to everyone else as Father Ryan, bursting with pride, happy that at last little Harri knew the truth. And when her dad walked her down the aisle, in her heart she carried with her a teenage girl called Liv.

1 May 1976 – Saturday

I woke up this morning dreaming of Kentucky. I saw horses and hay and trucks and land that went on for miles. I saw a big old farmhouse with a veranda and a swing chair big enough for six. I saw me in a meadow and Matthew riding a horse so fast he was a blur. It was really nice. I felt warm and whole and free and happy and safe. I felt safe. And when I looked down I saw a baby, just lying beside me, bald and thin and wrinkly, and although it doesn't sound like it, the baby was really cute with a squishy face. She was holding my hand and smiling. And then I saw another one! This one had hair and was a little bit tubbier and was yelling and didn't look one bit happy. So I picked it up and I think she was a girl but I'm not sure, and I held her and told her not to cry, and I stroked her and she listened to my heartbeat and she stopped. And I knew it was a dream and soon it would be over so I held her as tightly as I could and whispered into her ear but I couldn't hear what I said, which makes me think I didn't say anything because surely I'd know. Then she was gone. Dreams are weird. And I woke up. And all day I've been feeling a little nostalgic so I sat in my room and read my diary and I didn't realize how much I say 'anyway', and 'weird' and 'shit'. I say 'shit' a lot. And I switch off a lot too and I don't know if that's a good thing. Plus I really, really can't draw. I think I'm nostalgic because soon I'll be leaving here and endings, even the happy ones, are sad but then again every ending is a new beginning so that's okay.

Acknowledgements

Thanks to John Goodman for the excellent tour of Wicklow, and his wife Joanne Costello, for taking my husband horse-riding so that I could actually get some work done. Cheers, *amigos*! Thanks to my family: I love you all. To my husband: you still haven't a clue what I do but I wouldn't have it any other way. Thank you and I love you. To my friends: you make life so much sweeter. To everyone at Penguin Ireland and UK: thank you for your patience and support, and especially Patricia Deevy and Hazel Orme for all your hard work. And finally I promised a little lady that I'd be sure to compliment her beautiful eyes on paper so, Milly Kerins, you have the most beautiful eyes.